# WINTER SPELL

## Claire M. Banschbach

CAMPITOR
PRESS

**Winter Spell**

Published by Campitor Press


Interior formatting by Rachael Ritchey rachaelritchey.com
Cover by Magpie Designs magpie-designs.weebly.com


ISBN: 978-0-9992203-4-4

Other Books by Claire M. Banschbach

**The Rise of Aredor Series**
*The Rise of Aredor*
*The Wildcat of Braeton*

**The Faeries of Myrnius Series**
*Adela's Curse*
*The Wolf Prince*

Books by C.M. Banschbach

**The Dragon Keep Chronicles**
*Oath of the Outcast*

*For Margaret*

# Chapter 1

"Try again."

Tonya stared down at the jagged edges of coral. Her long dark hair swayed about her in the gentle current sweeping around the reef. A small orange fish darted out from an anemone, fixing her with a wide-eyed look that she chose to interpret as sympathy.

She looked back at the coral and then at her hands. Mihail sighed again, a faint stream of bubbles scurrying up towards the sun-kissed surface.

Tonya scowled. *I don't need another reminder that I can't do this.* Trying to reach the place of her elusive magic, she bent down to touch the coral.

Instead of revitalizing, another piece cracked off. Mihail hung his head. Tonya buried a scream.

*I can't even fix coral. The easiest job in the entire stupid ocean!*

Mihail coughed, gills on the side of his neck opening up for a split second before they vanished.

"Keep practicing until the tide turns," he said. He spread his rippling wings, more like fins, and swam away, shaking his head the entire way.

Tonya kicked at the coral, breaking another piece off in the process. A hermit crab scurried away from the debris, clicking its larger claw at her in displeasure.

*Even the creatures don't like me.*

She held her breath, letting the weight of it send her sinking down to sit cross legged on the ocean floor.

Vibrant colors of pinks, yellows, and oranges surrounded her. Bright flashes darted around the billowing coral outgrowths as the clustered fish swept in search of food. The ocean rocked around her with the waves on the surface hundreds of feet above. Sunlight swayed in time, the golden beams filtering down towards her — the lone spot of white and black in the world.

She frowned at the coral that still stubbornly remained broken and propped her chin on her hand. She couldn't practice until the next tide. She'd have to go up for air before then.

Other faeries flitted around her, effortlessly in tune with the ocean. Gills exposed themselves on their necks when they needed to draw in a deeper breath. Wings spread from their backs, as delicate and colorful as the fish that swam around them.

*But not me. I'm stuck in the space between waves.* She pushed to her feet, kicking up more sand than was strictly necessary, and swam towards the surface and her island.

Breaking the surface, she tilted her face to the sun and drew in a deep breath of the warm salty breeze. She treaded water and soaked in the warmth of the air and the sun and the sky.

A white gull dive-bombed the water nex
her face. Laughing, she wiped water fro
scolded the gull as it resurfaced. It squawke
retreated.

At least, it sounded like laughter. Lan
slightly easier to understand, but their language was all a
muddled mess.

Like her magic.

She struck out toward the island in the distance, sliding
through the waves with ease as long as she didn't try to use
her wings. The sand warmed her feet and she stood for a
moment to tilt her face back up to the sun, drawing another
deep breath.

Her bones just felt more *right* on the land. *My bones. That's
stupid. It's just the weight of the land pulling on me without the
water to push me up.*

She twisted the side of her mouth, squinting one eye before
pivoting on one foot. Water rose off her in shimmering
droplets. Her black hair floated around her head, wavering as
if caught in the waves before the water slicked from its dark
surface and it fell back to its slightly disordered mess —
completely dry.

Tonya plopped down to the ground, kicking her feet out
in front of her to bury in the sand. She scooped sand in her
hands, pouring it from one palm to the other in endless
motion.

This was the one place that she could be free of judgement.
The other faeries didn't need to come up to breathe. After
she'd been brought back to the ocean as an infant, her aunt
and uncle had been forced to move their dwelling closer to
the edge of the reef so she had a place to surface.

aunt had found plenty of ways to express her .inued unhappiness at the change, and at having to keep ner, over the last seventy years.

Tonya flopped back on the sand and flung one arm over her face to block out the sun. The heat of the day sank all the way to her core, drying her sharkskin trousers and woven kelp shirt in minutes. The sun baked her skin.

*What would it be like to be cold? To see a snowflake fall?* She'd only seen ice once in her life. A small iceberg had somehow found its lonely way from the far north down to their waters, bringing a strange cold that had stirred something deep inside her.

Something that belonged to her father—and the magic of his kind.

She couldn't touch it, just like she could barely touch the magic her mother had given her.

*Caught between the waves.* The product of the union of an ocean faery and an ice faery. The unexplainable. The warning to the other young faeries who wanted to try to swim in a monsoon's fury. Because they might get swept away like her mother, only to be washed up on the ice floes of the far north and found by a wild ice faery.

She sat up in a rush, flinging a handful of sand into the ocean, as if to make a difference in its depth.

*I wonder if they could have wanted me? Could have helped me pull out the strands of magic that are knotted up deep inside me? Or if they'd be ashamed of me, like everyone else.*

It was a hard thing, only having a secondhand story about her parents. Only having everyone else's opinions of them.

Tonya pushed to her feet, circling the small island. She paused at the northernmost tip, rising up onto her toes as if she could see the icy north. But she could only see the very tip of Myrnius, even if she strained her bits of magic. The

4

shoreline where her mother had last held her, before giving her to the ocean faeries and vanishing.

Three circuits of the island later, Tonya plopped back down to the sand. Thinking about her parents always woke a yearning inside her. A desire to see ice floes, narwhals, and leopard seals. Tundra, and glaciers, and wolves. Even if she had no idea where she'd heard those words before.

She stared out at the endless waves methodically marching towards her. Hemming her in. They always brought things to shore. Never took things away. Like the ocean was telling her that it would keep her here. That she could never leave.

The ache inside her churned restlessly. Half wanting to stay and dance with the waves, the other half wanting to touch them with ice and send it to play across the deep, cold sky. It twisted and turned around her heart so hard that her eyes stung with salty tears.

"I just want to be one thing," she whispered to the wind. "I just want to untangle myself and be free."

The wind carried her words away over the water, bringing back only the sighing of the waves in return.

She blinked hard in disappointment. Not like she'd really expected an answer. Not like she ever got any answers.

A shadow fell across the sand beside her. Mihail come to scold her back to the depths. The shifting sand cast the outline of his head into uneven spikes. She almost laughed. Mihail kept his hair in pristine condition.

"I'm going back down." She sighed.

"No." A deep, unfamiliar voice answered.

She froze as cold wrapped around her. Comforting at first, then stifling as it burrowed deep inside her and drove away the warmth of the sand.

The tangled thing inside her jerked tighter in response.

She tried to turn, but stiffness melded her joints.

A hand touched her shoulder. Her pounding heart leaped to her throat as she stared at the shadow. The cold wrapped tighter and tighter.

He spoke unfamiliar words. The sand shifted beneath her feet, tipping her over to meet the ground with breath-stealing force. She blinked and the world exploded in ice and cold.

# Chapter 2

*A*n ache pounded in Tonya's head, intensified by a strange cold wrapping around her. The ache migrated to her shoulder, shaking and pushing at her.

"Tonya!"

The ache apparently also had a voice.

"Tonya!"

Recognition pierced the cold. Sophie, her cousin.

Tonya peeled her eyes open, blinking at the harshness of the light against a strange white. Hands helped her sit up, and she stared in shock.

Snow covered the sands. Ice clung to the trunks and fronds of the trees in dripping spikes. It weighed down the scrub bushes, pushing their fronds into the snow. A crab scurried over the small drifts, leaving tiny prints in its wake.

The ocean had frozen in time, leaving a strange silence. Waves reared up, curling over themselves, halting in their tracks.

"What did you do?" Sophie asked.

Tonya met her wide-eyed gaze, an immediate defense leaping to her tongue.

But she sat in a small crater, a radius of snow and ice leaping away from her and spreading out across the island and ocean. *I'm the center point.*

"I don't know…" The words stumbled out of her dry mouth.

"What happened?" Sophie shook her shoulder again.

Tonya tentatively touched the snow. Her fingers met the slick of ice before she'd gone very deep. "I don't know."

"Whatever happened, you know they're going to blame you." Concern shone in Sophie's eyes. "You're the only source of ice magic here."

Tonya shifted her bare feet in the snow drifts. *Shouldn't I be cold?*

"Tonya, the Reef Guards will be here soon. They'll want to know what happened." Sophie tugged on her arm, helping her up from the crater.

"I was attacked by something. I think." Tonya slowly turned to look around her. Ice as far as she could see. *How did I make this?*

"What?" Sophie gave a low gasp and spun to scan the horizon. "Who?"

Tonya lifted her hands in a helpless gesture. "What do I tell them?" She pressed her hands to her cheeks. "What will everyone say? I'll have to go before the court…" Dread twisted her stomach.

"I'll stay with you," Sophie promised, touching her arm.

A bit of warmth sparked in Tonya's chest. Sophie had been a friend, a little bit of family among the whispers and glances and muffled comments of "half-breed."

*But I can't just run.*

"What if they want you to undo it?" Sophie whispered.

Tonya's heart weighed heavy at the lingering doubt in Sophie's voice. She'd never be able to undo — whatever had just happened. The magic didn't work for her.

She shrugged. "I guess they ship me off to some other deserted island to live out the rest of my six hundred years in non-magical isolation."

Sophie shook her head. "How is that different from how they treat you anyway?"

Tonya rubbed a hand across her sleeve. "How did you get out?"

"I wore a hole through the ice." Sophie pointed at a hole a few yards from shore. She could control currents with the touch of her hands, so it would have been the work of a moment for her to break through. But the hole was already icing over.

"Did I really freeze the whole ocean?" The question whispered from Tonya.

"It goes as far as I can see. Look." Sophie led her around to the northern shore. The ice crusted the waves all the way to Myrnius, and Tonya had a feeling beyond that as well.

"What did I do?" She sank down to her knees. *How did this all come from me? I don't have this kind of power!*

Sophie knelt beside her, her brow furrowing the way it did when she was trying to come up with the best possible argument.

"You said something attacked you? Maybe it caused this and you didn't at all."

"But ice?" Tonya lifted a hand to gesture around them. "We all know I'm the only one with even a hint of ice magic around here."

"All right." Sophie tossed her head. "Maybe it'll all melt, and we won't have to worry about anything."

Tonya managed a weak smile. Somehow, she knew it wouldn't melt. The warmth of the sun should have already sent the pristine crystals into watery puddles, but the ice and snow remained crisp, and the waves as frozen as ever.

A sharp crack echoed behind them. Tonya flinched. The Reef Guard had broken through.

"Just tell them about being attacked," Sophie said.

Tonya nodded, any scrap of bravery shriveling away into panic. *What if they don't believe me? What if this is their excuse to finally get rid of me?* What-ifs threatened to overwhelm her and only Sophie's tight grip on her hand kept her anchored to reality as two Reef Guards emerged from the ice and stalked closer, shark-tooth spears at the ready, their crusted armor casting bulky shadows over the shimmering ice.

"Tonya Freyr-dottir." The deep voice of one of the guards stumbled a little over the harshness of her name. The only thing she had of her father. The name her mother declared she had before giving her away.

"Yes?" Her voice trembled, and the iron face of the guard softened a fraction.

"You realize what this looks like?"

She nodded mutely, and Sophie's grip tightened around her fingers again.

"You'll need to come with us." His voice left no room for argument or pleading.

Tonya drew a shaky breath, darting another quick look around her. Whatever happened, at least she'd finally seen ice and snow.

\*

Tonya swam behind the Reef Guards, pulling herself along in sure strokes with her arms. She refused to humiliate herself further by unfurling her wings. Sophie trailed Tonya and the guards, keeping enough distance to not closely associate with them, but still close enough to lend support.

Faeries had begun to gather around the reef, gazing up at the sheen of deep blue coating the surface and distorting the light. A chill threaded through the water, sending fish darting away to hide among the coral.

The closer they swam to the center of the reef more and more faeries began to notice them. Tonya ducked her head as faeries clustered in groups, darting venomous glares at her.

*It won't even matter to them that I was attacked. I did this.*

"Tonya!"

She jerked her head up to see her aunt and uncle rushing towards them. Small currents from their wings swirled around her as they halted. Sophie shared their same angular features and light hair, though the hardness around her aunt's green eyes wasn't quite replicated in Sophie or her uncle when they looked at Tonya.

Her aunt grabbed her arm. "What happened? Where are they taking you? Did you do this?"

"Something attacked me. I don't know!" The answer bubbled from Tonya in a rush, the panic returning like a crashing tidal wave.

One of the Reef Guards swam back, gently pushing her aunt away. "We're taking her to the king. As her guardians, you will be allowed to come."

Tonya swallowed. Somehow their presence made it even worse. They'd taken her in, but against their will. They didn't approve of her mother's choice. Her father's blood was an irreversible taint upon her.

But her aunt and uncle nodded and fell in beside her. Sophie took that as an invitation to dart forward and swim next to Tonya. Sophie grabbed her hand again and squeezed.

Tonya mustered a smile and they followed the Reef Guard hand-in-hand.

Apprehension bubbled higher in her chest as they approached the twisting columns of coral that marked the entrance to the palace. Reef Guards stood beside each pillar. They fixed her with narrowed glances, then returned their attention to the reef.

Giant anemones swayed around the boundaries of the entry hall. Sand spread in ripples, stirring slightly as the group floated down to walk along the ocean floor into the main hall.

The sand shifted to patterned swirls of pearls and scalloped shells. Coral arches spread overhead, luminescent growths along them that would illuminate the hall once night fell. More Reef Guards lined the sides of the halls, all staring impassively. The king waited at the head of the hall, his queen clutching her hands together.

Tonya's two escorts halted five paces from the monarchs and bowed. Tonya barely remembered to do the same.

"We found her on the surface of the island," one of the guards spoke up. "It appeared to be the epicenter."

Tonya's aunt gasped and pulled away from her. Tonya kept her eyes fixed on a pearl at her feet. A faint swirl of pink wrapped around its creamy surface.

"What happened? Did you try to attack us?" King Stavros leaned forward, his narrow features creasing into an accusing frown.

Sophie stiffened, but Tonya tightened her grip on her friend's hand in warning. She risked a glance up at Stavros instead. He regarded her with distaste, and another little piece of her heart broke. But she might as well get it over with.

"Please, Your Majesty, if I may?" She pressed her hand to her chest in another bow, avoiding his glance of disgust. "I had gone up to the surface for some air." She tried not to wince as she gave them another reason to look down upon her. "I always go to the island. There's never anyone else but me there, except for today."

Stavros actually looked at her with something like interest. The queen only wrung her hands more vigorously.

"Someone came up behind me. I only saw a shadow. They touched me and I just — froze."

She shivered. The strange cold had placed invisible binds around her, sapping any strength or power she could muster. "Then they said something that I didn't understand, knocked me out, and then..." She lifted a hand almost helplessly. "When I woke up, everything was frozen."

"You're saying that you're not responsible for all this?" He gestured up at the surface.

Tonya swallowed hard. Maybe she was. In the brief seconds before she'd blacked out, she remembered the feeling of cold and ice coming from her and through her and around her. But the coils still wrapped and tangled within her.

Whatever it was, she was just as powerless as always.

"I don't know," she finally whispered.

Her aunt and uncle slid farther away. Sophie stayed next to her, still clenching her hand in a tight grip.

"Can you undo it?" the queen blurted.

Tonya stared helplessly at the queen. If she strained hard enough, a slight tingle of magic touched her fingertips. Maybe even enough to move the pearl at her feet and send it bobbing among the waves. Not nearly enough to unfreeze the ocean.

Stavros cleared his throat, stroking his chin and beginning to pace — little puffs of sand stirring in his wake. The guards didn't move. Neither did Tonya's heart.

"Until we can establish just what exactly you did, you will be placed under guard. You will be allowed up to the surface once every tide to take some fresh air." Stavros's lip curled in slight derision at her need. "We will have some of our strongest magic users investigate. And then we will decide what will be done with you."

Tonya's heart sank like a rock to the pit of her stomach. His words sounded ominously final. Like it had already been decided and she would never go up to the surface to see the snow and ice again.

She managed a bow. The guard gently took her arm, prying her away from Sophie, and led her from the throne room. She glanced back once. Her aunt and uncle stood together, a strange sort of relief on their face. Only Sophie watched her go, a faint quiver to her chin.

Tonya tried for a smile, but she felt just as frozen as the surface. Still just as powerless.

# Chapter 3

*Then wars troubled the mortals' lands. Count Stefan rose up and united them. He was named as the first king of Myrnius, and he ruled long and well. But that was long ago, and my ancestor's lands have since fallen into decay. The faeries have not been seen in these parts for many long years, and indeed, many doubt their existence.*

*But the forest still stands, and the mountains remain. As I sit among the ruins of my forefathers' castle, I hear a voice whisper a blessing through the wind. One day the lands will be restored, and Damian and Adela's children remain to watch over Myrnius.*

Diane paused, rubbing the quill along her chin as she re-read the passage she had just written. She shifted on her rocky seat and chewed the inside of her lip.

"Ralf!" she called.

Her guard circled back around the scattered masonry and picked his way towards her, climbing over fallen pillars.

"Yes, Your Highness?" he asked, his deep voice unerringly patient.

"How does this sound?" She read her latest effort out loud.

He cleared his throat and she braced herself.

"It's not exactly historically accurate, is it?" he said carefully.

She narrowed her eyes at him. "The ruins part is!"

Diane swept her arm to encompass the crumbling remains of a once-proud castle. It had been destroyed when she was a child, barely able to walk. She didn't remember its old glory. But the ruins were beautiful in a way.

Nature had begun to spring up around the tumbled columns and arches, and ivy clung to the remaining interior wall of the great hall like a leafy tapestry. But she liked to imagine what it had been like in her ancestor Stefan's time.

Ralf conceded her point with a gruff *hmph.*

"And the part about the faeries is technically true," she persisted.

He stood firm. "If by 'many long years' you mean three."

She sat taller on her rock and jabbed the quill at him. "Why do I ask you for advice anyway?"

A smile flickered across his face, making him actually look his young age, instead of the solemn guard he turned into whenever others were around.

"Because I'm stuck with you and have to do whatever you tell me."

She flicked the crumbly remnants of her lunch at him. He easily dodged the bits of bread.

"But really." Diane plopped her chin down into her hand. "Do you think it's that bad?"

He took a seat on a rock a few feet from her, adjusting his sword. "It's very poetic."

She flicked more crumbs at him.

His smile emerged for another half-second. "Maybe by the time it becomes one of the epic histories of our time, no one will bother to fact check to make sure that you weren't writing only three years after the second dark war."

Diane huffed a sigh. To have one of her tales considered as a historical document was a dream. But one that would likely not ever see fruition, as their country was still reeling from the war.

Instead of living in a castle, her older brother Edmund ruled from Chelm, the nearby township that had grown with refugees over the years. She had only one dress made from fine silk and it had been her mother's. The dress she wore now was made of more sensible materials, plain and with little to differentiate it from the common townspeople's clothing.

"Who knows? Maybe you'll see the re-building of this castle, or a new one, in your lifetime." Ralf's voice drew her back.

"Maybe," she agreed.

It wasn't like she knew what she was missing by not living in a castle. She'd lived in Chelm for as long as she could remember. And even though still a dreamer at eighteen after living through the war and its continued aftermath, she knew she would probably never see the ramparts and walls re-erected.

A breeze stirred her long brown hair. She looked up in confusion. It had a chill to it that didn't belong in the middle of summer.

Ralf stood, his brow furrowing in unease as he turned to the south. Another wind swept through, even colder this time. It grabbed some of her parchment and knocked it away. She didn't chase it, stepping closer to Ralf to stare with him at the approaching cloud.

It rose tall and white, shoving frigid air in front of it. Flecks of white peppered the front of her green dress.

"Snow?" she whispered in shock.

"Diane, move!" Ralf grabbed her arm in unaccustomed force and dragged her further into the ruins. She reached towards her pages in a desperate attempt to rescue them, but the wind scattered them all.

He pulled her, stumbling, through what had once been a corridor into the servants' quarters. They pushed into one of the rooms, and Ralf tried to prop the shattered door back up on its hinges as some sort of flimsy protection. The wind howled around the corners, sneaking around the corner and through the door to send them shivering.

"What is this?" she whispered. "Magic?"

The word sent a new chill through her.

"I don't know."

He shepherded her into the corner, sheltering her with his body and providing a little warmth.

A shriek of wind pummeled the door down, flooding the room with cold and stinging snowflakes. Ralf shivered against her, sheltering her from the worst of the blast. She curled frozen fingers into his tunic.

*Not again. Creator, please, not again.*

The wind built to a howling crescendo. She bit back a whimper. A freak snowstorm in the middle of summer reeked of magic. And she had too many terrible memories of magic used against her people. Fires that couldn't be quenched, twisted animals that preyed on the helpless, and sleepless nights spent listening to the distant thunder of battle.

She huddled against Ralf until the wind finally stopped howling, subsiding into an uneasy murmur. Ralf began to pull away, but she didn't release his tunic. His cold hands covered hers and she managed to look up at him.

"It's all right," he whispered. "I'm just going to look outside."

She jerked a nod and stumbled after him as he crept towards the door. Drifts of white poured through the door. He stirred it with his boot, and it came away crusted in snow.

Ralf kept her back with one arm as he peered around the door. She couldn't bear the eerie silence.

"What's out there?" she whispered.

He fixed her with a frown, the expression turning him back into the serious guard who had endured more combat than a young man of twenty-one should ever see. He drew his sword and she stepped back.

He'd been her guard for the past two years, and she trusted him with her life. He made her feel safe and he'd protected her on more than one occasion.

*I can trust him now.*

Still, she held her breath when he disappeared around the corner, only the soft crunch of his boots in the snow betraying him.

Her heart skittered around her chest at the silence that fell. *Did he leave? He'd never leave me.* She forced a calming breath. And another one. *I never thought I'd have to hide again while someone went to confront magic.* Her heart stuttered again. It wasn't like the war. It was too cold and quiet.

Ralf's quiet, "Diane," startled her so much she almost screamed. She composed herself as much as her shivering body would allow. Tucking frozen hands under her arms, she cautiously stepped out.

Snow covered the ruins, and icicles jutted out at odd angles as if the wind had blown them sideways. The sun shone again, sparkling off the snow. In the gardens, a fallen rose rested as a red blotch against the snow.

She walked towards Ralf, every step sending her sinking almost up to her knees. *Thank the Creator I decided to wear my boots today.*

Ralf stood on the rocks, where just minutes ago she'd sat surrounded by summer. He helped her climb up above the drifts.

"Look." He pointed to the north. A wall of ice and snow pummeled its way farther north, coating the land in white as far as the eye could see.

"What happened?"

He shrugged. "Come on. We need to go see if anything happened to Chelm."

Diane clapped a hand to her cheek. *Edmund! Matilde.*

She jumped off the rock, foregoing decorum and plunging into the snow. A bit of parchment poking out of the snow halted her. She gently freed it. The ink remained unsmeared and she read the paragraph she'd written only minutes ago.

It seemed silly now. She turned her gaze again to the south where the forest of Celedon loomed just out of eyesight.

*Whose magic is this, and will the faeries even help us?*

# Chapter 4

**R**alf insisted on taking the lead, plowing through the snow drifts towards the town half a mile away. For the first time ever, Diane regretted going to the castle.

*Creator, please let everyone be all right.* The prayer repeated over and over in her mind as she tried to fit her strides to Ralf's longer ones, misstepping into drifts more often than not. Finally, she stopped.

"Take shorter steps!" She propped her fists on her hips as he turned to look at her.

He flattened one eyebrow in mild exasperation. She never knew how he managed the look. She'd practiced in the mirror, but the closest she'd gotten was looking like a strangled griffin.

Still, he adopted a more reasonable pace.

Snow covered the red shale rooftops of Chelm. Mounds of white piled up against the southern sides of the houses. A relieved exhale puffed from Diane's lips as figures stumbled around the buildings.

One ran toward them and Ralf stepped aside to let her fling herself into her brother's arms.

"You all right?" Edmund demanded.

"I'm fine. Is everyone else?" She wriggled from his protective embrace.

His square jaw set in tense concern — a look that shadowed his young face all too often in the years since he'd been forced to take up the mantle of king.

"So far," he said. "We're trying to figure out what exactly happened."

"Magic is the only explanation," Ralf said.

He and Edmund exchanged a grim look. They'd fought together on the magic-ridden battlefields and held off the twisted creations that still roamed the lands. Diane had seen her fair share of it all.

They'd had relative peace for the last three years, and she hated to think that everything they'd tried to build back up had been lost.

She shook herself, crumpling the parchment in her hand.

"Let's evaluate the damage." She strode forward. *We'll need additional fuel. I'll make a list of houses that need extra patching to the walls to keep the cold out. Blankets. Food stores.*

Edmund caught up to her and together they went to each family, making sure they had enough blankets, inventorying food supplies, and staving off most of the panic that threatened. Diane used the back of her parchment to run calculations, scratching numbers with a bit of charcoal she'd left in her pocket.

Nearly an hour later, she and Edmund stood in the middle of the town square. Ralf waited a few feet away. He'd stayed at her side the entire time, even handing her a spare piece of charcoal when hers had rubbed down to an un-useable nub.

Edmund had smirked a little at his preparedness. An expression Diane had pointedly ignored.

Her brother looked over her calculations, biting his lip in a frown. "This isn't going to last long. We'll be lucky if any of the crops survived this freeze."

Diane's heart sank a little lower. In her immediate concern, she hadn't even thought about the outlying farms. Or the rest of Myrnius. She gave it until the end of the day before people began arriving from the nearest villages and towns to seek out Edmund.

He turned over the paper. "What's this?"

A smile touched the corners of his eyes as he read. She snatched it away, straightening the creases.

"Still enamored with the old tales of our ancestors and faeries who cared?"

She hated the despondence that tinged his voice. It didn't belong in a young man of only twenty-one. One who had already been king four years.

"It just seems a better thing to think on than all this." She swept an arm around them. "Not that this is terrible!"

He only smiled again. "I know what you mean. Sometimes I wish that we could have the wealth and peace that Father did before the war."

"If anyone can bring Myrnius back to her glory, it's you." She lifted her chin in determination. *I have to believe in something, and he's stubborn enough to do it.*

"That's why I'm glad I have you around. You manage to keep me a little bit optimistic."

She wrapped one arm around him in a hug. "Happy to help." She pushed him towards their house. "Let's go inside and get warm for a minute. Oh, Ralf! Go see your family and make sure they're all right. I'll be fine."

The guard gave a small smile and bow and left.

The sun shone down with the intensity of a summer day, but the snow remained, not even deigning to show signs of melting. Diane tried not to let it panic her. Gusts of cold wind scurried around the corners, only to be repelled by a bit of warmth.

She glanced up at the cloudless sky. Even the wind and sun didn't know what was happening.

Inside their manor house, a symmetric two-story structure, Diane's maidservant—Matilde—hurried to bring her a coat.

"You look chilled to the bone, my lady." She ushered Diane closer to the fire.

Diane rubbed her hands together, shivering a little as she took a seat by the wide fireplace. "You can't even rebuke me for not taking a coat out this time."

Matilde pursed her lips in a smile. "I'll bring you some tea. Sire, can I bring you anything?"

Edmund shook his head, eyes already distant as he stared into the fire. Diane kicked off her boots and tucked her feet up underneath her. She rested an elbow on the armrest and propped her chin in her hand.

"We'll figure it out," she said.

Edmund didn't look away from the fire. "With your unfailing optimism, do we have a choice?"

"No." She inserted extra cheerfulness that she didn't quite feel into her voice.

A faint smile tugged at the corner of his mouth. She hid a sigh. Everyone leaned on Edmund, and he in turn leaned on her, coming to her to provide the hopefulness that he couldn't quite seem to find.

She wished he'd be able to find it on his own. Wished she could be a normal eighteen-year-old for a day, not one helping with many of the burdens of state. Wished she could be a normal princess for once—have no bigger concern than parties, courtiers, and who she'd marry.

*Maybe for just a day. That all does sound a mite stuffy.*

"Wishing for miracles again, my lady?" Matilde extended a cup of tea to her.

Diane took it with a smile and inhaled the sweet fragrance of mint leaves. "Making my face again, am I?"

Matilde patted her shoulder and tucked another blanket around her before moving over to give Edmund a blanket as well. Diane sipped at her tea, watching with some amusement as Edmund didn't bother fighting Matilde.

The woman had been their mother's lady-in-waiting and had refused to be anything other than Diane's attendant as she grew older.

Her smile faded. Their mother had passed a few years before their father died in battle. In some ways, Matilde had filled that role over the last six years.

Warmth crept down to her toes with every sip of tea. She took a moment to forget all her current troubles while she drank. Her mother had once said that you couldn't possibly be worried with a cup of tea in hand. It just wasn't allowed.

It seemed like a good philosophy to adopt.

A pounding at the door interrupted the moment of calm. Edmund tossed away his blanket with a muttered curse. Diane took one last fortifying drink and slipped her feet back into her boots before she stood.

A guard entered, a look of bewilderment on his face.

"Sire, he just appeared out of nowhere and says he wants an audience with you."

"Who?" Edmund buckled his sword back on, shifting back into a hardened warrior with the action.

"He says his name is August." The guard shrugged almost helplessly. "I think he's a faery, sire."

# Chapter 5

€dmund recovered first. "A faery?"

Diane still stared, her jaw dropping open. Equal parts eager anticipation and apprehension rushed through her.

The guard only shrugged again.

"Show him in," Edmund ordered. The guard bowed and withdrew.

Silence lingered behind him. Diane attempted to compose herself into something more dignified than a staring, bemused princess. *What's a faery doing here?* They hadn't been seen since the war ended three years ago. *Did they have something to do with this?*

A minute later, the guard returned with the stranger behind him.

The man in front of her stood a fingers-breadth shorter than her. He wore a simple tunic and trousers made of green and brown fabrics. He regarded them with calm hazel eyes, and seemed ignorant of the unruly wave to his brown hair. He didn't look too much older than Edmund, though that didn't mean anything when faeries lived for hundreds of years.

*He seems nice.* Diane remembered faeries being taller, more ferocious, and awe-inspiringly terrifying. Something about the faery calmed her. Edmund, however, didn't seem to share her opinion.

He stood with arms crossed, glaring at the newcomer.

"Come to take responsibility for this?" Hardness edged Edmund's voice.

A slight twitch of humor moved along the faery's cheek.

"No, as a matter of fact." He spoke in a pleasant tenor voice. "I came on behalf of my king to see if your township survived the initial blast."

"Or if something here caused it?" Edmund caught the part left unsaid in the faery's reply.

Diane resisted the urge to smack his arm. Despite the human Myrnians being on fair terms with the faeries of Celedon Forest during and after the war, it still wouldn't do them any favors to anger them. Especially given the current predicament.

But the faery didn't seem to take any offense. "No, we've determined the origin came from somewhere south of here."

Edmund relaxed a fraction. Diane decided to step in.

"August, is it?" She came to stand with Edmund.

The faery's face melted into a pleasant smile. Another wave of calm washed over her.

"Yes. Pleasure to finally meet you, Princess Diane."

She came up short. "How do you know my name?"

"Your guards used it while I was waiting." August lifted an eyebrow.

Diane rolled her eyes. Obviously.

He grinned again. "My parents also happen to be your and your brother's godparents. So, I did hear a fair bit about you since they do check in occasionally."

"They — Who — what?" Diane stammered. *It can't be. I know faeries live a long time, but it can't be them!*

"Damian and Adela." August confirmed her wildest imaginings and the ramblings of her pen from only earlier that afternoon. Even Edmund raised an eyebrow.

"But..." Diane fought the sudden urge to sit down. "But they helped our ancestor! Hundreds of years ago! I thought it might just be a myth that they continued to bless King Stefan's descendants. Do I have a faery blessing?" Childish eagerness sent her leaning towards the faery.

Edmund cleared his throat and she knew a rebuke to contain herself was coming. But August only chuckled.

"Both of you do. And they'd have come themselves, but as you mentioned, they're getting on in years, and the king thought sending their over-eager son to check out a frigidly-cold magical spell was a better idea."

Diane flashed a smile. Edmund shifted forward and she swallowed her reply.

"So you're here to help?"

August hesitated. "In a way."

Edmund scoffed as if to say, "I knew it."

Since the time of King Stefan, the faeries had gradually become more open. Then the war happened.

Human sorcerers and witches, together with rogue faeries from Myrnius, Calvyrn, and Durne, turned on faeries and humans alike. War erupted as alliances and battle lines were drawn across all three countries. In the wake of magic, the humans suffered the most.

Ten long years later, the war ended. The faeries from each country went into deep hiding once again to sort out their own problems. Humans were left scrambling for aid against the magic still running rampant through the countries.

A bit of regret crossed August's face. "My parents and I didn't agree with the decision to withdraw. My entire family fought on the side of your people. We, too, knew suffering from the war."

A bit of shared respect passed between them for the war and those lost. That, at least, they could agree on.

Diane spoke again. "What are you offering us?"

"We're sending out scouts to the south to track the origin. From what we know already, this has extended east into Calvyrn, and north into Durne all the way to the Sandur Strait. After that?" August shrugged. "That's the boundary line of the far north. Even we don't know much about our kind past the Strait."

Diane shivered. The far north was said to be a place where wild and untamed magic abounded. Where strange creatures roamed, and reclusive faeries with the power over frost and snow lived in palaces of ice.

"So you don't think they did it?" She rubbed at her arm to bring some warmth back.

"We've never known of an ice faery to come this far south, so there's no reason for one to be out in the middle of the ocean," August said. "We've sent out messengers to the faeries of Calvyrn and Durne. We're hoping that we'll be able to put aside differences and figure out a way to undo this. All we ask is that you allow us to meet here, somewhere in your lands. Your family is still widely known among our folk to be friends of the faeries, and it is a neutral ground that we can all agree to."

Edmund crossed his arms tighter across his chest at this request. Diane didn't offer any advice. The uprisings had begun a few years after she was born, and she'd been brought up in war. She hadn't seen the battlefields, so her mistrust of magic did not run as deep as Edmund's. Perhaps because some part of her wished for a return to the old ways.

Finally, Edmund spoke. "When would this happen?"

"Four days from now. This strange ice affects everyone and our way of life," August said.

"Strange, how?" Diane interjected again.

"You've noticed it's not melting?" A divot appeared on August's cheek as he bit the inside in concern.

Diane and Edmund nodded.

"It reeks of magic, but it's like nothing we've ever seen. We have no idea what caused it."

"Wonderful," Edmund muttered. "Just when I thought it couldn't get any worse."

Diane pressed her arms across her chest as even her optimism began to vanish. This was something new, something strange. Something even the faeries didn't know about. And that just might make it worse.

# Chapter 6

Tonya sat on the ocean floor. Her black hair swayed about her to the gentle beat of the ocean. Despite the ice that still remained two days later, life went on in the ocean. The faeries were kept busier than ever trying to counter the effects of the ice on the ocean life.

She sighed and swirled a pattern in the sand with her finger. Even if she hadn't been kept under guard all lengths of tides, there was nothing she could do to help anyway. She just sat and tried to ignore the yearning to break free and see the ice again. It settled her in some way.

The guards were no help to try to pass the time. They just floated in stoic silence, not even facing her. The only time they acknowledged her presence was when it was time for her to go to the surface, or for announcing the arrival of the faeries appointed by the king to try to draw out her ice magic again.

The high walls of coral around her loomed closer at the memories of those encounters. Their magic of currents and ocean breezes and whispering tides only made the icy magic inside her wind tighter until it threatened to suffocate her.

She drew her knees up to her chest, flicking her fingers at an inquisitive fish that swam closer to investigate the tips of her hair. Some part of her wished that she was viewed more as a threat. Then maybe someone would at least look at her instead of just ignoring her.

A sigh escaped in a stream of bubbles. She tracked their path to the surface. They wouldn't pop. Just bump against the sheen of ice, then freeze. Most stuck, but sometimes the frozen bubbles would sink before the undercurrents, kept warm by magic, would melt them.

A pebble floated down in front of her face. She frowned and glanced up. Sophie floated a safe distance away. She dropped another pebble. Tonya made an irritated shooing motion. Sophie stuck her tongue out, then began waving her arms erratically.

*What's she doing? She looks like she's fighting off damselfish after wandering into their home.*

Sophie slowed down her motions, over-exaggerating what Tonya eventually decided was a query as to how she was doing. She lifted her arms in a shrug.

*I'd be better if I knew what was going to happen to me.*

Sophie's wings rippled as they kept her in place above the coral prison. She began trying to sign something else, then shook her head. A look crossed her face that meant trouble and Tonya tried to wave her off as she began to swim down.

Tonya's motions attracted the attention of the guard captain. He turned his gaze up, and an exasperated expression creased his broad features. He trilled a whistle to alert his fellow guards, but they stood relaxed as she approached.

"Can I please just talk to her?" Sophie asked.

"Do your parents know you're here?" Captain Kostis frowned at her.

A stubborn expression crossed Sophie's face. "No, but I'm old enough to make my own decisions, thank you very much."

"Sophie, you shouldn't be here," Tonya protested as she stood. It would just hurt Sophie.

Sophie swiped an irritated hand through the water, stirring it with a fresh current that coiled with her anger. "Tonya, this is ridiculous. You're about as harmless as a hermit crab. No offense."

Tonya propped her hands on her hips. "That is a little offensive, you know."

Sophie had more magic in her little finger than Tonya could conjure on a good day, but she didn't have to shout it.

A faint grin touched Kostis's mouth and he lowered his spear. "Five minutes."

Tonya shot him a grateful look. Sophie darted forward and touched down on the sand beside Tonya. She wrapped her arms around Tonya, nearly squeezing all her air from her.

"You're all right? They haven't done anything horrible to you, have they?" Sophie spun to glare at the guards.

"The worst they've done is ignore me." Tonya tugged Sophie back. The captain's smile softened in a bit of apology. Tonya ignored it. "Anything interesting been happening? Have they figured out how to get rid of the ice?"

Sophie shook her head. "No, but I heard some rumors that some land faeries made their way out here to try to find us."

"What?" Tonya stared. "Did I freeze the land too?"

Sophie bit her lip and slowly nodded.

Tonya sank to the ground and stared at the puffs of sand as it settled.

"I ruined everything," she whispered.

Sophie plopped down beside her, stirring more sand. "You did not. Someone attacked you. This could be their magic."

Tonya didn't have the heart to remind her that the faeries sent by the king had found nothing but threads of her magics in the ice. Albeit in wide swaths that entwined one another in a complex pattern they couldn't explain. It defied logical explanation that it could have come from her, but the evidence was there.

"What are the land faeries here for?" Tonya hoped it wasn't something dramatic like retribution against the incompetent faery who had somehow frozen the entire world.

"How am I supposed to know?" Sophie tossed her hands up in a swirl of water.

"Sophie." Tonya fixed her with a look. Sophie had always been notorious for eavesdropping and sticking her nose into other faeries' business.

Sophie rolled her eyes. "Fine. They did come to see what happened since they pinpointed the origin of the ice from here. And I heard that they're calling a meeting among all the land faeries to figure out a way to undo it."

Hope sprang in Tonya's heart. "Do they know how?"

In the extra second Sophie took to reply, Tonya knew there was no solution.

"They want you to go—to see if they can figure it out."

Hope sprang back up to shove at the despair. She'd be able to set foot on a different part of the land. She could see different faeries. Maybe someone would know something about her parents. It died with Sophie's next words.

"The king is deciding what to do right now."

She'd forgotten that someone else currently decided her fate. "Do you think he'll let me go?"

"He'd be stupid not to," Sophie declared, earning a faint look of disapproval from Kostis. "His advisors obviously can't figure it out."

Captain Kostis cleared his throat. "Your time is up."

Sophie scowled at him, daring him to make her take back her words.

Tonya nudged her. "You should go. And figure out what's going to happen and then come back and tell me."

Sophie smiled. "You know I will." Her wings appeared again, translucent and ruffling around the edges. She waved as she rose above the edges of the coral and swam away with the aid of a small current.

"There's a good chance he'll probably let you go," Kostis spoke.

Tonya floated a little closer to him, wrapping her arms around herself. "You think so?"

He cast a sidelong glance at her through the openings in his helmet. "As you said, our people haven't been able to figure out a way to undo it yet. Maybe we need some help."

Tonya raised an eyebrow. Ocean faeries were as wild and independent as the water itself. Help was not a word often used in their vocabulary.

"I'm just as surprised as you." A hint of a smile entered his voice, drawing a slight chuckle from her. "And I hope that you can figure something out."

She offered a wry smile. "I think you might be hoping for too much from me."

He turned to regard her more fully. "I don't think so. You remind me of Thalia. She never let anything stop her."

Tonya perked up at the mention of her mother. Kostis had been one of the soldiers who had gone to search for her mother after she disappeared. And the one to bring Tonya back to the ocean. He'd been friendly enough her entire life, but they'd never talked about her parents before.

"Did — did you ever meet my father?"

A brief frown creased Kostis's face. "I did."

Longing welled up inside Tonya. Part of her wished not to ask the question, since most believed the rumor concerning her.

"My mother and father—did they…"

"In the short time I spent with them, it was obvious they loved each other very much."

Relief crashed over her like a storm-powered wave. Maybe they did want her after all.

"How did you meet them?"

"I was on patrol when I caught a trace of her magic for the first time in almost two years. Hardly believing it, I headed inland to find her and your father on the Durnean coast, farther south than his kind had ever come. You were only a few months old. All she said was that they were fleeing from something and needed help to cover their trail. I escorted her farther south while your father backtracked."

Kostis paused and turned his gaze to a stingray swooping low above a bed of gently-waving sea grass. "He never came back."

Tonya blinked away the pressure that built behind her eyes. She'd never heard this and somehow it hurt even more than not knowing.

"What did my mother do?"

Kostis sighed and dug his spear into the sand, creating a small maelstrom of dirt around it.

"Against my counsel, she decided to go search for him. She gave you to me and left me to carry the news back to the ocean. And to ask your family to take you in and shelter you in the ocean. Then she disappeared and never came back."

A tear detached from Tonya's eye and floated away to merge with the salt water around her.

"Why didn't you ever tell me?" she whispered.

His light green eyes met hers, sorrow and regret furrowing deeper lines in his stern face.

"The king himself forbade it. What your mother did was unheard of, and the king had no wish to offend the ice king or draw the wrath of whatever was chasing them. And even from the start, you were a puzzling thing. Many thought you shouldn't have been able to exist. There's been no intermarriage between the different kinds of faeries, and certainly no children."

"But I could at least have known the truth about them!" Her voice gained strength.

"I'm sorry I never told you." His sincerity killed some of her anger. "But I did believe that it was to keep you protected. Whatever was after them, it scared your mother. And I'd never seen that before."

Tonya turned her gaze up to the icy blue of the surface, wondering and a little afraid. "Do you think that whatever was following them, found me?"

Kostis tipped a glance at the ice. "Perhaps."

She swallowed hard. *Maybe going with the land faeries is a bad idea. What if it's still out there and finds me? I could vanish like sea foam and no one would ever know.*

# Chapter 7

Tonya didn't have to wait long before the summons came to appear before the king. Kostis stayed by her side during the long swim to the king's court. Tonya stroked with her arms, fluttering her feet, pointedly not looking at Kostis as he effortlessly maintained pace beside her with rippling wings. The other guard with them was not so gracious, sighing heavily from time to time at their slow progress.

Tonya resisted the urge to stick her tongue out at him.

Word must have spread about the land faery's message, because the court was packed full of faeries, jostling one another for space as they floated, stood, or perched atop coral ridges. Tonya swallowed nervously as her guards began to push their way up to the throne. She kept her head ducked as whispers began to spread and a hush marked her progress towards the king.

She wobbled through a bow, barely managing to meet King Stavros's gaze. The queen once again sat beside him, though this time a bit of hope edged the constant fluttering of her hands.

"As you all know, this ice also covers the continent," Stavros said.

The whispers increased in intensity. Kostis rested a briefly comforting hand on her shoulder.

"Our land kin have called a summit. I have decided to send Tonya Freyr-dottir, with several representatives, to this council in the hopes that their combined magic will perhaps be able to undo this curse."

Tonya flinched under the word. *I didn't mean to curse anything.* But her guilt went unnoticed as louder conversation burst forth, arguments erupting like tiny storms among some faeries who didn't think that the ocean faeries needed any assistance.

"You leave by the next tide. Captain Kostis will lead the expedition." King Stavros deigned to look at her before swimming from the court, followed by his queen.

Sophie darted up, dodging a guard's halfhearted grab at her.

"They won't let me go with you!" Red tinted her pale cheeks and a scowl distorted her normally cheerful features.

"That's probably for the best," Tonya tried to say. She had the ability to breathe in and out of water, but for someone as young as Sophie, it would be more difficult, as she hadn't practiced spending extensive amounts of time out of the water.

But Sophie didn't let her finish. "It's ridiculous! Do they expect you to go marching overland like some prisoner?"

"I don't—"

"And what if you get attacked again?" Sophie jabbed a finger at her.

Tonya shut her mouth, pursing her lips and shifting hands to her hips while she waited for Sophie to finish railing about the dangers of the land and the supposed ineptitude of the faeries who would be going with her, and land faeries as a whole.

Kostis cleared his throat, a faint smile playing across his face.

Sophie broke off, glaring up at him. Tonya stared at him in mild affront. *I need to practice that sound if it'll get Sophie to shut up for a second.*

"As King Stavros said, I will be leading the expedition, so rest assured, she will be safe," Kostis said.

Sophie didn't look convinced, only narrowed her glare.

"Sophie." Tonya tugged on her sleeve. "I'll be fine. And, who knows, maybe I'll figure out how to undo the spell."

Sophie *humphed* a little, but flashed a smile, even though they both plainly didn't think it would happen.

"Are you going to keep her under guard while she goes to pack?" she asked Kostis. "The next tide is only in a few hours."

"No, I think you will do an excellent job keeping an eye on her," Kostis replied, voice suspiciously even. Tonya smothered a grin as Sophie tilted her chin up. Sophie grabbed her hand and whisked her away.

Tonya didn't have much to put into her bag woven of thick kelp strands. She had no idea what to bring to be on land for longer than a few minutes. She packed two spare sets of shirts and trousers, a comb, and a whale-bone knife.

Sophie sat on one of the rounded corals that bulged from the ocean floor, watching her. Tonya set aside her bag and sank down to her bed of sea grass. They stared at one another in silence.

"I'll miss you!" Sophie finally blurted.

Tonya blinked rapidly. There was no guarantee when she'd be back. "I'll miss you too."

Sophie darted to her side, wrapping her in a rib-crushing embrace. "You'll figure it out. I know you will."

A trembling laugh escaped Tonya.

"I don't have any magic." Nothing worth trying to use.

"Is there a rule that says you have to have magic to undo a crazy ice spell?" Sophie released her hold by a fraction.

Another giggle built in Tonya's chest. "I'm sure it's helpful."

Sophie cleared her throat suspiciously as she straightened and let go of Tonya. "Ice or no, I'm glad you're getting a chance to go onto the land. Maybe it'll help your magic."

"You think so?" Tonya twisted a bit of kelp in her fingers. *Maybe nothing can help it.*

Sophie jerked her chin in a nod. "You've always been half in and half out of the water. Maybe it's time to try something else."

Tonya slung her bag over her shoulder. "I hope you're right."

Sophie sniffed in superiority. "I'm always right."

Tonya bit back listing the many times Sophie had not, in fact, been right. Sophie rolled her eyes and gathered her in another hug.

"All right. Let's go meet Sir Shark Head."

"Kostis," Tonya corrected with a giggle.

"Whatever." Sophie smirked.

Their amusement dampened a fraction as they left the house and met Tonya's aunt and uncle.

"Be safe." Her uncle awkwardly patted her shoulder. Her aunt looked more reluctant, but finally gave her a small nod. Tonya returned it, understanding a little more in the light of the story that Kostis had shared. Her aunt had lost a sister twice. Once when the storms swept Thalia away, and then again when she married an ice faery before vanishing again.

Tonya began to swim towards the edge of the reef where she would meet with her escort. Sophie swam beside her, the silence stretching between them once more The shimmering blue of the ice crept closer and closer as they approached the surface, broken only by a circle of sunlight where the guards had managed to break through again.

Kostis and five other faeries waited. Three were soldiers, and the other two Tonya recognized as part of the king's council. They all carried bags similar to hers, but the guards carried extra bundles under their arms.

"Ready?" Kostis asked.

Tonya nodded. She accepted another hug from Sophie before leaving her behind to join the others. Kostis went first, disappearing through the hole with a mighty kick. A soldier followed, and then Tonya was next.

Sophie offered a small wave. Tonya drew a deep breath before kicking up towards the surface. A cold breeze swept around her as she broke the surface.

Kostis extended his hand and helped pull her up onto the ice. She slid a step on the ice before gaining her balance. One by one the other faeries emerged onto the ice, leaving a thin sheen of seawater over their skin.

Tonya bit the inside of her cheek and spun in a circle, slicking the water from her skin and hair in concentrated motion. She'd never needed to keep the seawater close to her skin when she was on the surface.

No one had seemed to notice her, engaged with unwrapping the bundles the guards had brought. Kostis handed her a bundle and she shook out a coat and soft boots made of shark skin and lined with sea otter fur.

The other faeries shivered as they shrugged into the lined clothing. Tonya pulled on the shoes, finding they gave her much needed extra purchase on the ice. But the coat she balled in her hands.

"Put that on," Kostis instructed. "You'll freeze."

Tonya hesitated, not sure if she should call their attention to the fact that she wasn't the least bit cold. In fact, the air was invigorating, like she wanted to fly and cavort with snow geese. No matter that she'd never seen a snow goose and definitely couldn't fly. She regarded the coat in her hands once more.

*I don't really want to look like more of a freak.* So, she pulled it on, but left it unfastened.

She settled her bag back over her shoulder, gripping the strap in nervous excitement as she stared around the waves frozen in tumbled curls. To the north lay Myrnius, and hopefully some answers. But maybe more importantly, a chance to explore the land that her mother had walked.

Kostis led the way, walking out over the creaking ice. A soldier indicated that she should follow. She slid a few steps before she found her stride. The others slipped and slid their way across the ice with muttered imprecations.

Not even hours of walking could wear down Tonya's excitement at being on the ice and walking toward Myrnius. A few seagulls swooped in to croak questions to the other faeries. Tonya caught snatches of their conversations—the animals were just as concerned about the ice.

Tonya quickened her pace to walk closer to Kostis.

"How much longer till we reach the shore?"

"It should be soon," he answered.

The sun hovered low at the western edge of the horizon, drawing extra sparkles from the frozen waves, when the ice gave way to the firmness of land. Snow crusted the sand dunes along the beach, ice crystals skittering across the tideline where waves had been frozen in their tracks.

Tonya sank up to her ankles in the snow. She bent to scoop a handful. Its chill sent tingles across her fingertips and the whisper of words just out of reach teased her. She tilted her head, closing her eyes as if to hear the words better, but they whisked away in the wind.

She let the snow fall from her hand in a miniature blizzard. Not really knowing what she was doing, she released a breath through pursed lips and the falling snow danced in a circle, swooping up in defiance of the breeze.

"What are you doing?" one of the soldiers snapped.

The snow collapsed to the ground and the tingle vanished from her fingers, leaving them a little cold.

"I—"

"Ice magic?" He kicked the snow at her feet as if it would come to life and attack him.

"I just wanted to see what the snow felt like." She lifted one shoulder, hoping it would appease him. *I don't know what I did. Except, maybe, it was a little bit of magic.*

The thought both exhilarated and frightened her. If she could control a fraction of snow, perhaps all the ice and snow *had* come from her.

"There's a sheltered cove up ahead where we'll stay tonight," Kostis broke in. He shepherded them down the beach toward a rocky outcropping. Tonya trailed along, turning her face away from the soldier who walked alongside her.

She pursed her lips again. But nothing stirred the snow and her fingers returned to their normal warmth. She sighed. Maybe she'd imagined the whole thing.

*

Tonya woke to the entirely new sensation of aching feet. She pushed aside her insulated whaleskin blanket to sit up. The other faeries huddled around the fire that one of the guards had started the night before. The dancing flames had mesmerized Tonya, and she'd stared at them until they sparked in her vision whenever she looked away. The faery hadn't even used magic to create it, all the more amazing to her.

She took a few minutes to comb her hair out and tuck it up with whalebone pins. She appeared to be the only one who had passed a somewhat restful night, as even the normally stoic guards had expressions of cold misery on their faces.

"Sleep all right?" Kostis came to stand by her as she folded up the blanket, brushing off some stray snowflakes.

She nodded.

"Cold?" he continued conversationally.

Tonya frantically snatched up her coat, discarded the night before, and pulled it on.

"Yes," she lied.

Kostis released another one of his grumbles, the sound compelling Tonya to shake her head.

*He's got to be using some sort of song magic in that noise.*

But Kostis smiled. "I thought you might not be. Perhaps that's the ice faery in you."

A little bit of the knot inside her eased, and a faint smile touched her lips. She'd always been compared to her mother while under the waves; she'd never really thought about the part of her that was like her father.

"I saw what you did with the snow yesterday."

Her mouth dried in alarm. If he knew, then the councilors knew, and maybe they'd poke and prod her with more magic.

"I think you should keep practicing."

"What?" She stared up at him. "But wouldn't that make everything worse? What if I cause a blizzard, or an avalanche, or freeze —"

Kostis held up a hand. "Calm down, Tonya. I don't think you're nearly that powerful yet."

She subsided with a sheepish grin. Her fears did sound ridiculous when he put it that way.

"I don't think practicing will hurt. Maybe it'll release some more of your power and help us figure out a way to undo this." He pointed farther inland where snow mounded in drifts as far as the eye could see.

Tonya drew a breath of the chill air and nodded. For the first time she felt some eagerness to try to use her repressed magic.

She edged a little closer to the fire and took her share of dried fish tucked in a thin wrap of pale pink kelp. She ate while the others packed and finished the last bites as they walked on.

After a quarter hour, square shapes with peaked tops appeared. Tonya stared at them, trying to puzzle them out. A tremendous noise split the air, and a dark shape ran towards them on all fours. It was covered in thick fur, muzzle bared wide to reveal teeth that were not at all friendly.

A figure ran from a cluster of humped dwellings and chased after the creature.

Kostis lowered his spear, holding off the creature as it snarled and growled. Tonya edged back a step, reaching for the knife stowed away in her bag.

The figure neared and Tonya caught her first glimpse of a human. He didn't look too different from the faeries. About two hand spans taller than Kostis, broader-shouldered, and without the aura of magic that surrounded her companions.

"Who're you?" he demanded in a gruff voice, resting a hand on his sword. The creature retreated to stand by him, still growling and showing its fangs. A few more men appeared from the dwellings to join him.

They all wore heavy coats, gloves, and expressions of mistrust. Tonya swallowed hard. *What if they find out I caused all this?*

"We are from the coast," Kostis said. "We're going to the council that your king and the faeries called about this winter."

The man relaxed a fraction. He snapped his fingers, and the animal subsided, its muzzle opening into a more friendly expression.

"Faeries?" he guessed.

Kostis nodded.

The man looked them all over again, pausing over her, possibly marking the differences between her and the rest of the faeries.

"Don't know that we've ever seen ocean faeries 'round here, even during t' war. Must be bad, then."

"Like it's not bad enough?" one of his companions grumbled.

"We're affected too," Kostis admitted. "I wish we could do something to help."

"First faeries in a while that've come around t' say something like that." The man shifted and reached down to ruffle the animal's ears.

Tonya couldn't jerk her attention from the animal as its furry tail swished back and forth, tongue lolling in pleasure. The man caught her staring, and a small smile softened his features.

"Ever seen a dog before, miss?" he asked.

Dog. Tonya filed the word away as she shook her head.

"Want t' pet her?"

Tonya glanced at Kostis for permission. The captain nodded with a faint smile and she hesitantly stepped forward.

"Let her smell you first."

Tonya stretched out her fingers as the man demonstrated. The dog stretched its nose closer to her, sniffing cautiously, then allowed her to brush a hand across its smooth fur.

A rumble of enjoyment broke from it as she scratched behind its ears. It butted her hand, reminding her of the dolphins that would sometimes come to seek out a faery or two to play among the waves.

"How far to the king's palace?" Kostis leaned on his spear.

The man barked a short laugh. "Palace? Our king hasn't had a castle t' his name since his father's time. You must really not know much about us."

"We knew of the war." A bit of defensiveness edged Kostis's voice.

"Aye, the war," the man scoffed. "King Edmund's doing his best after it all, but he's still young, and now all this?" He gestured around with a shrug of his shoulders. "I hear that Durne and Calvyrn are just as bad off as we are, so maybe that'll force us all t' work together again."

The dog pushed closer to Tonya, almost knocking her off balance as she stopped scratching to listen closer. The land war had only been stories to her. The ocean faeries had staunchly refused to get involved, sending out soldiers to protect their borders only.

But they did know that it had torn the faery clans and the human kingdoms apart and everyone had suffered for it.

"I hear maybe it's a rogue sorcerer from t' war casting t' spell," one of the other men spoke up.

"Or maybe some faeries trying t' exert their power again," another muttered.

A chill slithered across Tonya's heart. *Will this ice cause another rift if everyone casts blame like this?*

"My people have studied it, and we know it's neither of those things," Kostis said.

A bit of relief shone in the spokesman's eyes. "You know what it is, then?"

Kostis hesitated. "An anomaly."

The man's shoulders slumped again. "Aye, that's what most of t' rumors are."

"The council should be able to answer these questions, and hopefully find a solution," Kostis said.

"We wish you well, then," the man said. "It's about another two days' walk t' Chelm where you'll find t' king."

Tonya reluctantly stood and backed away to stand with Kostis as the dog returned to its master.

Kostis thanked the man and led the way around the village. Tonya glanced around at her companions. They all wore serious frowns.

*They're all worried about what that human said.* The thought came sobering and she turned her energy back to trudging over endless swells of snow and trying to coax some of it back to her hand.

# Chapter 8

"The faeries have arrived," a guard announced.

Diane reached over to straighten Edmund's coat lapels before buttoning up her own fur-lined jacket. She brushed a hand over her hair, making sure no stray strands had escaped from the narrow braid Matilde had plaited across the top of her head to fall into carefully-combed waves over her shoulders.

"You look fine," Edmund reassured.

They stepped outside together to greet the newcomers. Diane tilted her chin up to adopt the hint of regalness that her mother had taught her. It was a little difficult to attain while wearing several bulky layers of clothing and her thickest coat, but the faeries, it seemed, had also opted for warmth over fashion. What little fashion was left after the war.

Diane recognized August immediately. He stood beside two older-looking faeries, one a female faery with her hand tucked inside the male faery's. Diane stifled a gasp. Edmund looked down at her in confusion, then his eyes widened in shock.

Four parallel scars twisted down the right side of the man's face. She'd know that pattern anywhere.

It had been a shock to hear that August was the son of *the* Damian and Adela from the legends of her family, but somehow she hadn't actually thought they were still in Myrnius and would be coming to the council.

Edmund allowed her to pull him over toward them with no complaint.

August greeted them with a smile that turned to a knowing smirk as Diane tried to disguise her complete awe.

"King Edmund, Princess Diane, allow me to officially introduce you to your godparents, Damian and Adela."

To her lasting embarrassment, Diane uttered something more akin to a squeak, before being able to form a coherent sentence.

"I'm so pleased to meet you!"

"It's lovely to meet you as well." Adela freed her hand to reach out to Diane. Her voice had a lilting music to it as if she spent more time singing. Her long brown hair fell in effortless waves over her shoulders, but Diane caught a sheen of grey to some of the strands.

Damian offered her a bow and clasped Edmund's hand, who still hadn't been able to form a greeting himself.

"I'm sorry!" Diane finally burst out. "It's just—I've only ever heard—*legends*—about you and now..." She gestured widely with her hands before they fell back to her sides.

Adela's laugh caused the evergreens to shake snow from their branches and stand taller with new exuberance.

"I wish we could have met much earlier, but with everything that happened, we never really formally met your parents either. We all thought it was best to stay hidden in the forest."

"Certainly didn't stop her from trying to go explore in Celedon," Edmund finally spoke up. Diane nearly drove her elbow into his side for making her sound like a silly fool in front of them.

"We would have kidnapped you for a day, then," Damian said. The tease in his pleasant tenor voice carried up to his hazel eyes, and Diane once again felt a sense of calm and happiness

*If this is what faeries are truly like, then maybe there's nothing to fear.*

"You would have been stuck with her until you ran out of stories." Edmund smirked.

Diane dug her elbow into his ribs this time, decorum or no.

Adela chuckled and flashed a smile. "We'll have to sit down after this council. I've missed staying in touch with our godchildren. It makes me remember Steffan and Irena."

"I'd love that!" Diane said, taking a short breath to try to control the flush spreading over her cheeks.

"We wanted to thank you, Your Majesty, for hosting this council," Damian said.

"Edmund, please." Her brother shook his head.

Understanding crossed Damian's face and he nodded. "Something had to be done, and we appreciate your prompt response. It will be good for all of us to work together again."

Diane smiled and turned to the other faeries standing in a separate group. They wore earthy colors of browns and tans. The only female faery in the group offered her a tentative smile and Diane mustered one in return. These were the Durnean faeries. And while the faeries in front of her likely fought on the side of the humans, unease still rippled through her.

Two older male faeries stepped forward and greeted Edmund with slight bows. Diane nodded a tight greeting and snuck a glance instead at the fourth member. He looked about the same age as August.

He stood in tense alertness, gaze frequently straying around at the gathering townsfolk, the other faeries, Ralf standing comfortingly behind her. He carried himself much like Ralf, ready to spring into action at any moment.

Curious weapons were strapped across his back. The sheaths held some sort of slightly curved blade, but instead of hilts, a long piece of wood extended over his shoulder where he could grab it. The weapons gathered more than one curious, or scornful, look at their strangeness.

Edmund's touch on her arm brought her attention back.

"Please, come inside." Edmund gestured to the manor house. "Some of the other lords and stewards have arrived as well and we're all eager to hear what can be done about this ice."

Damian's mouth twisted in a frown and Diane's heart dropped a beat. *This already doesn't look like good news.*

\*

Diane chewed her lip as she stared down at the town. A warm breeze tickled her cheek, at odds with the snow still surrounding them. She flexed her gloved fingers, sore from writing notes late into the previous night from the brief council Edmund had held with the newly arrived lords and stewards, and taking more notes during the meeting with the faeries. The Calvyrnian water faeries hadn't been able to break through the iced rivers and lakes to come, but the human representatives had brought plenty of news.

"You trying to solve this problem yourself?"

Diane peeked a glance at where Ralf stood behind her. A half-smile curved his lips. She jerked her attention from the sight—something she'd been having to do more and more recently.

"Just thinking." She turned back to the village before she could flush. "There's so much to do, so much uncertainty…" She sighed and rubbed her eyes. Even the arrival of the Calvyrnian Lord Darek, descendant of Prince Killian the wolf prince, hadn't been able to truly distract her. Though she had determined to try to ask him about his line's rumored shapeshifting ability— especially after seeing the strange glint in his eyes when they caught the light.

The reports that the lords and stewards had brought were the same as what they already knew. Fields buried in snow and ice. Predicted crop failures if something wasn't done soon. Trade nearly nonexistent. Panic spreading among the people. A few riots quelled.

Then the news the faeries had brought.

The surprising revelation that there was a faery with ice *and* ocean magic, and a mysterious attack on her had caused the storm.

And the more sobering news that they had no idea how to undo it.

The Durnean faeries, strongest with earth magic, and the Myrnian faeries, whose magic was best with plants and animals had promised their aid to all three countries to try and avoid the worse. But if the ice wasn't removed…

"Diane." Ralf's voice held a bit of warning.

"I know." She sighed. "I can't do everything."

Even though she was perfectly happy with a pen and parchment in hand, helping keep Edmund more organized, it had overwhelmed her that morning when the faeries and humans had adjourned. She'd grabbed a coat and marched outside to the nearest hill to find some sort of relief.

But even the beauty of the glittering snow and ice taunted her. There was nothing she could do.

Messengers had said that the ocean faeries were on their way to Chelm. The council would meet one more time with them before deciding what to do.

"Damian said that we'd likely have to send someone north past the Strait. If that happens, they've already decided to send at least one human with the faeries."

Ralf stepped up beside her. "Did he say who?"

Diane shook her head. "No. But you should have heard the arguments from the lords and stewards trying to get someone picked from their lands." She rubbed her eyes. Whoever it ended up being, she pitied the poor faeries who'd be stuck with them. None of the options had sounded particularly appealing.

"Have you rested recently?" His concern drew her gaze back up.

She kept a hand pressed against her cheek to hide the quick blush. "When would I have time to do that?" Between councils and late dinners to discuss everything with Edmund in relative privacy, she hadn't had a full night's sleep since the ice storm.

His mouth puckered down in a frown and he gently touched her arm. Her heart paused. He never really touched her. *I must look awful.*

"You should go back and rest. I'll stand guard outside your door if I have to."

Diane allowed a slow smile. "All right."

His hand fell away from her sleeve and she fought a strange reluctance as she began the trek back into the town.

Men and women dipped bows and curtseys as she passed, most calling out greetings. She returned each with a smile and name if she remembered, but didn't halt her stride. Her heart lifted at the sight of children building snow castles across the square, their laughter teasing the breeze.

Smiles and laughter had been rare the past few days, but they were there, and that's all that mattered to her. Some of the higher-ranking townspeople stopped her to ask after news. She couldn't bring herself to tell them yet. The faeries didn't know what to do.

Matilde swept snow from in front of the mansion door.

"Wasn't expecting you back for some time, my lady." Matilde propped her broom against the wall.

"It's been strongly suggested that I come back and rest." Diane tilted her chin towards Ralf.

Matilde nodded. "Sensible young man. I knew I liked you."

Ralf's smile crept up around his eyes. Diane's lips curved in response.

"In you go!" Matilde shooed her inside. "Edmund's out, so I think you should be able to sleep for a bit. I'll make sure of it." She grabbed her broom again and shook it.

"Between you and Ralf, I think I should be fine." Diane retreated inside with a laugh. Inside her room, she pulled off her gloves and coat. Her desk tempted her, even littered with reports and papers. There was still so much to do.

Maybe she'd just do a little bit before taking a nap.

*

Matilde shook Diane awake two hours later.

"It's a miracle you didn't fall asleep at your desk, my lady." She wrenched open the curtains to allow offensively bright afternoon sunlight inside.

Diane groaned and lifted her hand to rub at her sleep-filled eyes, pausing before she stained her eyes with the residual ink from her fingers. It had happened more than once.

Matilde poured fresh water into the basin on her dressing table. "Come on, my lady. I already let you sleep too long as it is. Edmund's been asking after you for the past hour and rumor has it that the ocean faeries have been sighted."

That got Diane up and moving. "Matilde!"

"You needed sleep!" She waved a finger and ushered her to the dressing table.

Diane took a seat and automatically reached for the papers piled where she'd left them for review. They would be sent out to every lord and she wanted them to be perfect. Matilde frowned at her in the mirror, but didn't say anything as she ran a brush through Diane's hair.

Diane yawned as she read through the report, hoping Edmund wouldn't notice the spelling error on the second page. Matilde began a braid by Diane's left ear, bringing it over the crown of her head to wrap above her right ear before it swept across the back of her head in a loose trail. Matilde spent a few extra minutes fussing and trying to coax some extra curl from the ends of her hair.

Matilde finished before Diane could fall asleep again. Diane stood, rubbing her eyes before allowing Matilde to spread some cosmetics over her face and eyes.

"Beautiful!" Matilde declared. She brought out a white fur-lined cloak and carefully draped it around Diane's shoulders.

Diane wanted to protest that it was too much, but she traced a hand through the fur, remembering doing the same thing as a small child when her mother wore the cloak.

Matilde opened the door and ushered her out. "There's a snack waiting for you in the smaller sitting room."

Diane nodded, hoping for a few minutes of quiet in the room to eat. But Edmund paced in the small sitting room. Never a good sign when he was clearly waiting to ambush her.

"Oh good, you're finally awake." He barely paused to greet her before continuing his circuit.

"Then you should have let Matilde wake me up sooner." Diane dodged around him and headed for the tray of kaffe and strawberry scones.

She waited until he passed her by again. "Here," she mumbled around a mouthful of cream-covered scone and handed him the parchment.

He unrolled it and tried to read it as he paced, succeeding in ramming his foot into the same chair at least three times on his continuous route.

"You know you misspelled a word on page two?" He barely glanced up.

She huffed a few crumbs and rolled her eyes. "I know. I'd appreciate it if you didn't announce it to the whole world."

"The scones are hardly the whole world. Definitely less than once you're finished with them."

Diane scowled around her third helping. "If I wanted your opinion, I would have asked."

"How? You're too busy eating." Edmund managed a smirk and Diane didn't bother to warn him about the upcoming settee. She took a prim sip of kaffe as Edmund rubbed his shin with a barely muttered curse.

"Maybe you should sit down and try to read."

"If I wanted your opinion, I would have asked," he retorted in a poor imitation of her voice, but he plopped down into the armchair and kept reading.

She flicked a piece of scone at him. He caught it and ate it.

"I've allowed you to become a hellion," he said with mouth full.

She rolled her eyes and grabbed a fourth scone, debating on trying to store it somewhere within her dress or cloak. As they were both lacking in pockets, she ate it.

He rolled the parchment back up and tapped it against his knee. "It looks good."

Relief eased some of the tension in her shoulders. "How many copies do we need?"

Edmund rubbed his chin. "At least a dozen."

Diane looked sadly down at her fingers. There were scribes who could finish the copies, but there were few things she liked to hand off to someone else. Though in this case, she might just let them for the sake of her fingers.

"The ocean faeries have been sighted." Edmund tapped the parchment faster against his knee. "They're being directed to the council chamber. We'll meet there."

Diane took one last scone from the tray. "This will work. We'll find a way to undo it all, and then we'll get back to our lives."

"And then maybe I'll figure out a way to rebuild the castle like you want."

Diane smiled. Rebuilding the castle was a near impossible task with their current resources, but they both liked to dream about what life could be like.

Edmund stood and offered her his arm. "Shall we?"

She tucked her arm through his, still munching on scone.

"Are you going to finish that before we get to the council chambers?" he asked.

"Maybe. I can't exactly save it for later."

"Your dress doesn't have pockets?" He arched one eyebrow in surprise.

"No. Formal gowns have a sad dearth of pockets, leaving no room for hoarding food. Do you want to finish it?"

He gave a long-suffering sigh, but ate it in two bites. Diane dusted crumbs from her cloak and hoped that none lingered on her face.

Ralf and several other guards fell in behind them as they left the house. Diane shivered as a breeze whipped down the street towards them, cutting right through her cloak.

"I've never liked winter, and it's not fair that we get two this year," she groused, leaning a little closer to Edmund.

"Then walk faster so we can bring the summer back." He tugged at her arm.

"I would, but a certain amount of decorum is needed in public, wouldn't you agree?" She raised her chin a little, smiling at the townsfolk who had come out to watch and wait for the council results.

"You ate too many scones, didn't you?" he replied, giving a friendly wave to a young boy and girl who flourished their best salutes with wooden stick swords.

"And once again, your opinion isn't needed."

He gave a small smirk and kept walking.

The council chamber building was a two-storied structure with a foundation of smoothed white river rocks from the Nida River, and finished with darkened oak from Celedon forest. Frosted windows were spaced in even intervals between thicker beams worn smooth by age.

Soldiers stood by the doors and outside each window, most of them wearing the silver and red livery of the royal family. The others wore the colors of the visiting lords.

Edmund led the way inside where human men and women clustered in groups on one side of the wide chamber, their varied clothes marking them from Durne, Calvyrn, and Myrnius. Diane ignored them and the mistrustful glances they sent each other, looking instead at the odd company waiting a few paces away from the other faeries.

Blonde hair with reddish tints glinted bright in the sunlight streaming through the windows. All of them wore pale grey leggings and shoes, the rest of their clothing obscured by thick coats trimmed in strange silky fur. *Is that water on their skin?* Diane tried not to stare too intently at the extra shimmer around them.

The only female of the group stood with arms crossed over her stomach. Her hair was startlingly dark beside the paleness of her companions. The wet sheen seemed to be missing from her skin, also a shade darker than her companions. She glanced around nervously as if waiting for an inevitable attack. All but one of her companions notably ignored her, and Diane sensed an almost scorn in their glances to her.

"Poor thing." Adela came to stand by Diane, openly watching the female faery.

"Is she the one they said caused the ice?" Diane asked.

The faery looked too scared to have done anything big like freezing the ocean and at least three countries. She also didn't seem too much older than Diane herself.

"There is a different sheen of magic to her," Damian said meditatively.

Adela hummed thoughtfully. She took Diane's arm and headed toward the faeries.

Damian took the lead once they reached the ocean faeries. "Thank you for meeting with our messengers," he addressed the male faery who stood a half step ahead of the others and moved protectively towards the girl.

"We need a solution just as much as you do," the man replied. "I am Captain Kostis of the Reef Guard."

"Damian of Celedon Forest, and my wife, Adela." Adela dropped a curtsey. "This is Princess Diane of Myrnius. Her brother is the one who organized this council."

Captain Kostis offered a bow to Diane and she returned with a curtsey. As she straightened, she caught the female faery glancing at her with open interest.

"And this is?" Adela turned her smile to the girl.

"Tonya Freyr-dottir," Kostis said as if that would explain everything.

Tonya seemed to compress a little more. Adela offered her a hand, which Tonya hesitantly took.

"We'd like to see your magic, if that's all right?" Adela asked.

Tonya flashed a wide-eyed look at the faery before turning to Captain Kostis in something akin to panic.

Diane swallowed hard. It was fine to stand beside the faeries, but actually seeing magic still made her uneasy. The Durnean faeries came to join them and unease prickled along her arms.

"Maybe outside? Perhaps where not many of the townsfolk can see? I just don't want any trouble." She nearly tripped over her words, wincing as she realized how it might sound to a faery.

But Adela touched her arm and offered a slight smile. "I think that's a good idea."

Diane stepped back with a barely concealed sigh of relief. "Then I'll leave you to it."

# Chapter 9

"Should we go outside?" Adela gave Tonya a bright smile.

Tonya found herself reluctantly returning it as they escaped back into the frigid outdoors followed by two Durnean faeries, Kostis, and another ocean faery.

She took a deep breath, a sense of freedom rippling over her. The enclosed hall had felt stifling after the days spent trekking across the open countryside.

They walked in a silent procession to the outskirts of the town, the faeries from Myrnius and Durne keeping to their own groups, Tonya alone in the center. When they stopped, she pressed her arms over her stomach and stared down at the ice as Kostis and the other ocean faery explained everything they had already tried.

A light touch on her arm brought her chin jerking up. Adela stood close, a friendly smile on her face.

"I suppose we can start with the basics. You can do a little magic, correct?"

Something loosened a little around Tonya's heart at the openness in Adela's eyes.

"Very little."

She didn't know why she rushed to qualify it. Maybe because Adela looked like she might actually believe Tonya could do something.

"Have you tried with the ice?"

Tonya darted a glance at the ocean faery who wore his usual frown. Kostis, however, gave her a small nod.

"I've tried. When — when we first came onto the land, I was able to make some snow move, but I haven't been able to since."

"How do you control your magic?" Damian approached her.

Tonya furrowed her brow. *Control it?*

He raised an eyebrow. "Do you do things differently in the ocean?" He glanced to Kostis.

The captain shook his head. "No, we all have our ways of summoning magic, but she hasn't shown any proficiency for it."

Tonya winced and glanced away, finding the gaze of the younger Durnean faery turned on her.

He studied her, his head tilted slightly to the side. She pulled her gaze away, half-afraid to wonder what he saw.

*Or is he just trying to see how useless I am?*

"How do you use the little magic you have?" Damian asked.

Tonya hesitated, unsure how to explain it. She didn't use words like the others, or gesture with her hands as some did. *I just do.* Sometimes she had to move, pushing and pulling with her whole body to escape the knots smothering her, to squeeze even a drop of magic out. Other times, it rippled from her fingers as easy as whispering to the tides.

Faint heat tinged her cheeks as she tried to articulate it. But Damian and Adela didn't laugh. The second Durnean faery just raised an eyebrow. Tonya felt the other's eyes still watching her.

"You need something, boy?" Kostis growled, protectiveness rumbling in his voice. Tonya started as she realized he'd spoken to the young Durnean faery.

The faery glanced at Kostis, appearing unfazed by his gruffness. He stepped over to them and the knots re-coiled in her stomach.

*Here it comes.*

But he just held out a hand. "I'm Dorian."

No smile, no nod to accompany it. Just stating his name like a fact.

Kostis crossed his arms and glared. Tonya flushed, painfully aware she'd kept him waiting longer than appropriate.

"Tonya." She reached a tentative hand out to him, barely brushing his palm.

"Can I?" he asked.

She froze again, but didn't withdraw her hand. He didn't seem to be much older than her. What could he do that the older faeries among her people couldn't?

He looked down at her hand, his lips barely moving. Adela and Damian watched him in interest, but made no move to interfere. Warmth rushed over Tonya's arms, seeking, prodding. But it felt friendly, not like the frantic barbs of magic that the ocean faeries had sent out, trying to provoke her supposed ice magic.

Dorian didn't look up as he held out his other hand. Tonya bit her lip, bemused, but placed her hand in his.

"No wonder you can't do any magic. You've got some powerful warding spells placed on you."

"What?" Kostis spluttered.

Tonya's mouth dropped open and she stared. Dorian glanced up at her from under the tips of his curly brown hair. "They're clever. Well hidden. You can feel them, can't you? It's blocking you."

She nodded dumbly. *Warding spells? What does that mean?*

"How can you tell? Our people didn't find them!" Kostis frowned, concern in his voice.

"Did they even look?"

Tonya shook her head imperceptibly. They'd just tried to draw out her ice magic to get her to undo the spell.

"Should we just take your word for it?" Kostis still didn't sound convinced.

"Dorian is one of our best healers." The Durnean faery tilted his chin up proudly.

"He's young," the other ocean faery spat.

Dorian didn't drop Tonya's hands, but she felt him tense. His jaw clenched and the lines around his eyes deepened.

"When you spend a war trying to drive away the worst spells you can imagine from both faeries and humans alike, you learn to recognize different kinds of magic."

His voice didn't rise or fall, staying even as he spoke the words, as if reciting facts.

Dorian gently released her hands. "There's cold and sharp like an ice storm. Your father's magic, if I had to guess. And there's warm and gentle, like a summer breeze. Your mother."

His voice quieted a little over the words, meeting Tonya's eyes for the first time.

For some reason, tears budded at the back of Tonya's eyes. *There are parts of them with me, in me.*

Dorian looked at the other faeries. "I think the warding protected her whenever she was attacked."

"Protected? Isn't this a little overkill, then?" Tonya flicked a finger down at the ice.

A laugh bubbled from Adela. For the first time the hint of a smile cracked Dorian's face, crinkling a little around his light green eyes.

"If you're under warding spells, then your magic has been suppressed your whole life." Damian rubbed at his chin. "A serious attack could have triggered the spells to let your magic out to protect you. Resulting in this." He swept his arm out.

Tonya tucked her arms to her chest again. *So I still caused it. But what does it mean that my parents placed warding spells on me?* She met Kostis's concerned gaze. *Maybe they knew that whatever chased them would one day come for me.*

"And you don't know what attacked her?" Adela tucked her hands up into her coat.

Kostis shook his head. "Something more powerful than we thought, perhaps." His lips twisted in worry.

"Do you know how to undo the warding?" Damian glanced at Dorian.

The younger faery shook his head. "It's different than anything I know. But they feel like they were made to stay until whoever made them undid it."

"Meaning that my parents would have to undo them?" Tonya asked, her voice quiet. *I'm stuck like this. The ice will never thaw, and I'll have doomed the continent.*

The bit of bitterness toward her parents that sometimes surfaced on the loneliest of days reached up to claw at her heart. *It wasn't enough that they abandoned me? They had to leave me trapped and useless, too?*

"Or maybe someone with stronger ice magic could undo her father's warding."

A bit of hope bubbled inside her at Dorian's words.

"And if they can't, they might have a solution for this spell," Damian said.

Tonya lifted her chin a little higher. The faeries exchanged a glance, then nodded.

"We send someone north."

Tonya followed Damian's gaze over the gently-rolling hills. She had no idea what lay beyond, but somewhere — leagues away — was her father's homeland. The place where her mother had found something worth leaving the ocean — and her. And the place where something had hunted them down and forced them to leave her to the tides, all tangled in her own magic.

"Dorian." She mustered up her courage as the party trudged back through the snow to the council house.

He half-turned.

"Thank you."

He tipped a nod before lengthening his strides to beat the rest of them to the house.

Tonya rubbed her fingers together. *Maybe not useless, but still just as powerless.*

# Chapter 10

It didn't take the faeries long to come to a decision.

Diane quickly took her seat as the council convened. Edmund leaned on the table beside her, every line of his body tense in anticipation of the report.

She clenched her hands together under her fur wrap, praying to the Creator that it would be good news. That they'd find a way to get rid of the ice, so they could get back to their lives.

Movement shifted beside her. She glanced up at Ralf who met her look and gave a half-smile, despite the worry in his own eyes. Whatever came, she felt a little stronger with him there beside her.

Adela, Damian, and the other faeries clustered in the open square between the tables. Tonya stood a little off to the side, her hands twisting together.

Compassion rushed through Diane. The ocean faery didn't look like she had a malicious bone in her body.

She was only a young girl lost in herself, swallowed whole by a power that she didn't understand and didn't know she could wield. *A little like me.*

A light brush on her arm jerked her attention back. Ralf's stern features had softened again, this time into a real smile. He'd caught her staring at Tonya.

"Was I wearing my look again?" she murmured softly.

He nodded, eyes sparkling a deeper brown. Her heart skipped, an odd feeling that tended to happen when she caught a glimpse of the real man under his hardened exterior.

Whenever she felt like he saw the real her.

*Just a friend.* Diane shook herself. A friend who had been a constant at her side for the last two years. She tore her gaze away as Edmund coughed slightly, a slight frown leveled at her and then to Ralf. She tilted her nose up, focusing her attention on the faeries.

Damian spoke first, while Diane compulsively took notes, explaining the warding that had been placed around Tonya and what had likely triggered the ice.

"She needs to go north to the ice fairies. They might be able to undo the warding, or at least undo the ice magic." Damian stepped back.

A murmur rose from around the tables.

"As we discussed, then," Lord Darek sighed.

"My son, August, will go on behalf of the Myrnian faeries." Damian nodded to the young faery.

"Dorian will represent Durne," the elder Durnean faery spoke up. The youngest of their group gave a short nod, swapping glares with August.

Adela pursed her lips in mild irritation.

"And what of the humans?" One of the Myrnian lords who had pushed hardest for his own man to accompany the mission leaned forward.

Edmund paused a long moment. "Princess Diane will go."

She slashed a wide mark across the parchment, staring at Edmund with wide eyes.

"I'll do what now?"

Adventure had always appealed to her — from the safety of her armchair — but this wasn't what she had in mind. *I can't just leave!*

Edmund pretended he hadn't heard her.

"My sister is one of my most trusted councilors. She's personally overseen many of the reports gathered on the state of our kingdoms and has a comprehensive understanding of just how badly we need a solution. I trust her to see to the good of all our countries, no matter our differences in the past."

Heat flared along Diane's skin at the look of pride he turned on her. She ducked her head as the full attention of the council fell on her — some cautiously agreeing with the choice, others frowning.

Diane nudged her papers aside, lifting her chin, and returned the looks. Edmund had confidence in her, and that had always been enough. Behind the faeries, she caught the relief on Tonya's face and smiled at her.

"And who will you send?" Edmund nodded at the ocean faeries, speaking quickly to avoid the possibility of counter-arguments.

"Against my better judgement, Tonya will go alone from our people," Captain Kostis said. "I have been assured of the skill of August and Dorian. A smaller party will be faster and possibly less of a threat than sending a full guard." The words clearly pained him to speak.

Tonya didn't necessarily look any happier than him at the decision.

"Good. I will be more than happy to give you the supplies needed. Can we count on you, my lords, to ensure any aid they might need along their journey?"

One by one, the council nodded. No one looked truly happy as the council adjourned.

*At least I don't have to sit through more hours of arguing.*

As Diane pushed her chair away from the table and stood, she came face to face with Ralf's frown. His eyes had lost the humor of a few minutes ago, replaced by a storm of anger and worry. A sudden need to get away from the council, even from Edmund, filled her. She grabbed Ralf's arm and pulled him along as she headed for the nearest door.

It led into a scribe's room. Wide windows let in the sunlight, playing across the wooden desk and chairs in dust-filled rays. Diane went to the window, taking a short breath before turning. Ralf waited by the door he'd left open for propriety's sake. He stood tense, the cautious warrior back.

She waited.

"It's too dangerous, Diane!" he finally burst out. "You can't go."

"I'm inclined to agree." She crossed her arms. "I'll have you remember that my dearest brother volunteered me for this without even asking."

"I'll talk to him." He pivoted.

"Ralf!"

He halted. Diane sighed, her shoulders slumping. "I don't really want to go. There's too much to do here." *I don't want to leave you.* She swallowed the thought. "But I think Edmund's right, and I have to go."

"He's an idiot," Ralf growled. "He doesn't even want to send anyone along to protect you."

A smile twitched the corner of Diane's mouth. At least they could agree on the soundness of some of Edmund's ideas.

"Dorian and August look like they can handle themselves."

Ralf scoffed, taking a step closer. "Oh, and I'm just supposed to trust two faeries to look after you."

"I'm not necessarily happy about it either." Not about the faeries. She just wasn't sure she wanted to trek across several countries without the comforting presence of Ralf at her side.

"It's my job to look after you." He pounded a fist against his chest. "I just don't know what I'd do if anything—if…" He cut himself off, running a hand across his face.

A warmth sparked in Diane's chest. The memory of him leaning against her to protect her from the initial ice blast flashed. She hadn't been really focused on it at the time, but it suddenly seemed worth revisiting.

She stepped closer and wrapped her arms around him in a hug. He froze, before gently resting his arms around her, pressing a tentative hand against the back of her head. She closed her eyes. She'd never hugged him before. Never even really thought about it. But standing in the comfort of his arms, head resting against his chest, she wondered why she'd taken so long to do it.

"I'll be fine," she said, her words muffled a little by his tunic.

His scoff rumbled against her ear. She smiled. "I'll miss you."

His arms tightened briefly around her. "I'll miss you too." She tried to tell herself she imagined the hint of longing in his voice that lingered in her own heart.

She pulled back first, tilting her head up to meet his gaze, a tingle running down her arms to her fingertips from where his hands now rested on her shoulders. The lines around his eyes had softened.

"I'm going to worry about you every day."

"I'd be offended if you didn't."

A chuckle broke from him, a rare sound that she'd always treasured.

"And I'll be fine, really. After I go smack sense into Edmund for volunteering me."

"Need some help?" He grinned.

"I believe it's your solemn duty to assist me."

His hands brushed down her arms to rest around hers for a moment. "After you, then."

The tingle stayed in her fingers long after he released her and she led the way back to the manor house.

She stormed into the sitting room where Edmund waited, looking infuriatingly calm. He flicked a dismissive hand at Ralf which only served to irritate her more. Ralf left with a bow.

Diane watched him go, then turned to Edmund, hands on hips.

"You think you can just tell everyone I'm going without asking me first?"

He crossed his arms, jaw set stubbornly. "Yes. I don't trust anyone else."

"Heartwarming," she snapped.

"Diane, you know what we need. I trust you to see to Myrnius's good. And" —he shifted reluctantly— "everyone else's."

"What if I don't want to go?" She stood her ground.

Edmund narrowed his eyes.

Sudden boldness filled her. "What if I don't want to go alone with faeries?"

A frown sharpened his features. "No."

Diane crossed her arms, mimicking his stance. "No, what?"

"I've seen the way you two have been looking at each other. It's not good for either of you."

"And you get to decide everything for me, is that it?" Her voice began to rise.

"Diane," he said sharply. "Yes, I want you safe. Yes, I want you cared for. But this has to be done. And you will need to learn to do everything without him." He softened a fraction with each word.

Her heart squeezed. She'd just started to realize that she didn't want to. Wanted to keep Ralf's comforting presence by her side always.

She scuffed her shoe against the tile. *Does he know best?* Her heart said no. But her mind tried to reluctantly agree.

"I still don't want to go." She dragged her gaze back up to meet his.

He sighed, shoulders slumping. "I don't want you to go, either." A small smile tugged at the corner of his mouth. "I'll run the country into the ground without you."

New irritation flared. "You don't really need me."

Edmund tilted his head. "I've always needed you. Even when we were little."

She rubbed her suddenly smarting nose.

"Please. Do this for me?"

She sighed, defeated. It wasn't ever fair when he asked like that. His smile crept through a little sad, like he knew he'd won.

"Fine. But don't expect me to be happy about it."

He shook his head again. "I would never."

Diane rolled her eyes and moved closer, reluctantly accepting his brief hug. She tried not to think about the guard waiting outside. What she wanted had never really mattered. The country and Edmund came first. Even if that meant leaving Ralf, and everything familiar, behind.

# Chapter 11

"Is that all you brought?"

Diane critically eyed Tonya's belongings strewn across her bed. Grey trousers and a thigh-length tunic made from a woven fabric. They didn't look very thick. Tonya wasn't even wearing her coat. *How can she not be cold?*

The faery tucked her arms across her stomach. "Is that bad? I didn't know what I'd need on land."

Diane smothered a yawn and turned back to her wardrobe. Midnight wasn't far away, but she'd taken it upon herself to make sure Tonya was ready for the journey.

Not that she had any real idea what would be needed on a cross-country trek to the furthest reaches of the north.

"You will get cold."

Tonya paused, flicking a glance at her coat. "I won't, really. The cold doesn't seem to bother me like the others."

"That seems like useful magic." Diane flashed a smile.

Tonya lifted a dark eyebrow in mild surprise.

"But you might need some better shoes." Diane reached into the wardrobe and pulled out her spare pair of walking boots. "I'm a little taller than you, so they might be big."

The faery slid them on and stood, a frown touching her lips. "I don't really like these."

"Those boots, or just shoes in general?"

"Shoes in general, I suppose. We don't need them in the ocean." She sat back down, removing the boots and setting them aside.

"They're fairly useful on land."

Tonya allowed a faint smile. Diane took it as a victory. She pulled out her more practical winter dresses and laid them on the bed.

"Women typically wear dresses here, so a dress for you in case of any situation that doesn't involve endless walking."

Tonya rubbed her fingers across the cloth of the blue dress, edged with tiny embroidered flowers of yellow and red.

"But these are yours. And you're a princess. Surely I shouldn't take these? Is that right?"

She seemed to be asking after land etiquette.

Diane removed one of her finer winter dresses and added it to the bed.

"Normally, no. But I'm going to be gone for a few weeks, and I'd rather you use mine instead of them lying useless in the wardrobe. We need all our winter clothes here. No one else can spare them."

Tonya tilted her head and studied Diane with grey-green eyes. "You're very kind."

Diane shrugged, as if that would deflect the compliment. "People say so, but they don't see that I'm trying to be practical."

Tonya shook her head. "No, you're just a good person. In the ocean, no one would do this for me. Besides Sophie."

"Friend?" Diane dug out her traveling clothes.

"Cousin." Tonya tucked her knees up to her chest.

"I wish I had a cousin. I only have Edmund." Diane laid out her lined trousers and a short green woolen dress. Her thickest knee-length coat would go over the top.

Tonya smiled. "He seems nice. I sometimes wish I had a sibling."

"He drives me crazy most days." Diane grinned.

Tonya giggled, a sound that conjured an image of dancing waves along a shoreline. Diane passed Tonya her second pair of traveling clothes.

"You might not get cold, but these will hold up better than your tunic."

A knock announced Matilde and she pushed in, carrying two leather packs.

"I found a spare one for you, dear," she told Tonya. "I'm just not sure about that bag you brought."

Diane winked at Tonya. "Matilde doesn't trust anything that wasn't made here in the village."

Matilde hushed her and flicked her fingers at Diane's nose. Diane evaded with ease, and Tonya watched, amusement creasing around her eyes.

Matilde propped her hands on her hips and surveyed the clothes laid out. "For both of you?"

Diane nodded, smothering her offense at Matilde's sigh.

"In your parents and grandparents' time, you would have traveled in a carriage, with at least three trunks packed to the brim. Not on foot, with what you can fit into a pack."

"I agree, not walking would be better," Diane said.

Inexperienced riders would make their journey more difficult if trouble should arise, and they could not afford the extra burden of taking feed for the horses since ice would keep them from grazing. The faeries had agreed that attempting to summon griffons or the pegasi from the mountains in Celedon Forest might be too dangerous. The magic creatures had been even more wary since the war and didn't always listen to the faeries the way they once had.

Thus, the walking. It would take at least a week to reach the Strait.

"Boots?" Matilde crooked an eyebrow.

Diane held up her lined pair of walking boots and pointed to the pair she'd given Tonya. Matilde took over the packing, rolling clothes and other essentials into neat bundles and tucking them inside the bags.

Matilde picked up Tonya's bone-handled knife, pursing her lips with a nod of approval. "Elegant, and useful. You'll want to keep this on your belt, dear."

Tonya took it back without a word.

Diane glanced at the corner where her own weapon lay — a short staff that would easily double as a walking stick. The small weight in the bottom of her stomach grew a little heavier, the staff a reminder of the danger they faced on the road.

Bandits took advantage of the fact that the remainder of the army was spread thin. Rogue magic from the war still swirled in parts of the kingdoms, taking the form of terrifying creatures that would attack at random. Not to mention the distrust between humans and faeries, and the tenuous nature of the peace that lingered between Myrnius and Durne the last few years.

Their journey sounded less appealing by the moment.

Matilde fussed with the ties of the packs, sniffing a little, doling out advice as if she regularly undertook journeys to the north.

Diane gently pulled the packs away from Matilde and opened her arms. Matilde crushed her in a hug.

"Not that I'm happy with this whole arrangement. I'd much rather that young Ralf was going with you. But you'll do just fine. Take care of yourself." Matilde rubbed Diane's shoulder as her voice hitched.

Diane squeezed tighter, blinking back her own tears. "I'll miss you."

"You too, my lady." Matilde cleared her throat, back to her normal self. She glanced at Tonya, who'd looked away, her cheeks flushed.

"Take care of yourself too, lass. They said all this ice came from you, but I don't think you meant it. Not like some other faeries I've seen. And I don't know about those two faery lads, but I think you and Diane can solve the problem all by yourselves."

Tonya's face grew a little redder, a bit of a smile turning up her lips. "You think so?"

Matilde reached out to pat her arm. "It's an uncertain world we live in now. And like I tell my Diane, you have to take what you know and stare the problem in the face. Because who is going to make it better, if not you?"

"But what if we fail? What if I can't undo the magic?" Tonya whispered, her fear leaking out onto her face.

"Then you try again. That's all failing is. Something not done right the first time."

Tonya sniffed, flicking a hand across her nose. "Sure you don't want to come with us?"

Matilde's deep, rich laugh burst forth, then Diane joined her, and Tonya smiled.

"To bed, both of you!" Matilde waved her hand. "It's an early start planned."

A cot had been dragged in for Tonya, who'd initially shyly protested sharing a room with Diane. She ran her fingers over the blankets.

"You don't have to use them if you don't want," Diane said, sliding underneath her extra layers of blankets.

Tonya nodded and lay down on the cot, curling on her side to face the fire still blazing on the hearth. Diane snuffed the candles and lay down, crossing her arms over her stomach. Her thoughts ran rampant, filled with worries for the journey, and random details from the reports as she mentally traced their journey to the north again.

Tonya didn't seem in any hurry to fall asleep either. Diane eventually turned on her side away from Tonya, squeezing her eyes shut in an attempt to fall asleep.

*I hope Matilde is right.*

# Chapter 12

**D**awn came much too early. Diane dragged herself out from under the blankets, shivering in the cool air that rushed in to greet her. Tonya still slept atop her blankets, not even having the decency to look cold.

Diane frowned, hopping her way across the frigid floor tiles to the embers of the fire. She brought it back to a semblance of life before dashing behind the changing screen and exchanging her nightgown for the lined trousers and knee length dress she'd left out. She pulled on thick stockings, saving her toes from certain frostbite.

Tonya stirred with Matilde's knock. She sat up, rubbing her eyes in bleary confusion, as Matilde bustled into the room.

"Oh, good! You're both awake. Hurry and change, Miss Tonya. Breakfast is out already, and you don't want to miss out on the last hot meal you'll likely have for a while."

"Hot food?" Tonya tilted her head.

"Breakfast is meant to be served piping hot here on land." Diane pulled her boots on, tying the laces in perfect knots.

A frown lingered in the corner of Tonya's mouth, but she took the clothes that Diane had given her and went behind the changing screen. Matilde took a hairbrush and gestured for Diane to take a seat.

"Humor me, my lady." She brandished the brush.

Diane sat meekly and let Matilde coax the tangles from her long hair, plaiting it from her left ear across the crown of her head, and wrapping all the way around. Matilde removed the hairpins from her mouth and neatly pinned it.

Diane ran a finger across the smooth strands, trying to ignore the sudden stinging in her eyes. *I'll miss her so much.*

Matilde patted her shoulder. "That should keep you for a few days." She sniffed and turned away, exclaiming as Tonya reappeared around the corner of the screen.

"Those fit better than I thought they might!" Matilde straightened the dress and eyed the hem, which fell a few inches below Tonya's knees. The trousers piled around her ankles and she stood awkwardly clutching her old clothes.

The dark green color had coaxed a change in Tonya's features. Before, her narrow cheeks and chin had looked just as delicate as the other ocean faeries, but now they stood a little sharper and more wild, the green taking over the grey in her eyes.

"Have a seat, dear. I'm not sending you off to the wilds without a decent braid either." Matilde ushered her to the dressing table, and Diane hopped up to let Tonya take her seat.

Minutes later, a matching braid wrapped Tonya's head. She gently touched it, staring at herself in the mirror.

"Thank you," she whispered to Matilde.

The woman beamed. "You're quite welcome. Now, boots on, and to breakfast!"

Diane and Tonya carried their packs to the main hall, setting them down by the door before heading into the dining room. Edmund sat at the table, plate half empty already. The kitchen servant brought out plates for Diane and Tonya.

Tonya stared down at the warm toast smothered in jam, and the eggs and steaming links of sausage.

"It's delicious, trust me." Diane nudged her shoulder. Tonya raised her eyebrow, but tentatively lifted the toast to take a small nibble. She took a larger bite, a bit of a grin on her lips as she sampled the rest of the food.

"I think I could get used to hot breakfast."

"And you haven't even tried kaffe yet." Diane ladled sugar into her own steaming cup.

"Don't corrupt her with your kaffe-drinking ways." Edmund jabbed his fork at Diane.

She narrowed her eyes in a mock frown.

"How much do you drink?" Tonya asked.

Diane smiled around a bite of sausage. "I'd drink it all day if I could."

"Hasn't stopped you before," Edmund muttered with a smirk.

Tonya's smile turned to a grimace as she tried the beverage in question. "I think I'll leave it to you." She pushed the mug away.

"Good to see there's at least one sensible faery going along," Edmund said, not quite disguising the edge around the word "faery."

Diane frowned again. *If he's not happy with me going with faeries, then he shouldn't have volunteered me.*

All the same, she tried to draw out breakfast, eating slowly. Once she walked out the front door, she wouldn't be coming back for a while.

"Ready?" Edmund finally asked as the clock chimed the hour.

Diane nodded, finishing her kaffe in a last gulp. *I should have made sure to put some in my pack.*

They pushed back from the table and walked outside where a crowd of faeries and humans had begun to gather.

Edmund helped Diane shrug into her pack, making sure the straps set evenly against her shoulders. He extended her staff and she took it, rubbing it between her hands, the cold wind stinging her eyes.

He opened his arms and she lunged towards him, knocking him back a step.

"Be safe," he mumbled against her braid. "I'll miss you so much."

Diane shuddered a breath. "Don't do anything stupid while I'm gone."

"How am I supposed to do that? You're the one who keeps me sane." He pulled away and held her at arm's-length. "Come back in one piece."

She resisted the impulse to remind him there was a better chance of that if Ralf went along, but she forgot her irritation when she looked up at Ralf. He still wore his serious warrior face, but his eyes had softened around the corners. She gave into the strange impulse that had taken over the day before and stepped closer, happy to ignore Edmund's cautions. This time he pulled her into a hug and she leaned against his chest.

Ralf didn't say anything, just let his chin rest on the top of her braid. She closed her eyes, filing away the moment to think about later.

"Here." His voice rumbled against her ear as he pulled away. He held out his knife. "I'll rest a little easier knowing you have another weapon to use."

She took it with a smile and tucked it into her belt. His smile remained in the corners of his mouth.

"You know what to do if you run into any trouble?" His voice pitched back to his normal gruff, business-like tone.

Diane lifted her staff. "Hit hard and then run in the opposite direction."

He nodded. "And it's perfectly all right to leave the faeries behind."

Diane pursed her lips into a frown, staring pointedly at Dorian and August, who stood nearby and who had heard, judging from the looks of mild exasperation on their faces.

"I agree," Edmund said.

"Really?" Diane pursed her lips. "What about the part where we're supposed to be fostering new bonds with the faeries?"

Edmund lifted one shoulder in a shrug. "And it's so bad to want my sister back in one piece?"

Diane jabbed at him with her staff. He shied away with a smirk.

"Careful. If you hurt me, I won't give you your present."

Diane lowered her staff. "Fine. Truce."

Edmund grinned. "Works every time."

Diane leveled the staff at him again. His smile only grew as he handed her a new leather-bound journal.

A gasp of delight broke from Diane as she ruffled through the pristine pages just waiting for her pen.

"I expect it to be full when you get back," Edmund said.

She threw her arms around him again. "Thank you."

He released her after a moment, turning her to Adela and Damian.

"We wanted to wish you luck as well," Adela said. "And with your permission, give you something."

Diane perked up in interest as Edmund stiffened in wariness, a guarded expression falling over his features.

"What?"

"Some extra protection," Adela said.

Diane glanced at Edmund from the corner of her eye. She wouldn't turn that down.

She nodded her permission, and Adela reached out to brush her forehead with cool fingers. Damian's deeper voice joined Adela's musical tone as they spoke words that seemed just out of reach of understanding. But they made her want to laugh and cry all at once.

Adela withdrew her hand. "It'll keep you safe from all but the strongest magic."

Diane swallowed the fear that lurked in the back of her mind. "Thank you."

Tonya joined them, her hands twisting around the straps of her pack. She glanced back once at Captain Kostis, who gave a nod.

"Ready?" Diane asked.

The faery nodded, a bit of longing and excitement lingering in her face as she looked north. Diane wished she could share the same feelings.

Dorian and August slung their packs over their shoulders. They were similarly outfitted with thick winter coats and boots, and August wore his sword and a knife at his waist with the same comfort as Edmund and Ralf. Dorian once again carried his odd weapons.

Without a word, Dorian turned and began walking down the northern road that would lead them through town and into the wilderness beyond. August gestured for Diane and Tonya to follow before taking up the rear.

Diane looked back once, offering a last wave to Edmund and Ralf standing in front of the mansion, and to Matilde who stood huddled in the doorway.

The townspeople had turned out despite the early hour, calling well wishes to her, a few addressing the party at large. But they threw many cautious looks at Dorian and August, and stared curiously at Tonya.

Diane smiled back, waving a few more times as she projected a confidence she didn't really feel. *I can do this. We have to do this.* They broke free of the last houses where the road ran straight through the snow-covered fields and hills, calling them north.

# Chapter 13

Tonya huffed a breath, jerking at the straps of her pack that dug mercilessly into her shoulders. Her feet ached in the boots, despite the extra stockings that Matilde had given her since the boots were too large for her tiny feet. *I wish I'd just used my other shoes. Or not worn shoes at all.*

Diane trudged in front of her, head down as she methodically plunged her staff into the snow with every other step. Dorian kept walking, apparently unfazed by nearly three hours of continuous hiking.

The town and goodbyes had fallen behind them a long time ago. Kostis had simply patted her shoulder and wished her well, with a last admonishment to be careful.

She hefted her pack higher. He'd also told her to keep trying to use her ice magic. The same ice that spread uninterrupted for miles, barely cracking under their feet. Snow gathered in drifts, almost up to her knees in some places.

Tonya focused on Dorian's broad back again. He'd found the warding that bound her magic inside her. Adela had told her to try to find it herself and maybe push some of her magic through. *Maybe that's how I've been able to use magic before. I just have to remember what it felt like to use it.*

But all memory of whispering to the snow or spinning in the water vanished as soon as she tried. She kicked at the snow with a grumble, sending clumps of snow flying in the air to cascade back down in flurries.

"Can we stop?"

Diane's voice jerked Tonya's attention from her frustration. The princess had halted, one hand on her staff, the other propped against her hip. Dorian half-turned, a bit of surprise and confusion tilting his face into a frown.

"I'm not used to walking forever." Diane's voice held a hint of humor, but Tonya could see fatigue already wearing around her eyes.

"Sorry," Dorian simply said and moved to the side of the road.

Diane gave a small smile and followed, a frown contorting her entire face as she looked for a place to sit that wasn't entirely covered by snow. She sighed, her shoulders slumping before she shrugged out of her pack and sat on top of it.

Tonya allowed a small smile and went to sit next to her. She sank to her knees in the snow, gently pressing the indentation of her hand into the smooth, sparkling surface. A quick tingle brushed her fingertips, gone in an instant. She sighed. *I don't know why it surprises me anymore.* Brief flashes of magic were all she'd ever felt.

"Are you not cold?" This time August brought her attention up.

He sat on the other side of the road, also perched on his pack. The chill of the air had brought redness to his cheeks, making his eyes sparkle even brighter. Gloves covered his hands which he'd tucked under his arms.

Tonya allowed a slight smile. He looked only slightly more comfortable than Diane did.

She glanced down at her ungloved hands. She'd undone the buckles of her coat as soon as they were out of sight of the village, the heat from it oppressive to her.

"No. We don't really get cold currents where we live in the ocean, but I don't know that I've ever really been cold."

"Wish I could say the same. I hate winter." Diane tossed her head back, almost shouting the last words.

August half-laughed, but something in Tonya's heart squeezed. Diane hadn't meant it, but it was another reminder that Tonya had caused the ice and snow.

"Oh!" Diane slapped her forehead. "I didn't mean..." She waved to Tonya. "Sorry!"

Tonya shrugged, trying to hide the hurt that lingered under her skin. She glanced back to Dorian, who'd remained standing in what appeared to be his usual silence.

"How much farther will we go today?"

"Yes, are we planning to walk all the way to the Strait today?" August asked, the lightness of his voice not hiding the edge that sharpened his words.

Dorian returned August's glare with an intensity that sent an uneasiness twisting in her stomach. Diane frowned, her gaze darting between them. August hadn't argued outright when Dorian had taken the lead, but he clearly wasn't happy about it. The council had decided Dorian would be responsible for their path, as he was most familiar with the country they'd be traveling.

"We still have at least ten miles today, if we want to make it across the Strait in the quickest time possible." Dorian's voice was a little gruffer than August's, but it lacked the emotion that filled August's every movement.

Diane sighed, her shoulders slumping even more. The princess pushed up to her feet and picked up her bag with a grimace. Dorian quietly stepped up and helped her settle it back across her shoulders, brushing it free of snow. Diane edged away from him, her hands tightening around her staff.

"Thank you, but I'll try to manage on my own from here on out." Diane gave a little nod, as if to herself. "I know I'm a princess, and I have no idea what that means to you as faeries, but I'm going to do my part on this journey. So don't worry about me slowing anything down."

She lifted her chin, staring down both Dorian and August with a regal expression Tonya had seen in her own king and queen.

Dorian just gave a nod. "All right, then." He turned and began walking again.

"Sounds good to me." August paused by them, offering a smile. "But I'm here if either of you need help."

Diane's answering smile held a bit of hesitation. She waited until Tonya began walking to step out with her, side-by-side. Tonya gnawed at the inside of her lip, not sure what she was supposed to do.

*Am I supposed to talk?* Diane showed more friendliness to her than to the other faeries. A friendliness that made her uncomfortable. The uncertainty with which August and Damian regarded Tonya was almost a relief in its familiarity.

"What's life like in the ocean?" Diane asked, her eyes lighting up with a sparkle of interest.

Tonya hesitated. "I don't know if I can make it sound that interesting."

"Oh, come on! I need something to distract me from the fact that I have to walk another ten miles today."

Tonya reluctantly began to describe the reef, gaining a little more confidence as August dropped back a pace or two to join in Diane's questions. Dorian didn't speak, just kept walking in his even strides. But Tonya had the feeling he was listening anyway.

# Chapter 14

*I'm beginning to hate the land.* Tonya lay on her back and stared up at the gently-swaying green canvas above her. Two days of walking had left her feet aching and muscles sore that she didn't even know she had.

Diane curled up on her side next to Tonya, buried under her blanket and coat, still asleep. Tonya eased out from under her blanket. Even though she didn't really need it, she found the sensation of sleeping under it comforting.

Diane grumbled under her breath and disappeared further under her blankets as Tonya gently undid the flap. She winced in apology and stepped quickly out, turning to close it back up.

The small peaked tents had been a gift from August's people, spelled to provide insulation from the wind and cold. The tent that Dorian and August shared stood next to theirs, but only one of them would be inside.

They'd barely been civil to each other since leaving, exchanging barbed words only when necessary. On the first night, they'd managed to agree to split the watches so they didn't have to share personal space with each other.

She rubbed her eyes. It made for tense days, even if both were individually civil to her and Diane.

A step crunched on the ice that had formed a new sheen overnight. She pivoted, expecting to see one of her companions. Her breath caught in her throat. An animal crouched before her instead.

She recognized it as a dog, but this didn't have the same friendliness as the animal in the first town she'd encountered. Saliva dripped from its bared teeth and a wild light gleamed in its eyes. It slunk another step towards her.

Panic froze her feet. She didn't have a weapon. She'd left her knife in the tent.

"Don't move," a voice whispered behind her. *August.*

The faery edged around her, knees bent in a low crouch as he locked eyes with the dog. He whispered a few words, too low for Tonya to hear, but she still felt the tremor of magic within them.

The dog snarled, curling its lips further back from its fangs.

August persisted, sidling closer, a growl edging the unfamiliar words. The dog backed up a step, snapping in reply.

August stiffened, and before Tonya could blink, a silver flash streaked from behind the tent, slamming into the dog. It collapsed with a pained squeal, blood staining the snow as it thrashed, then went still.

Dorian stepped over, bending to grab the knife.

"What was that?" August demanded, fury darkening his face.

"What had to be done." Dorian wiped the knife clean on the dog's fur. "That wolf was too far gone to listen. Or is playing with forest plants the only thing you're good at?"

August lunged forward. "He was about to leave!"

Dorian's eyes narrowed. "He wasn't."

He turned away, but August yanked him back by the shoulder. "You miss killing things so much that you couldn't resist?"

Dorian shoved August's chest, breaking his hold. "You seem to like bringing up the war. Miss it as much as you say I do?"

Tonya didn't dare breathe at the rage on both their faces. *How do I stop them?*

"No, I just remember what your people did."

Dorian's normally stoic face twisted in a sneer. "I seem to remember plenty of Myrnians wreaking hell on the innocent."

August bristled even more. "I only saw Durneans at Monmarran."

Something flashed in Dorian's eyes that sent Tonya's heart skipping in fear. She licked her lips. *I have to do something.*

"What do you know about Monmarran?" His voice came terrifyingly even.

"More than enough. Were you there with your fancy sticks, or were you hiding somewhere pretending to be a healer?" August spat.

"Stop," Tonya said, her voice wavering.

Dorian shoved again, sending August back two steps. His hand moved towards the staffs on his back. An angry gleam answered in August's eyes and he grabbed his sword.

"Stop!" Tonya yelled, snow swirling around her.

They paused, not even looking at her.

"I don't know much about the war, but I know that this isn't helping anything!" She tried to muster some sort of command into her voice. *What would Diane do?*

"Please. The…" She searched her memory for the word Dorian had used. "The wolf is dead and we can't undo it. Please, can we break camp and move for the day?"

She softened her tone with a note of pleading.

Dorian sent her a long glance and brought his hand down. August relaxed a fraction and removed his hand from the sword.

Then they spun in opposite directions with one last glare, and left her standing alone.

Not alone.

Diane had exited the tent at some point during the commotion. She stared, eyes wide, curling her blanket around her shoulders. Her gaze flicked to the dead wolf, then after each of the men in turn, before settling on Tonya.

"Good thing they listened to you." Caution and a little fear lurked in her face, directed at the faeries more than the wolf.

Tonya nodded, pressure building up behind her eyes. She blinked hard, only serving to blur her vision more.

"Poor thing. Must be starving." Diane looked to the animal in pity.

Tonya gasped a short breath. She'd caused the ice. She'd driven the wolf to desperate measures. She'd gotten it killed.

"Tonya!" Diane's sudden closeness startled her. The princess laid a gentle hand on her arm, shaking it lightly. "The same thing might have happened during the regular winter."

Tonya looked at the red snow. *But it's not your regular winter.*

"Come. Help me pack up. We might have to do theirs too." Diane shook her head, muttering something under her breath about young men and ridiculous posturing.

Tonya understood some of it. There were plenty of young faeries in the ocean who sometimes didn't appear to have the brain the Creator blessed them with.

But whatever lay between Dorian and August was something different. Something raw and angry. What she'd seen in too many faces in the council chamber when the representatives of the different countries looked at each other. Something almost broken.

\*

Tonya sighed and nibbled at the corner of the tasteless travel bread. *What I wouldn't give for some fresh shrimp and sea moss.* Or even the eggs and toast she'd eaten the morning they'd left.

"I agree."

Diane sat next to her on the mossy log, legs sprawled out in front of her. Tonya raised an eyebrow. Diane lifted her own lunch in answer.

"It leaves something to be desired. I'd love some fresh meat."

"There might be some small game around here." Dorian flicked a hand around the small forest they'd entered a few minutes earlier.

"Killing one animal today wasn't enough?" August snapped from his seat a few feet away.

Crumbs fell from Dorian's hand as he clenched it around his meal.

"I know you're not opposed to meat, so you can get off your high horse." He looked pointedly at the dried jerky in August's hand.

"And I'm not hungry anymore," Diane muttered.

Tonya stared down at her bread, picking off another flake and bringing it up to her mouth. *How to get them off this subject? What would Sophie do?* She'd just start talking. But about what?

Tonya cleared her throat. In the two and a half days they'd been together, she still knew next to nothing about her two faery companions. Diane had been the only one willing to speak more than a few short sentences. She decided to start with Dorian, because she didn't like the hardness that tensed around his eyes whenever August spoke.

"Dorian, what's your home like? When it's not covered in ice?" She managed a lighter tone. They'd be at the border by nightfall and she'd no idea what they'd find.

Dorian glanced up, the lines around his eyes relaxing.

"There aren't as many forests as here." He cast a quick look at August that surprisingly wasn't angry. "More hills and rivers. Lakes. This time of year, the hills are emerald green and covered in every kind of flower you can imagine."

Tonya half-smiled. She'd like to see land flowers. The blooms under the sea were colorful and entrancing, but she'd always loved the few bright red blossoms on her island and wanted to see more.

"What are hippogryphs like?" Diane leaned forward, an eager light in her eyes. A welcome change from the caution that lingered around the faeries.

"What?" Tonya straightened in interest. This was a new word.

"One of our magical creatures in Durne. Half horse, half griffin," Dorian explained.

"Griffin?" Tonya tried out the word. "Those are those big bird creatures, right?"

August snorted in mild offense. "They're a little more than just big birds."

"They're terrifying." Diane shivered.

"I've only seen small glimpses of them flying above cliffs," Tonya said.

"Be glad that you haven't seen them up close," Diane said.

But Tonya wanted to know everything. August's face softened into a smile. He dug in the snow, scraping through the thin sheet of ice until he reached a patch of grass. He pulled a handful of blades free and took some pine needles to add to the pile in his palm.

He spoke a few merry words that Tonya didn't quite understand, but the grass and needles swirled in the air, taking the form of a creature suspended in flight. Wings spread from a body like the cats she'd seen in the town, but the face sharpened into a beak like the parrotfish.

"That's a griffin?"

"Aye," August said. "They're almost as tall as that tree you're sitting under, and longer than you and Diane put together."

Tonya now understood Diane's fear. "How does that turn into a hippogryph?"

"It doesn't." August smiled patiently. He flicked a glance at Dorian, then spoke another few words. "This is a hippogryph."

The griffin kept its head and wings, but the hindquarters shifted to the animal Tonya now knew as a horse.

"They're about the size of a griffin," Dorian spoke up again. "Just as mean."

"How does an animal like that come to be?"

"Legend says that a sorcerer tried to cross a pegasus and a griffin." Dorian shrugged, his tone indicating he didn't put much stock in the tale. "They live in caves by the lakes, so you have to be cautious when around water. They're more likely to capture and keep human prey than a wyvern."

Tonya shook her head. "Too many creatures to keep track of."

Diane laughed. "Every country has a few different ones that rarely cross over the borders. We have griffins and pegasi here. The griffins live along the cliffs and sometimes in the forests. The pegasi live up in the mountains. They're generally harmless."

"Unless you come too close to their eyries," August put in with a chuckle.

"Thankfully the Rusalka, the vicious water spirits, have all been exterminated." Diane shivered again.

"There are still a few living in our rivers," Dorian said, his mouth twisting into a grim frown.

"What do you have besides hippogryphs, and these water spirits?" Tonya asked, ready for his frown to leave again.

"They're rare, but there's still a few phoenixes around. The war was hard on them too." Dorian didn't look at August for once. "If you can find one, and catch it in the right mood, it might grant you a small wish or two."

"Really?" Diane perked up. "I thought that was only a myth."

Dorian shrugged, but a small smile peeked out at the corner of his mouth. "I'm assuming it's true, since I've had one or two wishes granted."

"How? What?" Diane leaned further, almost falling off the log.

Dorian shrugged again, clearly not about to tell.

Diane pursed her lips into a pout. "Fine."

"What about these wires—wyv..." Tonya stumbled over the word.

"Wyverns?" August supplied with a grin.

"That."

"They live in Calvyrn. They have some nasty creatures there. Baedons, trolls, wyverns." Diane shook her head. "I'll take griffins over those any day."

August and Dorian both nodded in rare agreement.

"I fought a Baedon once. Don't want to ever again." Dorian shook his head.

August looked up in quick interest, before he remembered he was supposed to hate Dorian. Tonya barely resisted rolling her eyes.

*Boys.*

"What about the ocean?" Dorian shifted more comfortably against the tree.

"Sea dragons live in the darkest part of the waters. They come to eat young faeries who try to sneak out of the reef at night." Tonya smiled at the bedtime story. "Gilled deer live on islands, but come into the water to hunt. They look like smaller versions of the deer you have here." She pointed around to the forest. "But with gills along their nose. And their teeth are savagely sharp."

She thought a moment more. "Echo seals can mimic any sound and try to lure you to your death." She paused, confused. *Where have I heard that one before?*

"What?" Diane asked.

"Nothing." Tonya hesitated. "Well, it's just that I don't think that the seals are something I learned about growing up in the reef."

Diane's brows furrowed and she tilted her head.

"You think they're from the north?" Dorian tipped his chin up, revealing more of the curiosity in his green eyes.

Tonya rubbed her fingers together, and slowly nodded. *Now they'll all think I'm crazy. Just like everyone did when I accidentally said something like that in the reef.*

"Does that happen often? Knowing things from the north like that?" There was no judgement in Dorian's voice. He simply wanted to know.

Tonya looked away from him, unsure of how to react to his different response. But Diane and August also looked at her with the same genuine curiosity.

"Sometimes things just pop into my head. Like how I know about eagles and polar bears. And narwhals with their horns that will grant your heart's desire with one touch. And sometimes I think about glaciers and—" She clamped her mouth shut. They wouldn't want to hear all of that.

But a glance up showed all three of her companions focused on her every word.

"What else?" Diane's eyes sparkled with delight. "I don't know anything about the north!"

Heat crept up Tonya's neck and cheeks.

"I don't know if any of that's really there. I don't even know how it pops into my head if I've never seen it. Kostis said I was no more than a baby when my mother left me with him. And…"

Her throat locked up for a moment. "I've never had anyone to teach me about it."

Diane pressed her hand around Tonya's arm, a smile of sad understanding crossing her face.

"Maybe you'll find someone to when we get there."

The annoying pressure built up behind Tonya's eyes once again. She couldn't quite understand Diane's eternal optimism that almost rivaled Sophie's.

She sniffed and put away the last of the bread that she still couldn't quite stomach. "Should we keep going?"

Dorian tipped a small nod and rose to his feet in a smooth motion. Tonya pulled her pack back on, trying not to wince as the straps settled into the permanent grooves she was sure were etched into her shoulders.

"And how many hundreds of miles do we still have to go today?" Diane asked, a playful smirk on her lips. She stretched her arms overhead before picking up her pack and staff.

"Only two hundred," Dorian replied in his usual serious voice, but a hint of laughter lay underneath.

Diane laughed and Tonya let the smile creep across her face. August rolled his eyes, but didn't make any comment. Dorian led them back to the road, which wound between towering pines and oak trees. A few squirrels scampered down the trunks, clutching the bark with their paws as they craned their necks, chattering at August.

He replied in words Tonya couldn't understand. But, like with the wolf that morning, they rang with magic.

"What are you doing?" She turned to face him, walking backwards.

"Telling them we're trying to fix the strange weather." He whistled at a magpie that fluttered along beside them, cawing madly at him.

"How?"

He quickened his pace to walk beside her, allowing her to face forward again.

"My magic is strongest with animals. I inherited that from my father. I can speak their language."

A pair of gleaming eyes in the undergrowth startled Tonya and she grabbed at her knife, but August waved her hand down.

"Just a fox," he said calmly. A smaller, reddish-brown version of a dog slunk out of the bushes, running a few steps beside August before vanishing again.

"Are—are they going hungry because of the ice?" Tonya swallowed hard, remembering Diane's words that morning.

August's sideways glance held quick pity. "They're managing. When my people begin to journey out to help our countries, they'll make sure the animals are taken care of as well. It's our job to take care of all living creatures."

"Even those terrifying creatures you told me about?"

"Sometimes. My father once befriended a griffin to help it. But that's more the exception than the rule. I'm sure it's the same with your people."

Tonya nodded. A specific contingent of the Reef Guard trained to fight the sea dragons and keep the human ships safe in the waters. But they'd also helped a herd of gilled deer find a new island when a storm destroyed their previous home.

"How do you like the land so far?" August tucked his hands under his pack straps.

Tonya took a breath, letting the forest fill her senses — the gentle rays of the sun that brought faint bursts of warmth despite the icy breeze, and the ongoing crunch of footsteps of the companions she'd never really expected to start to feel comfortable around.

"Besides my feet hurting all the time?" She raised an eyebrow.

August laughed. "Besides that."

"I'd have to come up for a few minutes every change of the tide to be able to breathe. There was a small island where I'd sit and stare at the distant coastline of Myrnius. It's so much bigger than I imagined. So different. There's so much to learn." An embarrassed laugh escaped.

"You seem to be doing well so far." He nudged her arm with his elbow.

The friendly gesture took her by surprise, but she smiled. "I'd like to see it without all the ice and snow."

"I'm sure you will. Soon, right?" He winked, as if willing her to believe it too.

She offered another smile and watched her feet take step after step. She didn't know how to respond to the optimism that they would find something to untangle the magic inside her. The hope she could figure out a way to undo the magic when she didn't even know how to do a simple spell.

August nudged her arm again. He tilted his head, concern in his hazel eyes.

"I think I'm just tired." She lifted one aching shoulder in a shrug.

He nodded, a divot appearing under his lip where he bit the inside. He didn't appear convinced. She quickened her pace to get away from the look and ran into Dorian's back.

He'd stopped Diane, pushing one arm in front of her. He stood tense and alert, glancing around them. August immediately mirrored the stance.

"You hear anything?" Dorian murmured.

Tonya clutched at the straps of her pack in the sudden eerie silence. August moved his hand to his sword, the steel gently grating as he began to ease it out of its sheath.

"Animals are gone," he whispered.

"I can't feel anything from the ground." Dorian edged his feet apart to widen his stance.

A word that was definitely a curse edged from August as he slowly turned his gaze up to the sky. "Let's get under cover."

Prickles ran along Tonya's skin as the strip of sky above the road suddenly seemed a mile wide. For the first time, she felt cold.

"Easy now." Dorian tugged Diane's sleeve and began to move towards the trees to their left. Diane followed, her pale face set in grim determination as she gripped her staff and mimicked the way his feet slid across the ground.

Tonya tried to do the same, but her boots suddenly felt even heavier and more unwieldy.

"Keep moving." August's hand kept a gentle pressure on her elbow. A swallow caught in her dry throat.

Dorian kept them moving into the treeline and over ten feet from the road, under the thickest branches he could find. He had yet to draw a weapon, but his stance stayed ready. August's sword rested free, angled towards his body to prevent it from glinting in the light that crept through the heavy foliage.

"Anything?" Diane's whisper ended in a slight squeak.

Dorian shook his head, but August slowly pointed up.

The heavy rush of wings broke the stillness, and the trees surrounding them swayed in the gust as a large *something* passed overhead.

Diane shrank back against the trunk. August's throat bobbed. Dorian wore an even grimmer expression.

*What is out there?* Panic welled in Tonya. A hand on her arm startled her, and she relaxed a fraction at Dorian's touch. He brought his gaze from the sky a moment to give her a slight nod of reassurance.

"You see it?" he asked August, barely moving his lips.

"Coming back for another pass," August returned.

A guttural shriek tore through the canopy, sending Tonya's fear spiking like a lightning surge on the water. She stumbled back a step into Dorian. Diane clapped her gloved hands over her mouth, squeezing her eyes shut as her chest heaved in a suppressed breath.

August clenched his free hand into a fist, but his eyes stayed trained on the sky.

They remained frozen as gradually the wingbeats faded, and one last cry sounded in the distance.

Tonya jumped as a blue bird shook itself in a nearby tree and gave a low trill. With that, life returned to the forest. August relaxed and sheathed his sword. Diane slid down into a crouch, keeping her head bowed for a moment.

Dorian released Tonya's arm. Heat flashed across her face as she realized she'd been pressed up against him without even realizing it. She stumbled a step away with a fumbling apology.

His features softened into what she decided was his smile. His mouth barely moved, but the skin around his eyes crinkled, coaxing a brightness to the light green.

"What was that?" She jerked her attention from the sight.

"Remmiken," Dorian said.

Even the name sent a shiver down Tonya's spine.

"They're even more terrifying out here." Diane shivered again before taking Dorian's proffered hand and rising back to her feet.

"That explains why neither of us could sense it." August addressed Dorian, his eyes holding no malice.

"We should probably stay off the road for a while in case it comes back around," Dorian replied.

Tonya rubbed her arms, pushing away the goosebumps the cry had raised. "What happens if it comes back?"

"Just pray it doesn't." Dorian took a few steps away, staring in the direction of the road for a moment before checking the position of the sun. "Let's go."

Tonya fell in beside Diane. She hated to bring it back up, but the name remmiken didn't mean anything to her.

"What was that?" She tried to keep her voice low.

Diane shivered again. "A creature that some of the worst sorcerers made during the war. It's some of the nastiest parts of those creatures we told you about smashed into a flying monstrosity."

She didn't say anything more, leaving Tonya to her own imagination as the others walked in silence.

After nearly an hour of picking their way through the forest itself, Dorian finally led them back to the road. There'd been no sign of anything but the usual forest life. The rest of the day passed much the same way.

It was only when they came to the edge of the forest, as the sun sank low in the western sky, that Dorian announced they'd reached the border. August stiffened back up and their glares returned.

Tonya bit back a sigh. *Back to normal, then.*

# Chapter 15

The endless hills of Durne spread out before Tonya, their rugged bulk gentled by the sparkle of the morning sun against the ice. They'd camped the night in the shelter of the forest before beginning the next stage of their journey. At least another five days' walk across Durne lay ahead of them before they reached the Strait, and then the north beyond. *And then finding the ice faeries and praying they can do something.*

"Trying to see it from here?" Dorian's voice carried a bit of a tease as he came to stand beside her.

She turned a quick smile up at him before glancing back at the horizon. "Maybe. Glad to be back home?"

He paused for a long moment, a muscle along his jaw tensing. "A little."

*I said something wrong! How do I change the subject?*

"What did you mean yesterday, when you said you couldn't feel anything through the ground? Was it because of the ice?"

Dorian shook his head, his features easing back into relaxed lines.

"Here in Durne, we actually live underground. Earth, stone—we're naturally strongest with it. If you train right, you can sense something coming towards you by listening to the earth. The remmiken flies, so the ground wasn't able to tell me anything."

Tonya brushed back a few strands of hair that escaped from her braid which had somehow still stayed in place for the last few days. Matilde must have her own special magic. "Are you trained for earth? August said he was strongest with animals. What's your magic strongest with?"

His face lost some of its lighthearted expression.

"Healing," he finally said.

*Making everything worse again. Just stop talking.*

"I wish I could use my magic for something," she said. *Why can't I stop talking? He doesn't want to hear this either!*

"I'm sure you'll find a way."

"There's not. I've tried." Tonya crossed her arms, automatically preparing for pity or condescension.

Instead, he pulled off a glove and held out his hand.

"Can I?" he asked, much like he had the day of the council.

She slowly placed her hand in his calloused palm, her mouth tucking into a frown. He spoke some words in a lilting cadence she didn't quite understand, like they were mumbled, despite how clear she heard them.

The knots inside tugged in response, then eased a little. Her eyes widened in surprise. He glanced up, his eyes sparkling in amusement at her reaction. She extended her other hand towards the snow. *Find the holes in the warding.*

She closed her eyes. It felt like Dorian had opened the gaps a little wider.

She caught a whisper in the breeze beckoning her toward fjords and glaciers and mountains. She whispered back and a tingle pricked her fingers. Hesitantly, she opened one eye and saw ice crystals dancing in an invisible wind and the ice thinned under her feet to expose hints of green.

*It worked!*

"Tonya!" Diane exclaimed in delight, breaking her concentration. The knots tightened again and the ice fell.

But the spot of green remained, a bit of hope in the frozen waste she'd created.

She turned to Dorian and caught her breath. A full smile had broken out over his face, a bit lopsided, but triumphant. *For me.* The heat returned to her face at the realization. She pulled her hand away as Diane clapped her hands.

"That was amazing!"

"I don't even know how I did it." Tonya rubbed her hands together, trying to remember the way the magic had felt. She looked at Dorian again. The smile had faded back to the corners of his lips, but still danced around his eyes.

"What did you do?"

"Started off by saying I wasn't going to hurt you." Dorian pulled his glove back on. "Then tried the strongest anti-warding spell I know."

Tonya's heart fell. If that was the strongest spell he knew, and it had only barely suppressed the warding enough for her to do that small bit of magic…

"At least you could practice a little, right?" Diane nudged Tonya's arm, her voice still bright and cheerful.

Dorian shrugged. "I could keep trying to see if there's anything I can do to let you use it more."

Tonya's heart flipped a beat. "You would?"

He tilted his head, puzzled amusement taking over.

"Yes." He said it like it was the most natural option in the world.

*He means it.* A grin spread across her face before she could stop it. *He actually wants to*—can—*help me. I'd be able to do some magic.*

Dorian tipped a nod and moved away. Tonya propped her hands on her hips, standing a little taller. Suddenly her aching feet and the miles ahead of them didn't matter. Even frequent slips and slides along the sides of the hills couldn't dim her new confidence.

Until the shriek sounded.

August whirled around, focused up on the sky. He drew his sword.

"Run!"

Diane grabbed Tonya's hand and hauled her into a dead sprint. A sharp wind knocked them off their feet and Tonya's knees scraped against the ice.

The remmiken landed in a spray of white. A narrowed head and snout like a sea dragon swung low on a long neck. Taloned feet gripped the ground, and giant wings spread wide to balance it. Its dull brown hide shimmered in the sunlight. Saliva dripped from curved fangs, sizzling when it hit the snow.

It opened its wide maw and shrieked. Tonya stumbled back, but Diane remained frozen in place. Her staff trembled in her hand as she stared at the creature. Then her face went slack. The remmiken made a noise like a purr of contentment as it turned red eyes to Diane.

"Make her look away!" August landed in front of Diane, a pair of dusky brown wings spread wide.

Dorian stepped up beside him, unsheathing the weapons strapped to his back. He slammed the blunt ends together with a sharp word of command, transforming it into a double-bladed staff.

He twisted it in his hand, bringing it to his side. He and August exchanged a brief glance.

"Take left?" August asked.

Dorian nodded. "Tonya, you and Diane stay back. And don't look at its eyes."

Tonya nodded dumbly, even though they couldn't see her. Her heart froze in her chest as they charged forward.

Diane took a step, tugging on her arm, and Tonya remembered what August had told her to do. She pushed in front of Diane who still stared vacantly at the remmiken.

"Diane!" Tonya shook her shoulders. Nothing. She placed her hands on Diane's cheeks and forced the young woman to look into her eyes. "Diane! Look at me!"

Diane's pupils dilated, then shrank as she focused on Tonya with a gasp. "What…?"

Her gaze slid past Tonya and her eyes widened. They both turned to watch the battle.

Dorian moved in a series of fluid sweeps and slashes, twisting the double-bladed staff around himself with ease, fending off the remmiken as it snarled and struck at him like a sea snake. A few feet away, August pushed himself to his feet, straightening his wings with a snap.

The remmiken pumped its wings, the force of it pummeling Dorian back. A pair of short, broad wings exploded from his back, giving him traction to remain on his feet.

August darted forward under the remmiken's wings as they raised again. He stabbed up with his sword, eliciting a scream of rage from the beast. It swiped toward him. August ducked to the ground, rolling out of the talons' reach. Dorian extended his hand, clenching his fist in a grabbing motion, and pulled back with a shout.

Tonya watched in shock as the remmiken's wing crumpled. Part of it broke off, disintegrating like crumbling sand. The creature howled and spun, lashing out with a barbed tail. It moved too fast for Dorian to react, and the tail caught him across the arm, flinging him to the ground to slide a few feet.

August charged again with a shout, dodging the slashing talons and landing multiple blows of his own. Dust dribbled from each wound he cut in the beast's hide.

Dorian struggled to his feet, keeping his arm tucked close to his chest. He hit his knee again. Tonya cast a glance at the remmiken, wondering if she dared run over to help him. August cried out, stumbling a step before taking the remmiken's head in his chest, throwing him back several feet.

The creature snarled in triumph and whipped towards Tonya. Fear rooted her to the ground. Some tiny bit of herself tried to fight back, and she reached a trembling hand for her knife. Diane brought her staff up in front of her body, a small whimper escaping.

It prowled forward, tail swishing like one of the village cats she'd seen stalking a bird. It rumbled deep in its chest, bringing its snout closer and exhaling a sickly-sweet breath over them.

Diane yelled, a surprisingly warlike sound, and lashed out with her staff, cracking against its teeth and breaking one of the larger fangs off in a puff of dust. Its eyes glowed brighter as it snarled again.

A shout echoed and something dragged it backward. It writhed and shrieked as its talons skidded across the ice. Dorian appeared, his face twisted in concentration, his extended arms shaking with effort as he backed away, somehow taking the creature with him.

It fought back, twisting until it could fix him with its eyes. His arms slowly lowered and a blank look crossed his face.

"Dorian!" Tonya screamed and he shook free of its control.

The remmiken growled in frustration and spun, flinging its tail toward her.

"Down!" Diane screamed and threw herself at Tonya, knocking her to the ground as the tail smashed into them.

Tonya sobbed for a breath as Diane shuddered beside her. Dorian grabbed his staff again and ran forward, flicking a bolt of magic that knocked the remmiken's nose away and ramming one of his blades into its chest.

It screamed, impaling itself further onto the blade as it pushed forward to try to get him. Dorian gritted his teeth, struggling to hold on with his injured hand, his wings flapping uselessly as his feet skidded backward.

Another shout came from overhead. August launched into a dive, his sword held out in front of him, aiming for the base of the creature's neck. His wings opened at the last second, steadying him as he slammed into its neck, burying his sword all the way to its hilt.

The remmiken froze like a statue, one remaining wing spread wide, its head arched mid-strike before it crumbled into dust. August's wings fluttered, bringing him safely to the ground outside the pile of debris.

Dorian shakily stood taller, wiping some of the dust from his face with his sleeve.

August leaned over, resting hands on his knees. He tilted his head up to look at Dorian.

"Griffin's tailfeathers, healing magic is your strongest magic."

Dorian took another breath. "You always go for the dramatic kill?"

A slight grin quirked in the corner of August's mouth. "Looked like you needed some help."

Tonya helped Diane sit up, but the princess slumped against her. A faint whimper escaped Diane as she reached toward her right leg. Panic jolted through Tonya. Red blood soaked through Diane's clothes.

"Dorian?" Her voice scraped out in a whisper. She tried again, fear cracking the word as she reached to help staunch the blood.

"Don't touch it!" Dorian's voice came sharp.

August cursed as they ran over.

Dorian shrugged out of his pack, fumbling with the straps as his left hand seemed to be giving him trouble. August grabbed the pack, undoing the buckles in seconds. Dorian pushed the flap back, yanking out a smaller bag, and began digging through it with his good hand.

"Wash it off," he instructed August without looking.

August took his canteen and gently poured water over the oozing cut across Diane's calf, careful not to touch the wound or the blood. Tonya wrapped her arms around Diane's shoulders, letting her squeeze her arms.

"How are you feeling?" August turned a smile at Diane, not quite hiding the concern in his eyes.

"Um..." Diane sniffed. "It was hurting. But now I can't feel my leg. That's not normal, right?" Her wavering voice began to rise.

Dorian uncorked a small vial, using the back of his left hand against her boot to gently rotate her leg to expose the cut.

"This will help drive out the venom. I want you to tell me when you can feel everything again," he instructed gently.

Diane nodded as he gently poured a few drops on the cut. Now that it had been mostly cleared of the blood, it didn't look as deep as Tonya had first thought, but it ran nearly two handspans down the side of her leg. Some blood still dribbled from the edges of the cut.

"Nothing yet," Diane said. Dorian poured a few more drops on. August bit his bottom lip as he watched. Tonya tried to take a calming breath, even though the sight of the red-stained snow and the open wound was beginning to make her nauseous.

Dorian kept administering the medicine until Diane's foot jerked. He flinched as she kicked him in the thigh.

"Sorry!" she blurted, curling her leg back with a wince. "It definitely hurts now."

He smiled, but it didn't quite reach his eyes. "All right. I'm going to clean it again and get it bandaged up."

Diane nodded. Dorian pulled the glove off his right hand with his teeth, and took the canteen from August, rinsing the wound again.

"It's not deep enough for stitches," he said, but spread a paste over the wound, pressing the edges together. August moved in to help, keeping Diane's leg elevated as Dorian wrapped a bandage neatly around her calf. He fumbled a bit with his left arm, using the back of his hand to keep things in place.

Diane kept her lips pressed tightly together during the process, face pale. Tonya kept her arms around Diane as August gently helped her move away from the stained snow.

Diane drew a shuddering breath, a broken laugh escaping. "I'd make a terrible warrior."

August smiled again, his shoulders relaxing. "I've seen men laid low with scrapes smaller than that, believe me. And none of them would face down a charging remmiken like you two did."

"I think I might have frozen my feet to the ground," Tonya said, trying to blink away the sudden urge to sob in relief.

August laughed, the sound finally breaking the tension inside her.

Diane wiped her eyes as a giggle broke from her. "And this is why I'd rather write about the adventure than have it."

Tonya turned to where Dorian packed away his things. She caught a brief wince of pain before he shuttered it away.

"Are you all right, Dorian?"

He nodded, not quite meeting their gaze. "Just sprained it a bit." He lifted his arm.

August narrowed his eyes. Quicker than the remmiken, he flicked out his hand, catching a light blow to Dorian's injured arm. Diane yelled and smacked his shoulder as Dorian sat back with a huff of pain.

"Let me see."

"Why do you care?" Dorian snapped, any trace of friendliness gone.

August clenched his jaw. "Because I'd rather not have you hold us up by pretending that it's not as bad as it is."

Dorian glared back, but pulled his empty sheaths overhead and shrugged his left arm out of his jacket. He rolled up his sleeve and Tonya winced. Dark bruises mottled the skin of his forearm from his wrist up to his elbow.

"Did it cut you anywhere?" August asked.

Dorian shook his head, stiffening as August gently took his arm to check the extent of the bruising.

"Broken?" August pressed around his elbow and forearm.

"Don't think so." Dorian's voice strained as August rotated his already swollen wrist and fingers.

"Your wrist looks like it got the worst of it." August dug in the bag until he pulled out another bandage.

Dorian cocked an eyebrow. "I'd noticed."

He said nothing as August began wrapping the bandage around his palm, then up around his wrist and forearm.

Dorian gave a small nod as he finished. "Can you hand me another bandage?"

"Not good enough for you?" August's lip curled in a slight sneer.

Dorian rolled his eyes. "Ice."

August grudgingly nodded and handed another bandage over. He scooped handfuls of ice crystals, holding them against Dorian's arm as he wrapped the second bandage over it all.

"What does that do?" Tonya watched in confusion.

"Helps with the swelling and some of the pain." Dorian tucked the tail of the bandage in place and managed to get his arm back through the sleeve of his coat.

"You can't just heal yourself?" Diane tucked her hands under her arms, shivering a little in a cool breeze.

He pulled the sheaths back over his head, settling them across his chest. "We can't instantaneously heal ourselves or humans." He gestured to her leg. "We can speed up the process, though. We should both be fine in a few days."

August stood, brushing snow from his knees. Diane accepted his help to stand, wobbling a little on her bandaged leg. Dorian reached for his double-bladed staff. He rested his hand in the center of the staff, spoke a word, and it separated again. He sheathed one blade over his right shoulder, then tried to pick up the left blade, but his fingers wouldn't cooperate enough to wrap around the staff.

August stepped forward, picking it up and carefully placing it in the sheath. He paused a moment more, then held out a hand to Dorian.

The other faery regarded him, then clasped his hand and let August haul him to his feet. Tonya pushed upright and handed Diane her staff.

"Ready?" Dorian asked, as if he'd never been injured himself. Tonya nodded and Diane experimented with putting some more weight on her right leg.

"I can manage," she said.

Dorian shouldered his pack and started walking. They skirted the pile of what had once been the remmiken, already blowing away in the light breeze. Tonya kept close to Diane as they walked. The princess limped gamely after Dorian, using her staff to compensate for her injured leg, but their progress slowed considerably.

She finally halted in the early afternoon. Tonya rested a hand under her arm as the princess took a few short breaths, her head bowed. Dorian and August gathered around.

"Not to be dramatic, but I don't know that I can keep going right now." Diane's voice sounded miserable.

"Sit down a minute and let me check your leg," Dorian said gently.

Tonya kept a steadying hand under Diane's arm, helping her lower herself to the ground. Blood streaked the bandage and Tonya caught a glimpse of worry in Dorian's face.

August crossed his arms. "Make camp here?"

"I just need to rest for a bit," Diane said, but she rubbed the skin just above the bandage, not quite hiding the slump in her shoulders.

Dorian removed his pack again and dug another vial out of his healer's kit.

"Small sip for the pain." He held it out to Diane. Hesitation showed in the twitch of her hands. Dorian didn't flinch, keeping it outstretched towards her. She slowly took the vial and drank. Her face contorted in a grimace as she swallowed.

She smacked her lips together and shook her head. "You couldn't make it taste better?"

Dorian gave a slight smile. "I'll make a note of that." He stored the vial away. "There's a Hold a few miles from here. We can head there and spend the night."

"What's a Hold?" Tonya and Diane asked in unison.

"A community of his people." August didn't attempt to hide his reluctance of the idea. He dragged a hand through his hair. "Would they even let us through the door?"

Dorian shifted enough to look up at him. "This one will."

August chewed the inside of his lip. "Fine. What do you think?" He looked down at Tonya and Diane.

They shared a glance.

"If it means sleeping inside, then yes," Diane said. Though she seemed about as excited as August.

Tonya nodded as well. *It means a delay in the trip, but it would help both Diane and Dorian.*

"All right, then," Dorian said.

Diane shifted her injured leg and dug the end of her staff into the ground, prepared to try to get up. She got far enough to bear a little weight, then shook her head, sinking back down to the snow.

"I feel ridiculous. It's a small cut." She tipped her head back with a sigh.

"I can take your pack," Tonya offered, not sure if she actually could manage another when her shoulders and back already ached, but if it wasn't that far to the Hold...

"You want me to carry you for a while?" August asked.

"What? No!" Diane jabbed a finger at him.

"Why?" August smirked a little.

"Because it'll be humiliating. And I won't make you do that, Tonya."

"Be honest. Is it because I don't have dark green eyes and brooding good looks?" August tilted his face up in an aggrieved expression, but his voice and eyes danced with mischief.

Diane glared and threw a handful of snow at his face, only making him laugh. "Leave Ralf out of this."

"Seems an appropriately grumpy name." August dodged another clump of ice.

Tonya began to smile. A muffled sound like a chuckle came from Dorian, for which he received a snowball to the chest.

"I bandaged your leg!" he protested.

Diane flicked more snow. "It's the principal of the thing."

A burst of cold and white hit Tonya in the face and she yelped in surprise.

"Don't think I didn't see you smiling." Diane glared, but her lips twitched in amusement.

Tonya grabbed a handful of snow and dumped it into the hood of Diane's coat. Diane shrieked and tried to brush it out, only sending it further down her neck. She gave up and tossed more snow at Tonya, who retreated behind Dorian.

Diane began to gather snow into a larger ball, a fiendish look on her face as she eyed them both.

"No." Dorian stood to leave Tonya to her fate, but she rose with him, hopping along behind him.

Diane smiled wickedly and threw the snowball anyway, managing to pelt both Dorian and Tonya with snow. August lobbed a snowball at Diane, which she barely dodged.

"Oh, throw at the crippled girl!" She retaliated with startling accuracy.

Tonya threw snow at August, still behind the relative safety of Dorian. He tilted his head to look back at her, raising an eyebrow.

She grinned back, suddenly wanting to see his smile spread from the corners of his eyes all the way across his face. It started, then abruptly shifted to shock as she shoved a handful of ice into his collar.

Tonya backed away, terror mixing with elation as he deliberately brushed it away and bent to scoop up a handful. She took off at a run, feet whispering effortlessly over the ice, dodging between the snowballs August and Diane were now sniping at each other.

A snowball whizzed overhead and she spun to face Dorian who bent to gather more snow. A frantic giggle broke from her as she scooped more snow into a ball. Dorian was unfairly fast despite only having one good hand.

Ten minutes later, Tonya sat breathless on the ground. Diane sprawled in the snow, having conceded eventual defeat to a triumphant August who looked like he'd survived a miniature blizzard. Dorian brushed snow from his coat, eyes still dancing.

"I haven't had a decent snowball fight in ages!" Diane slowly sat up.

Tonya rubbed some flakes between her fingers, almost imagining the tingle of magic coming stronger. "This was my first one."

Diane smiled. "You have good form for a beginner."

Tonya struggled to her feet and went over to Diane, who preemptively scooped some snow.

Tonya laughed, spreading her arms. "I come in peace!"

Diane smirked and took Tonya's extended hand and levered herself up to her feet. A wince cut through her smile as she placed weight on her leg.

"My offer still stands," August said.

Diane took a short breath, nodding almost to herself. "How far to the Hold?"

"Two miles maybe." Dorian pointed off to the right across the hills.

"Are you sure?" She turned back to August.

"I'm stronger than I look." He winked.

"Hmm." She pursed her lips in a doubtful expression.

He only laughed again. "For that, I might just make you walk."

Diane chuckled, her shoulders visibly relaxing. "I'll take you up on your offer then, kind sir."

August gave a flourishing bow. "I live to serve."

"Perfect. What else can I make you do for me, since I'm so grievously injured?"

"Don't press your luck," he warned good-naturedly. Tonya took Diane's pack for her as August scooped the princess up into his arms.

Tonya swung the pack over her shoulder, staggering a little under the extra weight. Dorian tipped a questioning glance at her, and she nodded, determined to carry it for as long as she could. He retrieved Diane's staff and rested it against his shoulder as he again led the way.

Two miles crept slowly by, lightened only by the friendly bickering between August and Diane, managing to bring a few quiet chuckles from Dorian. Tonya lagged under the extra weight, but they kept a slow enough pace that she didn't fall behind.

Finally, Dorian paused by a hill that stood a little taller than its nearby counterparts. He used Diane's staff to dig in the snow until it rammed against something. He bent to brush off a sizable grey rock cut through with faint streaks of some pink mineral. He rapped his knuckles three times against it, then twice more before standing back and waiting.

Diane tapped August's shoulder. "You can put me down now."

"Sure?" He glanced at her in light concern.

"Yes, I'd rather not show up at a faery door, declaring I'm a human princess, and looking like I'm making you carry me around. Not sure what that does for first impressions." August laughed and gently set her back down on her feet, letting her lean against his arm.

Dorian shifted between his feet, and Tonya realized with some surprise that he seemed nervous. The air around the hill shimmered and revealed a bright red door inset into the earth. Even cleared of snow, ice still clung to the hinges.

It swung open to reveal a male faery. He stepped out, a flat expression on his face as his gaze flicked over all four of them before settling back on Dorian.

Dorian didn't say anything, just held the other faery's stare.

*This doesn't look very welcoming.*

"Dorian," the faery finally said.

Dorian shifted again. "Endre."

Before Tonya could blink again, Endre punched Dorian across the face. August started in surprise and Diane lurched as if she'd take on the stranger with her bare hands. But Dorian just wiped some blood from the corner of his mouth.

"Had that coming, didn't I?" He tilted a glance up at the other faery.

Endre sniffed, shifting his hands to his hips. "That you did."

Dorian softened a fraction. "Good to see you."

Endre shook his head, lunging forward to wrap Dorian in a hug. "You too."

*What is happening?* Tonya stared, as bewildered as her companions.

"What are you doing with these Myrnians?" Endre asked, bitterness coating the name. "And a human?"

"We're on our way north," Dorian said. "We ran into a remmiken this morning."

"North?" Endre raised an eyebrow.

"To see about undoing this ice."

Endre glanced back over all of them. "Remmiken, you said?"

Dorian nodded. Tonya squinted at both of them, beginning to see some similarities in their sturdy features, the way they held their emotion around their eyes and away from their voices and mouths.

"Aye, they've been out more, along with the hippogryphs, since the ice came." Endre stood aside. "Come in, then, and get warm."

Dorian waved them ahead as Endre led the way through the door into a tunnel. Small cylinders hung along the walls, glowing in a gentle golden light. The lights brightened as the door creaked shut behind them.

Ten paces later, the hall opened into a wide chamber that looked much like the greeting area in Diane's house. More lights hung around the walls, illuminating the tiled floor and benches. Three doors opened off the room, leading deeper into the hill. Carvings etched the tiles along the floor and spread up into the walls — intertwining vines and flowers wrapping around large birds that appeared to be on fire, and creatures that looked like August's grass creation.

*Hippogryph.* Tonya traced the outline of the carving under her feet, the lines and crown of flowers softening it into something less terrifying than she'd imagined.

"This way."

Endre led them through the door on the far left. A few slits opened through the side of the hill, allowing natural light to creep through and illuminate the same designed tiles along the walls. Alcoves with cushioned benches nestled beneath each window, and occasional doors branched off into other corridors.

But still Endre led them on, taking a few more turns with sure steps. Tonya clutched at her sleeves, hopelessly turned around, and not sure how she felt about her first experience underground.

Their footsteps echoed off the floor, drawing a few curious faeries toward the hall. They greeted Endre, stared at the others, and whispered when they saw Dorian.

Tonya twisted to look back at Dorian. He smiled in a pained way the first time, and then kept his eyes slightly above her head every other time.

*What is this place that makes him so nervous?*

Endre halted before a door, carved and painted in bright reds and yellows. He knocked and stepped back, grabbing Dorian and hauling him forward a few steps. Dorian jerked his arm from Endre's grip with a huff.

"We all missed you," Endre said.

Dorian swallowed hard, his reply cut off as the door opened to reveal a faery woman in a bright yellow dress, a few streaks of grey in her dark hair. Her eyes widened as she looked at Dorian.

Tonya thought she was going to mimic Endre's greeting and punch Dorian again, but she pulled him into a wordless hug.

Dorian's words came so soft, Tonya nearly missed them.

"Hello, Mum."

# Chapter 16

"Mum?" Diane mouthed to Tonya. She lifted a shoulder in response. August watched in silence as the woman released Dorian and noticed them.

She swept sharp dark eyes over them, assessing in a way that reminded Tonya of Dorian.

"Friends?" Her gaze lingered on August with a harder edge.

"Yes," Dorian replied. "This is Lady Diane of Myrnius."

Diane managed a curtsey, wobbling and bumping into August, who graciously steadied her.

"She was injured in a remmiken attack this morning."

His mother's eyes widened a little and her hand pressed to her stomach.

"This is August of the Myrnian faeries." For once, no bitterness coated Dorian's voice. August flicked a glance at him, but gave a nod of greeting. "And Tonya of the ocean and ice faeries."

Tonya still wasn't sure what the proper greeting was on land, so she settled on mimicking August and offered a small nod, striving to hold the curious study of both Dorian's mother and Endre.

"I'm Ilka," his mother said. She opened the door wider and stood aside. "Welcome to Csorna Hold."

Dorian gestured for Diane to go first and she hobbled forward, still clutching August's arm. Tonya followed them into another wide, circular room. The ceiling rose higher than the entrance and halls, giving Tonya the feeling that she could breathe a little better. The same decorative tiles covered the walls and ceiling, painted in bolder colors and designs. Three doors split off the main room.

"How long will you be staying?" Ilka asked.

"Just the night. If that's all right?" Dorian seemed hesitant, a little wary of his greeting.

Ilka nodded, her hand still pressed against her stomach. "Will you want to see to her leg?" She nodded to Diane.

Again, Dorian hesitated. "I can in the kitchen?"

"Yes." Ilka placed a gentle hand under Diane's arm and pointed to the open door to the right. "I'll take her."

She glared a little at August. He nodded and stepped back, his movements stiff.

"The women can have the spare room. You two can share Dorian's old room." She glanced between August and Dorian.

Dorian tipped his head down. "That will be fine. Thank you."

August made no argument, only gripped the strap of his pack, adjusting it on his shoulder. Tonya's own load suddenly took on new weight, and she fought the urge to dump it all on the ground, sit down, and not move for at least a tide.

"Endre, show them." Ilka disappeared with Diane into the kitchen.

Endre reached for Diane's pack, which Tonya willingly surrendered.

"You remember where your room is?" A hint of bitterness still coated Endre's voice, even after his greeting.

Dorian nodded, his face melding back into something harder than his normal expressionless mask.

"This way."

Endre led Tonya through the left door and into another hall. The short passage dead-ended in a comfortable-looking room, lined with cushioned benches and a small black box in the center with a rounded tube reaching up to the ceiling. Galloping horses suspended in motion ran the walls, vines and flowers trailing from manes and tails.

Endre opened the last door on the left. The same glowing lights hung from the ceiling on short chains. Two beds rested against the far wall, complete with carved and painted wooden chests sitting at the foot of each. Endre placed Diane's pack on one chest and Tonya shrugged out of hers and laid it on the other chest.

"Washroom is through there." Endre pointed at another door inset a few paces from the foot of the bed. "My room's on the other side, so make sure you latch the door before using it."

Tonya nodded, although she had no idea why she'd need a wash room.

"Could you show me how to get to Diane?" Her heart twisted, longing for a familiar sight.

Endre wordlessly led the way back out the door, turning into the sitting room, not back into the main hall like Tonya had expected.

Heat emanated from the black box and the glimmer of flames shone through a glass pane. The warmth eased the ache in her body and she almost just took a seat in front of it to fall asleep. But Endre kept walking through an open doorway and another short hall into the kitchen.

The kitchen was nearly as big as the entry hall. A long wooden table and benches took up one half. Long counters and shelves ran the length of the other side. Ilka stood at a broad surface of metal, watching a pot of steaming water.

Diane sat sideways on one of the benches, Dorian kneeling beside her. His healer's bag lay open on the table.

Diane's face brightened at the sight of Tonya.

"I'll stitch it this time," Dorian said.

"I fainted last time I had to have stitches, but I'll try not to fall on you." Diane gave a wobbly smile.

Something in Tonya's stomach eased a little at the return of the smile to Dorian's eyes.

"That's appreciated," he said.

Tonya went to sit behind Diane, letting her lean against her. She swallowed hard at the sight of Diane's leg—bruised and bloody as the gash lay exposed again.

"Hopefully I won't pass out either." Her light tone brought a chuckle from Diane, and the princess relaxed a fraction more.

Diane gently squeezed her hand. "Thank you."

August entered and took a seat on the other side of the table.

"Doing all right?" he asked Diane.

"Ask me after Dorian chops my leg off."

August chuckled and Dorian tilted a glance up at her, the smile deepening around his eyes.

Ilka set a bowl of steaming water on the table along with several clean cloths. Dorian handed Diane the vial of medicine again. He began gently washing the cut after Diane had taken a few sips. She stiffened against Tonya, stifling a faint whimper of pain.

"So, Diane, where did you learn how to use that staff?" August rested his elbows on the table.

Diane's head whipped to face him so fast, she nearly smacked Tonya's nose with her braid.

"Edmund wanted to make sure that I could protect myself. We settled on the staff after I nearly took my arm off with a knife."

"Last round of stitches?" Dorian's voice rumbled in amusement.

Diane's giggle pitched a little too high. "Yes. Although it's been awhile since I've practiced like I should have. Ralf hasn't been happy about that."

A smirk played across August's face.

"*You* can keep quiet over there." Diane jabbed a finger at him.

August spread his hands wide, still grinning. "I'm sure we can work in some training around the endless walking."

Diane sat a little straighter in interest. "You think we — ooh, that's a big needle!"

August rapped his knuckles on the table, regaining her attention. Tonya swallowed hard, looking away before Dorian started stitching.

"Do you think you might be able to teach me how to use my knife?" Tonya tipped her head towards August.

"That's a good idea." Diane tried to turn to see her until Dorian tapped her knee and she settled back.

"I agree," August said. "I can take care of the knife fighting. I think Dorian might be better suited to practicing with you, Diane."

Diane pressed a hand against her chest. "Do my ears deceive me? Did that really just come out of your mouth?"

A wry smile puckered August's mouth. "Careful. You widen those eyes any more, they'll fall out."

A rumbling chuckle came from Dorian, drawing another laugh from Diane. Tonya smiled and a bit of tension eased in her chest. Diane told a few more self-deprecating stories about training mishaps, warning the faeries what they'd be getting into with training her, drawing more laughter from August.

A brief clatter brought her attention back to Ilka. Dorian's mother leaned against the counter, her arms folded across her chest, a curious look on her face as she watched Dorian work.

Careful not to let her eyes stray to the stitches, Tonya looked to Dorian. He was still intent on his work, but the smile still remained. It settled her again.

"All done," Dorian announced, winding a new bandage around Diane's leg.

"That was quick!" Diane perked back up. "It feels better."

She gently swung her leg off the bench to rest on the floor.

Dorian folded up the towel from under her leg, and the damp cloths he'd used to wash the wound.

"Let me know how it feels once that medicine wears off." He tucked the vial back into his pouch.

Ilka came forward and took the dirty linens. "Dinner will be in a little over an hour. There's enough time for you all to clean up."

Diane glanced down at her fresh bandage, a frown on her face.

Dorian rested his hand on the bandage and whispered a few words.

"It'll stay dry now."

Tonya tucked a hand under Diane's elbow as she pushed to her feet, picking up her boot as she did.

"I'll see to a bath for you two." Ilka nodded to them.

Dorian slowly wiped his hands on the last clean cloth. "Go ahead." He looked at August.

The other faery tipped an almost imperceptible nod. Tonya didn't know if she preferred the way they were tiptoeing around each other now. But at least the air was free of the crackling animosity.

She and Diane slowly made their way after Ilka, back through the sitting room and to their assigned bedroom. Ilka pushed through into the washroom. The same tile coated the entire room, an extra lamp hanging from the ceiling. A chest of cabinets stood against one wall, and a copper tub against the other.

Ilka crossed over to it and began pumping a handle up and down. Tonya stared in fascination as water began to pour through the spout into the tub. Once full, Ilka dipped her hand in the water, speaking a few words. The water bubbled for a moment and then steam began to gently wisp from the surface.

She pulled cloths from the cabinet and placed them on the short table by the tub, along with a white block.

"It'll stay warm and clean for the both of you," Ilka said. "Need anything else?"

"No, this is perfect," Diane said. "Thank you."

Ilka stepped out, leaving the two of them. Tonya swallowed, heat already creeping up her neck before she even asked her question.

"What are we supposed to use this for?"

Diane hopped around to face her. "You've never had a bath before?"

Tonya shook her head. "I've lived in water my entire life."

"I forget!" Diane clapped a hand to her forehead. "Well, then you're in for a treat. Soap." She held up the block. "For washing your hair and skin. Towel for drying off. Make sure you bring clean clothes to dress in after."

"You can go first." Tonya half-stepped back.

"Are you sure?" But Diane eyed the tub eagerly.

Tonya smiled. "Yes. Need help with anything?"

Diane limped out and grabbed her pack, digging out her clean, slightly-wrinkled dress. "I think I can manage."

Tonya sank onto the bed as Diane went back into the washroom. She unlaced her boots, wiggling her toes after peeling off the socks. She reached for the pins in her hair and combed out the braid with her fingers. Her dark hair fell in crinkled waves over her shoulder, her scalp tingling with the sensation of finally being released after spending days in the confines of the braid.

She set the pins on the small table between the beds. *How can I get out of having my hair done like that again?*

She lay back on the bed, eyes closing almost against her will as she waited for Diane.

The princess had to nudge her awake twenty minutes later. Her hair hung damp and loose around her shoulders as she pressed the towel around the strands.

Tonya took out the dress that Diane had lent her, pausing a little over a clean pair of sharkskin trousers and light shirt. But it didn't seem like the appropriate thing to wear.

Her doubts about the bath slipped away as she sank into the warm water. Her muscles gradually relaxed and an embarrassing amount of dirt floated away from her skin to dissipate in the water.

The knot of magic loosened a little in response to her skin once again being coated in water. She slid under the surface, closing her eyes at the familiar sensation of her hair floating free. Her breath released in a cloud of bubbles as she fought the sting in her eyes.

*I miss the ocean and the Reef more than I thought.*

The part of her that always ached in the ocean felt at home among the ice. But the ocean still claimed her, the tide whispering to her with every beat of her heart now that she stopped to listen.

*Do I go back if I don't find a solution in the north?* As much as she missed the sighing of the waves and the crying of gulls, she knew she couldn't wade back into the breakers and leave the land behind. It had stolen a part of her heart, and she hadn't even seen the north yet.

She ran her hands through her hair, finding more tangles. She sighed in another burst of bubbles and emerged to grab the slippery bar of soap to wash.

When she finished, she hesitated between the towel and trying to use her magic to dry off like she would have if she'd just emerged on her island. She decided against it as soon as her hand sank into the softness of the towel.

She dried and dressed and went back out into the room. Diane sat on her bed, still combing out her damp hair. Tonya sank back onto the bed, enjoying the sensation of being clean and having her feet and hair free. She tucked her legs up under her skirts.

Tonya patted her towel over her hair one more time, then decided to try. She reached for the bit of magic that always seeped through in the water. Tongue sticking out slightly from the corner of her mouth, she closed her eyes and felt for the water. Her hair rose in response, shaking itself free of water drops, which disappeared as they slicked off.

"That seems like a practical use of magic." Diane's voice jerked her eyes open.

Now dry, her hair fell back around her shoulders. Tonya shrugged. "It's about the most I can do with water."

"But I see it doesn't take care of knots either." Diane smiled. She beckoned Tonya over, holding up her comb.

Tonya went and sat with her. Diane turned to sit cross-legged on the bed and began combing Tonya's hair.

"Can you really not use much magic?" Diane asked after a moment.

Tonya pilled the skirt between her fingers. "No. It feels all tangled up inside me. I can't even shift into an animal like other faeries. I'm just sort of — me."

"Well, I like this version of you." Diane tapped her shoulder with the comb. "Even if you did accidentally freeze everything."

Tonya turned enough to see Diane out of the corner of her eye. The princess took up another section of her hair, tugging a little at Tonya's scalp as she untangled it.

"You're one of the few people who do." She twisted to face the princess. "Thank you for — everything. You and Dorian and August..."

She shrugged. Their glances the first day had faded away to be replaced by an almost foreign acceptance.

"I wasn't expecting to find — friends, especially after what I did..." Her eyes burned again. "No one has ever really accepted me for anything..."

Diane tapped her shoulder again. An understanding smile softened her face. "Then they've missed out on an amazing faery. And I think you're going to be even more amazing after you, what did you say? Untangle your magic."

Tonya turned away to hide the tear that slid down her cheek.

"Do you really think we can figure out a way to undo it?" She tried to steady the wobble in her voice.

"We're going to." Determination hardened Diane's words. "I made a promise to my people and to Edmund that I was going to help fix it. And I can't let them down. Besides, this is what friends do. Help figure out a way to undo magical ice spells."

Tonya smiled a little at the tease in Diane's voice — also at the word "friends."

"Do you think that's what you could be with August and Dorian? Friends?" she asked. The slight undercurrent of tension between Diane and the faeries had faded to almost nothing since the remmiken attack.

A sigh broke from Diane and the comb paused for a moment in Tonya's hair. "I think—maybe. I know they both fought on our side during the war, but I didn't realize how hard it is to trust them sometimes."

"Or me?"

The comb tugged at a new patch of tangles. "No. I know you didn't mean the spell. Maybe it's just because I know your people weren't involved in the war, like that somehow makes it easier..."

Tonya faced Diane again. "Can I try?"

She pointed to Diane's wet hair and the princess arched an eyebrow.

"I suppose." She let Tonya place a hand on her head.

*Find the holes in the warding.* Tonya reached for the same thread of magic that she had earlier. She kept one eye cracked open as her tongue once again escaped in concentration.

Diane bit back a giggle as her hair began to lift and wave about her head. "It tickles!" she whispered.

Tonya tried to shush her around her tongue and her own triumphant laugh as the water slid free and melted back into the air.

She took her hand away from Diane's head. The princess gingerly felt her hair.

"Dry. And poufy." A grin lit her face. "You have no idea what it takes to achieve this without magic." She squeezed Tonya's hand. "I guess magic's not so bad."

"Glad to help." Tonya grinned. *I did it. I actually used my magic for something. Even if it was just hair.*

Her stomach rumbled in agreement.

"I concur." Diane returned her comb to her pack and stood. "Should we go see about dinner?"

*

Tonya slid onto the bench beside Diane. August sat next to her, and across from them sat Dorian and Endre. Ilka took the head of the table. The opposite end sat empty.

None of the Durneans looked at the seat.

Ilka blessed the food in an even voice and asked the Creator's favor over their continued journey. Tonya stared down at her clasped hands and added the prayer she'd been praying since the day the ice had appeared.

*Creator, please help me figure out a way to undo this.*

Dishes were passed around in silence. Tonya spooned roasted potato chunks smothered in herbs and slices of meat Ilka had called stone quail onto her plate. Dorian passed her the basket of golden crusted bread and offered his slight smile again.

She ducked her head and focused on the meal. The potatoes' crisp skin broke on her tongue in a burst of savory flavor, combining wonderfully with the light sweetness of the roasted meat. It endeared her a little more toward the land.

"Tonya, you have lived in the ocean your entire life?" Ilka broke the silence.

Tonya dabbed her mouth with a napkin as she nodded. "It's where my mother wanted me to live."

*Before she left me.* The bitter voice surfaced again.

"And what happened to her?"

Tonya shrugged. "I don't know. I don't know about my father either. I just know that he came from the north."

"Dorian told me about your journey and the reason for the ice." Ilka took a small sip of her pale wine.

Tonya swallowed sudden nervousness. Ilka set her cup back down and gave a small nod, sorrow lurking in her gaze as it settled for a moment on the empty seat.

"I hope you can find out what happened to them."

"Thank you," Tonya whispered. It was something she'd thought about often enough over the long miles, but something she didn't know if she dared hope for.

"He also told me that you are more than just Lady Diane." Ilka looked to Diane. "I don't know much about human royalty, so I hope that you will be comfortable enough here." She gave a small nod.

Diane carefully swallowed. "I will be." A bit of something passed between them, and Diane seemed to settle more. "Thank you for your hospitality."

Ilka gave something closer to a smile that didn't fade as she turned to August. "Dorian says you killed the remmiken."

August's head flew up and he darted a glance between her and Dorian. Dorian didn't look up, tearing a piece of bread in two.

"He did just as much as I to bring it down," August finally said, the same caution in his words.

Pride lingered in Ilka's smile.

"So you didn't forget how to use your staff, then?" Endre stabbed at a potato chunk.

Dorian's hand tensed around his fork, but he just quietly shook his head. Tonya nibbled at her bread, confused by Endre's constant changing mood.

"We've heard of your parents even here." Ilka turned again to August, whose features relaxed into a smile at her more friendly tone. "You must be proud of them."

"They leave a great name to live up to," August said.

"Do you have any siblings?" Diane poured herself some more wine.

"Two older sisters. And..." August paused, nudging a piece of meat around his plate with his fork as he flicked a glance toward Dorian. "I had a brother."

Dorian leaned his elbows on the table, still only picking at his food.

"How did he die?" he finally asked, meeting August's half look.

Tonya held her breath as a deeper silence covered the rest of the table. Ilka pressed her lips together. August prodded at a potato.

"Killed by a Durnean faery who'd turned," he said.

Dorian nodded, his jaw set a little crookedly.

Ilka watched the two of them, one hand pressed flat against the table.

"I lost a cousin to a turned Myrnian faery." Dorian flicked his hand in and out of a fist. "And a friend to a patrol of both Durnean and Myrnian soldiers who didn't stop to see what side she was on."

Endre scowled and pushed away from the table. Ilka closed her eyes as he strode through the door back out to the entry hall, slamming the main door behind him. Dorian tracked his path and laid his fork down. He stood.

"We've got some things we need to talk about. I'll be back later." He paused at the other entrance to the kitchen and looked back to August.

"I'm sorry."

"Me too," August replied, but there was no trace of anger, just sadness in his voice.

The air finally seemed to clear between them, the tension fizzling to nothing like sea foam on the warm summer sand. Raw understanding the only thing left in its place. The entry door closed gently behind Dorian, and Diane released a quiet sigh, her shoulders slumping.

"I hate what the war left," she whispered.

Ilka leaned across the table to touch her hand. Her eyes held the same sadness as Diane's.

"Me too." She nodded to the seats her sons had vacated. "Me too."

They finished their meal in silence. Diane offered to help with the washing up, but Ilka gently turned them down, saying she wouldn't make her guests work in her kitchen.

They slowly filed out into the sitting room where the fire still burned steadily in the box, though Tonya had not seen anyone tend to it.

"I think I'll go to bed," Diane said. She wobbled a little on her leg and August steadied her.

"Walk you to your room?" He flicked an exaggerated wink.

A smile teased Diane's face. "I'm flattered, but you're not tall or handsome enough."

His eyes widened in mock affront as a laugh escaped. She tilted her nose smugly in the air as she tugged him along, Tonya following a few steps behind. Diane halted at their door. She impulsively flung her arms around August.

"Sorry about your brother," she murmured against his shoulder.

He gently folded his arms around her, tapping her shoulder. "Thank you." He blinked rapidly a few times as he pulled away.

He cleared his throat. "I'll think I'll turn in too."

Diane sniffed and rested her hand on the latch.

"Tonya?"

Tonya rubbed her arm with one hand, feeling suddenly like she was just standing on the outside again.

"I will in a little bit." She took a step back into the sitting room.

They both wished her good night and retreated to their rooms. Tonya sat on the cushioned bench, drawing her knees up to her chest. She wrapped her arms around her legs and rested her chin on her knees, watching the flames dance through the small window.

Eventually Ilka finished her gentle clatter in the kitchen and came to stand in the doorway.

"Do you need anything?" she asked.

Tonya shook her head. "I'll likely go to bed soon."

A smile gentled Ilka's narrow face. "I wouldn't wait up for him. He and Endre have a lot to work through."

A bit of warmth crept up Tonya's neck as she realized that's what she'd been waiting for — Dorian to come back in so she could make sure that he was all right after the stifling looks and the words with harsh undercurrents.

"I wouldn't be surprised if they came back with some bruised knuckles and bloody noses."

Tonya straightened in mild alarm. But Ilka just smiled again.

"The hazard of having boys."

Tonya offered a tentative smile.

"I'll be in the library for a bit if you need anything," Ilka said.

"Thank you." Tonya rubbed a hand over her sleeve again.

"I didn't think I'd be grateful for this ice, but it got him to come home again for the first time in a long while, so maybe I'll be thanking you." Ilka rested a hand against her stomach. "Good night, Tonya."

"Good night," Tonya murmured as she left.

The Hold lapsed into silence, only the occasional creak of the pipe or deeper snap of the fire breaking the quiet. Despite the fatigue covering her, Tonya's eyes refused to fall heavier towards sleep.

Eventually, the scrape of a door opening and closing at the end of the hall announced that Ilka had gone to bed. Tonya rubbed her eyes, sliding her feet down to touch the floor. She sighed, not sure why she was still up. Her mind wasn't even thinking of anything important, just staring at the fire that still burned, sending out a comfortable warmth that seemed to stretch into every corner of the house.

The heavier creak of the main door sounded. One set of footsteps briefly paused before the door next to the guest room closed. Endre.

Tonya leaned forward, her hands gripping the edge of the seat, listening for Dorian. A full minute later the door closed again, and his even tread approached.

She suddenly wished that she'd gone to bed. She'd be plainly visible in the light from the fire and the cylinders that still glowed softly. Her cheeks burned a little hotter as he paused by his door.

He stepped out of the shadows of the hall, solidifying back into his normal form that was all quiet edges. A bit of relief nudged her heart at the absence of any bruising or blood on his face after Ilka's prediction.

"Still up?" He didn't seem to quite know what to do with his hands. But his shoulders sloped into a more relaxed position, and his smile rested closer to the surface.

"Not tired yet, somehow." She shrugged, tucking her own hands into her lap.

"Wait there." He went into the kitchen. She drew up her legs to sit cross-legged on the bench, not about to leave for all the magic in the ocean.

He returned a few minutes later, carrying two steaming mugs. She gingerly took one from him as he sat beside her.

A creamy drink filled the mug, a dusting of something sweet-smelling floating on top. She took a cautious sip, sighing as it slid smoothly down her throat.

His eyes crinkled at the corners as he sipped at his own drink. She settled back against the cushions. He followed her stare to the fire, and they sat in companionable silence, savoring the beverage.

"Is everything all right with you and Endre?" She cautiously asked the question burning in her throat since he'd walked in.

He slowly rotated his mug in his hands. "I think it's finally starting to be."

He drank again, wiping the corner of his mouth with a thumb. "August is right. I haven't left the war behind. It still has a hold on me that I can't shake. And I let it come between me and a lot of people."

Dorian shook himself as if embarrassed at having spoken that much.

Tonya traced the curling handle of her cup. "We heard some of what happened in the ocean. The Reef Guard kept scouts along the coastlines, making sure that our waters wouldn't be touched. There were some that wanted us to get involved, but the king refused. And I'm glad he did, because it seems like the war still snares around everyone and everything like a strangling eel."

Dorian's chest rose and fell in a huff of a laugh. "That's true enough. Nothing like it had ever happened before and I pray that it never does again. But Endre's anger at me is for more than not coming home for the last few years."

He shook his head. "I'm sorry. You don't want to hear about this. We don't really know each other that well, do we?"

Tonya bit back a quick wish that she did know him that well. She shrugged a shoulder instead. "Does it help to talk about it?"

He tilted his head enough to regard her from the corner of his eye. "It does a little."

She took another sip, the warmth of the creamy drink spreading all the way down to her toes. "How's your arm?"

He held out his left hand, spreading his fingers. The swelling had already reduced, and the bruising was not as noticeable.

"Already better. I told you." A gentle tease entered his voice.

"How do you do it?"

He raised an eyebrow. "Heal?"

She nodded.

"I suppose it's like any other magic. You just have to find the right words."

"That's very helpful," she commented into her cup.

His huff of a chuckle came again. "What makes sense to me doesn't always make sense to others."

She reached over and nudged his arm. "I didn't say it doesn't make sense. I was just expecting a long and lyrical explanation."

His eyebrow nearly disappeared under his hair. "Long and lyrical? From me?"

Tonya nearly snorted her drink through her nose. "You're right. What was I thinking?" She wiped her mouth.

His smile stretched across his face as he took another drink.

"What about your magic?" he asked. "How do you do it?"

Tonya rubbed her thumbs over the gentle curve of the mug. "You mean the little bit I can barely squeeze by the warding spells?"

This time he touched her arm in response to the bitterness in her voice. She turned her head to stare at him. He looked back, seriousness in his face and open curiosity around his eyes.

She hesitated. She'd never tried to explain it to anyone. No one had cared enough to really ask her about her magic.

"It's like I have to wait until I hear it whisper to me and then I can whisper back. If that doesn't sound silly?"

"No," he said simply. "Does it feel different when you use either kind?"

This time the curiosity leaked out into his voice.

She sat back to better look at him.

"I'm sorry, I don't mean to offend. I just find it fascinating."

She tilted her head in confusion.

"But not in a bad way, or…" he began stammering and a flicker of amusement tickled her chest, finally breaking out in a giggle.

He rolled his eyes.

"You don't think having two kinds of magic makes me some kind of—freak—or anything?"

His eyes widened. "Why would I think that?"

"Well, because I'm…"

She focused on the rearing horse on the opposite wall. Some in the reef didn't care about her magics. Others made no bones about the fact they found it offensive she even existed. Those were the ones who made the worst comments about her parents, some going so far as to call her mother a traitor to all faery kind for marrying outside her magic.

Very, very few found it interesting that she held two magics inside her, no matter how poorly she could use them. But none had ever tried to help her like Dorian.

His gentle touch on her arm brought her back. She stared at his hand for a moment before raising her eyes to meet his. "Ocean magic feels smooth, flowing. Like the swell of a tide or the brush of a sea breeze. Ice magic tingles and nips. Though I don't remember what it felt like when all the ice burst from me."

"It's a little amazing that it all came from you." But his voice held no bite.

Tonya scoffed a little. "Amazing or confusing that the girl with barely any magic could have made something like it?"

He frowned. "You have plenty of magic. The warding is just blocking it, trying to protect you."

A sigh brushed past Tonya's lips. "But why'd they have to ward me? Why couldn't they have just outrun whatever was chasing them and kept me?"

The words slipped out before she could stop them.

His hand wrapped around hers and she squeezed his fingers, blinking away the sting in her eyes.

She cleared her throat.

"Sorry." She moved her hand, but he still held it. He released her slowly. She tucked her hand back into her lap, skin suddenly cold.

"If it helps at all, the way the warding feels, they poured as much love and protection as they could into their spells."

Tonya pressed her fingers over her eyes for a long moment. Even with Kostis's reassurance that her parents had loved each other, the doubt that had been present over her entire seventy years wasn't so easily banished.

"Thank you," she whispered. "I've never known them, so I don't know why it affects me so much."

"They're your parents," Dorian stated. "They should always be there to protect and look after you."

Familiar hurt tinged his voice. This time he stared at the opposite wall, jaw tensed hard for a moment. Her heart twisted at the memory of the empty seat at the table and the way they didn't look at it.

Tonya searched for a way to break the sudden silence and bring both their minds away from the painful topic.

"Did you really mean you'd keep helping me use my magic?"

He shook himself slightly and focused back on her, the smile returning to the corners of his eyes.

"I'm just a little nervous that if we can get the warding removed, my magic won't know what to do with itself and just..." She lifted her hands helplessly.

"I'm happy to," he said. "And I don't think your magic will just burst out of you. It just needs you to help it sort itself out."

"You make it sound so easy." She rubbed her hands.

What would it feel like to have instant access to both her magics without having to coax it past the warding? What would it be like to call to the tides and fly on a blizzard's breath? *Except I can't fly.*

He shrugged. "I just believe that you can."

She had to clear her throat again. Even Sophie hadn't stated that level of belief in her before the freeze. She drank the last of her beverage to hide the way her eyes blinked in rapid succession.

"I think I'll head to bed now. We have a long day again tomorrow." She pushed a smile to her face as she stood.

Dorian seemed to understand and took her mug from her.

"See you in the morning, then."

She nodded and retreated to the hallway, pausing to look back at Dorian. He hadn't moved yet. Her heart flip-flopped in her chest.

"Thank you." She hoped that he knew why.

He tipped his head. "You're welcome."

She slid the door to her room open as quietly as she could to avoid waking Diane. All the lights had gone out except for one by her bed that had dimmed to almost nothing, as if waiting for her.

She wriggled out of the dress, changing to her more comforting woven shirt and trousers, suddenly needing a little reminder of the only home she'd ever known. The light winked out as she lay down and pulled the blankets over herself. She curled her hand against her chest, the warmth from Dorian's hand returning as she fell asleep.

# Chapter 17

**D**iane stretched under the soft woven blankets, squeezing her eyes shut to deny one final time that she was truly awake.

*I had no idea how much I'd miss sleeping in a real bed.*

She peeled one eye open. The soft light was back. It startled her the night before when they'd dimmed all on their own as she'd gotten into bed. Tonya slept, curled on her side in the opposite bed, burrowed in a pile of blankets.

In the absence of natural light in the room, Diane had no idea what time of day it was. But she felt refreshed enough to have slept through the entire night. And hopefully not too late into the morning.

*Although I think we'd have been woken up if it was too late.* Unless the boys had similarly overslept.

She sat up, pushing the blankets away with a reluctant sigh. Thinking of the boys reminded her of the chilliest dinner she'd been part of in a long time. *I hope the mood has thawed for breakfast.*

Her movement woke Tonya, who stirred and blinked owlishly.

"Morning!" Diane said cheerfully.

Tonya rubbed her eyes and nose, looking a little offended at the brightness of her tone. "Can we stay in bed forever?"

Diane laughed, and a smile peeked out from Tonya. "I wish. But I need food."

That brought Tonya sitting up. "How's your leg?"

Diane swung her legs over the edge of the bed. Her shift fell to her knees, exposing the bandage winding about her lower leg. No blood stains peeked through, and the constant throbbing from yesterday had completely abated.

She gingerly set her toes on the tile floor, expecting a chill like the floors back home, but a faint warmth lingered. It gave her the courage to stand up. Her leg held steady beneath her and only a slight twinge of pain shot up her calf.

"Much better. I guess Dorian knows what he's doing after all."

Tonya nodded, a thoughtful little smile curling about her lips. Diane lifted an eyebrow in interest and filed it away for later. *What happened after I went to bed?*

Tonya hopped out of bed, straightening her loose tunic and fitted trousers.

"Is this all right to wear for breakfast?" she asked a little doubtfully.

Diane unpacked her spare set of trousers and travel dress and began to change, leaving the right trouser leg rolled up above the bandage.

"I have no idea what Durnean faery propriety says, but I suppose it might be. It's what you'd wear in the ocean, correct?"

Tonya's face cleared in relief. "I've just never really worn dresses before. The skirts get in the way in the water."

She tipped a glance over at Diane, as if afraid of offending her.

But Diane saw the practical appeal of just wearing trousers and a shirt and avoiding the extra material of a skirt altogether.

"I'd imagine so. I did consider asking to borrow some of Edmund's shirts." She slid the travel dress overhead, the skirts settling comfortably around her knees.

Tonya pulled out a white bone comb and began running it through her hair. She gathered the long strands and began twisting it, gathering it up behind her head, and tucking it into place with whalebone pins.

Diane watched jealously as the hair didn't immediately come tumbling down. Instead, it looked almost pleased with the new arrangement. She plaited her own hair in a long braid, not having the patience or skill of Matilde to redo the crown braid again.

"Do you think I can leave my boots off until Dorian looks at my leg again?"

A hopeful expression creased Tonya's face. "I won't wear mine either, if that makes you feel better?"

Diane giggled. "Don't like shoes, do you?"

Tonya shook her head with a grimace. "We don't really need them in the ocean. Only the Reef Guard wear light boots for their uniforms and for protection if they have to go fight."

"Unfortunately, they're routinely useful on land. Hopefully we won't offend everyone by not wearing them *just* yet."

Diane couldn't quite bring herself to stuff her feet back into boots. Back home, if she had a few hours of privacy, she'd shuck her shoes and go barefoot to Matilde's eternal dismay. She hadn't realized how much she'd missed the bits of freedom throughout the day.

Tonya gave a sunny smile and waltzed to the door, looking ridiculously pleased for having gotten out of wearing shoes. Diane grinned as they retraced their way to the kitchen.

August and Dorian were already up and eating at the table, talking almost conversationally. Ilka turned from the stove.

"I was just wondering if I was going to have to come wake you two up." She smiled, a more open sight than the night before.

Diane returned the smile, enjoying the feeling of being well-rested for the first time in days. And feeling more at ease in the faery Hold than she had the night before.

"We were contemplating how to try to stay in bed all day to avoid more walking."

Ilka chuckled, a rich, low sound. Dorian gave a quick smile. *If it's been anything like home, I wonder how long it's been since she's really smiled?*

"How's your leg feeling this morning?" Ilka took down two plates.

"Still attached." Diane stuck her foot out.

"I'll look at it in a few minutes," Dorian said.

"Breakfast first." Ilka handed her and Tonya full plates and shooed them over to the table.

Fresh fruit, bacon, and more fried potatoes piled alongside flatcakes. August shoved a jar of honey towards them as they sat on opposite sides of the table from each other.

"Morning!" Tonya greeted them both with a smile that got a little brighter when she turned it to Dorian.

Diane spooned honey onto the cakes with interest. August caught her glance and smirked a little.

"What is this?" Tonya took the jar as Diane passed it over, tilting it to look at the amber liquid.

"Honey," August said. "Trust me, just put it on the flatcakes."

Tonya pursed her lips in mock suspicion, but dabbed a spoonful on her flatcake. Diane dug into her meal in unladylike haste. Her appetite had only grown with the miles they'd traveled. Tonya ate a small forkful of flatcake and her eyes widened appreciatively. She spooned more honey on and tucked in with impressive speed.

"I think we need to take you on a food-tasting tour of all three countries when we're done, Tonya." Diane smeared a strawberry through some stray honey. "It has occurred to me that we are missing out on so many opportunities."

"Like what?" Tonya dabbed her mouth with a napkin.

"Fried apple cakes," August said.

"Walnut pastry rolls," Dorian supplied.

"Or savory roast goose and caramelized potatoes." Diane sighed.

Ilka chuckled as she sat down with her own plate. "If you decide to come back this way, I'll celebrate with a pot of paprikás."

"I don't know what that is, but it sounds amazing," Diane said, fully prepared to call off a day of traveling to eat.

"It is," Dorian said in his quiet voice, a smile flickering just out of sight. Ilka softened and returned his almost smile.

Diane cut off a piece of bacon, glad to see things seemed to have smoothed out a little between Dorian and his family. Though it could have just been the absence of Endre. It hurt more than she thought it would to hear Dorian and August talk about the war, even if it helped them through whatever they held against each other.

"When are you leaving today?" Ilka covered another plate and set it aside.

They all looked at each other, and Diane's own reluctance to resume traveling showed in her companions' faces. "I suppose it will depend on how my leg is?" She turned a questioning glance to Dorian.

He nodded, rising to place his empty plate in the wash tub. "How's your arm?" Diane asked, suddenly remembering the horrible bruising and swelling.

Ilka looked up sharply. "You were hurt too?"

"I'm fine."

Dorian frowned a little at Diane and she gave a little wince of apology. She hadn't realized he was hiding the bandage from his mother, like he'd tried to hide the injury from them. He rolled his eyes a little and pulled up his sleeve as Ilka went over to him.

He'd left the bandage off. The swelling had diminished, and the black and purple bruises were already fading to a greenish color in spots. At least a few days of healing had been compressed into one night. It gave Diane hope for her leg.

August narrowed his eyes as he looked at the injury, seeing something else Diane hadn't.

"You keep your scars?" he asked, a slight edge under the curiosity. Diane looked closer, finally seeing scars tracing their faint way across the bruised skin.

Dorian glanced down at his arm, opening and closing his fist a few times before nodding. The look on August's face suggested it wasn't much of an answer. Ilka gently took Dorian's arm and looked over it.

"Dorian is as reckless a healer as he was a warrior."

But pride laced her words.

Dorian kept his gaze on his arm. August nodded slowly, as if that meant something to him. Diane finally understood August's disbelief the day before. Dorian showed just as much experience as August when battling the remmiken—yet healers were not usually trained in combat, human or faery.

"Ocean faeries keep their scars," Tonya said, a confused frown in the corner of her mouth.

"We don't always here on the land," August replied. "My father was forced to keep the scars on his face because the king at that time thought he might turn to the Nameless Ones for what he'd done to save my mother."

Tonya shivered, and a chill scurried down Diane's back at the mention of the Nameless Ones. Clearly, the ocean also had faeries who turned to evil and used their magic to harm rather than help.

"We think them a symbol of pride," Tonya said.

"Guess we're a little more vain here." Dorian rubbed his hand over the skin. Diane caught a faint shimmer around his hand and thought she might have imagined it, but the bruising turned a little lighter and more yellow.

"You ready?" He looked to her.

Diane reluctantly finished the last of her potatoes and bacon. She nudged the plate out of the way and turned sideways on the bench, bringing her leg up onto the wood.

"I suppose."

Dorian took his bag from where he'd left it on the counter the night before and crouched beside her. He was able to use both hands this time to undo the bandage, gently tugging it away from the wound.

Diane hissed a short breath as it tore free with a quick jab of pain. The bruising and swelling around the wound had faded, much like Dorian's arm. The wound itself remained closed in the neat line of stitches, the skin already looking like it was trying to knit back together.

Dorian gently washed the cut again and spread more ointment before wrapping a fresh bandage around her leg.

"I think it should be fine to walk on today."

Diane pushed her bottom lip out into a pout. "You sure?"

His green eyes twinkled with laughter that barely showed on his face.

"Unfortunately, yes. And I'm afraid I'm not as chivalrous as August. I won't carry you for the next fifteen miles."

"No?" Diane pressed a hand to her chest. "What good are you, then?"

The laughter shone again as he stood.

"Fifteen?" August raised an eyebrow. "You might be out of luck, princess. Although I do seem to remember a conversation about you not wanting to be helped too much." His grin puckered one half of his face.

Diane smiled. "Some friends I picked."

Another pleased smile spread across Tonya's face at the word "friend," and Diane's heart again went out to the faery.

"Shall I pack you some extra food, then?" Ilka gathered the empty plates with murmured thanks from August and Tonya.

"That would be fine." Dorian gave his mother one of his rare full smiles.

She patted him on the shoulder as she passed.

Diane and Tonya returned to their room to re-pack their bags and reluctantly stuff feet into boots. Tonya stayed in her ocean clothes, shrugging into her fur-lined jacket and leaving the buckles, as always, undone.

They brought their packs to the kitchen, along with Dorian and August, and Ilka found room for small bags of food to supplement their stores.

The boys had also returned to their travel clothes, coats, and weapons. August shouldered his pack, running a hand under the straps and along the collar of his jacket to straighten it out. Diane accepted his help this time to pull hers on. He helped Tonya next, who looked at her bag with an expression of distaste.

Ilka folded Dorian into a long hug before letting him pick up his own pack. She walked with them to the main entrance of the Hold, where a different faery stood guard.

"Stop and say goodbye to Endre," Ilka said, leaving no room for argument from Dorian. "You all are welcome back here any time."

She looked at each one of them, giving August a slight nod.

He pressed a hand to his chest with a deeper incline of his head. "Thank you."

"Take care of yourselves out there." Ilka pressed Diane's and Tonya's hands.

"Thank you," Tonya murmured, the same wide-eyed look of surprise on her face anytime someone offered an overture of friendship.

The guard faery opened the door for them and August led the way out, Dorian pausing a moment more to accept one last hug from his mother.

The door creaked shut behind them. When Diane looked back after a few paces, the hillside was covered in snow, no trace of the door or the signal stone to be found.

"The faery veil is back in place. You won't be able to find it again without help," Dorian said. "This way first."

They trailed after him without question as he trekked around the base of the hill and wound through another small gap toward a smaller knoll.

Several faeries walked the hills, eyes cast down to the earth and ice. A few stood in a cluster, heads bent towards each other in conversation. They all wore loose trousers and long coats that flared about the knees. The same bright colors painted on the walls were embroidered through the fabric.

"Wait here." Dorian held out a hand and moved towards a lone faery kneeling in the snow, hacking at the ice. The crack of it parting ricocheted through the hills and Tonya couldn't hide her wince.

Endre placed his hands in the crack, bowing his head. A faint swirl of pale magic covered him, racing down his arms and into the ground. A glimpse of green showed beneath the ice before it lunged back to cover the grass.

Endre pulled his hands away with a frown. He looked up, his expression easing a little at the sight of Dorian waiting a few paces behind him.

He stood, the snow not even sticking to his clothes. He and Dorian exchanged a few words, the lines easing again around Endre's eyes into something nearly friendly. He looked over at them and gave a slight nod. Dorian held out his hand, and Endre pulled him into a short hug before releasing him.

August twisted his hands around the strap of his pack, digging the toe of his boot into the ice. Sorrow nudged Diane's heart again. She couldn't bear the thought of losing Edmund, and from the sound of August's voice the night before, he and his brother had been close. It softened her a little more toward the faeries.

Dorian's even tread jerked her from her thoughts.

"Ready?" He shifted his pack.

They nodded and he led the way back to the indentation of the road. Diane sighed, hitching her pack higher on her back. Her leg gave a slight twinge and she frowned down at it. *I'll have to press through if I can.*

The road ran away from them, winding through the hills, ever north towards the unknown.

# Chapter 18

"**W**hat is it?" Diane stared out across the flat expanse. The hills had vanished, leaving nothing but open space and eddies of gusting snow.

"A lake." Dorian squinted as he stood at the very edge of the change.

August took a cautious step forward, tapping his boot on the spot where the snow rippled to a stop and the flat took over. The ice echoed back and, in response, a kind of groan ran out ahead of them.

Diane shivered, curling her hands around her staff. "Do we go around?"

Dorian shook his head. "No. That'll take too long. It's miles around to the other side if we do. We go across. Can I see your staff?"

Diane handed it over. *What's he after?* Dorian moved another few steps, sliding each foot forward as he tested the ice. He rapped the end of the staff against the ice, eliciting another hollow knocking sound.

Tonya stood a short distance away, both feet spread wide in a supporting stance, an almost dreamy expression on her face. She blinked slowly, her eyes coming back into focus.

"It can hold our weight," she said.

All three turned to her.

"How do you know?" August asked.

A bit of snow scurried about her feet. Her grey-green eyes sharpened and a small smile twitched at her lips.

"I used the right words."

A huff of amusement came from Dorian. "All right, then."

Diane accepted her staff back and leaned on it as she studied them with interest. They'd seemed a *little* closer since leaving Csorna Hold almost two days ago. It wasn't much, but they walked alongside each other more, Dorian now no longer leading the way alone. Shy conversations initiated by Tonya, and then those glances.

*Something happened at the Hold and I missed it.* She didn't know if she was more peeved at that, or the fact that Tonya hadn't said anything to her. *But* — she reluctantly dug her staff into the ground — *it's not like we're that close either.*

"So we can cross it?" August twisted to look at them, unaware of Diane's musings.

Dorian nodded, shielding his eyes to look across the ice. "It'll still take us most of today to get across. We should probably push to the other side before stopping for the night."

August grunted agreement. "Aye, I don't really want to camp on the ice, no matter how thick it is. We need to rest first?" He tilted his head to Diane.

She shook her head. "My leg's still holding up. I should be able to walk a few more miles before needing to stop."

Since leaving the Hold, it hadn't bothered her much. Dorian had announced he planned to take out the stitches that night and let it heal naturally from then on.

Diane felt the odd imbalance in her body as it had begun to change from the miles they'd walked to something harder and leaner, but her injured leg still scrambled to catch up.

"Let's go." Dorian stepped out onto the ice, Tonya behind him. August gestured for her to go next, taking up the rear in their normal marching pattern.

The ice creaked and moaned beneath their feet, creating an uneasy twitching sensation on the bottom of Diane's feet, as if to remind her that just underfoot lay a vast amount of water waiting to swallow them up in a heartbeat if the ice felt like cracking.

She slipped, wincing as she dug her staff into the ice harder than she intended. She regarded the ground around the staff with a cautious eye, waiting for cracks to appear. Tonya stepped back and helped her regain her balance with a touch under her arm.

"Even though we've been walking on ice this entire time, somehow this feels different." Diane slid her feet forward again.

Tonya's boots whispered effortlessly over the ice, almost like she was skating. "I know. I'm not sure I like walking across a lake like this."

A curse broke from August, and they twisted to see him, wings outstretched to balance as he hit the same treacherous patch as Diane had.

"Careful," Diane said unhelpfully.

He pursed his lips into a frown and flew a few paces, setting down gingerly before his wings folded and vanished from sight. The ice groaned and he froze. Diane's heart thudded in response. Dorian tensed beside them.

Only Tonya seemed unaffected. "It's just shifting."

"Shifting? That doesn't sound good." August kept his hands extended by his sides, to balance or possibly sprint away.

Tonya pressed her lips together in a way that made Diane think she was holding back a laugh. Diane prodded the faery's side and Tonya skated away with a squeak.

"All right, ice whisperer. Are we going to plummet into the freezing depths, or can we keep walking with only minor heart palpitations?"

Tonya giggled. "It's safe to keep going, I promise. The water's shoving against it, but the ice doesn't want to crack."

August tilted his head, the frown still twisting his lips. "I don't know if that makes me feel better."

"Might agree with you on that one." Dorian took a hesitant step. The ice held its peace.

Shaking her head, Diane followed, holding her breath every few paces. August had to use his wings repeatedly to steady himself, his usual grace deserting him on the more treacherous surface.

"I'm about to leave you all behind and just fly to shore," he grumbled after nearly falling again. He didn't bother tucking his wings away to *wherever* they went.

"Must be nice to fly." Diane carefully skirted around the shimmering patch that had nearly taken August down.

"It is," he agreed, sliding his feet forward with more caution.

Dorian spread his wings a moment later, a murmured explosion of words coming from him as he steadied himself. Like August, he kept them open.

Diane studied the difference, watching for the tell-tale shimmers that meant the ice was just waiting to try to trip them up. She'd begun to think that the lake had a personal vendetta against them.

The faeries' wings looked similar—a toughened membrane stretched over a rigid bony framework reminiscent of a bird. But August's were long and broad like an eagle's wings, made for flying. Dorian's were shorter and more compact, like the stone grouse they'd seen running over the snow, flying only in short bursts if they needed.

Both were a solid brown color, but she picked out different shimmers in the membrane in the sunlight, and the way they shifted colors ever so slightly.

The colors shifted to a lighter brown in August's wings, shading almost green around the edges to match his coat as he walked with more confidence. Dorian's took on a dark blue tint at the tips, the same as his trousers, as he accepted August's cheerful ribbing with a roll of his eyes in response to an almost fall.

Tonya walked along with quiet grace on the ice, untroubled by anything the lake threw at them. But Diane had yet to see her use her wings. It had been briefly touched on in the meetings before they left that Dorian and Tonya couldn't fly long distances, but she still wondered about Tonya's.

"Dorian, can I ask you a question?" Diane skidded forward a few steps.

He didn't even pause to nod. Diane debated a moment longer, hoping he wouldn't be offended somehow. Since the Hold, she'd felt a little more at ease with him, but he was harder to read than August.

"Do Durnean faeries fly?"

He tilted a glance over his shoulder, no anger in his eyes. "We can, but in short bursts only, and we don't really get very high above the ground. We use them more for digging."

"Digging?" Diane raised an eyebrow as she studied the delicate-looking membrane again.

"Our wings are tougher than they look." August chuckled. "It takes a lot to even break their surface."

Dorian paused for a moment, expanding his wings again with a slight arch to his back. This time Diane saw the small claws at the apex and the ridges along the edges.

"Comes in handy when you live underground and you don't want to use up your magic to shift the ground."

"Couldn't just use a shovel?" Diane teased.

Dorian's eyes sparkled. "What's the fun in that?"

*I think I understand what Tonya sees in him.*

"What about you, Tonya?"

Amusement vanished from Tonya's face.

"I don't fly either." She walked on, a tenseness in her steps.

Diane stared helplessly after her, exchanging a bemused glance with August and Dorian. They followed in silence, Diane trying to figure out some way to apologize without making it worse. She eventually settled on waiting for Tonya's shoulders to relax.

It took nearly half an hour before Tonya slid back to join her. She briefly sighed, tipping her head back and forth before speaking.

"Sorry."

"No, I'm sorry, I didn't mean to —"

Tonya shook her head. "It's all right. My wings are just — sort of — broken?" She shrugged one shoulder, a bit of red creeping up her pale cheeks. "I can't really swim and I can't fly with them, so…"

Diane blinked. She hadn't considered what ocean faery wings were like before.

"Well, speaking from experience, feet are just as good to get around on."

A smile flickered over Tonya's lips, and she nudged her shoulder into Diane's, but not hard enough to threaten her footing.

August swore again as he slipped. "Better than we're doing anyway."

"Than *you're* doing," Dorian corrected with a hint of smugness that was erased as August dove at him with a smirk.

They rolled to the ground, August coming up first on his knees. Dorian pushed up onto his hands, his wings pulsing in a quick beat that sent a blast of air at August to send him skidding backwards.

August retaliated by flicking his hand in a wave. Dorian easily dodged the gust of colorful magic, twisting so one hand was still planted on the ground and scraping his foot along the ice as if pushing it toward August.

August smirked as nothing happened. "Forgot we weren't over earth, didn't you?"

Dorian grumbled, flicking his fingers instead, sending some dusky green light towards August that he couldn't quite evade in time. It pushed against his chest, sending him into a partial roll. He used his wings to get himself back on his feet. Dorian pushed up off the ice, smirk in place.

Diane rolled her eyes and started walking again. The roughhousing was a welcome change from the chilly words, but it didn't mean they had to stop walking. Especially when walking on ice that she didn't particularly trust, even with Tonya's reassurances.

Tonya watched August and Dorian in amusement as they mock-fought their way across the ice with plenty of mishaps and falls. Though this time laughter accompanied it. Diane smiled as she and Tonya stayed well out of the way. Dorian's deeper laugh accompanied August taking flight before dive-bombing him.

"I think that's the first time I've heard him actually laugh," Diane mused.

Tonya's cheeks tinted red. "Me too."

Diane cleared her throat, and Tonya looked up at the unremarkable cloudy sky, the blush deepening.

"I see the appeal," Diane said, trying to keep her face straight.

"It's not like that!" Tonya's voice squeaked.

"Hmm." Diane raised an eyebrow.

"It's—he's—he's just one of the first people to seem to care about me, and it's spinning my head is all. I mean how is it different than you and August doing the same?" Tonya somehow managed to speak without taking a breath.

"It's not so bad to make friends, is it?" Diane nudged her arm.

Tonya flashed a smile. "No. Maybe I'm just not used to it."

Diane nodded. "And he's not so bad on the eyes."

Tonya squeaked again and shoved her hard enough to send her slipping a step. Tonya caught her arm.

"Sorry!"

Diane nearly fell over as she giggled. Tonya narrowed her eyes in a frown, but seconds later a chuckle broke through.

"No, he's not."

"But?" Diane prompted as Tonya fell into silence.

Tonya watched the boys as they walked a good thirty paces ahead.

"Well, I'm—me. I'm two kinds of faeries put into one and who knows if that's natural or not? There's plenty that think what my parents did by marrying was wrong. And even if he felt something for me, I wouldn't want his people, his family, to look at him the same as I've been looked at my whole life."

She stared down at her boots as they took step after step. Diane had to clear her throat. "I think that's stupid."

Tonya cast her a sideways glance. "But you don't know faeries," she whispered.

"How is it different from me marrying a Calvyrnian, or a Durnean?" Diane asked. "Just because we're from different countries doesn't mean there's anything wrong with loving that person."

"But it's different with magic!" Tonya waved her hands and an eddy of snow rose in response.

"How? You obviously turned out all right."

Tonya shoved her hands into her coat pockets. "Only because my parents warded me off with spells. Who knows what I'd be if my magic were free? Oh, this would happen!" She freed a hand to jab at the ice.

Diane snorted. "I hardly think that you would intentionally freeze the world if you had full access to your magic."

"You don't know that." Fear lingered in the purse of her lips and the hunch of her shoulders as she returned her hands to her pockets.

"Tonya," Diane said patiently, hooking her arm through Tonya's. "Even though we've known each other for all of a week, I know that you're a kind, caring faery with a sense of humor I wish you'd let out more."

"Really?" Tonya raised an eyebrow. "Sophie used to say some of the same things."

Diane smiled. "I think Sophie and I would get along quite well."

Tonya snorted a laugh. "The Reef wouldn't survive the two of you."

Diane tossed her head back with a laugh. August and Dorian stopped to wait for them. Diane kept her arm looped through Tonya's as they took their time to catch up.

"Maybe I'm not the best person to be giving advice, as I've been studiously avoiding my feelings for my guard for the last two years." Tonya's giggle interrupted her and she nudged the faery. "But Dorian's not totally oblivious to you. What could it hurt?"

"Him, maybe," Tonya replied softly, but she smiled and let Diane lead her on.

They all fell back into the sort of quiet, companionable silence that came with walking all day. Eventually, hills reappeared on the horizon, and their pace quickened.

But the lake played tricks once again and the hills seemed to move no closer in an hour's walk. Diane sighed and stretched her neck from side to side against the pull of her pack straps. *I should be used to Dorian being right by now.* She glared at the rebellious hills.

They agreed to eat dinner rations on the move, all eager to be off the ice. Even Tonya, who seemed more energetic than she had the entire trip. The clouds had obscured the sun all day, but their grey bulk had grown even darker by the time they reached the hills that had finally deigned to move closer.

Bits of forest covered the hills, welcome splotches of green and brown against the never-ending white. Diane stepped onto the shoreline with a sigh of relief. Even though she still stood on ice, she felt more *solid.*

She was ready to throw her pack down and sleep, but August looked around, body tense and alert.

"I think we should move out from here." He looked to Dorian. "Smell that?"

The Durnean faery tapped his foot against the ice, lifting his chin into the light breeze.

"You're right. There's a hippogryph cave around."

Diane's heart dropped into her stomach. She managed a swallow around a dry throat.

"It's just the one, and it's asleep right now." August dropped his voice lower.

"Which way is the fastest out of here?" Diane clasped jittery fingers around her staff.

Dorian pointed straight ahead and started walking again. Adrenaline whisked away the fatigue in her muscles and joints, keeping her going for another hour until Dorian stopped in a small forest that ran ragged over the hills away from the lake, connecting enough in its random copses to earn the title.

"We should be safe here," he said.

Fatigue came crashing down around Diane, as if it had just been waiting for the words. Tonya sank down into a crouch with a sigh of relief.

"Don't get too comfortable. We still have to set up the tent," Diane reminded her.

"I can sleep outside. I don't get cold."

Diane shook her head against a smile, letting her pack thud to the ground before bending over to free the neatly-wrapped tent from its bindings. Another benefit of faery magic allowed the tent to be folded up into a neat square no bigger than a dinner plate.

Tonya struggled to her feet and helped Diane shake out the canvas. Diane yawned as they set the canvas on the ground and watched it begin to build itself, a sight that had been shocking the first night, but now seemed almost ordinary.

*Maybe I'm getting too used to magic.* Even the magic Dorian and August had been using on the ice hadn't elicited fear the way it would have days ago. *Was this what it used to be like to live peacefully and as friends with faeries?*

The tent finished with a final snap, joining the boys' tent, which always seemed to build itself faster. Tonya shoved her pack through the flap.

"What would it take to skip training in the morning and sleep?" Diane yawned again.

Dorian and August had held true to their word and began to include an hour of training in the morning between breakfast and starting on the day's walking.

August stretched his arms overhead, his spine cracking with the motion.

"At this point, not much. I'll take first watch?" He looked to Dorian, who nodded, a bit of relief in his eyes.

Diane felt a smidge guilty about not being asked to participate in the watch rotation. August and Dorian had just taken it upon themselves, letting her and Tonya get a full night's rest. But the relative comfort of her bedroll called. Maybe she'd offer the next night.

August dug out his blanket before disappearing out into the trees. Diane followed Tonya into the tent, laying out bedrolls in the dark by habit now. Diane barely kicked off her boots and slid into her blankets before sleep claimed her.

*

The unmistakable brightness of late morning woke Diane. She sat bolt upright, startling Tonya awake.

"I think we overslept." Diane rubbed her eyes, scraping grit away. She slid her feet back into boots and went outside, stepping over the staff she'd left at the entrance. August stumbled out of his tent, rubbing his arms in the absence of his jacket.

"You just woke up too?" He stomped his feet against the ground to wake himself up.

"Where's Dorian?" Diane turned to search their little camp.

"Here." Dorian appeared through the trees, rubbing the back of his neck. "I fell asleep. Sorry."

"Good to know you're not perfect." August's little smirk held no trace of judgement.

Dorian rolled his eyes. "I think we should be fine with a fire for breakfast."

Diane clapped her hands together, the cold already finding her in the few minutes she'd spent out of the tent's warmth.

"You're a treasure, Dorian."

He raised an eyebrow, shaking his head slightly. "You haven't talked yourself out of training this morning yet."

"How does hot sausages and toast sound for breakfast?" Diane sent him her sweetest smile.

"I'm listening."

Diane chuckled, and turned to retrieve her pack.

"You going to share with us?" a new voice asked.

She stifled a surprised cry as eight figures stepped out of the trees to surround them. She stumbled back into Dorian's steadying hand. August spread his feet wide in a whisper of sound against the ice, guarding their back. Tonya retreated to his side, clutching her knife.

The strangers all wore heavy, dirt-stained coats. Slim packs were slung over shoulders, and all carried drawn swords or axes that gleamed uncomfortably bright in the morning sunlight. Diane shivered as the tallest man sized them up with flat blue eyes.

"So, what, exactly, are three faeries and a human doing all alone out here?" He spoke in a friendly manner, but his voice stayed as cold as the ice around them.

# Chapter 19

"We're just passing through." Dorian edged in front of Diane, his voice neutral.

The leader tipped his scruffy chin up to regard him. "Faeries don't just travel in packs anymore. Especially not with humans."

He scowled at Diane. Diane narrowed her eyes back, wishing she'd brought her staff with her.

"This one looks Myrnian." Another of the men jabbed a blade toward August.

Tonya bumped Diane's shoulder. "What do we do?"

"What do you want?" Diane lifted her chin higher, infusing authority into her voice.

"Ooh! Maybe a fancy human!" The leader smirked. "We'll take you for starters, once you tell us where to get a ransom for you."

Diane scoffed. "I *don't* think so."

Several of the bandits chuckled.

"And we'll make sure the faeries are locked up nice and tight so they can't come after us once we take the rest of your supplies as well." He reached to his belt and undid a curious-looking shackle. Iron inlaid the steel cuff in swirling patterns that shifted and changed the longer she stared at it.

Three other men brought out the same contraption.

Diane swallowed hard. The dark metal would be infused with powerful spells that would eat away at a faery's magic if they tried to use it. Sorcerers had worked in conjunction with rogue faeries to make them during the war. Even amid the other horrors, the thought had made her stomach turn.

"Tonya," Dorian murmured, "do not let them touch you with those."

Diane felt rather than saw Tonya's nod of agreement.

"August, you have a weapon on you?"

"A knife. Don't worry about me." August shifted his stance again, a tight eagerness in his voice that sent another shiver down Diane's spine.

"Last chance to walk away," Dorian warned the men.

"Admirable." The leader smiled. "Give us the girl. We could even find a use for the other one too. You don't want to tangle with us, boy."

Dorian whipped one of his blades from its sheath. "Try me."

Diane pressed closer to Tonya. "Stick together and head for my staff," she whispered, her voice wavering.

Tonya nodded again, her hand trembling where it gripped her whalebone knife. Diane hoped that the faery could remember her two meager hours of training with August.

"Jakab, make sure the girls don't run." The leader nodded to the bulky swordsman closest to Diane and Tonya. "Tomi, help take these two down."

Diane tracked his look to the shortest of the men. Tomi nodded, not quite meeting Dorian's furious glare.

"Traitor!" Dorian spat. The faery met his glance for a second before shoving his fist forward in a punching motion. Dorian threw his arm up, blocking the blinding flash of light. He spun, kicking out with one foot. The ground rumbled in response, sending two of the men staggering into each other.

August jumped forward, disappearing as a snow leopard took his place and pounced on the startled bandit closest to him.

Jakab strode forward, his sword lowered by his side, beady eyes fixed on Diane.

*No you don't.* She grimly clenched her hands. There wasn't room to run and follow Ralf's precise training instructions. She'd have to settle for the backup plan.

Tonya thrust forward with her knife, but he caught her wrist and twisted. Rage filled Diane at Tonya's cry of pain. She darted forward, forcing the full weight of her body through the heel of her hand in a punch to his sternum. He wobbled, and she followed up with a knee to his groin.

He stumbled back with a colorful swear. She shoved Tonya out of his fumbling reach and ran around him to the tent, where she scooped up her staff. Tonya set into a stance beside her, breath coming in quick gasps.

"That was good, Tonya. Just keep moving and don't let him get too close." Diane twisted the staff comfortably in her hands.

Dorian had formed his bladed staff and took on a bandit and the faery. They struck at him with swords, batted away by the quick thrusts and swipes of his blades. He spun it in a quick circle, somehow deflecting another burst of magic.

August shifted back to his faery form mid-leap, his wings forcing him into a spin to avoid a sword snaking toward him. He landed in a crouch, a knife appearing from somewhere.

He slowly rose to his feet, wiping away blood that dripped from the corner of his mouth.

The look on his face unnerved Diane—ferocious, focused, *eager.* Nothing like the cheerful faery of moments ago. She jerked her gaze away as his knife flashed and his opponent fell with a cry.

"Diane!"

Jakab had gained his feet and approached, a little more warily this time. Diane took the initiative, sliding her feet wide and jabbing out with the staff. He lunged for it, and she whipped it out of reach to smack him on the shoulder.

He cursed, stumbling sideways under the force of the blow. She narrowed her eyes, readjusting her grip on the lower end of the staff. He retaliated in the way Ralf predicted he would. With a more careless swing toward her.

She spun the end of her staff up to connect with the blade, knocking it away. Before he had a chance to recover, she swung again, overpowering his weak block and shoving the blunt end of the staff at his head.

It contacted solidly with his forehead, sending him staggering a step before his eyes rolled back and he fell to the ground.

"Put the knife away." A condescending voice jerked her attention away from her victory to another grubby bandit approaching Tonya. The faery held her knife out in one hand, the other extending toward the ground.

The man dangled a shackle in one hand and waved his sword with the other.

Tonya's free hand trembled as nothing stirred the ice. Diane stepped up beside her, bringing the staff to level at the new threat.

"You can do it, Tonya," she growled.

The man raised one eyebrow in question, and kept advancing.

Tonya swept her hand up with a hoarse cry and the bandit jerked to a stop, ice creeping up his legs to his knees, freezing him to the ground.

Diane's wild laugh scared her as she jerked Tonya away from the man's frantic sword thrusts. August appeared in front of them, a sword in one hand, and knife in the other. Blood streaked his shirt and the hard glint hadn't left his eyes.

"All right?" His voice didn't sound right — harsh and even. He glanced at the man Tonya had frozen, his lip curling in a savage sneer.

"We're fine," Diane stammered, her fear rushing back.

"Stay here." August stalked toward where Dorian still battled the other faery. The bandit leader and his last remaining brigand faced off with August, the leader swinging the cuff.

August drove into the second bandit with a blast from his wings, slashing out with the sword and cutting a scarlet streak across the man's chest. The man fell to the ground, scrambling away.

The leader swung out with the cuff, the chain wrapping around August's left arm. He stiffened, a cry strangling in his throat. August yanked down with his left arm, his wings swirling a small snowstorm as he launched himself into a spinning kick that pummeled the man to the ground.

August shook the chain free, flicking his hand contemptuously and knocking the man to the ground in a burst of magic. He lay stunned in the snow. August leapt toward him, sword raised overhead.

"August!" Dorian's sharp voice halted him before he could plunge it into the man's chest.

Dorian stood, half-turned away from where his staff blade rested at the other faery's throat. August jerked a breath and slammed the sword into the ice beside the leader's cheek instead, cutting a thin line through the scruff of his beard. August stepped away, hands clenching in tight fists. "Get out of here."

The bandit scrambled to his feet, taking in the sight of his men. The man Tonya had frozen had almost chipped free of the ice. Jakab stirred a few feet away. Dorian had only wounded the other man and the faery seemed almost grateful to surrender.

But two lumps lay unmoving at the other end of the clearing. The bandit broke free of the ice and lunged towards Tonya, cuff extended. August whipped his hand out.

The man stumbled to a halt, staring at his empty hand. August's knife quivered in the nearest tree, the cuff dangling from the blade.

"I won't miss again," August snarled.

Dorian disengaged from the faery, jabbing with the point of his staff to shepherd the wounded men together. The bandit leader sneered as he staggered past.

"Maybe I'll report you to the nearest garrison. Know what they'll do to faeries who attack and kill humans?"

August shoved forward and the man flinched away. The bandits stumbled into the forest. Diane loosed a shaky breath and released aching fingers from around her staff.

Tonya made a faint sound in the back of her throat and Diane turned her from the sight of the bodies. August faltered a step before sinking down to the ground, elbows on knees and hands clenched in his hair. His shoulders jerked in gasping breaths as his wings lay limp behind him.

Dorian held his hand out by his side, a quick look telling them to stay where they were. He placed his staff in the snow and knelt a cautious pace away from August.

"All right?" he asked quietly.

August slowly unclenched one hand and rubbed it across his face. "I'm fine."

But he didn't sound convinced.

"You hurt?" Dorian eased forward.

August shifted, bringing one knee down and straightening enough to show a cut along his left side. Tonya made the small noise again and clutched at Diane's arm. The blood stain spread across August's shirt and began to ooze into his trousers.

Dorian pulled up the shirt to expose the cut. August didn't flinch.

"Diane, will you get my bag from the tent?" Dorian's voice didn't show any alarm.

Diane ushered Tonya back a step or two until she sat unsteadily on the ground. Taking a deep breath, Diane went towards the tent closest to the bodies. Keeping her eyes fixed on the tent flap instead, she went inside and found Dorian's pack. She dug out the healers' bag, pausing a moment more to grab August's coat from the top of his bedroll.

Dorian helped August take off his shirt as she stepped back outside. His wings had disappeared somewhere along his muscular back. One long scar traced his side above the new cut, and a patch of skin like an old burn scar wrapped along his left arm.

Diane swallowed hard. It matched the shape and size of the iron cuffs. A fresh stripe of red wound about his forearm where the bandit leader had caught him.

"Looks like I'm not the only one who kept some scars," Dorian said as Diane placed his kit beside him.

August kept his head half-turned away, jaw clenched as he stared at the snow with the same distant expression Ralf and Edmund would sometimes wear when they thought no one was looking.

Diane placed his coat over one shoulder, tucking it around him enough to still leave his injured side exposed. He briefly looked up to give her a nod of thanks. She retreated a few paces, near enough to let Dorian know she'd help if she needed to.

Dorian extended the vial of pain medicine, but August shook his head. Dorian didn't argue, just began cleaning the wound.

"It's how my brother died." August finally spoke, a shiver running through him as if he was waking up. "Some Durneans like—like them caught me after a battle went bad. Eryk—" His voice faltered before he went on. "Eryk came after me. We barely got out, but some renegade faeries and human were after us. It was a deep cut."

He briefly touched his side. "I couldn't do much with the cuff blocking my magic. He took the next blow that was meant for me."

August lapsed into silence for a moment. Dorian kept working, threading a needle and pulling the edges of the wound shut. August barely flinched.

"My father and some others were too late. He'd already died. I was nearly there myself. I told them to leave the scars, because I didn't want to forget that I was the reason he died."

Dorian's hands faltered. Diane pressed a hand to her aching chest.

Dorian resumed his task, tying off the last stitch, and placed his hand against the wound. But August nudged it away.

"No magic. Let it heal on its own. It's the least I deserve." He nodded to the dead bandits.

Dorian silently acknowledged his wish and wrapped a bandage around him. Standing, he extended a hand to August.

"Go change before you catch cold as well."

August took a long moment before he clasped Dorian's hand and pushed to his feet, shuttering away a grimace of pain and limping to their tent, his coat clutched around his shoulders.

Diane went over to Dorian as he carefully wiped his hands clean. She'd seen the look on August's face, heard similar things before, but still had no idea what to do. Somehow the thought of it being the cheerful, vibrant August made it worse.

"What do we do?" she asked.

Dorian folded the cloth in his hands. "Break camp, get away from here."

Diane crossed her arms, tucking her hands against her sides to stave off the sudden rush of chill.

"And I'll talk to him if he wants. No offense, but you didn't live through the same thing we did."

But Diane only nodded. "I know. But it hurts almost as much to watch someone go through it. Just tell me what I can do to help."

Dorian offered a brief smile that crooked the corner of his mouth. "I will."

He left her and went to Tonya, who still sat with her knees tucked up against her chest.

"You all right?" He gently touched her arm.

She turned a watery smile up at him. "How soon can we leave?"

"As soon as you're ready."

She accepted his hand to stand, dusting away the snow that clung to her clothes. She and Diane ducked back into their tent to do up their packs and bedrolls. The tent folded back up as soon as they undid the ties. Dorian did the same with the other tent. August stood over the dead bandits, who were now laid out, side-by-side.

Diane held her breath as he extended a hand and a faint golden glow covered the bodies for a moment before abating. August turned away and helped Dorian fold up the tent, his face still a cold mask.

They left the clearing without a word and walked for nearly two hours before they stopped to share out breakfast.

"What did you do with them?" Tonya bravely asked.

"The ice won't stay back long enough to bury them, so I made sure that their bodies would stay safe until their friends came back." August rolled a few crumbs of waybread between his fingers. A bit of blood still stained the cracks around his knuckles.

"That was kind," Tonya said.

August offered a ghostly version of his normal smile and returned to picking at his food. He still hadn't eaten by the time they'd finished and packed away the remnants.

Diane caught the look Dorian gave her and tugged Tonya out in front to lead the way. Eventually a murmur of conversation began behind them, and when she glanced back, August strode beside Dorian, hands wound about the straps of his pack, head down as they talked.

"What do we do?" Tonya migrated closer to her, giving a quick look back.

"Keep walking north," Diane said. "How are you doing?"

Tonya took a deep breath. "All right, I think. I've never been in a fight before. And it appears that fighting combined with blood makes me nauseous." She tried for a smile.

Diane rested her staff against her shoulder. "My knees have finally stopped shaking, so you're in good company."

"Really?" Tonya lifted a disbelieving eyebrow. "You seemed very confident while clobbering that whale head."

Diane giggled at the unfamiliar term. "Thank you. It's the first fight I've been in, so either Edmund and Ralf will be happy to hear that I handled myself well—or will begin running around like headless chickens because I was in a teensy bit of danger."

"I'd hate to see what you consider a normal amount of danger." Tonya smiled.

A smirk teased Diane's mouth and the tension that still lurked in her muscles began to ease.

"As you know, remmikens are no match for us. And neither are oversized—whale heads, was it?"

Tonya's smile built into a laugh.

"And you!" Diane wrapped an arm around the faery's shoulders. "Using your ice to freeze that man's legs!"

A flush spread over Tonya's cheeks, but a triumphant grin livened her eyes. "I didn't think I could do it, but whatever Dorian's been doing has helped, I think."

"It was genius." Diane squeezed her in a hug before releasing her.

"But." Tonya's face fell just as quickly. "It's still not strong enough to undo any of this."

"Patience, young faery. Small steps." Diane tried for the superior tone of a master scholar.

The brightness returned with Tonya's snicker, and they trudged on with a new lightness in their steps.

*

As the sun swept lower to the horizon, Diane beckoned to Dorian. He jogged forward, leaving August trudging along in their wake.

"Is there a place we can rest and have a fire with dinner?" she asked.

Dorian rubbed at his chin, scanning the open hills around them. "There's an abandoned Hold about half a mile away we can probably stay."

Diane hitched her pack higher. "Perfect. Can we please go there?"

He offered his slight little smile and adjusted their path to the northeast. Tonya and August didn't argue. Dorian finally stopped at the base of a hill that, at first glance, looked larger than its neighbors. But then Diane blinked, and it seemed nothing out of the ordinary in a sea of rippling earth.

Dorian shuffled around the base of the hill before finding a stone like he had at Csorna. A rap sent the fairy veil shivering and peeling back to reveal a broken door. Its green and yellow painted surface still presented itself boldly against the cold, despite the gaping wound down its center. Diane shivered, hating to think what could have broken the door like that.

Dorian's face remained unreadable as he gently moved the door back and ushered them in. Unlike in Csorna, the entrance hall remained dark. No cylinders of magic sprang to life at their approach. Something clattered and Tonya stifled a soft cry.

"I kicked something!" Some panic edged her voice. The fading light didn't penetrate far inside and Diane clutched her staff as the darkness weighed oppressive around her.

"Give me a moment. I can find some of the lights and maybe restore the magic." Dorian cursed as he kicked something else and his boots thudded heavier in a stumble.

A flicker of light came from behind Diane and she turned to see August holding up a hand illuminated in gentle golden light. It snapped out just as fast, and a sharp cry of surprise came from his direction as he fell.

"Someone warded this place against magic," August panted, a scuffling announcing him rising uncertainly.

"Should we leave, then?" Diane turned her head, as if she could see any of her companions.

Any reply was cut off as another gentle light appeared. For a moment, Diane couldn't make sense of what she saw. A luminescent glow hovered on either side of Tonya, rippling in an odd pattern around the lower edges of a swooping outline. The light illuminated Tonya's face and the hall around them, shimmering and dancing like light through water.

"Is—is that your wings?" A bit of breathless wonder coated Dorian's voice.

Tonya ducked her head as she nodded. "Will it help figure out a way to get some light?" Her voice was edged with cold.

"There's nothing here, except that spell. We should be able to stay here fine." Dorian jerked his eyes from Tonya to Diane and August.

The other faery didn't argue, just set his pack on the ground. The thing that Tonya had kicked was a bit of smashed pottery. Bits of broken furniture were scattered around the Hold. The doors leading deeper into the mound had been torn off hinges and lay in pieces.

"What happened here?" Diane couldn't repress the question.

Dorian pointed up at the walls. Curled script that seemed to shift just outside her understanding had been painted across the carved stone.

"Sorcerers and rogue faeries attacked this place. It's a curse against anyone who dared fight against them," Dorian said.

Tonya stepped a little closer, her wings rippling again as the light brightened. August sniffed and grabbed his water flask. He nodded to Dorian, who stepped forward and braced himself against the wall. August placed his foot in Dorian's laced hands and balanced precariously as he splashed water across some of the words and rubbed them away with his coat sleeve.

Once the curling pattern was disrupted, a shiver cut through Diane. The air seemed to lose some of its weight and a flicker of light sparked next to Dorian. August jumped down, leaving Dorian free to press his hand against the cylinder. It sprang to life, blazing brightly as if in thanks that it had been allowed to serve again. August stepped over to the next one. He tapped the surface and it did the same.

As if realizing they were free to shine, the rest of the lights around the room flared into life. They stood blinking in the sudden light. Tonya backed away a step, her cheeks flushing as they looked back at her.

"They're beautiful," Diane breathed softly.

Tonya's wings held the same basic bony structure as the boys' wings, but the edges curled and rippled like a fish's fin. Dark spots scattered across the pale membrane in some sort of pattern. The luminous glow along the bones and edges shone brighter in the curled folds.

Tonya tilted a glance at her. "They're absolutely worthless, is what they are."

Her shoulders jerked and her wings disappeared, leaving the room a little dimmer.

"It looks like the same camouflage as my snow leopard pelt," August offered. Diane smiled to hear his voice back to normal.

"Which is helpful in the ocean, how?" Tonya snapped. "I can't fly, and I can't swim, but I can glow and blend in like a land animal." She retreated another step and wrapped her arms around her stomach.

They stared at her.

"They helped just now," Dorian said gently.

She sighed and rubbed her forehead. "I'm sorry. No one's ever called them beautiful." She looked to Diane. "Or thought of a way they might actually work. They're just another part of me that got mixed up at my birth."

"You seem to have done all right so far."

Diane's jaw dropped at the abruptness of August's voice. Tonya's eyes widened.

"Let's go find some firewood." August gestured over his shoulder. She hesitantly joined him.

"Mind if we use your wings again for more light? I don't want to go around turning all these on just to find wood."

Tonya mutely nodded and let her wings unfurl as she and August went into one of the tunnels. Dorian watched them go, nodding to himself with a slight smile. The expression wasn't exactly what Diane had expected.

"Tough love?" Diane guessed.

Dorian shrugged one shoulder. "Maybe it's what she needs."

*And I wonder if you'd be able to say the same thing to her.* Diane bit her lip against the sudden giggle.

Dorian rolled his eyes as if he'd guessed what she'd thought. "Help me clear out this corner?"

They'd cleared a space in the corner opposite the smudged curse by the time August and Tonya came back with arms full of wood pieces. Dorian shifted the earth into a small divot and August kindled a fire inside.

The flames sparked in varied hues as the painted wood caught, then returned to their normal red and gold as they ate into the wood. Diane toasted the last of the fresh bread from Dorian's mother and handed it out, along with slices of cheese to go with the inevitable dried meat. She leaned against the wall as she ate, grateful for a stable shelter from the wind and cold. The lights gave off a slight heat along with the fire.

"I wonder why no one ever came back," she mused.

Dorian wiped his hands clean. "Likely found other homes during or after the war."

"Aye, it looked like whoever lived here was able to clear most of their belongings before, or after, it was attacked. And this far north, I doubt anyone wanted to risk coming back to re-settle during the war." August bit at the inside of his lip.

Diane nibbled at the last of her cheese. The borderlands had seen most of the heavy fighting, but central Durne had been ravaged as well. The north had been held by the rogue alliances. She shivered, hoping that one day someone would come back to the Hold and fill it with good magic again.

"How far north are we?" Tonya stared at the colors still burning off at the base of the flames.

"We'll be at the Strait tomorrow," Dorian said. "After that, I'm not entirely sure where we go."

"I wish I had something that could help, but the things I know about the north don't include maps." Tonya's lips quirked.

August huffed a laugh as he unfolded his sleeping roll.

"I'll just be glad to have finally made it somewhere and be a little closer to our goal." He set aside his sword. "No offense, but I'm wishing you'd had the eternal summer spell locked away inside you."

Tonya's features shifted into a full smile and Diane caught Dorian staring at the young faery. She smothered a grin as he jerked his gaze away.

"Let me check your side." He turned instead to August.

Diane took out her journal as Dorian began to re-bandage August's wound. Tonya shivered at the raw stitches and scooted closer to Diane as she began journaling.

"What do you write in that?"

Diane didn't look up, focused on her notes. "Recording our trip. It's an obsessive habit of mine to write down anything and everything. It's about the only thing that makes me useful in Chelm."

It was a fact she'd told herself to stop herself from dreaming and wishing for other things. And a skill that helped keep the kingdom running when nothing else she did would really contribute.

"I don't believe that." August tugged his shirt over the new bandage and lay back on his blankets.

Diane flashed him a smile. "As far as humans go, I'm afraid I'm not very special. My only talent lies in keeping my brother organized."

"And being the voice of reason in a room?" Dorian said.

"And seeing value in everyone and everything around you?" Tonya put in.

"Or giving everyone hope for a better tomorrow?" August shifted one arm behind his head.

Diane cleared her throat, blinking rapidly against some sudden dust mites in the air. She focused on the blurring words under her pen, tracing over the last letters she'd written until her nose stopped smarting and her eyes ceased watering.

"It's not such a bad thing to dream." August's next words coaxed her head up. A guilty smile touched his face. "I found some pages of your story in the snow when I first came to Chelm."

Heat once again tinged Diane's cheeks. "Was it completely ridiculous to read a human's story of your parents?"

He shook his head. "Obviously pages were missing, but it's your family's account. I'll tell you the faery version sometime."

Diane turned to a new page. "What about now? Unless telling stories around a fire is only a human tradition?"

August smiled. "If it is, faeries willingly adopted it." He pulled his knees up to rest more comfortably as he stared at the ceiling. "How am I supposed to start?"

"Once upon a time?" Diane winked.

Tonya leaned forward on her knees, eagerness brightening every angle of her face. Dorian settled back against the wall, arms crossed over his chest. August grinned back at Diane for a moment before beginning.

"Once upon a time…"

# Chapter 20

**W**e'll *be at the Strait today.* A shiver cut down Tonya's spine, tempting her wings to wriggle free. It had been a long time since she'd let them out. She shook her head as she remembered Diane's breathless, *"They're beautiful!"*

Though it was nice to be considered useful, for once.

Ice crunched beneath her boots. She squinted her eyes against the brightness of the sun on the sparkling crystals. Dorian and August once again walked side by side, engaged in a less-serious conversation from the sounds of their voices and the way August tossed his hands about in enthusiastic gestures.

At least he seemed to have cheered up from the day before. Another shudder cut across her skin at the memory of the hard light in his eyes. Diane yawned, trudging along beside Tonya. True to her word, she'd compulsively scribbled notes throughout August's story the night before as Tonya sat spellbound.

He'd glossed over the romantic bits between his parents, focusing instead on the battles, but Tonya hadn't minded.

They'd slept late, the doors protected by new warding spells that August and Dorian put up. But no one seemed to mind after the strain of the previous day.

"Look!" Diane's sudden words jerked her attention to follow the line of Diane's pointing finger.

Up ahead the hills compressed to flat land. A wide something cut through the plain—and across? Tonya caught her breath. Across was another vast expanse, but this one called to her with a heart-stopping cry. Wild and free and cold and—home.

She pushed forward, her feet flying into a run. Her companions didn't call out, just picked up their pace to follow her to the edge of the Strait.

Unlike the lake, the dark water wasn't frozen. Massive chunks of ice floated among the gently lapping waves. A sleek figure surfaced to stare at them over a whiskered snout before diving again with a gruff bark.

*Seal.*

Her fingertips tingled with the nearness of magic. Magic that leeched from the broken ice, deeper threads calling from the mountains just out of eyesight, from the tundras that draped across the mountains. From whispers of the forests and the gentle lapping of the frigid water as it wound its way to the ocean—her other home.

"How do we get across?" August asked, breaking the spell the north had begun to spin on her.

She cast a closer look at the strait. *I could make it across.* The wild impulse to dance her way across the shifting ice surfaced and her wings nearly burst forth to help her balance and skim across the waters. But her companions wouldn't be nearly as graceful, or lucky, to make it across in one piece.

"How about that?" Diane pointed farther down the bank.

An unbroken swath of ice remained as a bridge across the water. They headed toward it and Tonya pressed a tentative hand to its surface. She caught the reassuring whisper of its sturdiness before the twisting warding around her magic shut it out.

"It's safe."

Her companions looked back at her with trust. A thrill skimmed through her as Dorian gestured to the ice with a smile. She stepped out onto the ice, leading the way across.

A breath of cool air brushed across her skin as she placed her feet on firm land again. She drew in a deep breath, tasting the distant pine and the *wildness* of the country around her. The first time she'd touched ice weeks ago, she'd felt a little more awake.

Now, a new awareness pulsed through her, starting in her feet and working all the way up to the tips of her hair. She felt alive in the way she did after a storm at sea. Like her magic was waiting at the edge of her fingertips, desperate to create.

Not for the first time, she wondered what she could be if her magic was free.

"What now?" August looped his hands around his pack straps and tilted his head.

Dorian shrugged. "The plan was a little hazy after getting to the Strait."

They glanced at her. Tonya stared back.

"Don't look at me. I have no idea what to do." *Besides explore this whole place.*

"I can't believe I'm going to be the one to suggest that we just keep walking." A laugh cut through Diane's voice.

Dorian's smile took up one side of his mouth. "If there are any faeries around, they'll probably come find us. Our magic stands out like a sore thumb here."

"They'll be friendly, right?" Diane raised an eyebrow in worry.

Dorian shrugged again. "I have no idea."

Tonya stared out over the tundra. The ice felt different. Like it wasn't quite soaked through with her magic. She began to move without consulting her friends. Now that she was there, she couldn't stop. Something told her the ice faeries would be friendly.

*Or maybe that's just me being stupidly optimistic. They could hate me just as much as everyone in the Reef.*

But her father had welcomed her mother. It sounded like her mother had stayed for some time in the north. Maybe that meant the ice faeries weren't as harsh as the others seemed to believe.

She kept walking and no one argued. They continued in silence and Tonya took the opportunity to keep drinking in the wonder of the north, even if the landscape hadn't changed too drastically from before.

"Tonya..." The sharp edge came back to August's voice.

She pivoted to look at him. He stood, arms loosely by his sides, squinting toward the horizon. Dorian edged his feet farther apart, a frown twisting at his mouth a second later.

"Someone's coming."

A soft gasp broke from Diane, and Tonya retreated a few steps to stand by them.

"Who? Where?"

August pointed. Dark shapes appeared on the horizon, moving toward them, sprays of snow and ice kicked up in their wake.

The boys exchanged a nod and kept their hands away from weapons. Tonya stared at the advancing figures. They were beginning to solidify into outlines that didn't make sense. The closer they got, the clearer they became—whoever approached rode bulky animals with sprawling horns and curiously bowlegged hind limbs.

Dorian and August edged forward until they sheltered Tonya and Diane between them, presenting their strongest sides to the approaching strangers. Tonya peered around August's shoulder, hopelessly intrigued.

Four riders split and swept around them, circling in constant motion. Dorian's shoulder matched the tallest animal's withers for height. Tooled leather embossed in reds and greens cinched a saddle in place and wound about the creature's muzzle and curved horns in a bridle. The riders all wore matching knee-length coats of deep blue, trimmed in spotted fur. They guided their mounts with leg cues as carved spears lowered.

"Who are you?" A rider halted her animal in front of Dorian, her spear a handsbreadth from his chest.

He spread his hands wide in a placating gesture. "Travelers. I'm Dorian." He introduced the others. "We're looking for the ice faeries."

Her angular features didn't relax. Dark hair swept over her shoulder in a braid, the tips icy white. Her skin was a shade darker than Tonya's browned skin and every move she made reflected the wild energy of the land.

"You are faeries yourselves." Her sharp grey eyes fell to Diane. "Except for that one. What do you want here?"

Dorian shuffled a half-step to the side and waved his fingers in a signal for Tonya to come forward. The woman shifted her stern gaze to Tonya and the spear wavered.

"You..." She transferred her spear to Tonya, ignoring the way Dorian tensed. "Do you know who you are?"

Tonya swallowed hard under the unyielding stare, suddenly afraid that even here she might always be ashamed of her father's name.

"I'm — I'm Tonya Freyr-dottir."

The woman caught her breath and something like a smile softened her features for a moment.

"Stand down," she said to the others.

They reined in their mounts, bringing their spears to point up at the sky. The leader slid from her animal and came forward a few steps. Now at eye level, she wasn't much taller than Tonya, but she carried herself with the same dangerous grace as Dorian and August.

Two daggers were strapped to her belt in colorful sheaths, and fur-lined boots laced up to her knees over trousers.

"You wouldn't know me, but I'm Lilja. I was once a good friend to your father."

Something broke in Tonya, like rock finally succumbing to the pressure of a glacier.

"You knew him? What was he like? Is he still here? What —"

Lilja held up a gloved hand and Tonya stumbled to a halt. Her grey eyes softened again.

"There will be time enough to talk about Freyr later."

Tonya's heart stuttered. From the way she said the words, it was plain that he was gone. She blinked hard. *It's not like I really expected him to be alive.* But the hole inside yawned a little wider.

"Why have you come back?" Lilja leaned on her spear, her head cocked slightly to the side as if she knew, but still wanted them to say it.

Diane's hand nudged into Tonya's and squeezed. She glanced to the side to see Diane's sympathetic smile before the princess nodded back to Lilja. Tonya shuddered a breath.

"I've lived in the ocean my entire life. A few tides ago, I was attacked while on land. It seems my parents had given me wards of protection."

She paused long enough to catch Dorian's brief nod of support.

"But in protecting me from the attack, it somehow triggered my ice magic that, until then, I'd had no ability over. It froze everything." She swept a hand behind her.

Lilja pursed her lips, exchanging a quick look with her still-silent companions. "Aye, we know of this strange phenomenon. Despite what you might think, there is still summer here in the north. We were not happy to see a spell of this magnitude sweep through."

"She still can't use her magic because of the warding," Dorian said. "Our people have no way of breaking the spell. We've come to see if you could help her, or find some way to undo the ice in our countries before it destroys everything."

Lilja focused on some point beyond them before giving a sharp nod.

"You will come with us to Konungburg."

"What's that?" August broke his silence.

Lilja's frosty glance came back. "Our city. You will see our king and he will determine how to proceed. If there was no magic user powerful enough among your people to undo this, then I'm not sure what we can do. Come." She strode back to her mount. "You will ride behind us. I do not intend to walk the entire way."

"Ride? On those?" Diane raised a brow at the creatures.

A hint of a smirk stirred Lilja's features. "Our caribou are more than capable of handling two riders."

She swung up onto her caribou's back and it shifted in response, the four toes of its hooves spreading wider to grab more purchase on top of the snow to balance her weight.

"Tonya, you will ride with me."

Lilja's tone brooked no arguments, and she directed the others to her companions. Tonya sidled forward, reaching a cautious hand out to the caribou. It cocked its head to regard her with large brown eyes, nostrils flaring as it took in her scent. It shook its head and she reflexively backed away from the heavy antlers waving in her face.

Lilja extended her hand. "Foot in the stirrup to help yourself up," she instructed.

Tonya obediently placed her foot in the tooled stirrup and managed to pull herself up with the aid of Lilja's hand to sit behind the other faery.

"Hold on," she needlessly instructed and turned the caribou.

They lunged forward in a rocking gallop. Tonya wrapped her arms around Lilja until the faery tapped her hands.

"Not so tight." But she sounded faintly amused. "Jyri won't let you fall."

Tonya relaxed a fraction, bravely lifting her head from Lilja's blue coat to see the others racing alongside. Diane clung just as tightly as Tonya did, but August wore a slight grin as he hung on with one careless hand. Dorian looked slightly less at ease than Tonya felt, but still sat behind the saddle with more grace than Tonya with every powerful leap forward.

They ran across the tundra for nearly an hour before stopping to rest the caribou. Tonya slid off, her knees wobbling a little on solid ground again.

Just ahead of them, the tundra shifted into hills, and those to forests sprawling across the snowy landscape like evergreen giants.

Lilja stepped up beside her. "We'll reach Konungburg in another hour of riding."

Tonya nodded, her eyes still searching out the boundaries of the landscape, imagining she could see the low ridges of mountains in the distance.

"It's so beautiful," she whispered.

A smile softened Lilja's features. "You should see it in its summer glory."

She extended her hand and snow and ice swirled away from the ground for a moment, revealing soft green grass and purple and pink flowers that had been crushed under the weight of the snow. Tonya sank to one knee, gingerly touching the ground.

The north whispered back and she closed her eyes, listening to the storm of magic thrumming through the earth, wind, and sky. The ice rushed back to cover the ground. She drew her hand away and dabbed at her eyes and the unexpected tears.

"It's so strong here." Not even the ocean at the height of a summer storm carried this much magic.

Lilja waited until she regained her feet. "It's the Creator's Lights."

Tonya tilted her head. Even with everything her father's magic whispered to her, that was unfamiliar.

"They're lights that touch down in the furthest tundras and mountains, pooling their pure magic into the earth and air and spreading throughout the world. They're an amazing sight."

"You've seen them?"

"They're bright enough to be seen from a distance. You'll see them from Konungburg. They come nearly every day. They're the reason we live here. To protect them and the wild magic they leave."

"Do you have to very often?" Tonya rubbed her sleeve. "Protect it?"

Lilja half-turned to look at the others standing close by and listening to their conversation. "We did our fair share during the war. Even if you didn't see us."

Dorian and August nodded, and the three other ice faeries relaxed a fraction.

"Come." Lilja gestured back to the caribou. Tonya grimaced behind her back, but followed and remounted behind the faery.

This time they raced across the gentle hills, turning to the northwest. Swaths of trees, out-flung from the main bulk of the forest, passed beside them. Bright eyes watched them from the shelter of the trees and a wolf howled to the faery who carried Diane behind him. A straggling V of geese honked overhead before wheeling away to the south.

The terrain began to slide into a gentle decline. The caribou planted their forelegs into the ground, giving themselves purchase as they continued their dash. The path furrowed between two hills and they rounded the northern mount to reveal an icy bay and Konungburg.

Lilja slowed Jyri to a walk. Tonya shifted her seat to better see over Lilja's shoulder. Diane audibly caught her breath.

Forested hills topped with a dusting of snow surrounded a valley. Peaked roofs with swooping carvings above the doors gathered in circles. Even from the top of the valley, figures were visible in the open circles between the houses, or walking the paths that connected each of the commons.

A castle dominated the landscape, nestled in among the hills. Tall white towers reached towards the sky, their tops the same color as the achingly blue sky. The entire structure glistened in the sunlight, making it look made of ice. A causeway stretched out from the stone walls toward the bay.

Several figures paced its length or knelt at the water's edge. One daring faery jumped from burg to burg, wings stretched wide for balance.

Lilja urged Jyri on and they clopped towards the castle. Tonya whipped her head from side to side, taking it all in.

Women in dresses of bright reds and greens and blues, the edges and belts embroidered, mixed with men in trousers and tunics of the same colors. They all had the same dark hair and lightly-browned skin. Some, like Lilja, had streaks of cold white in their hair, but most looked too young for it to be from age. The men wore their hair short on the sides and longer on top, the edges spiked and sometimes tipped in white.

A few children dodged about the corners of the longhouses, pausing to wave at the riders or stare in open curiosity at Tonya and her companions. One male faery landed in the street in front of them, taking a moment to furl his black- spotted wings before stepping out of their way.

Tonya stared at him. The coloring of her wings wasn't so strange after all.

Pelts stretched on frames, caribou lowed to each other, small foxes in patchwork fur of white and brown chased faery children around. A grey wolf peered around a longhouse corner, staring at August with curious amber eyes before it whisked away.

A honking bark drew Tonya's attention back to the causeway. A sleek spotted figure hauled itself from the water onto the stone, slapping flippers against the surface before rolling to its back to soak in the sun.

They clopped across another stone bridge spanning a narrow inlet of water that bobbed its way in front of the castle and up to the hills. Two male guards in the same deep blue coats as their escorts stood on either side of the open gate, spears in hand and axes on their belts.

An eagle fluttered its wings from its perch above the faery on the left, peering at them with the same intensity as the guard.

"Commander Lilja." The guard on the right nodded, his gloved hand gripping the spear a little tighter as he scanned them.

"We found them on the southern tundra today," Lilja said. "They seek an audience with King Birgir."

The guard nodded again and waved them in.

Grey stone paved the courtyard, with lines of white sweeping through in a pattern that made no sense to Tonya. Lilja and the guards handed off the caribou to other faeries in simpler coats of grey.

"Come." Lilja waved her hand and strode up the steps to the doors carved with the relief of polar bears facing each other on hind limbs and surrounded by geometric shapes of fishes and whales and seals.

More guards opened the doors at their approach. Lilja didn't stop in the wide hall, leading them on to another set of high wooden doors. Carved creatures arched over each doorway they passed. Thick furs lay on the floor by wooden benches placed below windows of clear ice. More faeries in blue coats walked the halls, weapons in hand, standing out of the way of any approaching faery.

The faeries in the castle wore finer clothes than those outside, a more refined elegance to the embroidery and subtle differences in the shades of the standard blues, greens, reds, and greys.

Many stopped in their tracks and stared at the travel-worn companions and their clothes which seemed strange in comparison. Tonya ducked her head against the scrutiny. Most seemed intrigued, but she knew deep down that it would turn to disinterest or disgust as soon as they found out what she was.

The doors swung open before them, allowing Lilja to keep her purposeful stride as she entered.

Wooden columns, draped in evergreen garlands, stretched up to the arching ceiling. More carvings took up every visible space on the wood and even leapt across the ceiling as birds and swirling ribbons. Tall icy windows lined both sides of the hall and inset the ceiling, allowing a clear view of the sky.

A raised dais stood at the end of the hall. Colorful banners draped the stone behind the wooden chair covered in thick white fur.

"Wait here." Lilja paused a few steps from the empty dais and strode off.

Tonya rubbed at her sleeves, turning back to her companions who looked around the hall in wonder.

"This place is amazing," Diane whispered. "I'd live here if it weren't so cold."

"I don't think it's cold year-round. They did say it was summer here too." August tilted his head back to regard the windowed ceiling.

"I guess I really did freeze the whole world." Tonya crossed her arms across her chest.

"Not the entire world," Diane said. "Just the ocean and nearby landmass."

"Oh, that's so much better." Tonya tried to bite back her harsh words.

She was treated to three concerned stares. She dropped her gaze to the patterned floor for a moment, taking a deep breath.

"Sorry. I think I'm just a little too nervous to finally meet my father's people, and—and..." She couldn't finish.

Diane wrapped an arm around her shoulders. "It will be fine. They'll love you."

Tonya sniffed, embarrassed at how obvious her desire to be accepted by some form of family shone through.

"Thanks."

Diane released her, and a hand nudged into hers. She looked up to Dorian. He offered his quiet smile. The sight helped drive away the worst of the doubt and fear, leaving it to linger in a back corner of her mind. He loosened his grip and she reluctantly let him go, turning back to the dais.

Brisk footsteps announced Lilja's return. She strode over to them.

"The king is coming to meet you."

Tonya brushed at her coat in sudden anxiety. Voices sounded and a male faery entered from a side door flanked by two guards in blue coats. A slender silver circlet sat around his forehead. He wore a sleeveless knee-length robe of the same blue, edged in white fur. Silver swirls embroidered the length of the tunic and Tonya picked out caribou, eagles, and bears in the designs before they shifted to something else.

His fitted dark grey tunic and trousers showed a surprising bulk compared to the more slender guards who stood with him.

Lilja pressed a clenched hand to her chest and bowed. Diane swept into a curtsey and the boys bowed. As she still wore her sharkskin trousers, Tonya settled for a bow as well.

"King Birgir, may I present Tonya Freyr-dottir, and her companions, Princess Diane of Myrnius, August of the Forest Folk, and Dorian of the Plains Folk," Lilja announced in a crisp voice.

"Greetings!" King Birgir's voice boomed throughout the hall.

Tonya darted a glance up to meet his curious gaze.

"Commander Lilja tells me you are responsible for this ice?"

Tonya swallowed hard. "Yes, Your Majesty. It was an accident."

A smile quirked at the corner of his mouth. "I'd hate to see what you could do on purpose."

Tonya relaxed a fraction. So far, he didn't look too mad.

"Not much, sire. My magic is trapped."

He nodded. "Yes, the commander mentioned something about that as well." He stared at her again until Tonya nearly squirmed. "Creator's Lights, you look so much like Freyr."

Tonya's eyes widened. "You knew him?"

The king's features softened, much like Lilja's had when she first saw Tonya.

"He was a good friend. And because of that, I'm welcoming you to Konungburg. I want to hear the entire story of what happened. I'll have our strongest ice casters meet here in an hour, which should give you enough time to refresh yourselves. Lilja."

Lilja bowed again. "I'll see to it, sire."

"Tonya." King Birgir's voice halted her. "You should know that there are many who didn't approve of what Freyr did, marrying your mother. I would have spoken against it had I not seen how much they loved each other. I am welcoming you, but there are many who won't."

Tonya bobbed her head. "Thank you, sire. But it's nothing I haven't faced among my mother's people."

His blue eyes softened, and he tipped his head in a slight bow to her. "I'm sorry it's like that for you. I'll see you in an hour."

He turned and left the hall, with Tonya staring after him. Her father had been friends with a commander. Had been friends with a *king*.

"Lilja." Her voice wobbled a fraction. "Who was my father, exactly?"

"Here we have a king, and we have other noble families
that carry some royal blood and more powerful magic along
with it. Your father was the second son of the Ísbjörn family."

Tonya staggered a step, her knees threatening to buckle
beneath her. Royal blood. Her father was a noble. *I have noble
blood?*

# Chapter 21

*H* steadying hand closed about hers and Dorian stood by her side. The same surprise showed in his eyes, but he said nothing, only offered his quiet support. Tonya drew a breath.

"That's—unexpected." A nervous laugh broke from her.

Lilja chuckled. "Aye, I suppose it would be. Follow me, and I'll show you to your rooms." She waved them on and nearly left them behind with her brisk stride.

Tonya nervously freed her hand from Dorian's for the second time in only a few minutes and tugged at her sleeves as she hurried after Lilja.

"I wish she'd slow down," Diane whispered as she half-jogged to keep up. Tonya nodded, still distracted by the recent revelation about her father.

Lilja took a staircase off the main entrance hall, taking them up another broad staircase and corridor, where it wound up into one of the towers. Two turns around the tower and Lilja halted at a door.

"Guest quarters that should suit the four of you. I'll send one of my guards to escort you down in an hour."

And she left them standing at the door.

"Well!" Diane said briskly and opened the door.

They stepped into a circular room with carved wooden pillars around the edges that branched into a latticed pattern along the domed ceiling. Benches and low couches were placed around an inset firepit and furs spread over the stone floor. Large windows took up the wall opposite the door, allowing a view of the snow-dusted hills. Arching doorways opened off into three other rooms.

Diane took charge, peering into each room.

"Looks like there's two bedrooms. You two take that one." She pointed the boys to the room on the right. "And Tonya and I will take this one."

"Sounds fine to me." August shrugged out of his pack with a groan, rubbing his injured side as he headed towards their room.

The chamber next to Tonya and Diane's appeared to be a dining room with a heavy table and four chairs. Tonya followed Diane into the bedroom and sat down on one of the two beds.

"How are you doing?" Diane unbuttoned her coat.

"You mean after finding out that my father was a noble and there are plenty of faeries here who might hate me?" Tonya slowly pulled her arms out of her pack. "Fine, I suppose."

Diane huffed and came to sit by her. "Even if anyone gives you trouble, the king formally welcomed you, so they'll have to be nice."

A smile quirked at Tonya's mouth. "I'm not so sure that's reassuring."

Diane giggled, and nudged her shoulder. "And you'll have a princess on your side, so there."

Tonya relaxed into a full smile. "Thank you."

"Now." Diane pushed to her feet. "Washroom's through there. You can go first this time."

Tonya pulled her hair out of the pins, letting it tumble free. She undid the laces of her bag.

"Dress this time, probably?"

Diane nodded. Tonya sighed and dug out the dress.

A low pool of water, gently steaming, was inset in the floor of the tiled washroom. Fluffy towels sat on a low bench. She likely didn't have enough time for a full bath, so she knelt at the edge of the pool and splashed water over her face and neck, plunging her arms into the pool and scrubbing with the block of soap. *Later,* she promised herself.

Tonya pulled on the dress, grimacing at her boots in distaste as she picked them up and headed back to the bedroom. She plopped onto her bed and combed her hair out while Diane went to wash and change.

Once finished, she reluctantly did up her boots again and tiptoed into the common room. Dorian and August already waited on the benches in fresh clothes. August's hair was damp and on end, and he sat slightly hunched over.

"You all right?" Tonya took a seat next to him.

His hazel eyes crinkled a little around the edges as he nodded. "It's just started hurting a bit now that I sat down."

"If you'd let me help it along, it'd feel better," Dorian grumbled.

August pressed his hand against his side as he straightened. "I'm fine. How are you holding up?" He raised an eyebrow at Tonya.

"I'm fine." Tonya deepened her voice, mimicking his short reply.

A smirk flashed across his face. "Would it help if I start bowing to you?"

She shoved his shoulder. "Don't you dare! Besides, I'm only—half noble, or something."

He righted himself with barely a wince, his smile still twinkling in his eyes. "How's the north holding up to your expectations?"

Tonya wrapped her hands around her knees, glancing around the room and out the window.

"I don't know. Some parts of it feel familiar, almost like coming home. The rest is me panicking about everything." Her smile spread in response to August's chuckle. Across from her, Dorian's eyes crinkled, and she relaxed more.

All too soon a knock sounded at the door, and a serious faery in a blue coat announced he'd escort them to the audience with King Birgir. August edged forward on the bench. Dorian stretched a hand down and helped him to his feet.

August frowned. "If I make you hate me again, will you stop hovering?"

Dorian rolled his eyes and shoved him towards the door. August laughed as he left. Tonya pursed her lips and followed.

"Is he really all right?" she asked Dorian.

"He will be with a few days' rest. Don't tell him, but I've been slipping in a little bit of healing magic whenever I change the bandages."

"Good." Diane pursed her lips as she stepped up beside them and shut the door.

Tonya tried not to stare like an ignorant puffer fish at every new sight as they trod down the stairs to the chamber where the king awaited them. More faeries paused in the halls as they passed, some in the grey coats appearing to be servants, others in the blue coats that marked the soldiers. Some female faeries paraded with their spotted wings proudly trailing behind them, casting shy glances at August and Dorian.

Diane rolled her eyes and looped her arm through August's as he winked back at a young faery, who fell into a fit of giggles as they passed.

"You know, for being snobbish about Tonya's parents, they certainly seem eager to flirt."

Tonya ducked her head to hide a grin when Diane tilted her nose up in the air as they passed a murmuring group of faeries who cast sharp glances at Tonya. Somehow, surrounded by her friends, the familiar looks didn't sting quite as much.

*Although I'm sure they will later. It's not like they're going to stop even after meeting with the king.*

They followed the guard through the main hall again and down a smaller corridor to a private room. He rapped once and opened the door, stepping aside to let them in.

A firepit took up the center of the room, flames crackling merrily. Cushioned benches sat around three sides, brightly-colored blankets tossed across their backs. The king sat on the bench directly opposite the door. Tonya bowed again, along with the others.

"Please, take a seat. Food should be along shortly." Birgir waved them to the benches.

To Tonya's pleasure, Dorian took a seat beside her. The door opened again, and Lilja entered. A bit of red crept into the commander's cheeks at the smile the king directed her way.

"We'll have a more formal council meeting later, but I wanted to hear it all from you first. Lilja and I were some of Freyr's closest friends." Birgir looked to Tonya. "From the beginning, if you don't mind."

She swallowed, rubbing her hands along the smooth fabric of her dress.

"I've always lived in the ocean among my mother's people," she began haltingly. "I've never been able to use my magic, except in tiny bursts."

She paused, expecting a protest as the ice and snow surrounding them told a different story. But Birgir leaned forward, elbow on one knee, chin propped on hand, staring at her intently.

Tonya forced another swallow. "I can't stay longer than a tide underwater without having to come up for air. There's a small island on the reef where I'd go for a few minutes every tide. Many tides—I mean days—ago, I was sitting on the island, dreaming about the north." She gave him a faint smile.

"Then I saw a shadow behind me. I thought it was my teacher and told him I'd be back down shortly. There was deep voice that just said 'No,' and then—" She faltered. "He said something else, and everything became cold, like all the warmth was sucked from me, and I passed out. When I woke up, the waves and island were frozen."

She stared down at her dress, pilling the fabric between her fingers.

"Interesting." Birgir sat up and looked to Lilja, who sat with her arms crossed over her chest. A frown puckered the corner of her mouth.

"And then what?" she asked.

"They blamed me for it and tried to draw out my ice magic." Tonya twisted her fingers together. A snort drew her attention up to the look of disgust on August's face. She darted a glance at Dorian, taken aback by the bright bit of anger showing in his eyes.

"But they couldn't?" Birgir guessed.

Tonya shook her head. "No. They couldn't figure out why, or how, it came from me. At least until we went to Myrnius to King Edmund's council. Dorian was the one who found the warding spells on me."

Birgir shifted forward. "Warding spells?"

"Powerful spells, placed by her parents to keep her hidden," Dorian said.

Birgir tapped his chin. "To keep her safe from whatever chased them from here?"

"Yes, sire."

Tonya whipped her attention back to the king. "You knew why they fled? What was chasing them?"

Birgir shrugged. "Freyr only indicated that something with powerful magic and anger was after them. He didn't say anything else, just took Thalia and ran. He only told me that they would go south, hoping that crossing the Strait would deter whatever it was from following them. It seems he was wrong."

"So—so he never came back?" Tonya fought the whisper that clogged her voice.

"No, little one. I'm sorry." Birgir dipped his head. "We sent warriors after them when we could no longer sense his magic, but they found nothing. I'm afraid he's—left this world," Birgir finished with some difficulty.

Tonya sat back, staring at the never-ending dance of the fire.

"Do—do you know what happened to my mother?" Her voice refused to climb any higher than a strangled whisper.

This time Lilja shook her head.

"No. I tried to find her myself. It was well known that she was with child when they left. I knew she would not abandon you, and so I went south to try to seek both of you among your kind. But nothing."

"Kostis couldn't find anything either." Tonya rubbed her nose. Lilja tilted an inquisitive look.

"He's one of the Reef Guard who knew my mother. He said that he met my father, and that he was returning north to try to fight off whatever chased them, to give my mother time to escape with me. But my mother gave me to Kostis on the southern shores of Myrnius, telling him to keep me safe while she returned to find Freyr. She never did."

"Strange." Birgir rubbed his hand along his chin. "He still didn't say who or what was chasing them."

"You know I have my theories," Lilja grumbled.

"And there is no way to prove any of it." Birgir frowned.

"Prove what?" August spoke up, his sharp hazel eyes flicking between the two ice faeries.

"Some were outspoken against their marriage when it was made known. Others weren't as obvious, but Freyr could sometimes be oblivious to subtlety," Birgir said. "And some people very close to him didn't approve either as they felt it weakened Ísbjörn's standing among the nobles."

"But anyone we suspected was well accounted for during the time they went missing," Lilja broke in. "We still think to this day that perhaps it was a Draugur, a —" She paused with a frown. "How would you say a faery that has turned from the Creator's Lights?"

"Nameless One." August twisted his fingers in a sign to ward off evil.

"But the ones that we have managed to pry from the crevasses in the furthest reaches of the mountains deny anything." Birgir leaned back against the bench.

"You can't trust a Draugur," Lilja muttered. "They knew something."

A muffled knock at the door dispelled the discomfort that prickled along Tonya's arms at the mention of Nameless

Ones. A grey-coated faery entered with a tray and set it down on a low table within reach of Birgir, before bowing and leaving the room.

"Oh, let me." Lilja tugged his arm away from reaching for the steaming kettle. "You manage to spill every time."

Birgir surrendered with a faint smirk. Lilja handed out clear mugs of hot tea all around, with plates of thick biscuits, caribou sausage, and frosted berries to follow.

Lilja settled back down with her own cup of tea. She pursed her mouth and a faint puff of white came from her lips, icing the golden rim of the cup before sipping.

"You said a shadow. What did it look like?" she asked.

Tonya winced as she scalded her tongue on the liquid as she drank. She traced the rim, wishing she could summon enough ice to cool the drink as Lilja had done.

"I don't know, I…"

"Just tell us what you can remember," Birgir said kindly.

Tonya closed her eyes, shivering a little as she conjured up the terrifying moments before her world had turned on its head.

"It looked like a faery, because I thought it was my teacher," she began slowly. Something else niggled the back of her mind. "But the head was wrong and strange. I thought that Mihail might have mussed his hair."

"Why do you think that?" Lilja's question opened her eyes.

Tonya stared at the king, dread storming in her chest. "Because — because it was spiky — like…"

Lilja looked to Birgir, the same understanding lightening in her eyes at the white-tipped points of the king's hair. He sat back, rubbing a hand over his head.

"Lights! It *was* one of us, then…" He trailed off.

"What does that mean?" Diane demanded.

"That it could have been anyone." Lilja's mouth tightened again and she set her mug down. "Unfortunately, there are only a few male faeries who don't wear their hair like that, and they're usually nearing the time to take the path to the Creator's Halls."

"At least we can rule out at least a score of faeries." Birgir tipped a wry smile.

Lilja rolled her eyes. "How do you want to handle this? I can start inquiries to see who was away from Konungburg when the ice storm began, but that will take time. Or it could have been a faery from one of the outlying settlements." She tugged at the white-edged tip of her braid.

"Aye, that's too much ground to cover. Keep your eyes open once it's announced that Freyr's daughter has come back."

Dorian stiffened. "You're using her as bait."

"You have a better idea, lad?" Birgir raised an eyebrow.

Dorian slowly shook his head. Tonya stared down at her lap, afraid to ask if that would actually pare down their search for the culprit.

"Our strongest magic users should be here shortly, and we'll start looking at this warding. Perhaps we can undo Freyr's side of it to allow you access to your ice magic."

Tonya's heart leaped in quick hope. "You think you can?"

Birgir gave her a warm smile that didn't seem to ever be far away from his face. "We'll try. Ice in summer is never a good thing. Even our lands are suffering from it, so I know that yours are as well." He looked to her companions.

"The faeries from Myrnius and Durne are doing what they can, but we're in danger of losing animals and crops in famine-inducing numbers if something isn't done soon," Diane spoke up.

"Oh, is that all?" Lilja raised an eyebrow. "We'd best get busy, then."

Birgir pushed to his feet. "Indeed. Tonya, would you come with us? Lilja and I will both be among the faeries who will test the warding and your magic. The rest of you can return to your rooms, or I'll have a guard escort you wherever you want to go."

Tonya set her cup aside and stood.

"Is this all right?" Diane mouthed the question and Tonya nodded.

Both Birgir and Lilja had professed to be friends of her father. She supposed they could be lying, but she couldn't manage to feel anything but warmth toward them. Dorian looked less pleased to be letting her go. He now stood protectively beside her.

"I'll come find you later?" Her fingers twisted in her skirt again.

He slowly nodded and stepped back enough to let her pass between him and the firepit. She followed the king and commander from the room.

# Chapter 22

Tonya clutched at the edges of her sleeves as she stared back at the five faeries standing opposite her. At least two looked at her in distaste. The third male faery didn't appear to care one way or the other, and Birgir and Lilja were continuous pillars of support and encouragement as she tried to summon the faint threads of her magic.

Even standing so close to the heart of the ice magic, she could still barely pick out the whispers of her power. Nerves smothered the bits she could hear and twisted her tongue so she struggled to whisper back.

She fought to maintain her composure as she failed and failed again at the simplest spells and tasks.

*It's like trying to train at the Reef all over again. As if I needed another reminder that I'm about as useful as a crab.*

Lilja sparked a bit of magic against her, and Tonya gasped as cold rippled down her skin.

"Found Freyr's warding," Lilja said. "He did a good job on it, too."

Tonya glanced down at her arms as if the warding would appear there.

"Hm." The unconcerned faery flicked magic at her without even asking. She flinched away, an extra tingle prickling her fingertips.

"It doesn't like any sort of magic," he said.

"Protecting against all magic?" Birgir crossed his arms, propping one hand against his chin. Lilja shot him a sharp look, but he ignored her. Tonya rubbed her hands together, wondering if she had the courage to ask about it later.

"Possibly. Although he likely didn't know she had ice magic. That may be why her magic reacted so violently to the attack."

"What do you mean?" Tonya furrowed her brow. "We thought it was just my suppressed magic finally having some way to escape."

"Aye, I could agree with that," Lilja said. "But Freyr's warding is against any northern magic. So it's working against yours as well. It seems to affect your ocean magic in the same way. Northern magic attacked you, forcing the warding to defend, and that allowed enough room for your magic to sneak out. I suppose we now know what happens if someone tries to suppress their ice magic."

Birgir huffed a laugh. Tonya didn't find it funny at all. The two other faeries listened with pursed lips.

"I don't see a way to undo the warding. Not without Freyr here." One shook his head.

Birgir slowly nodded. Tonya's breath caught in her chest, her heart beating harshly against her ribs in response.

"So…"

Lilja rested a steadying hand on her shoulder. "We'll keep talking amongst ourselves before we jump to the worst conclusions."

Despite the kindness in her tone, Tonya already knew the answer. There was nothing else to do. Their journey had been a waste and she'd doomed a continent.

"Do I need to stay?"

Lilja and Birgir exchanged a look.

"No," Birgir said. "Why don't you rejoin your friends, and we will discuss it all this evening."

Tonya nodded. As she retreated toward the door, it flung open and another faery strode in. The red of exertion darkened his cheeks, and his dark hair was even more disheveled than the normal style. His scarlet and white coat still had dustings of snow on the shoulders. Sharp grey eyes swept around the gathered faeries, who stared at him in surprise at his sudden appearance.

Tonya felt frozen as his gaze found her. Something about him felt familiar. It took a moment to realize it was the high cheekbones and restless grey in his eyes that stared back at her in the stillness of water.

"You!" His voice pitched low like a distant storm. "I heard rumors, but didn't believe them. You—you look just like them." Emotion caught in his voice.

Tonya looked to the king and Lilja for help. A flicker of something crossed Birgir's face before it smoothed in welcome and he stepped forward.

"Steinn."

The faery broke his stare from Tonya with a start and whirled to give the king a hasty bow. "Your Majesty, I apologize for the intrusion, I—"

Birgir raised his hand. "I think under these circumstances it's easily forgiven. Tonya, this is your uncle Steinn."

Tonya stared. *Uncle.*

"Tonya!" Steinn smiled and extended his arms.

Tonya hesitated before stepping into his embrace. A cold prickle ran down her arms and she withdrew. Steinn still smiled as if he hadn't noticed her shivering.

She looked to Birgir and Lilja, wondering why they wouldn't have told her about Steinn immediately. They must have known him, since they were friends with Freyr. But the frown lingered in the smallest corner of Birgir's mouth, and Lilja watched with her keen eyes.

"Steinn has searched for you these last seventy years," Birgir said.

Steinn's wide smile didn't falter. "I knew you must be out there somewhere. And after Freyr disappeared…"

For the first time, his expression broke and sadness hunched his shoulders.

"Thank you," Tonya said, not sure what else to say. Confusion whirled about her mind.

After what she'd said, surely Birgir and Lilja would have known how important it would be for her to know that some family had been actively looking for her? That she would want to meet her father's family?

"Your Majesty, may I speak with her when you are done?"

"You were just in time, Steinn. I was about to send for an escort to take her back to her friends. They are in the northwest tower. I'm sure you would like to catch up with your uncle, Tonya?" Birgir's smile came devoid of the strange tenseness.

Tonya nodded. *Maybe I'm reading this wrong.*

Steinn flashed a smile again and gestured to the door. She stepped out first and Steinn closed the doors behind them. He took her hand and settled it around his arm. Her fingertips tingled in response.

They walked down the hall, Steinn staring at her the entire time.

He finally shook his head. "I'm so happy to have found you."

"You really looked for me?" Tonya tilted her head up towards him.

"As often as I could get away from my duties here. I know Freyr would have wanted you protected."

"Do – do I have any other family here?" she blurted.

He inclined his head. "Yes. My parents live here in the castle, but..."

Tonya steeled herself at the long pause.

"They were greatly distressed by Freyr's sudden disappearance. And honestly by the fact that he married your mother. I'm assuming they at least told you of your heritage here?"

Tonya nodded. "Yes, that my father was a noble."

"Aye, and here in the north, we take bloodlines seriously. Freyr was my younger brother, but still expected to marry well. He took the form of our polar bear like I do, so we knew the blood ran strong in him."

She tightened her grip on Steinn's arm. *There's so much I don't know about this place. Blood lines, heritage – everything.*

"Ísbjörn. Polar bear?" she guessed.

"That's right." He smiled again. "Do you know any of the language?"

Heat tinged her cheeks. "No. But all my life I've known some things about the north. Like if the wind is coming over the waves in the right direction, I can hear it whisper about the magic of this place. I never knew *how* I knew, but maybe it's because of his warding?"

"Warding?" Steinn raised an eyebrow.

Tonya explained all that she knew of her parents' warding. A hard glint came into Steinn's eyes as he listened, but it vanished in a blink. Tonya thought it must have been the light shining through the ice windows as they walked.

"Perhaps he did find a way to give you something of our people before he disappeared. It sounds like something Freyr would do." A bit of tension came into his voice. "And perhaps that's why I could never find you. I tried every tracking spell I could think of with what I could remember of you, and your parents."

"What was Freyr like?" Tonya flexed the fingers of her left hand as the prickle stung her fingers again.

The smile bloomed again, and Tonya relaxed under the sight. "He was kind, generous. Loyal. A bit more than impulsive. Once he got an idea for something, it was hard to talk him out of it."

A smile curved its way across Tonya's face. She'd longed her whole life to learn about her father, and so far, she liked what Steinn said.

"But I feel I should confess. We did not often get along, and it took him disappearing to make me realize that I did love my brother. That's why I looked so faithfully for you. Maybe I could get part of him back through you."

Tonya tightened her grip. Steinn shook himself a little. "He loved being outside, even in the dead of winter when our most hardy ice casters stay indoors by the fires."

"You get cold?" Tonya interrupted in surprise. She'd seen the fires, but assumed it was for her companions.

Steinn turned a puzzled glance at her. "Yes. Do you not?"

Tonya bit her lip and shook her head.

"Interesting. Must be a side effect of the warding." A curious gleam lit in his eyes as he stared at her, and the prickle stirred along her arms.

"Can I meet my grandparents?"

It broke Steinn's glance and he shook himself.

"I don't know. As I said, they didn't take too kindly to Freyr marrying your mother. And even less so to the news about you. It might be best to stay away for now. At least, until I break the news to them and tell them what a wonderful young faery you are."

He patted her hand, and heat assailed her face again.

"I'd still like to meet them," she said, finding the *desire* deep in her soul. If she could meet them, she could see more of the place that her father called home.

Steinn smiled. "I'll see what I can do. Now, how did you come to be here? Tell me about these friends of yours."

# Chapter 23

"**H**e seemed nice." Diane took a seat next to Tonya. The door had just closed behind Steinn, leaving the four companions alone.

Tonya drew her knees up to her chest, nodding slowly. Her uncle had been all attention during the story of their travels, and the shorter stories she'd told about growing up. He'd expressed some disgust at the way she'd been treated among her people, and a part of her heart had warmed even as the strange tingle returned to her fingertips.

"What's wrong?" Dorian's voice startled her from his seat to their left. August sprawled on the remaining bench, his head propped on a pillow.

"I don't know. He is nice, but..." She rubbed her fingers together.

"Something seemed a little—odd about him." August lazily flicked a bit of magic at the fire, sending it snapping higher.

"You think so?" Tonya said, glad that she wasn't the only one overthinking everything.

"It could just be nerves from reuniting with a long-lost niece who everyone thought was dead." Diane smirked.

August shrugged, lacing his hands across his chest and tapping his thumbs together. Tonya didn't really think that was it either. There were also the looks that Birgir and Lilja had given Steinn. *Like they don't really trust him. And Birgir said some people very close to Freyr didn't approve either. Steinn or my grandparents?* She rubbed at her arms.

"How do you feel about him?" Dorian asked. She settled her gaze on him, half-wishing that he wouldn't always ask the direct questions. She leaned her chin down on her arms and lifted a shoulder in a shrug.

"Maybe it's reuniting with an uncle I didn't even know existed and appears to actually want to get to know me."

Diane leaned against her shoulder for a moment. "He tell you much about your father?"

Tonya flicked a finger up against her nose to ward off a sniff.

"He did."

She couldn't bring herself to say more than that. Freyr had sounded like everything she would have wanted in a father. And the one constant in any discussion about her father was the fact that her parents had wanted her.

She blinked hard. She hadn't even realized how much hearing that from someone who actually knew both of them would heal the ragged bits of her heart.

Tonya tilted her head back to look up at the stars glittering sharply on the other side of the ice panes in the ceiling.

"How do you get to the stars from the land?"

"Find the star path beginning from the highest mountain in Celedon Forest," August said.

"From the lake that reflects the purest night sky." Dorian shifted to lean back and better look at the stars. "How do you get to it from the ocean?"

Tonya stared at scattered stars linked in a bright constellation. The Running Bear.

"We follow the fastest current to the place where the sky meets the sea and enter into the Creator's Halls," she murmured.

A soft sigh broke from Diane. "It sounds so easy, and so beautiful for faeries. Being able to just leave the world and walk to the Creator's Halls without dying first."

She tilted her head up, firelight flickering over her features, finding the sadness that lingered in the shadows.

"We can still die." August didn't break his stare from the sky. "But getting through the Halls of Death to the stars isn't easy."

"How long do you think it takes to find your way through the Halls?" Tonya asked, tightness filling her chest.

"I don't know." Raw understanding filled August's voice. "When my brother died, I made myself a promise. That if I died, I'd find him in the Halls and we'd go together."

Tonya squeezed her eyes shut for a long moment. *I'm afraid he's left this world.*

"I hope that they've found each other and have made it to the stars."

"My father always said that death never really separated anyone. That they were always just waiting a little out of reach. And that if you really loved someone, they'd be there waiting when you died." Diane's voice hitched and she sniffed.

"I like that." August's voice was rough.

"Me too," Tonya agreed in a small voice. She looked at Dorian, who had yet to say anything. He still stared up at the stars, jaw tense.

"Dorian?"

He inhaled quickly and looked at her.

"You all right?" Diane asked before she could. He nodded, his tension obvious.

"Sometimes it's hard for me to still believe in all that," he finally said. "My father left. He was one of the ones to first go rogue. He tried to get me and Endre to go with him. I couldn't. Endre did, until he saw what they'd really started doing to humans and to our people."

His hands clenched against his legs.

"Is that why you became a healer?" Tonya softly asked.

He nodded imperceptibly. "One day after a battle, I just couldn't pick up my staff anymore. It made me sick. So I turned to healing, hoping to try to undo some of the damage."

He paused for a long moment. "We're taught from birth that the Creator put us on earth to protect and nurture, so I couldn't figure out how He allowed faeries to turn like that, to do those things."

"When you figure it out, let me know?" August said wryly.

Tonya didn't know what to say. They'd all lost something. Her to something unknown, and them to the shared experience of the war. All left with questions that might not find any answer.

A soft gasp from Diane made her blink.

"Look!" Diane pointed up.

A flicker of light shot across the sky. Tonya held her breath. Another followed. And another. Ribbons of green and blue and purples darted across the sky in quick succession, leaving a green aura in their wake.

"The Creator's Lights," Tonya murmured in awe.

They watched in silence, the glimmering light finding its way down to dance off their faces. The lights came slower and less often, fading completely and leaving the stars to shine brighter in their absence.

Tonya dabbed at her cheeks, embarrassed, until Diane sniffed next to her. Lilja had said that they carried the Creator's magic with them to earth. After seeing them, it was easy to believe.

"This entire trip might have been worth it just to see that," August said.

Tonya swallowed hard. There had been a short message from Birgir, that they were still discussing ways to undo the warding. Dread had dogged her all evening, whispering that it could never be undone and the ice would stay forever.

Or until she died.

Her heart stalled. *What if that was the only way to undo it? Would they agree?* She glanced at her companions, still sitting in silence around the fire pit.

*No. They never would.*

She felt silly for even thinking it. "I think I'll go to bed. It's been a long day." She pushed to her feet, extending her hands once more to the warmth of the fire. *Will I feel cold if the warding is removed?*

Murmured "good nights" were returned. Dorian reached out to touch her hand as she passed his bench.

"You all right?" he asked, his voice barely audible, but concern loud in his eyes.

She smiled, her heart thudding in a different way. "I'm fine. Just tired."

She forced herself to walk away. Now, more than ever before, she couldn't let herself get attached. She was already the half-breed faery, the outcast, and she couldn't tangle Dorian up in that.

But now she'd be known as the faery who destroyed an entire continent. Dorian, August, and Diane deserved to be able to walk away from her shame. Soon she'd get the final answer that there was nothing to be done.

*

"There might be an option," Birgir announced the next morning.

Tonya nearly spit out her tea.

"What?" she said in unison with her companions.

They sat around a large table in a dining room somewhere in the castle. Tonya had barely paid attention to where they were going, swallowed up in the fear of the expected answer. Lilja and Steinn also sat at the table, along with a few other faeries who had been introduced as members of Birgir's council.

Birgir tipped a slight smile at their reaction. "As you already know, there isn't anything that we can do to undo Freyr's warding. We consulted Steinn as well, thinking maybe that his magic might be similar enough, but it appears not."

Tonya pressed her hands against the table, wishing he'd just get to the point.

"You saw the Lights last night?"

Tonya nodded.

"They touch down on the furthest northern tundras, where they pour the Creator's magic into the earth for all of us to use." Birgir leaned forward. "They could undo the warding."

"What do you mean?" Tonya whispered, glancing between Birgir and Steinn. Her uncle had a thoughtful look on his face.

"The Lights contain pure, unfiltered magic, untouched by any creature before it soaks into the ground," Steinn's gravelly voice picked up. "If you touch it, they will wipe away the warding, and any other magical working on you."

*Wiped away.*

"What about my magic?" Tonya asked.

"Your magic will be fine. Probably enhanced for a while after touching them." Lilja offered a half-smile. "There's not much out on the tundras. Not even animals. It'll be a safe place for your magic to be released."

Tonya pressed her fingertips harder against the table. What if her ocean magic decided to unleash itself and reveal itself as deadly as her ice magic? She could drown Konungburg if she wasn't careful.

"When do we leave?" August paused from his food long enough to ask.

"Steinn has offered to take Tonya," Birgir said. "We'll put together an escort. The journey there will take two days, and it's not an easy trip."

"It might be easiest if you three stayed behind," Steinn said.

"No." Dorian and August spoke at the same time. Diane looked up, ready to argue as well. Warmth spread down to Tonya's toes.

"We started this together," August said. "We're going."

"Sounds like you have an escort, Steinn." Birgir chuckled. Faint disapproval tightened the corner of Steinn's mouth, but he nodded.

Tonya sent a small smile of thanks at the boys. August tipped a lazy wink back. Dorian's eyes softened and she forced herself to look away after a glorious moment.

"When can we leave?"

"Tomorrow morning will be best," Steinn replied. "It will take some time to prepare for the trip. The nights will be cold out in the open and we'll need enough supplies to get us there and back. And King Birgir didn't clarify—it's two days by caribou. You'll have to spend some time today learning how to care for your own mounts and how to ride."

Diane and August were the only ones who looked pleased about that.

"We won't need anyone else to go along with us?" Dorian asked.

Steinn shook his head. "I'd only planned to take along two other faeries anyway. There isn't much danger from anything but wild animals, and I'm well equipped to deal with them. I think you are as well."

He looked to August. The younger faery eyed him for a moment, as if seeing him in a new light.

"The animals here speak a little differently than I'm used to, but it shouldn't be hard to translate if I need to," he said.

Steinn nodded. "Good. The hardest part of the journey will be the hills we have to cross to get to the tundra. The ice will make it more treacherous, but the caribou have sure footing. There should be nothing else to worry about."

A breath of relief escaped Tonya. Something could be done. A sudden horrible thought struck her.

"How do you know when the Lights come back? What if it takes weeks, or—"

It was already two days longer than she wanted, but what if it stretched into days too late?

"Not to worry," Lilja said. "The Lights come nearly every night."

Tonya wilted back into her chair. There was a way to undo the warding, to access her magic. She could figure out a way to undo the ice later. Or ask one of the numerous ice casters sitting around the table.

"Then that's settled." Birgir thumped a hand on the table. "I'll oversee the preparations myself."

"That's not necessary, Your Majesty," Steinn began, but Birgir waved him off.

"Anything for Freyr's daughter."

Tonya returned his smile, warmth shooting through her. It couldn't even be dimmed by the small frown of irritation that quirked Steinn's lips.

Maybe she'd also get a chance to know her uncle better over the next few days and help him make a convincing case to go meet her grandparents. Maybe even stay? She set her mug down, surprised by the thought. *So far this place has been more accepting of me than the Reef ever was. But would I truly be welcome to live here?*

Diane and August laughed over something, drawing her attention back to the table. She'd be welcome in Diane's house, she knew that. Would be welcome back in Csorna Hold. *With Dorian?* Her cheeks heated again. *No. It's better to part ways with him after this.*

"We'll head down to the stables after breakfast," Steinn said.

Tonya nodded her agreement, her excitement fading away into nervousness. There were many things which still fascinated her about the land. She wasn't sure learning how to ride the antlered beasts was one of them.

But she had no choice if they wanted to make good time to the tundra. She was the last to finish eating. Her appetite had been non-existent that morning, and had yet to return with the promise of riding lessons. She drank the last of the tea and followed the others from the room.

Steinn led the way through the wide corridors and staircases out into the crisp air. Tonya paused on the top step, tilting her head back to the sun that seemed a little closer, and inhaled deeply of the pine, and salty bay, and wild tang of magic swirling through the air.

"You look at home here," Dorian said as she opened her eyes.

He'd hung back to wait for her while Diane and August walked with Steinn, already pestering him with questions from the mildly-irritated look on his face.

"I feel more at home here," she admitted. "Maybe my ice magic is stronger than my ocean magic? I just—don't know why anyone would want to leave here."

He nodded slowly, his eyes sweeping across the view of the valley the castle steps afforded. "You should go out to the bay as well. It's the place where both of your magics meet."

Tonya turned her attention out to the dark waters of the bay, chunks of ice bumping into each other with each gentle sway. Seals basked on the furthest point of the bay, their honking conversation audible with the shifting wind.

"Would you go with me?" The question burst from her.

A smile tugged at his mouth. "Of course."

"That's if I survive trying to ride a caribou."

His smile turned to a wince. "Glad I'm not the only one dreading this."

Tonya giggled. "Let's get it over with. Going down to the water sounds infinitely more interesting."

They hurried to catch up to the others. Diane half-turned to catch Tonya's gaze, wiggling her eyebrows in a ridiculous question. Tonya rolled her eyes and turned her nose up in the air in a pointed refusal to rise to Diane's teasing. Diane snorted a laugh and looped her arm through Tonya's.

The stables were long, low buildings of grey stone, sheltered by the castle's bulk from the worst of the winds that swept off the bay.

Steinn flagged down two faeries in grey tunics edged with red.

"Ingvar, we need some caribou for a short journey to the northern tundra tomorrow. But they will need to learn to ride and care for them today."

The older of the faeries nodded, rubbing a hand through his dark hair that lacked the white tips.

"All new to riding?" Ingvar asked.

"I've ridden horses," Diane supplied.

"I'm experienced with horses and pegasi," August said.

Tonya shook her head. Ingvar tipped a smile at Dorian's long-suffering expression.

"I think I've got some animals that will suit the four of you just fine." He beckoned them into the stables.

The sweet scent of animals and hay greeted them. Gentle lowing crooned from the corners. Antlered heads emerged over carved stall doors to watch them with curious brown eyes.

Ingvar walked beside the stalls, murmuring back. A few of the caribou looked at them in more interest.

"Niko." Ingvar opened a door and a large male caribou stepped out. Ingvar pointed down the mow and the caribou trotted off.

Ingvar kept walking, opening three more doors for a female and two bulky males. "Raakel and Ransu are siblings." He sent a male and the female off. The last male stretched its head out to curiously sniff at Dorian.

Dorian held out his hand and the caribou butted it with his nose, sliding his cheek along Dorian's hand to present a furred ear to be scratched. Ingvar slapped the caribou's rump. It jumped and trotted off with a snort of irritation.

"Arvo will be yours," Ingvar told Dorian. "Be warned, he likes attention a little too much."

"I noticed," Dorian remarked dryly.

Ingvar and his companion stopped only to load them up with saddles and bridles and brushes before following the path the caribou had taken out into the arena behind the stables.

The caribou waited patiently, except for Arvo who knocked his antlers against Niko's. Niko snuffled and butted him back a pace until Ingvar clicked his tongue and they ceased. Arvo made a beeline for Dorian again, sidling closer and keeping one eye on Ingvar and the other on Dorian as he rubbed his chin against the faery's arm.

Tonya stifled a giggle. Dorian rolled his eyes and rubbed under the caribou's chin as Ingvar began a basic lesson on grooming.

Nearly thirty minutes later, after fumbling her way through saddling and bridling Ransu, she wobbled precariously along with his rocking walk around the arena.

"Just relax a little," Diane said, looking disgustingly at ease on Raakel as they trotted around.

"Just relax a little," Tonya muttered under her breath, tensing instead as Ransu jogged a few steps to try to keep up with his sister.

Ransu stopped, huffing at August as the faery passed. August reined in, chuffing back. Ransu's ears flicked and he tipped his wide antlers back and forth. Tonya recoiled from the movement of the branching prongs so near her face.

August chuckled, turning to her. "He says that he's not going to let you fall."

"That's easy for him to say. He's not up here feeling like driftwood in a storm." Tonya tightened her grip on the reins. Ransu snorted again.

August leaned over, tapping her hands. "Loosen up."

She nearly dropped the leather. August bit the inside of his lip.

"Shut up," she muttered fiercely.

"Keep about this much slack." August demonstrated with his reins. Tonya managed to mimic the swoop of his leathers. "Now let's start walking."

Tonya's muscles froze up as soon as Ransu stepped out.

"Let yourself move with him." August smiled again, his words encouraging. "Don't you ride whales or something in the ocean?"

Tonya snorted a laugh. "No, and I'm sure they'd be significantly safer than this."

Ransu shook his antlers again.

"He's offended you think a giant water worm is safer than him."

"Water worm?" Tonya arched an eyebrow.

August lifted a shoulder. "His words. But I could be translating it wrong."

Tonya tentatively unlatched a hand from the reins and patted Ransu's neck. "Sorry."

He snorted back. August grinned.

"Am I forgiven?"

"I think so," August replied. "And don't look now, but you just relaxed."

A laugh burst from Tonya as she realized that she was finally moving along with the gentle sway of Ransu's clicking walk, her knuckles not so white around the reins.

"Let me know when you feel comfortable enough to go faster." August reached forward to scratch around Niko's antlers.

"We can't walk all the way there?" Tonya pursed her lips in a mock pout.

"Fortunately, no." August grinned.

Tonya rolled her eyes. "Should you be the one helping me? We're going to be jumping castle walls next, aren't we?"

August tossed his head back with a laugh. "If they were shorter, you can bet we'd try it."

Tonya laughed, gathering her courage. She reached to pat Ransu's neck again.

"Don't let me fall," she admonished, and nudged her heels against his sides as Ingvar had instructed. He gradually quickened his pace to a slow trot. She gripped with her knees and tightened up on the reins before remembering to try to relax.

Ransu snorted gently as she began to move more in time with his stride.

"Good!" August kept pace easily. "He promises to take care of you. Let him."

Tonya swallowed, bouncing hard in the saddle as she lost the rhythm in another burst of nervousness. August nudged Niko on faster, leaving her on her own. She set her jaw, keeping her focus between Ransu's antlers, and gave him another little nudge. He obligingly quickened his pace. She survived two laps around the arena before pulling him back down to a walk.

"You're a natural." Steinn leaned on the rail. She steered Ransu over to him.

"I don't know about that," she said. "I'm sure he has a few pointed things to say about my riding." She scratched under the harness that looped from the saddle around Ransu's chest. He stretched his head forward, wiggling his antlers slightly in response.

Steinn chuckled, rubbing the caribou's chin. "He likes you. They're good creatures, but can be a bit picky about riders."

"Is that supposed to make me more relaxed?"

Steinn laughed, his eyes crinkling up at the corners. It drew a smile from Tonya. *What did my father look like when he laughed?*

"Keep practicing. We'll have to ride faster than this if we want to make it to the tundra in two days."

Tonya sighed, shifting her feet in the stirrups. Her legs already felt sore. But she obediently turned Ransu and kept riding.

They broke for a quick meal at noon, sitting on the rails of the arena to eat. Arvo lurked a pace away, his gaze trained on Dorian.

"Did I get the brain-addled one?" Dorian muttered under his breath. August nearly snorted tea through his nose. August broke off some bread and handed it to the caribou, who chomped it with a blissful blink of his eyes.

Tonya sipped at her tea, rolling her head back and forth to relieve some of the stiffness. *I'll be lucky to be able to walk tomorrow.*

"I haven't ridden this much in a long time." Diane kicked her boots against the railing. "This might be a long few days."

Her companions had taken off their jackets, staying warm enough with the riding. Tonya had jumped at the opportunity to shuck her coat without looking strange. She stretched her arms out, her fingers itching to call the ice and snow on the stable roofs. But the warding clamped down on her magic before she could try.

Dorian nudged her arm and held out his hand. His eyes were soft with a smile. She rested her hand on his and closed her eyes as the knots loosened in her chest. She lifted her hand again and felt the tingling rush spreading from her fingers. Arvo half-reared and plunged through the miniature snowstorm as she called snow down from the roof.

"So you can do some ice magic!" Steinn's voice sent the snow collapsing to the ground in harmless piles. A gleam shone in his eyes before it was shuttered away in a smile. Tonya tucked her hands back into her lap.

"A little. Usually if Dorian tries an anti-warding spell first," she said.

Steinn passed a quick glance between the two of them. The prickle stabbed her fingers at the look. She rubbed her fingers against her sharkskin trousers, the roughness chasing the feeling away.

Ingvar pushed back into the arena. "Last lesson before we're done for the day. Then you'll help me pack up the feed for them."

Tonya huffed a sigh and slid down from the railing. One more lesson and then she could go down to the pier.

# Chapter 24

**W**aves lapped against the wood, sending shivers of magic through Tonya. A light breeze teased at her hair hanging loose around her shoulders. The ice floes tempted her, but she remained on the solid pier. She let her arms dangle by her sides, stretching her fingers wide as if to catch strands of magic that floated in the space where the saltwater and the ice met in the mouth of the bay.

It teased at the fringes of her mind. Beckoning to her, as if saying that it was the one place she could exist as a whole. Where she could belong. Except she didn't know how to get there.

Dorian's shadow fell across the gentle waves. The sight anchored her back to the land. He had yet to say anything since they'd come to stand on the pier, content to let her be as she pushed the boundaries of her limited power, ready to help if she needed.

Endless waves swelled outside the bay, stretching across the far horizon, their darkness interspersed with the white of ice floes. The land spread away in a sea of white-tipped green, and the whispers of the open tundras beckoned beyond.

Both calling to her magics. Both trying to claim her. She reached for Dorian's hand, wanting something to help fasten her back to herself. He squeezed her fingers in his gloved hand.

"Would you ever leave Durne?"

"I did a few days ago." His voice carried the barest hint of amusement as he kept staring out at the bay.

She brushed at the strands of hair that fell into her eyes. "Permanently?"

A short intake of breath came from him. "Sometimes I think about it when I have to walk across old battlefields, or through towns that still bear the marks of the war. But there's nowhere else to go that doesn't carry that same stain."

He paused for so long she thought that was all he had to say.

"But," he continued, "it's my home, and it will always have a part of my heart. I think I'd always go back."

A distant whale breached in a gush of white foam. Tonya smiled, resisting the urge to dash across the ice floes to call to it.

"I thought I didn't want to go back to the ocean. But standing here, I'm not so sure. I've always felt caught between the waves, not quite in sync with the ocean."

His grip tightened a little. "And now?"

She lifted a shoulder in a quick shrug. "I think maybe I can see the place I could be. Balancing between both where the waves brush the ice." Quick heat tinged her cheeks. "That sounds stupid."

"No." He shook his head, glancing down at her. "I like the way you describe things. Like you can say the things that people feel but never explain." He shifted slightly. "Now I sound stupid."

Tonya leaned a little closer so that their arms touched. "Never."

A smile crept its way down to his lips. "It sounds like in two days, you'll get to find that place you were talking about, to balance your magic."

"Is it stupid to say that scares me more than the remmiken?"

She should be dancing with joy at the chance to free her magics, but the thought that everything might go wrong and she might trigger another disaster had latched into the forefront of her mind. She hadn't been able to shake it.

"No." His quiet assertion warmed her.

He kept staring across the waves and she tipped her face to study his profile. Strong, quiet, but the rage of a summer monsoon still glimmering beneath the surface. Even becoming friends with August hadn't diminished it. But she knew if she studied August, she'd see the lonely fury of a blizzard whirling through him.

Both were storms she didn't know how to calm.

He shifted, startling her as he suddenly stared into her eyes. Her breath caught. He'd always looked at her different, but now she felt *seen*. Like he saw the tangles inside her and didn't care about it. Not like every other faery who looked at her and only saw that she was half and half.

Stuck between the waves.

"Tonya..." he started, his throat bobbing nervously.

Her heart thudded hard.

*What could it hurt?* Diane's words echoed.

*Him.*

Her hand felt clumsy in his. *I can't do it to him.* She pulled her hand away.

"We should go back." She tried to lighten her voice, like she hadn't been straining to hear what he'd been about to say. Like her heart wasn't cracking at pulling away.

The smile around his eyes dimmed and faded away. He nodded once, flicking his hand back up the pier, indicating that she could go first.

She ducked her head, fighting against the sting in her eyes from a sudden chill wind and hurried back to the castle, not turning to see if he even followed.

This time as she walked through the halls, she saw the stares. The glances, the sneers, the disgust. She'd been so caught up in the moments of acceptance from Birgir and Lilja and Steinn that she'd forgotten.

They were the rare few. The rest hated who she was. What she was. The product of a union between their noble son and an ocean faery.

Unwanted.

The faery who cursed the lands with unbreakable ice.

She'd been a fool to think that she could stay. That anyone could want her. Birgir and Lilja and Steinn could be lying to her. Using her to undo the ice and then waiting to cast her out, laughing at her naivety.

"Tonya!" Her name spoken in a deep voice startled her and she barely stopped herself from running into her uncle.

"What's wrong?" Steinn rested a hand on her shoulder.

She rubbed her hand across the sleeve of her coat. "Nothing."

But her trembling voice betrayed her.

"I saw you walking with that plains faery healer. Did something happen?" Her heart cracked a little more at the faint sneer in his voice over the word *plains*. Not Dorian. Just the *plains faery*. As if he wasn't even worth the consideration of a name.

And hearing it from her uncle who had greeted her with kindness, previously greeted her companions with friendliness, made it worse. Like maybe he'd been pretending all along.

*I'm right to keep away from Dorian.*

"No. Just tired from today." She forced herself to look at him, blinking when his features melted back into kindness and compassion.

"Of course. I forgot how exhausting learning to ride can be. There's some time before dinner if you wanted to rest?"

She jerked a nod, shifting awkwardly on her feet as she finally realized she didn't recognize the hallway.

"I got a bit turned around." She gave an embarrassed laugh. "I think I was a little overconfident in getting back."

Steinn smiled, but it didn't quite warm his face like before.

"Just like your father. Always rushing into things."

He tucked her hand in the crook of his arm and turned her gently back around. He kept his hand over hers as they walked. Her fingers stung with repeated prickles. She shifted her fingers in discomfort and he let his hand fall away.

They walked in silence. He turned down a wide corridor to the winding staircase that she'd walked past in her haste to get away.

"I know the way from here." She released her grip on Steinn's arm. He looked down at her.

"You sure?"

She nodded, suddenly needing to be alone.

"All right." He stepped away. "I'll see you at dinner?"

"Yes. Thank you." She mustered a small smile and hurried up the staircase. She hesitated outside the doors to their chambers, but silence lingered on the other side. She slipped through into the empty common room. The door to the boys' room was closed.

Tonya tiptoed to her room. The faint splash of water from the adjoining chamber announced Diane was washing. Tonya slipped off her boots, threw her coat across a chair, and slipped under a heavy quilt. She pulled it up to her chin as she curled on her side.

Not cold. Never cold, but needing the feeling of closeness and security.

She closed her eyes. *Plains faery.* It was said the same way most of the faeries in the reef said *ice faery*. The way she imagined so many faeries here saying *ocean faery*.

Their kind weren't supposed to mix. Supposed to fall in love and have children. Children who weren't even proper faeries, with strangled magic and mismatched wings that served no function.

Diane didn't understand. Not really. August acted like he didn't care. But what if he did? What if he and Diane were only pretending so that she would undo the ice and not cause any further damage?

"Tonya?" Diane asked tentatively.

Tonya dabbed at the tears leaking from her closed eyes. She pulled the quilt up higher to block her face. "I'm fine."

The bed shifted as Diane settled beside her. "I don't think so. Dorian came up a few minutes ago. He and August growled at each other and then they left to go hit each other in the courtyard. Something happened, otherwise you wouldn't be in here like this."

Tonya shifted a bit of blanket with a finger to peer at Diane. The princess leaned close, concern filling up every corner of her open face. But Steinn acted concerned about her, then derided Dorian in the same breath.

"You wouldn't understand," she whispered.

Diane got up and Tonya closed her eyes again, hating that she'd been right. She froze as Diane flopped down on the other side of the bed, comfortably close.

"So tell me."

But Tonya stayed curled under the quilt, hoping her silence would drive Diane away. Even if she was sincere, being close to Tonya would only hurt her.

"I hide too."

Tonya half-turned in surprise at Diane's sudden pronouncement. An embarrassed laugh broke from Diane as she stared up at the ceiling.

"I never feel like I have much to offer. Even if people say differently." She briefly glanced at Tonya. "I feel like I can't live up to what my parents were, because I remember them as larger than life. I dream of things and adventures, but never reach for them."

Tonya slowly rolled over, keeping the blanket tucked up to her chin. "Everyone's always looked at me different. Never really giving me a chance. I think I've believed that I'm a mistake for so long that I really don't know how to fix that."

A breath shuddered from her. "I thought it would be different here, but then today, I started seeing it again, hearing it all again. But this time Steinn said something, and it made me realize that even liking Dorian is a mistake."

Diane laced her hands across her stomach. "Liking someone for who they are is never a mistake. Anyone who says otherwise can eat snow."

Tonya snorted a giggle. Diane's chuckle faded and they lapsed into silence.

"Tonya, you're not a mistake. Everyone has said that your parents loved each other. They wanted to keep you. And I'm sorry that they're not here anymore. I know what that feels like."

"Even if I've never met them?" Tonya whispered.

"Yes."

Tonya sniffed and dabbed at her cheeks with the blanket. "Is it stupid to be afraid of finally having my magic freed? What if I drown the land next?"

Diane flicked her fingers carelessly. "I can swim."

"But really?" Tonya pressed.

"When my brother asked me to be on the council, I refused. I'm only eighteen, no real experience to contribute, and the only woman in the room. He didn't make me. Ralf actually found me after that conversation." A bit of red touched her cheeks. "He told me that experience didn't matter at first. Soldiers learn by fighting and figuring out what skills are their strongest. How would I know what I had to offer, if I didn't at least try?"

She took a breath. "It all scared me, until I saw how unsure Edmund was about everything too, but he did it anyway. I had no excuse after that. It helped me become a better version of myself."

Tonya moved the blanket down a little further.

Diane rolled, propping up on one elbow. "It's all right to be scared. Anytime we have to change ourselves, it's frightening. But usually we come out better and stronger for it."

"What if I don't? What if ocean and ice magic aren't meant to mix and once the warding is gone, they—?"

"They didn't put the warding on you at birth, right? So, if tiny baby you didn't explode with magic, then I don't think you will now."

A laugh nudged Tonya's chest. The words helped, but the fears still swelled like storm-caught waves. "Thank you."

Diane flopped back down. "Tonya, I meant what I said before about being a friend. Am I here to make sure the ice is undone? Yes. But just know that after this, if the northern and the ocean faeries are still idiots, you can come to Chelm. I can't promise it wouldn't be some of the same there, but I'm learning to not be afraid of magic so much anymore. I think we all could do the same."

Tonya pressed her hands over her eyes. "I don't really have many friends." Her voice hitched over the words, making it hard to get through. "So thank you. For everything."

Diane's arm draped over her, squeezing tight in a hug. "You're welcome."

The pressure eased and the bed shifted again as she sat up.

"And I think you should talk to Dorian." Diane nudged her shoulder, tugging the blanket down. "Avoiding people you like isn't the answer."

Tonya sighed, propping herself up on an elbow. "Know this from experience?" She wiggled an eyebrow.

Diane poked Tonya's stomach, sending her falling back on the pillows with a smirk.

"Believe me, the first thing I'm going to do when I get back is talk to him. If I don't lose my nerve first." She offered a wry smile.

"I'll freeze your feet to the ground so you can't run off."

"I doubt I'll need any help with freezing when it comes to admitting certain things." Diane pulled her damp hair over her shoulder and began braiding it.

Tonya straightened. "What's it like for you?"

Diane's fingers paused.

"With Ralf?" She lifted a shoulder when Tonya nodded. "I don't know. I miss him when he's not there. I like seeing his smile come through, because I know that it's the real him coming out." A shy grin curved across her lips. "He's never been afraid to tease me, to push me to be better."

Tonya drew her knees up to her chest, rubbing a fold of the quilt between her fingers.

"Maybe that's what it is. Dorian's been one of the first to help me try to be *more* than what I am now."

"Then give him a chance. Forget what anyone else says or thinks. Their opinion doesn't really matter, does it?" Diane finished her braid and tied it off with a bit of ribbon she pulled from the pocket of her dress.

"Maybe I'll wait until after we find the Lights," Tonya said. "I don't want to mess it up."

Diane's mouth twitched downward in quick disapproval. Despite Diane's words, her fears couldn't be quelled so easily. She wanted to see who she was after the warding was gone before doing anything.

Diane scooted to the edge of the bed. "Just as long as you tell him."

Tonya leaned forward, resting her chin on her knees. "I will."

"Good. Now go take a bath before dinner. You smell like caribou."

Tonya gasped in mock outrage and shifted to prod Diane's side. The princess dodged with a laugh. Tonya crawled out from under the quilt. She pulled out fresh clothes from the chest at the foot of the bed and headed to the wash room.

After bathing and dressing, she placed her dirty clothes on the bed and reached for her boots. She froze at the sounds of masculine voices in the common room. She tiptoed over to peer through the partially-open door.

Dorian and August were fresh back from the training court. Dorian had folded his coat over his arm. August's was slung carelessly over a shoulder.

Sweat streaked both their shirts and plastered their hair. They both seemed more relaxed and at ease.

Diane sat in the window seat, writing in her journal. She greeted them both with a smile, drawing them into a conversation. Tonya watched Dorian, taking the chance to study him without the coat and weapons.

His shirt couldn't quite hide his muscular build. His shoulders were broader than August's, fitting with the overall compact strength of his frame. She'd forgotten how smooth his movements were, how quietly he walked like a snow fox stalking its prey. *How does anyone think he's just a healer?*

He half-turned to the door, as if knowing that she stood behind it.

Tonya backed a step away from the door, flushing a little at peering through the crack like a timid fish. Her heart leapt at the sound of his light laugh. It dropped in her chest just as quickly as she remembered the way his smile died when she'd pulled away at the pier.

She closed her eyes. *I'll tell him after. Once I figure out who I am with the warding gone.*

Tonya waited until their footsteps receded and the common room fell silent before slipping out to join Diane on the window seat. Tonya stared out the window, watching figures walk or fly through the courtyards and town as Diane journaled.

August reappeared first, nodding a greeting to her before flopping on one of the benches and closing his eyes. Tonya sat a little taller, waiting for Dorian.

The dinner bell rang through the castle as he emerged from the room. He came up short when he caught sight of her. She swallowed hard, her tongue twisting at the sight of him. Diane prodded her hip with her foot before setting her journal aside and joining August at the door.

"Dorian!" Tonya blurted as he neared the door. Dorian half-turned, hand still on the latch.

She swallowed hard, not sure what she was going to say. He waited, caution in his stance.

"I—thank you for going down to the pier with me today." It wasn't what she'd meant to say at all. *I'll tell him later,* she promised herself again.

Dorian's face smoothed, and he offered a small smile. It wasn't much, but it was better than the mask that had fallen over his face earlier.

"You're welcome."

He opened the door wider in an invitation for her to go first. She hurried forward, flashing a quick smile before ducking her head as she passed him. His smile stretched a little wider before he followed her.

# Chapter 25

"**G**ood luck!" King Birgir pressed Tonya's hands between his own.

"Thank you." She smiled.

His expression never faltered. He turned to the others standing in the stable courtyards, wishing them well by name. *How could I have doubted him?* Tonya shook her head. The king exuded friendliness and cheer like the small pups that bounded around the stables.

Steinn waited beside his caribou, checking the leathers and turning a glance up at the early morning sky.

"We should be off," he announced.

Tonya went to her caribou, patting its nose. Ransu snorted, breath pluming in the chill. Diane swung up onto Raakel, tugging the collar of her coat up a little higher against the light breeze. Dorian mounted, keeping Arvo still with a touch. He'd kept his distance since the night before.

It left a curious ache in Tonya's chest, but it gave her the space she'd wanted.

August mounted last. Lilja pulled him aside, their heads bent low together. The murmur of their voices was barely audible, but August nodded a few times. His serious expression melted back into something more carefree as he turned to them and vaulted onto his caribou without using stirrups.

"Show off," Dorian muttered, his movements stilted at first as Arvo stepped out.

"Safe travels and may the Lights guide you." Birgir lifted a hand. He turned another smile to Tonya. "See you in a few days, Tonya Freyr-dottir."

Lilja stood beside Birgir, arms crossed over her chest, a frown remaining in the corner of her mouth as she swept one last glance over them.

"Stay cautious," she said. "The ice has thrown things into disarray."

"I'll make sure they stay safe." Steinn lifted a hand in a salute. Lilja lifted her hand as well, her frown unwavering.

He led the way through the town at a brisk trot. Hooves clattered over the stones, echoing loudly in the empty streets. The few faeries already awake and outside watched them ride out with either curiosity or disinterest.

But Tonya still saw a few sneers thrown her way.

She ducked her head, keeping her eyes on the road until they passed out of Konungburg and into the hills beyond. Unlike Csorna Hold, the town and castle didn't disappear when they left the valley. It seemed the northern faeries were less concerned about being found by anyone who would happen to wander by.

Steinn turned north into the hills. They spent the morning winding through hills at a walk, then sprinting across flatland between.

The sun hovered at its midpoint when Steinn finally reined in. They'd stopped at the base of a large rise. A shallow valley stretched out before them. Tall fir and spruce trees marched their way down the hills, stretching into the valley like long green fingertips that parted only for a meandering frozen river.

Dark bulky shapes with broad horns paced slowly through the valley, stopping to paw at the ice and snow before moving on to nibble at the low-hanging boughs.

"What are those?" Diane shielded her eyes to look at the animals better. Even from that distance, the creatures were obviously taller and broader than their caribou.

"Moose," Steinn said. "We'll give them a wide range. They can be territorial. But first, I think it's time for lunch."

Diane's stomach growled audibly in agreement and she flushed. Tonya giggled as she slid down from the saddle. Her legs swayed underneath her and she grabbed hold of the leathers to keep her feet.

Ransu tilted a look back from the corner of his eye, snuffling a question. She scratched under the chest strap and he stretched his neck low, wiggling his antlers back and forth in appreciation. Dorian briefly caught her gaze across the backs of their mounts, but she looked away quickly.

*Later,* she promised herself again.

August stood beside Niko, feet braced wide and fists on hips as he stared out across the valley.

"I wouldn't mind getting lost out here."

Steinn paused to follow his gaze. "Aye. Once the ice is gone, then you will surely never want to leave. The mountains to the east and north are even more beautiful."

The frank honesty in his voice calmed Tonya. The derision from the night before had been absent all morning. *Maybe I imagined it.*

"What's past the tundra?" August asked.

Steinn lifted his chin as if to see farther. "More mountains, more tundra, then freezing ocean and shifting ice. Not many creatures live past the mountains on the other side of the tundra. We very rarely go there ourselves."

"How much longer are we in these hills?" Tonya dug out a treat for Ransu.

"Such impatience!" Stein chided. "We'll reach the tundra by tonight. The sun sets later out over the tundras, so we'll ride longer today."

A strange eagerness lit his eyes. The prickle teased along Tonya's arms again. She rubbed her hands over her sleeves, unable to shake the feeling of unease that had been lurking since the night before.

*I'm just anxious to get to the Lights and am seeing things.* She glanced to Dorian again as the urge to tell him reared up. She pushed it away before her storm-tossed emotions could overwhelm her.

Steinn insisted on letting the caribou rest for at least an hour. After the food had been packed away, Diane took out her journal and began writing. August strode off down the hill with a caution from Steinn not to go too far. Tonya took one sideways glance at where Dorian sat and hurried after August.

August tilted a curious look at her, but didn't question. A brief flicker of amusement touched his face as he looked past her up the hill, before turning into the forest. She imagined Dorian sitting slightly apart from the others, waiting patiently.

She followed August into the trees, inhaling a deep breath of crisp spruce. Small flakes of snow fluttered to the ground as they brushed past branches. He didn't appear to have any destination in mind, just wandering through the forest and letting her walk in silence beside him.

"Do you miss your home?" she finally asked.

He reached up to knock a drooping branch free of a heavy casing of ice. It sprang back to its former height. Tonya caught its shiver of gratitude from the corner of her eye.

"I do. I spend a lot of time walking the forest back home. It's my duty to look after the forest animals, but it also has plenty of quiet places to spend hours."

Tonya flushed. "I'm sorry. I didn't mean to intrude if you wanted some peace and quiet."

He quirked a grin at her. "It's all right. I never thought I'd have a plains faery to thank for showing me that it's all right to talk about things." He tipped a nod at her. "Or just be quiet with someone because you can't hoard your silence and space forever."

*Plains faery.* Where once there had been animosity in August's voice at the term, there was nothing but friendliness.

"Thank you for coming to the tundras with me," she said.

"Like I said, I wanted to see this finished through to the end." His grin returned. "And the rest is purely selfish. I want to see those Lights up close."

Tonya laughed. "I'd ride all night to get there if I could."

August's chuckle quieted as he half-turned his head. He stood poised like a cautious animal, chin tilted slightly up as his gaze swept the forest.

"What is it?" Tonya whispered, hoping it wasn't some angry moose about to charge through the trees.

"Not sure," he murmured back, lifting one hand with fingers spread wide to feel the breeze as it swept in around them. Then he blinked and his posture shifted.

"But look." He crouched and pointed into the underbrush.

Tonya knelt beside him, looking under the bush where bright eyes peered back. August murmured something and a small fox cautiously stepped out. A smile broke over Tonya's face as the fox tiptoed its way to August, stretching out its nose to sniff around his hand before nuzzling his fingers.

Its brown fur stood out in stark contrast to the white around them. *Summer coat.* Patches of white still lingered, perhaps trying to change back to its winter camouflage.

It gave a small bark and trotted back to the brush, emerging a moment later with four small kits pouncing along in her wake.

"Hold out your hand," August instructed. The fox performed the same cautious assessment of her before allowing Tonya to stroke her soft fur. The kits sidled forward, jumping up against August's knees, tumbling through the snow, or snapping at the trailing edge of her sleeve.

"Is the ice giving them too much trouble?" Tonya fondled the ears of one of the kits.

"Not too much. She's just glad to hear that it's going to be fixed soon." August gave her a reassuring smile.

Tonya sat back on her heels with a sigh. "Tell them sorry."

August did, then kept murmuring to the fox. It replied in barks and yips and tail swishes. It went on longer than Tonya thought a simple apology should take. One of the kits clambered up into her lap, distracting her from the myriad expressions crossing August's face as he listened.

He rose to his feet, no trace of snow on his trousers or coat. Tonya shooed the kits away and stood, brushing her knees off.

"What was all that?" she asked.

August shrugged, his expression clearing once again. "Nothing. Just asking what life in the north is like."

Tonya didn't believe it for a second. "Anything interesting?"

"Apparently it gets cold here." August grinned before beginning to walk back the way they'd come.

Tonya rolled her eyes and jogged the few steps to catch up with him. "What did Lilja want to talk with you about before we left this morning?"

He gave another shrug. "Just telling me to keep an extra eye out with Steinn for any trouble. They've had some problems with the bigger animals out here since the ice has disrupted normal summer hunting and feeding routines."

Tonya hummed a noise of understanding. Her fingers rose to rub her sleeve. *If that's the case, why did it have to be a private meeting like that?* She didn't like the fact that August might be keeping secrets from the rest of them.

But before she had a chance to question him any further, they'd come within earshot of their companions. Steinn and the others had the caribou ready by the time they'd walked back.

"We'll run across the valley. The ice on the river is thick enough that we'll be able to ride right across without stopping and continue up into the hills." Steinn glanced over them. "Ready?"

Tonya mounted Ransu and gathered up the reins. Her muscles already felt sore and they still had hours to go. She nodded and Steinn clucked to his caribou. It sprang forward in a spray of white to thunder into the valley. They followed two by two, forced back into silence by the clicking and pounding of hooves.

Moose barely glanced at them as they passed. An eagle hovered on the breeze before wheeling away. A young wolf darted alongside them for several bounds, sending Ransu skittering to the side with a nervous snort.

Steinn barked something to the wolf and it leapt away with a cheerful bay, rejoining other wolves lounging in the distance.

Once in the hills on the other side of the valley, they stopped for a few minutes to let the caribou catch their breath before continuing on at a walk for half an hour. True to his word, Steinn pushed at the same quick pace all afternoon and the miles fell away under hooves as they passed over hills and streams and another valley.

Tonya shook her head at her earlier optimism of wanting to ride all night when they finally stopped on the edge of the hills. A wide expanse of white stretched before them. The sun hung low in the sky, painting it in vibrant splashes of pinks and purples and darker blues.

"Is this it?" Diane staggered forward a few steps.

"No. We still have miles to go. Nearly to the foot of those mountains." Steinn pointed ahead.

What Tonya had initially mistaken for darker clouds or sky shadows was a low line of mountains, ragged points barely visible in the fading light.

Diane grimaced and pulled her packs from behind Raakel's saddle. "I'm not moving for the rest of the night."

Steinn chuckled and helped her ground tie Raakel. Tonya reached for her bags and paused as a whisper of something caught the wind as it teased around her face.

She froze, searching out on the tundra. A movement caught her eye—a lumbering shape that nearly blended into the white around it save for the long shadow that stretched towards them.

*Polar bear.*

Her fingers curled around the leathers, anchoring her in place as the wind whispered something enticing from the bear's direction.

"Look!" Diane pointed, breaking the wind's spell.

A cold look crossed Steinn's face at the sight of the bear. August stood, one hand on Niko's reins, leaning towards the bear, head tilted in confusion.

"Polar bear." Steinn said the word almost like a curse. "Stay here. I'll send it on its way. They're dangerous to have around." He strode off, one hand on the long knife at his belt. Tonya watched him go, misgiving stirring in her soul.

"August?" Dorian's quiet question jerked her attention back to the forest faery. He stood stiff and alert, watching Steinn stride toward the bear that now paced back and forth with audible grunts.

August shifted, his expression staying thoughtful. "Nothing. Just never seen a bear like that before."

Dorian stared at him a moment, solemn features calling August a liar louder than any words could. An unexpected shiver cut across Tonya's skin as she again had the feeling that there was more going on around her than she knew.

"It's leaving," Diane said.

The bear lumbered away from Steinn. Her uncle stood with arms crossed, his posture rigid as he watched the bear retreat toward the trees that marched out onto the tundra from the hills.

August made a thoughtful hum as he watched Steinn walk back to them before turning to care for Niko.

"I cast some warding around us to keep out any other dangerous animals," Steinn announced as he returned. "We should be safe enough out here now."

Diane breathed an audible sigh. Tonya couldn't shake the feeling of disappointment. *Maybe it's because polar bears are the sign of my father's house and I wanted to see one up close.* But the wind felt lonely and empty as it tugged at her loose braid, nothing like the almost warmth it carried when the bear had appeared.

She helped Diane spread out their tent to allow it to build itself. August did the same, and this time Tonya caught the slight flick of magic he sent into the tent to make it grow faster. Steinn watched in interest as he erected his own sealskin tent.

Dorian headed up into the hills to collect firewood. August walked after him, but they parted ways a few steps into the woods. Steinn's eyes narrowed briefly until August stooped to pick up a fallen branch before disappearing further into the trees.

Dinner was a quiet affair. Tonya's eyes drooped shut as her sore body called for sleep. Steinn insisted they didn't need a guard as his warding spell should be sufficient. Dorian and August didn't argue overmuch, appearing grateful to be able to get a full night's sleep.

Tonya crawled into the tent along with Diane, curling up under the extra blankets that had been provided. Wind off the tundra rattled the tent in sporadic gusts. The caribou shifted against their ground ties with soft snorts and shuffles. A wolf howled somewhere in the distance, joined one-by-one by the rest of its pack.

Tonya closed her eyes and let the sounds of the north lull her to sleep.

# Chapter 26

The low rumble of voices stirred Tonya awake. Diane was already sitting up, rubbing her eyes and yawning.

"When we get back to Konungburg, I'm going to sleep for a week," she declared. "And then never leave the house when I get back to Chelm."

Tonya pushed back her blankets with a laugh. "It's been a long journey."

Diane stretched her arms overhead, her fingers brushing the canvas.

"But!" She turned to Tonya. "We'll find the Lights tonight!"

Tonya's insides twisted up in nervous excitement. It leaked out into a shaky grin. Diane began rolling her blankets up. Tonya did the same, hands trembling. Magic might soon be able to fall freely from her fingers.

Diane pushed out of the tent first. Dorian and August had already collapsed their tent, packs sitting in neat piles beside them. Steinn was nowhere to be seen, but his caribou waited patiently beside the others.

Tonya placed her bag by the boys'.

"Where's Steinn?" She took in a deep breath of the crisp air.

"Said he wanted to go make sure that bear wasn't around." Dorian extended both of them dried jerky.

Diane grimaced as she tore off a strip. "I'm also never eating anything dried ever again when we get back home."

Dorian chuckled and Tonya tore her eyes away from the way his face came alight. She focused instead on August, who sat more alert than Dorian in a strange contrast. His gaze flicked around and he occasionally spread his fingers wide as his hands dangled over his knees as if testing the wind.

Tonya swallowed another bite of the flavorless jerky, clearing her throat.

"When is he coming back?" The jittering hadn't left her joints and the tundra begged to be raced across.

August shifted his shoulders in a shrug, his features relaxing into something more easy. "I don't know. But he's been gone awhile."

"We should get ready so we can leave when he gets back." Dorian stood, slapping snow from his coat.

Tonya muddled her way through saddling Ransu and fixing her pack in place. She undid his ground tie like the others did and slipped the bridle in place. August walked among the caribou, touching their noses and whispering a soft word. They stood still in obedience, nickering to each other as August returned to wait with the others.

Another ten minutes crept by. Tonya got up and began to walk around. August and Dorian also stood, exchanging worried glances.

"What if something happened?" Diane wrapped her arms across her stomach.

"I'm sure he's fine." Tonya tried to force assertiveness in her voice. Diane nodded, pursing her lips in worry and walking away to go rub Raakel's nose.

Tonya turned to face the north. The mountains were taller in the full light of the sun. Maybe a half day's run across the flat tundra.

A sharp snort turned her attention to the caribou. They began to mill about, pressing close and grunting to one another. Diane backpedaled from the increasingly frantic waves of their horns.

August darted forward to place himself between her and the anxious animals. Steinn's caribou tossed his head towards the sky and gave a louder snorting honk, sending the others into a more restless state.

August stretched out his hand, but Niko slammed his forefeet down and lowered his horns. August backed away. Without warning, Steinn's caribou bolted, taking off parallel to the hills and heading west in a spray of snow. The others followed, leaping away in frantic haste, ignoring August's call.

"What?" Diane gasped as they disappeared with all their supplies and packs.

"August, can you get them to come back?" Tonya asked.

A heavy crunch disturbed the snow behind her. A shadow fell alongside her. She froze. Faery-like, the head outlined in uneven spikes.

"They're not coming back," a deep voice growled. The same as on the beach, but now she knew it as Steinn's voice. A hand clapped on her shoulder.

Her companions turned at the voice. Steinn murmured under his breath and ice leapt up around her legs and knees, pinning her in place.

"I should have done that before," he whispered in her ear.

"What are you doing?" She futilely tried to move her legs, teetering precariously.

"Finishing what I started seventy years ago."

Cold horror swept over her.

"Let her go!" Diane shouted, grabbing her staff. Steinn stepped around Tonya, allowing her full view of his face, a sneer twisting him into something nearly unrecognizable. He flicked his hand almost contemptuously, and a block of ice slammed into Diane.

Tonya gasped as the ice rebounded off Diane, throwing her backwards to skid almost ten feet away, where she lay frighteningly still. The ring of steel brought her attention back to August and Dorian.

August had his sword drawn. Steinn shoved both hands, palms out, sending shards of ice flying towards them. August jumped in front of Dorian and Diane. He twisted, sweeping his arm up in front of himself like a shield. The ice halted in midair, trembling as it hovered.

Steinn curled his lip in derision. August's arm shook under invisible strain. Tonya tried to jerk her feet free again. She stretched her fingers towards the ice pinning her in place, but the holes in the warding had shrunk in her panic.

Dorian drew his blades, snapping them together with a sharp word. Sweat beaded August's face.

Steinn stepped forward, keeping his hands outstretched. "Give it up, boy. I'm stronger than you."

"Dorian!" August gritted.

Tonya's eyes widened in horror as Dorian settled his feet into a ready stance, prepared to run.

Steinn pressed forward another step. The ice shards bobbled in the air, inching forward. August's legs began to buckle under the strain.

August dropped his arm. The ice flew forward, targeting him before he could raise his hand again. His grunt of pain as they impacted echoed across the tundra. Tonya screamed as he crumpled to the ground, ice sticking from his chest and arms. His hand sprawled limply beside him.

Dorian sprinted forward, swinging his bladed staff. Steinn brought up his spear to parry. The crack of wood on wood shattered the horrified silence. Dorian slashed his staff in a wide sweep, pivoting to drag his foot along the ice. The earth rumbled in response. Steinn staggered a step.

Dorian swept his foot out again, knocking Diane's fallen staff towards Tonya. It skittered to a halt a bare pace away. Tonya bent to reach it, the muscles in her legs and back screaming at the tension as she tried to reach it.

Desperate, she stretched out her hand and the ice jittered in response, shoving the staff precious inches closer. Her fingers closed around the polished wood. Straightening with an effort, she began smashing the blunted end against the ice.

Sobbing breaths broke from her in time with each strike. A crack appeared and she dared risk a glance up at where Dorian and Steinn still battled. Steinn struck down with his spear. Dorian blocked the overhead blow, but Steinn kept up the pressure, bearing down with all his strength.

Then he let up. Dorian staggered under the sudden release.

Steinn swept his hand out at the ground. Dorian slid on the sudden slickness of new ice, hitting his knees. Steinn made scooping motion with his hands. Smaller shards of ice leapt from the ground. Their razor sharp points glittered in the sun before Steinn hurled them forward.

Dorian's eyes widened, and he threw himself down, twisting to place his back to the oncoming assault. His wings spread wide to protect him.

The ice impacted. A hoarse scream broke from him, pummeling its way through Tonya as the shards tore through his coat, embedding in his back, leaving scarlet streaks. A horrible tearing sound came from his left wing as the ice ripped holes in the shining membrane.

Steinn continued the onslaught until Dorian went still. His bloodied hand slipped away from where it had tried to protect the back of his head. His left wing slumped to the ground, twitching weakly. His legs and waist were buried under the piles of snow and ice kicked up by Steinn's attack.

Tonya's hands tightened around the staff as Steinn turned to her.

"It wasn't supposed to happen exactly like this," he said. "My hand was forced last night."

Her vision blurred around the corners. She swung the staff at him with a strangled cry. He caught it almost contemptuously and ripped it from her grip. It clattered to the ground.

He grabbed her hands, encasing them in cuffs of ice with a word edged in sharpness. The prison around her legs fractured with another command and she stumbled forward as he tugged her hands.

Only the wind stirred the camp site. Something in her heart twisted it harder than her strangled magic ever had at the sight of Dorian's torn and bleeding form lying limp in the snow.

Steinn whistled and his caribou trotted out from the woods. Tonya stared at it, but the other four made no appearance. She staggered under his grip as he led her to the animal.

He shoved her into the saddle and sprang up behind her. Tonya tried to twist against his unyielding bulk as if to reach out to her companions. Shock had robbed her of her will to fight.

He grabbed her arm in an iron grip and pinned her in place. She fell forward as the caribou sprang to a run and they raced north across the tundra, leaving the destruction behind them.

# Chapter 27

**D**iane came slowly back to consciousness. A groan edged past her lips. As if her body had been waiting, she began to shiver. She forced her eyes open to see the wide expanse of blue sky. Her entire right side throbbed.

*What happened?* She rolled over and caught her breath.

August sprawled on his back, slender shards of ice protruding from him. Dorian lay a few paces from him, unmoving. Tonya was nowhere to be seen.

Diane pushed to her hands and knees with a sob as memory rushed back. *Steinn. He attacked us. Why?*

The question had to wait. She forced her limbs to carry her in a crawl to August, dread mounting at what she would find. Blood oozed in patches around the wounds in his chest, stomach, and arms.

"August?"

Her voice cracked as she rested a hand on his neck. A cry of relief broke from her as she found a sluggish pulse. A second later his chest barely moved in a breath.

"Just stay there," she said stupidly as she moved to Dorian.

He lay on his side, half-buried in snow and ice. The wind gently moved his limp wing, pushing through tears in the membrane in a horrible fluttering sound. Beads of blood edged the rips. A streak of red cut across his pale cheek. Small, palm-length shards of ice embedded in his side and back.

"Dorian, wake up." She shook his shoulder. "Please?"

He stirred and jerked awake. Pain furrowed his face as he moved. She grabbed his shoulder again.

"Careful!"

"Diane." His voice slurred. "You're all right?"

"I'm fine."

He pushed himself up on his right elbow, grimacing in pain. His wing jerked with his movement. She caught the exact moment he saw the damage. He froze, turning his head a little more to see as he shifted his wing.

A shuddering breath broke from him and he turned his head, pressing his forehead against the ground. His jaw tensed and his left hand clenched in a bloody fist.

"Dorian?" she whispered shakily, placing a tentative hand on his.

He moved again, teeth clenched against another cry as he shoved to his hands and knees.

"Where's Tonya?" His voice came hoarse.

Diane glanced around. A mound of ice glistened in the sun. Her staff lay discarded near it. One deep set of caribou tracks led out across the tundra.

"Gone. Steinn must have taken her."

Dorian made a noise in the back of his throat that tore at her stomach as he tried to move again.

"Dorian, August's hurt. We have to help him first."

His head flew up. Diane shifted to reveal August behind her.

"No." Dorian breathed out in horror. She helped him crawl over to August. The forest faery still hadn't moved, only faint gasps marking him as still alive.

Dorian slumped beside him, keeping his left arm tucked up against his chest. He laid his right hand on August's chest, wincing a little as he murmured some words of his magic.

"Help me pull these out." He glanced up at her.

"Are you sure?" Diane scooted around so she knelt on the opposite side of August.

"They're not that deep." He winced as he tugged at a strap across his chest. "I kept my kit with me since he's been acting jumpy."

Diane returned to his side to help him pull it over his head and maneuver it around his uninjured wing.

"What about you?" she asked as blood dripped to the snow in tiny red stains around him.

"I can take care of him first."

But he winced as he pulled his left arm down and wrapped stiff fingers around the first shard.

Diane bit down hard on her lip as she helped remove the ice. Blood spread in wider stains. She undid the buckles of August's tunic as Dorian dug into his kit.

August jolted awake with a little gasp. Diane jerked her hands away before recovering enough to press him to the ground as he tried to move.

"Easy." Dorian rested a trembling fist against August's shoulder.

"W-what happened?" August croaked.

"It was Steinn," Dorian replied shortly, tugging a bandage free.

August tried to move, crying out before his head thudded back down to the ground.

"W-where's T-Tonya?"

"Gone." Diane's throat clenched. A disconcerting blue had begun to appear around August's lips.

Shivers began to wrack August's body. "You h-have to g-go after her."

"The caribou are gone." Diane began to rub at his arms to try to warm him up.

Dorian pushed aside August's coat and tunic to expose the wounds. His hands shook.

"Diane..."

Diane reached to help as Dorian pressed his fingers around the wounds. His lips moved soundlessly.

"D-Dorian, you're hurt..." August's hand fumbled at Dorian's sleeve.

A bit of a smile pushed past the creases around Dorian's eyes. "Can't feel too bad if you're still stating the obvious."

August tried to lift his head again, but failed. His lips turned a deeper shade of blue.

"G-go after T-Tonya." He tried to shove Dorian's hands away.

"They're long gone. We need to get you taken care of first."

"D-don't be an i-idiot."

"Says the faery who let himself get impaled on ice," Dorian muttered.

"T-to save your s-sorry wings. R-regretting it now." August somehow forced a smile past the pain etched in his face.

Dorian didn't answer, the lines around his eyes deepening.

"What?" Diane whispered.

"I've never seen this before. The ice *melted* inside his blood. It's starting to freeze him from the inside." Dorian kept his hands pressed against August. "I can't get it out. Steinn must have warded it against this."

Desperate horror filled his eyes, mirrored in Diane's heart.

"What do we do?" she asked.

Dorian hung his head and Diane knew the answer.

"No." Tears stung her eyes, freezing their way down her cheeks.

August closed his eyes, his shivering increasing in intensity.

"Just g-go," he said.

"No," Dorian snapped, sudden intensity in his voice. "There's one more thing I can do."

"N-no." August pushed at Dorian's wrists as he began to say something. "S-stop, Dorian!"

"No!" Dorian fisted his hands in August's tunic. "No one else is dying!" he shouted. "You understand? No one else is dying. I can't watch it again!" A sob broke through. "I can't. Not if I can stop it."

August grabbed his wrist in a trembling hand, understanding breaking through the pain. "All right. J-just not too m-much. T-Tonya needs you. D-Diane needs you. Not too much."

Dorian nodded.

"What are you talking about? What are you trying to do?" Diane asked.

"Giving him some of my magic to help fight it." Dorian focused on his hands.

Diane touched his arm. "Will that really help?"

Dorian turned a haunted look at her. "For a little bit. Until we can get some help." He sounded like he was trying to convince himself.

"I-idiot." But pained relief strained through August's voice.

Dorian closed his eyes. August's shivering abated and the blue receded a little from his face. Together, Diane and Dorian wrapped bandages around his chest and arms.

"We need to keep him warm." Dorian buckled August's coat back on.

"With what?" Diane asked, helplessness filling her until she looked past Dorian. Hope flickered.

"Look!" she whispered.

Dorian turned with a sharp gasp. A caribou cautiously approached, horns lowered. As it got closer, a strangled laugh came from Dorian.

"I never thought I'd be so happy to see that animal again."

*Thank you, Creator!* Diane recognized the bright green leathers of Arvo's tack.

Dorian pushed to his feet, listing to the side with each step toward the caribou. His wings flapped behind him. Arvo grunted and shuffled back a step.

August reached a hand out toward Arvo. The caribou came forward and let Dorian take the bridle and lead it over. His knee buckled and Diane sprang up.

"Sit down. We're taking care of you next."

Somewhat to her surprise, Dorian didn't argue. He half-collapsed back into the snow. Diane nearly cried in relief when she saw the green square of the tent attached to the saddle along with the blankets.

She spread out the canvas and managed to help August move himself over to lie on the tent. She tucked a blanket over him, then folded the rest of the tent around him.

"I'll get a fire going in a minute," she promised. He gave a ghost of a smile before his eyes slid closed.

Dorian undid his coat. He smothered a groan, back arching in agony as he tried to fold up his wings.

"It's all right!"

Diane rushed to his side, even though it was anything but all right. She finished undoing the buckles and tugged his shirt up, managing to expose all the cuts on his back and side without taking the coat off. She inhaled deep through her nose, trying to keep her nerves steady for a few more minutes.

He touched her arm. "I'll walk you through it."

She jerked a nod, pulling his kit toward her. He gave short instructions, flinching with every touch.

"The ice that hit you, did it do the same as with August?" She tied the last bandage off with trembling fingers.

Dorian shook his head. He pulled his shirt back down over the bandages and buckled his coat again.

"What about your wing?" She brushed the top edge of the wounded wing. An unexpected softness met her fingers before it jerked away.

"We can't do anything for it right now. I don't—don't have the right supplies."

He bowed his head again. Diane grabbed his spare blanket and tucked it around him as best she could, wings and all.

"All right. What should we do?" She sat back on her heels.

He looked up at her.

"You said you could help August until help came. We're the only ones out here. Help isn't coming. What are we going to do?"

Diane hated the cold logic that came from her mouth. All she wanted to do was curl up and cry.

"We could go back," Dorian eventually said.

"How? We have one caribou. Who knows where the others went? It'll take us several days to get back through the hills to Konungburg with both of you wounded. And what about Tonya?"

Dorian slammed his fist against his thigh. Diane didn't flinch.

"K-keep going." August's voice came barely audible. "I'll slow you d-down. G-go after her."

"We're not leaving you," Dorian growled.

"He's right, August," Diane said, her voice nearly the same aggressive pitch as Dorian's. She looked north, following the tracks.

"What if we keep going forward? It looks like they headed north. Maybe we can catch up. The Lights are supposed to break the warding on Tonya, right? What if they do the same for August?"

Dorian met her gaze again, a bit of hope stirring in his green eyes. "It's a chance."

"I'm just not sure how we're all supposed to get there with just one caribou." The words slipped from Diane.

A nervous huff came from Arvo. The caribou looked at something past Dorian and Diane, and he shuffled away. Only a quiet word from August stayed him.

*What now?* Diane exchanged the same look with Dorian. Tension knotted her shoulders. A heavy crunch sounded behind them. She reached for her staff, whirling on her knees and freezing.

The polar bear had returned.

It stood a few paces away, head up and ears pricked as it studied them. Diane swallowed hard. It stood nearly as tall as Arvo. The giant paws could take her apart with one swipe. It grumbled deep in its throat, coming forward a step. Diane locked away a whimper of fear, raising her staff.

"D-Diane," August's quiet voice sounded. "It's all right. That's not a bear."

# Chapter 28

"That ice must have hit you harder than I thought," Dorian growled.

Diane didn't take her eyes from the bear. It stared back at them, nose twitching.

"It's not—" August huffed. "Just help me sit up."

Diane slid backwards, laying down her staff and slowly exchanging it for Ralf's dagger. She got to August's side where Dorian joined her, his heavy hunting knife in his hand.

The bear came forward another step. It huffed and snorted, shaking its head back and forth. Diane slid a hand under August's shoulders and pulled him upright with a grunt.

"You're heavier than you look."

"And here I was hoping that you'd offer to carry me." The tease in August's voice sounded so normal that tears threatened Diane's eyes.

*Focus!* She kept her arm around him to prop him up, the other hand gripping her knife. August fumbled his arm free and beckoned to the bear.

"You're sure that's not a bear?" Dorian muttered.

"T-trust me."

Diane and Dorian exchanged a tense glance over August's head, but held still as the bear approached. It halted a few paces away, chuffing deep in its throat. August made a reply. It shuffled its feet, mouthing a series of grunts and growls.

August huffed back.

The bear swung its head back and forth, digging its claws into the ice. Diane caught her breath.

"Trust me," August said again and reached out a trembling hand. The bear came forward and touched his hand with its nose. August hunched forward as he sank his hand into the thick fur around its neck.

He closed his eyes, mumbling a little around stiff lips. He broke off in the middle of several sentences, shaking his head. The bear waited patiently, not moving and keeping dark grey eyes fixed on August. It finally growled a little. August nodded.

"T-that could w-work," he agreed with no one in particular.

He started speaking again, his voice rising in command. Then his hand fell away and he slumped to the side. Dorian cursed and barely caught him before he could tip into the snow. The bear snorted and leapt back a pace.

Diane helped lay August back down. The blue had deepened around his lips again, and tremors wracked his body.

"What in all the earth were you thinking?" Dorian snapped, pressing a hand on August's forehead and giving him more magic, judging from the way August relaxed and new paleness emerged in Dorian's face.

*As reckless a healer as a warrior.* Ilka's words came back to Diane. She shook her head, but couldn't bring herself to be upset.

The bear shook its head as if to clear its ears of water. It growled deep and gave great chuffing coughs. It flung itself side to side, paws swerving on the ice as if trying to shake free of something. A roar broke from it, sending Diane and Dorian reaching for their knives again.

The bear turned and padded back over.

"Thank you," a gruff voice said.

"Creator's Hands!" Diane yelped. "It's talking!"

Dorian stared wide-eyed at the bear. "August...?"

A small groan came from August as he tried to move and gave up. "That's a f-faery trapped inside a b-bear's pelt."

"Yes." The bear growled again as if trying to clear its throat. "My name is Freyr."

Diane's jaw dropped. *That's not possible — Maybe I didn't hear right?* She stiffly turned to Dorian who looked as if he'd seen a ghost.

"Phoenix fire..." he whispered. *"That's...?"*

August managed to get up on an elbow, watching the bear as if he'd been expecting this all along.

"I think he might be able to help us."

"Lie down." Dorian shoved August's shoulder without preamble. "Start talking." He jabbed a finger at the bear.

August tugged the blankets around himself with a grumble. The bear — Freyr — sat back on his haunches.

"You first," he countered. "I've been wandering the wilds for a long time, not quite remembering who I am. Until I saw you yesterday and caught my brother's scent, and — something else."

Diane hovered on the edge of a breath, not sure how to say that the something else was likely his daughter. The same uncertainty reflected in Dorian's eyes. He showed no sign of starting to talk. She licked her lips.

"We've been traveling for almost two weeks now. Since the ice appeared."

Freyr grunted. "That's when I first started to come back to myself."

Diane shook her head slightly. She'd puzzle that out later. "There was a young faery with us. She was the cause of the ice."

Freyr shifted, the bulky ridges of his body going still. He stared at her with unnerving intensity.

"She'd been living in the ocean. But something attacked her and released her ice magic. There was nothing to be done among my people, or among the land faeries, so we journeyed here. King Birgir suggested that we continue to journey north to seek the Creator's Lights. They're supposed to undo the warding on her and let her access her ice magic again and somehow undo all this."

Diane stumbled over the last bit of the explanation as Freyr came closer, pressing his narrow snout into her face.

"What is this faery's name?" he growled.

"Tonya."

Freyr backed away, whipping around to face north, head high as he stared at the single line of tracks.

"Tonya."

Another roar burst from him that sent Diane reaching for her knife again. But Freyr turned.

"What happened here?"

Dorian told the quick tale of the ambush, as Diane had been unconscious for most of it.

"Your turn." Dorian wrapped a blanket around himself, wincing as the cloth brushed his injured wing.

Freyr sat back on his haunches. "From your story, I assume you know who I am?"

Diane nodded. "Tonya's father. Everyone thinks you're dead."

He snuffled. "Not dead. Maybe worse. I learned a short time after fleeing the north that it was my own brother who was after Thalia and me. My choice to marry her caused some of the nobles to shun our family. Steinn felt the loss of standing keenly, and argued with me. I wouldn't listen." His head dipped.

"After I left her and the babe — Tonya" — his gruff bear's voice softened somehow over the names — "I turned back to confront him. Hoping that maybe since we'd left, he would leave us be. But he ambushed me not long after I crossed back over the Strait. He had several other faeries with him. He trapped me in this form and placed a warding over me — to make me forget everything and become a bear."

He ground his claws into the ice. "There was one thing he still gave me. A sense of searching. Looking for someone. But I never remember. The only thing I remember is him when he sometimes comes to find me. Until a few weeks ago."

He lifted his head to sniff at the wind again. It ruffled the white fur around his shoulders, and his skin twitched briefly.

"The ice came and brought a whisper of something familiar. It carried a hint of my magic with it and that made me start remembering. The warding he placed on me keeps me away from any other ice faery, but when I sensed him yesterday, I followed."

"Y-you were in the valley," August said. "I caught a sense of you there. And last night. An animal that wasn't quite right."

Freyr dipped his head. "You have good instincts. Yes, I followed. And then heard the whisper of the almost familiar magic again not long ago."

Diane rubbed at her eyes. "Of all the things to happen on this trip, I didn't really expect to be talking to a bear who's really a faery and the not-dead father of my friend."

Freyr nudged her knee with his damp nose. "You seem to be handling it all well."

Diane's chuckle came out a little strangled. "Only because I think I'm still in shock from everything." She glanced to Dorian. "What now?"

Dorian looked north as if he could see Tonya there in the distance.

"Freyr, you know Steinn better than we do. He's been after Tonya for years. What would he do to her?" His voice hardened over each word, until they cut at Diane.

A growl rumbled in Freyr's chest. "We warded her against any attack. You said the ice was the result of something attacking her?"

Diane nodded. *Probably Steinn, though we have no way to prove that other than asking him. And I don't think he's going to just let us walk up and do that.*

"Then he'll have to get rid of the warding to do anything to her. He didn't kill me, so I don't think he'll kill her. He'd be risking the crevasses if he did. I wager he'll try to take her to the Lights to break the warding before he does anything."

August grunted again as he moved. "So that gives us until tonight to find them."

"Just where do you think you're going?" Diane leveled a glare at August.

"Were we not just talking about heading north to find the Lights ourselves?" He glared back, his eyes dark circles in his pale face. "Dorian. We have to go after her."

The way he said it sounded like Dorian was the one who needed to go after her.

Dorian shook himself, looking back at them. "Can we make it in time?"

Defeat warred with pain in his face. Diane reached out and squeezed his arm.

"We're going to do our best." *Because she still has something to tell you.*

"You have the caribou and me." Freyr pushed up to his paws. "I can follow their scent."

"Freyr." A thought struck Diane. "Why can't you change back now?"

Freyr swung his head to look at her. "Steinn's spell is a strong one. He's the only one who can undo it..." He paused, his snout wrinkling as his nose twitched. "No, that's not right..." He shook himself, chuffing. "He can undo it."

But he didn't sound certain.

Diane reached out a tentative hand to rest on his shoulder.

"I'm sorry. We'll find a way to undo your spell, too." A frantic sort of laugh burst from her lips. "We'll just add it to the list."

Freyr nudged her arm with his nose again. "I'm sorry. I think all this is my fault."

Diane shook her head. "No, Steinn did this."

"He felt panicked last night. If you could sense what I was, what's to stop you from telling everyone? Then they'd find out what he'd done."

"He might have done this anyway before we got to the Lights," Diane said. "Obviously he didn't want to help Tonya either."

"Still." Freyr lowered his head to touch her arm. "I'm sorry."

She gingerly rested a hand in his thick fur. "Thank you for helping us."

"All right." Dorian moved his blanket away with a grimace, his wounded wing jerking involuntarily before returning to its limp position. "How do we do this?"

Diane bit her lip, assessing, making a mental list of resources. This was something she was good at. Spreading thin resources out, making sure things were provided for in the best manner.

"Arvo can carry two of us. August, do you think you can ride? I don't know that either of us will be able to help very much."

In answer, August pushed back his blankets and sat up, hunching over with the effort.

"Dorian, you and I can ride Arvo. Freyr, we have some rope. Do you mind if we rig up a harness on you to help August?"

Freyr tipped his head back and forth. Diane pushed to her feet. She retrieved the rope from Arvo's saddle. Dorian took over, cutting several lengths and tying them together around Freyr's broad chest and behind his forelegs to loop over his back. Freyr sank down to his stomach to help August struggle onto his back.

Diane tied a blanket around August as Dorian looped rope around the faery to keep him on Freyr. Diane rolled up the tent and Dorian's cast-off blanket and shoved them back among the packs.

Arvo snuffled at Dorian. The faery leaned against the caribou's shoulder, closing his eyes for a moment.

"Are you going to be all right?" Diane whispered, gently touching his arm.

Dorian opened his eyes, but his smile was nowhere to be found around them. "Ask me when we get to the Lights and get her back."

Diane nodded, pulling him into a gentle hug, careful not to stir his injured wing. He tapped her shoulder with his good hand.

"Let's go," he said.

She pulled away, and mounted, extending a hand down to help him clamber on behind her. Arvo adjusted his hooves against the ground, compensating for the extra weight. August sat hunched over on Freyr's back as the bear began to walk. Diane tightened the reins and kicked Arvo up into a trot, pulling him alongside the solitary line of tracks.

Freyr loped along in their wake, August leaning down on his back. Diane refused to look at the sun to see how much time had passed since Steinn had first attacked. She focused instead on the mountains, willing them to come closer with each jolting step.

*

They kept the same steady pace of trotting and then walking. The hours passed in silence. Diane alternated between staring at the tracks and staring at August, who leaned further and further down on Freyr's neck as the day progressed.

Finally, Freyr padded to a stop where the tundra began to shift up into hills, rocks strewing themselves like dark sentinels in the snow. Diane reined in, fear jolting through her as August barely stirred. Dorian slid down from behind her, grunting as his boots hit the snow.

"He can't go on," Freyr said, lowering himself to the ground. Diane dismounted and followed Dorian to their side.

August lifted his chin, a shudder wracking his body. Diane clapped a gloved hand across her mouth. The blue had deepened around his lips, but an eerie paleness had spread across his cheeks—frost swirling across his skin like a newly frozen lake. Tiny flakes of white touched the irises of his hazel eyes.

Dorian cursed, ripping open August's coat and tunic to pull at the bandages.

"A-at least o-offer to c-court m-me first." August managed a smile through chattering teeth.

"Why didn't you say anything?" Dorian demanded.

"I-it's n-not going to m-make a d-difference."

"Shut up." The look Dorian gave him could have melted an ice floe. His breath left him in an audible *whoosh*. He staggered and Diane leapt forward to grip his elbow to steady him.

August's face regained a little color and the blue receded. He grabbed Dorian's shoulder.

"No more!" His growl matched Freyr's for intensity.

Dorian swayed under their hold. "Can you keep going?"

August jerked a nod and released him. Diane helped Dorian stumble back to Arvo and mount, biting her lip under the strain of hauling him back up behind her. He turned his face away from her searching gaze, but not before she saw the faint blue outlining the cut on his cheek.

"Let's go," he said.

Diane checked the position of the sun where it hung low in the sky. "How much farther, Freyr?"

Freyr brushed the tracks with his nose.

"We're getting close." His voice rumbled deeper with eagerness.

That was all Diane needed to hear. She urged Arvo on, Dorian clinging a little tighter to her belt this time. "Close" turned into another hour's ride. The rocks clumped larger together and the hills rose higher. The deep purple and greens of the mountains distinguished themselves as trees and rock formations tumbling down from the soaring heights to strew across the hills.

Finally Freyr stopped, paws poised mid-step. He turned his nose to the wind. He swung his head back and forth.

"Here."

The tracks curved around a grove of trees and rocks. A flash of movement in the trees revealed Steinn's caribou grazing on the low pine branches. The wind shifted towards them, masking their scent, but still Diane held her breath. The darkness of a cave opening loomed beyond the caribou. Nothing stirred.

*Where is Tonya?*

# Chapter 29

The rhythmic stride of Steinn's caribou over the bleak tundra finally broke through Tonya's shock. She twisted against Steinn, trying to turn to look at the ruin behind her. He grabbed her shoulder and forced her back in place.

Wind tore hair from her braid to whip across her cheeks and mingle with the tears. It had been Steinn all along.

Rage at having been deceived and attacked flared through her. Magic pressed up against the warding, filled with the fury of the ocean and the mountains. She jammed an elbow back into his stomach.

Steinn's breath left him in a rush and he released his grip for a precious moment. Tonya twisted again, trying to pitch herself off the side of the galloping caribou, ready to worry about consequences later. Steinn clicked and the caribou slid to a stop. Tonya barely stopped herself from striking the horns as she was thrown forward.

Steinn grabbed her braid and wrenched her head back to look at him from the edge of her vision.

"Stop. I found a way to skirt some of your warding. I will hurt you if you try again." His voice came colder than the wind before a blizzard.

She swallowed hard against the pressure in her throat.

"Did you kill them?" She barely recognized her voice, tight and angry.

"No. But the ice and cold will finish them off."

Moisture stung her eyes. "Why?"

He shoved her head forward and jabbed his heels into the caribou's sides again. Tonya grabbed on to the front of the saddle with her ice-bound hands again as the caribou leaped back into its ground-eating gallop.

No answer came from Steinn. Only occasional jolts of magic that slithered its way around the warding to remind her not to fight.

Steinn didn't stop for the midday meal, only to rest the caribou. No words passed between them, only glares on the rare opportunity when they came face to face. Her stomach growled in hunger as they galloped into the beginnings of hills, but still Steinn did not stop.

Fatigue weighed on Tonya by the time they entered a small copse of trees that shielded the open mouth of a cave. Even her anger had died to a flicker. Steinn dismounted and dragged her from the saddle. Her legs buckled as she hit the ice.

He cursed at her and pulled her upright, halfway dragging her behind him into the cave. She pitched to her knees on the cold, stony ground. She glanced around as Steinn stepped away to light a lantern that had been left by the entrance.

It wasn't a large cave, maybe twenty paces from the door to the back of the cave. The southern side opened into a rough-hewn corridor that wound somewhere deeper.

When she turned, her breath froze in her chest. The north wall of the cave was covered in ice.

Suspended in the ice was a figure.

Tonya pushed up higher on her knees, straining to see in the afternoon light that trickled into the cave.

Steinn stepped closer, lifting the lantern to better illuminate the ice wall.

It was a woman. One hand lifted up in front of her, palm outward. The ice bubbled around her fingers. Her other arm stretched out behind her, framed in a similar distortion of ice. Long blonde hair flung about her head. But Tonya locked on to her face. Slender features, sea-green eyes, a look of fear and determination frozen in place.

*It can't be...*

A dress of blues and blacks, edged in polar bears and wild berries stitched in deep red, clung and fluttered about her in the same frozen wind that tangled her hair. The lighter blue of a kelp-woven bodice overlaid the dress.

"Meet your mother," Steinn spat.

A sob of disbelief broke from Tonya. She lurched to her feet, pressing one hand against the ice. The woman's eyes stared past her, unseeing. *Mother...*

Her ice and ocean magic twitched through her fingers and she desperately tried to find the right words to whisper to the prison, to break it open. Steinn yanked her back.

"You don't have the strength to break it," he sneered, his hot breath on her ear somehow making her shiver.

"Is she even still alive?" She forced the question around the tightness of a hundred wild currents smothering her chest.

"She is."

Tonya jerked a breath.

"But she's never getting out."

"Why?" Tears threatened to overflow.

"Because she's more useful right here. Don't worry. As soon as we break that warding around you, you get to keep her company for the rest of your life."

He shoved her back down to the ground. The ice chains unlocked from her wrists, but before she could move, they reformed around her feet, anchoring themselves to the floor.

Steinn headed for the entrance.

"Wait!" Tonya cried. He pivoted. "Why couldn't you have just left them alone? What did she ever do to you?"

"Because he fell in love with her, that's why!" He threw his arms wide, jerking a step back to her. "An *ocean* faery. He sullied the blood of the north with her. With you! It's disgusting. Even if he wasn't the son of one of the oldest noble families in Konungburg, he should have married better. Kept the strength of the north where it belongs."

She squeezed her eyes shut, forcing the tears to run down her cheeks. The words cut deeper than ice shards or shark teeth.

"He wouldn't see reason. Wouldn't see that he could alienate us from our own people, had already begun to, by his actions. Bring our house to its knees. No one else would stop him. So I had to." A frantic note came into his voice. "I was too late to prevent you, but I swore to put you away just like your mother. So the world would never know the shame of you. If not for that warding, I would have found you years ago! Lucky for me, I finally found a creature willing to talk about the abomination that lived under the waters."

The hate-filled words threatened to crush her under their weight. She covered her mouth with her hands, refusing to allow him the satisfaction of actually hearing her cries.

He turned on his heel and left the cave.

Tonya scooted back against the wall, drawing her knees up to her chest, burying her face in her arms as her body jerked with helpless sobs.

By the time Steinn returned, her tears had dried to salty tracks on her cheeks. She stayed curled up, half-afraid to meet his gaze and see the hate openly shining in his eyes. He'd pretended, lifted her hopes, all the while planning *this*.

Anger warred with the shame and humiliation his words had wrought on her. And a little bit of resignation that she was truly nothing more than a disgrace, a blight among faeries.

Something that shouldn't exist.

Between the rushes of emotion, she stretched and curled her fingers, trying to summon the bits of magic that stayed stubbornly out of reach. Her stomach growled again.

Steinn flung a bag down at her side. "Eat. We'll leave in a few hours for the Lights."

She waited until his boots retreated through the hallway in the southern wall before uncurling her stiff joints. Drawing dried seal jerky and soft biscuits out, she tried to settle more comfortably against the wall, but the ice chains made adjusting her feet difficult.

Tonya tipped her head back and studied her mother again as she slowly ate. Steinn had left the lantern on the floor by the ice wall, its light still burning brightly.

*What were you like? What was he like? What was so special about him and this place that you decided to leave the ocean behind and have me?*

She rubbed at tired eyes to prevent another outpouring of tears. *What would you have done in my place? Kostis said you were a powerful wave dancer, but you are so far from the waves here. What chance do I have?*

A sigh broke from her, along with a few rogue tears. The light cast long shadows through the door. Sunset would come soon and then they'd leave.

One shadow moved, shifting and dancing across the floor. Tonya held her breath. A figure slumped against the entrance. Broad shoulders, quiet edges, light green eyes.

"Dorian?" she whispered in disbelief.

"Tonya!" He lurched forward, crashing to one knee beside her.

Without thinking or caring, she flung her arms around him, burying her head against his shoulder. He held her just as tightly.

"You're alive," she mumbled against his coat.

"So are you." His voice shook a little.

She fisted her hands tighter in his coat. This time he flinched.

"Not so tight," he said almost apologetically. She pulled back, keeping a grip on his arms as she swept a glance over him. Blood stained around rips in his jacket. His wings hung awkwardly behind him.

She reached a tentative hand over his shoulder to touch the edge of the torn wing. He shifted just out of her reach.

"Dorian…" She brought a hand to his cheek, not even caring about her fears and doubts regarding him. Blue rimmed a cut on his other cheek. She swallowed tightly. "What about the others?"

"Diane is fine. The warding August's parents put on her protected her. August is…" He reached up to squeeze her hand with weak fingers. "He's not doing well. We need to get him to the Lights."

Tonya took a deep breath. "We need to get out of here. My uncle is through there." She jerked her chin at the passage. "I think he might be asleep. We just need to get these undone."

She tugged at the ice chains. They rattled against the ground with light *clinks*.

"Tonya..." Dorian's horrified whisper brought her head back up. He stared past her at the ice wall and the faery trapped within.

"That's — that's my mother..." She yanked at the chain again.

"Your..." He jerked a breath. "Tonya, we found — "

A faint scuff was the only warning she had before Steinn kicked Dorian in the back and knocked him to the ground. Dorian curled against the ground, face twisted in agony.

"Dorian!" Tonya tried to get to him, but Steinn kicked her away. She gasped for breath, forcing her arms to push herself up to her knees.

"You're persistent, I'll give you that." Steinn curled his lip in a sneer. He raised his hand, light forming around his fingers in colorful swirls.

"Don't!" Tonya grabbed at her uncle's arm. Steinn jerked his hand away, cold anger in his eyes.

"You would try to save his life? For what? To be with him?" Disbelief filled his voice. "I've seen the way you look at him. Half-breed yourself, you'd sully your blood further? Spend your days digging in the dirt?"

He stomped the heel of his boot on Dorian's injured wing.

Dorian's back arched with his cry. Tonya flung herself against Steinn with a shout. It knocked him off balance enough to let Dorian drag himself away.

"There's nothing wrong with her," Dorian gritted, getting an arm underneath him.

Steinn kicked him back down. "What would you know about it?"

He grabbed Tonya's upper arm, hauling her awkwardly to her feet. The ice melted with a command from Steinn. She stumbled after him as he strode towards the door, overcoming all of her efforts to pull back toward Dorian.

They broke into the early twilight.

"Tonya!" Diane stood outside, staff held in front of her. August slumped against a rock, disconcerting paleness covering his cheeks. *Frost?*

A shadow moved behind Diane.

Tonya reflexively jerked against Steinn as she recognized it as a bear. She opened her mouth to warn Diane, but a voice spoke first.

"Steinn!"

Tonya stared, trying to track the owner of the growling voice.

"So they found you, then?" Steinn sneered at the bear.

Tonya stopped struggling in her shock. *It's talking!*

"They gave me back my memories and my voice. What have you done?" The bear lunged at Steinn.

Steinn threw up a hand and a blast of light hit the bear, sending it skidding backwards on wide paws.

"What needed to be done, Freyr!" he yelled. "It should never have been allowed to go this far." He jerked Tonya's arm. "But you always thought you were better than anyone."

Tonya jolted, her limbs losing their stiffness. *Freyr?*

She stumbled in the snow as Steinn kept retreating. His caribou snorted.

"Give it up," he said to Diane, nodding at August. "That one won't last much longer. And there's nothing Freyr can do to stop me."

Another blast of light prevented the bear from lunging again. Steinn slung her over the caribou's withers like a sack of provisions and sprang into the saddle.

"I'll deal with you all when I get back."

He flicked his hand and ice sprang at Diane. Tonya cried out as if that would stop it. The ice hit Diane and puffed into harmless powder. Diane's wide eyes met Tonya's, then she charged Steinn.

He simply wheeled the caribou and galloped off, Tonya watching again as her friends vanished in the distance.

# Chapter 30

**D**iane stared helplessly after the snow cloud kicked up in the caribou's wake as Steinn once again escaped with Tonya. Freyr ran a few steps and loosed a thundering roar. A faint sound behind her turned her away from their failure.

August slumped against the rocks, arms wrapped across his stomach, his chest barely rising and falling.

"August…" Dorian staggered over to his side, hitting his knee with a heavy thud. Diane swallowed hard and crouched by the faeries.

The curling frost had spread over August's cheeks and now dusted bits of his hair. Another little wheezing gasp edged past his blue lips.

"We have to get him to the Lights," Dorian said desperately. But fatigue bowed his body and blue edged the cut along his cheek and had begun to touch his lips.

"Dorian, are you affected by the ice, too?" Diane asked quietly.

Dorian looked at her for a long moment, defeat in his eyes. "I've been trying to fight it, but can't much longer *and* give my magic to August..."

Diane took a steadying breath. She gripped her staff in a white-knuckled grip.

"All right then, let's get moving." She rested a hand on August's shoulder.

He shook his head slightly. "No, I c-can't...k-keep g-going. I-I can't."

Freyr's bulk loomed over them.

"He's right," he said softly. "I remember. If I were in my human form I'd be able to help, but I cannot access my magic like this."

Diane latched on to that. "How? Dorian couldn't draw the ice out and he's a healer."

A bit of hope gleamed in Dorian's eyes and they both looked desperately to Freyr.

"You don't know ice magic. And I know my brother's spells. He's strongest with animals, but I taught him some ice casting. I could undo it."

"How do we break your spell? Would touching the Lights undo it?"

"There's a way..." Freyr lowered his head, snuffling like he was searching for something. "Yes, it would, but..." His body stiffened and his head whipped towards the cave.

Diane lurched after him as he charged the cave mouth. She stumbled into his bulk just instead the entrance.

"Thalia..."

She followed his stare and her mouth dropped open in shock.

"Thalia!" Freyr lunged forward, rearing up on hind paws to drag his claws across the ice. The woman didn't move. The ice barely scratched.

"No!" Freyr shoved his entire weight against the ice wall, claws skidding across the ice.

"Freyr!" Diane reached a hand out into his fur. It calmed him enough to start him pacing instead of shoving at the unmoving ice.

Diane fought a shiver.

"This is your wife?" she whispered. *Tonya's mother? Did she know?*

An agonized groan came from Freyr.

"What has he done?" He bowed his head and pressed it against the ice.

Diane rested her hand in his fur. "I'm sorry. We'll find a way to free her."

"How?" His growl pitched deeper. "None of you have the magic to undo this ice. Her touch is the only thing that can return me to my faery form. You have enough to worry about right now. And Steinn's still out there with my daughter..."

His growl broke over the last word.

Diane tried to think. She automatically reached for paper and charcoal. When none came readily to hand, she half-turned as if expecting to see Ralf there with charcoal already extended. She bit back a sigh.

"Stay here," she told Freyr, but he looked in no hurry to leave.

She went back out where Dorian still sat beside August. They looked even paler in the fading light.

"Let's get him inside. Can you help?" she asked Dorian.

The faery struggled to his feet, biting his lip as he nodded.

"Come on, August. We're just going a few feet and then you can rest." Diane managed to control the tremble in her voice. August's eyes cracked open a fraction and a shadow of his smile appeared.

They took him under his arms and pulled him to his feet. Diane's knees almost buckled under his weight, but she staggered forward step after step until they laid him down at the back of the cave. She went back out to retrieve the tent canvas and blankets from Arvo who still waited patiently.

She wrapped the insulating canvas around August and covered it all with a blanket. The other blanket went back to Dorian. Several more trips outside the cave yielded enough firewood to last a few hours.

"All right, here's what we're going to do." Diane stacked the last of the wood. "Freyr and I are going after Tonya. We'll try to get him into the Lights to break his spell. We'll need his help to deal with Steinn. Then we come back here and he can draw the ice out of both of you. We can free Thalia, and then go home."

Determination that she didn't quite feel filled her words. The faeries and Freyr looked back at her.

"All right," Dorian said quietly. He tipped a glance at August. "Just hurry."

Diane nodded, digging her nails into her palms to keep from crying.

"D-Diane?" August managed to reach out a hand to her. She felt the icy cold of his fingers even through their gloves as she took his hand. "I-if I d-don't make it, p-please tell my parents t-that I-I'll find Eryk, and we'll g-go together."

Dorian bowed his head, pressing the heel of his hand against his forehead. Diane squeezed August's hand.

"You'll make it, August. We won't be gone long."

His cheek twitched in something like a smile before a grimace overcame it. Several shudders wracked his body before he stilled and cracked his eyes open again.

"P-please?"

She leaned close to him, gently tucking his hand back under the blankets. "I will," she said softly. "But hold on for me, all right?"

He gave a small nod and let his eyes slide closed. Her heart galloped in panic as it took a second longer for him to jerk another breath. Diane pressed Dorian's arm, bringing his pained gaze back up.

"We'll be back as soon as we can."

"What if the Lights don't come tonight? What if you don't make it in time? What if—?"

"Dorian!" She shook his arm gently. "It's going to work."

She had to believe it because there was nothing else to do.

"Take Arvo," Dorian said. "You might need him on the way back."

Diane swallowed. *Because they won't need him here.*

"All right." She glanced up at the bear. "Ready, Freyr?"

He lowered his head, nudging both August and Dorian before padding from the cave. Diane followed after one more last look behind.

"Do you think the Lights will come tonight?" She undid Arvo's tether.

Freyr lifted his nose to the sky. "Yes. The air always feels different in the hours before, telling you when they'll come."

Arvo chuffed as if he didn't believe it.

*It does sound a little far-fetched.* Diane swung into the saddle. She rubbed Arvo's shoulder in apology for another run. He shook his antlers and snorted, looking at the cave and then north.

"They're not coming, boy," she murmured. "It's just the three of us now."

He gave a louder chuffing honk of protest, but responded to her tug of the reins. He didn't even shy away when Freyr came close. Diane set her jaw and jabbed her heels into his side. She wasn't going to stop until they found Tonya and the Lights.

*

This time Tonya fought back.

Even through the lashes of magic from Steinn. Her struggles made the caribou stumble more than once, and Steinn's face grow darker in anger. Darkness overtook the last vestiges of the tundra, covering the mountains in a protective shroud.

The stars shone brighter and the moon reflected its brilliance off the snow. Ice sparkled back in more mesmerizing glimmers under the moon's touch, small eddies kicking up in a breeze like the magic was trying to escape to the sky itself.

Finally, the caribou slid to a halt in a broad open circle between two out-flung roots of a towering peak where the flat tundra ran straight into the mountainside cliff. Steinn shoved her off the caribou, ice leaping up to lock around her before she had a chance to move.

He thumped to the ground, sending the caribou skittering back a few steps with a flick of his fingers. He paced a wide circle around her, ignoring her glares as he turned his gaze up to the sky. Waiting.

After a long moment, she caught a shift in the air. Something static like lightning about to strike. Something sharp like the frigid bite of a storm in the dead of winter.

Something *magic*.

A green ribbon darted across the sky. She caught her breath. She'd almost hoped the Lights wouldn't come, but they had.

Her magic leapt up against her chest, straining towards the Lights. The warding locked it back down.

Another streak of light shone, disappearing before she could blink. Brilliant violet darted past, touching the mountainside and dancing among the trees in an eerie display before it leapt back into the sky. Green and yellow together brushed against the tundra.

They kept coming, longer and brighter, dancing through the sky or skimming low into the mountains and hills. Tonya held her breath, her magic pressing hard against her skin, trying to escape to join the Lights in their dance.

Then brilliant pinks and purples and greens surrounded her, swirling about her in a maelstrom of magic. Tingling ran the length of her arms. Her hair loosed from her braid to whip about her head, stretching toward the lights.

A thin tendril of green snaked out to brush her right arm. She tried to touch it, but it melted away from her fingertips, returning as soon as her hand stilled. Another slender ribbon of purple wrapped around her left arm, leaving behind a trail of warmth.

She flinched as the heat began to increase, burning at her arms and legs and waist where the lights now encircled her. With every new shimmer of light, she grew hotter and hotter, until it felt like her skin would melt away.

Tonya stumbled away with a scream, ice no longer holding her captive on the ground. The Lights followed, though dimming in intensity. They pressed close around her, seeping under her skin, the colors leaking out of her fingertips. She felt a shift inside of her. Like something snapped, the edges of herself whipping away to let something through.

*Magic.*

The roar of an ocean storm, the gentle sigh of waves, the stillness of tide pools.

The rage of a blizzard, the chill of ice, the quiet after a snowfall.

It all rushed in her and through her at the same time.

She fell to her hands and knees, gasping for breath.

"Tonya!"

The Lights fled, revealing Diane and the bear racing toward her. The crackle of magic disturbed the air. Steinn launched a beam of light at them. Diane threw herself from Arvo and lunged in front of the bear. The light refracted off her and into the sky.

Tonya clenched her fingers in the ice. Cracks appeared in response. The individual particles begged to be returned to their liquid state, to dance in waves. The ice clamored to be formed under her careful hands.

A shudder cut through her. It was like two loud voices shouting for her attention, neither willing to give way until she called forth blizzards and monsoons, currents and ice shards.

Another cry came from Diane. She stood hunched over in front of the bear, one arm out-flung as if to hold off Steinn's steady attack. Rage filled Tonya and this time her magic leapt unhindered to her touch. She didn't know what she wanted, just to stop Steinn.

She pushed to her feet, flinging her hands toward him with a scream. Ice and snow swept up in the wave of power that came from her, whirling and spinning at Steinn and knocking him back.

Tonya ripped her hands apart, halting the storm. She stalked forward as Steinn scrambled to his feet. He pushed his hand to her, palm out. Her feet slipped on a new sheet of ice.

She stomped her foot hard, and it shattered.

Steinn backed away. He lunged a step forward, shoving his hands out again. The gust of wind and magic pummeled into her chest, knocking her down to the ground. She shook off another attempt to bind her with ice and stood.

She spun in a circle, dragging the toe of her boot along the ice like she'd seen Dorian do. Her magic flooded up to her hands, forcing her fingers wide. She threw it at Steinn as she faced him again. A rumble cracked the ice beneath his feet, catching him off guard when her green and violet lights hit him in the chest.

Steinn got to his feet slowly, backing away for each step she now took forward. The bear leapt closer, coming up on his left side. Its teeth were bared to their full extent, ears back, and a thundering growl reverberating across the mountains and tundra. Diane crept to his right with her staff raised, a look of determination on her face.

Steinn looked between all three of them and backed away again. He whistled and his caribou ran to him. It didn't stop as Steinn grabbed the harness and hauled himself up into the saddle to gallop away.

Tonya's knees buckled in relief. She tipped a glance up at the sky where the Lights still formed and danced. *Thank you.*

"Freyr, quick!" Diane's shout brought her back.

The bear lunged at the nearest light that sent its magic into the ground. It retreated into the air before he could reach it. Then, as if that was the signal, the lights flickered one more time in the sky and then vanished.

Diane cast a stricken look at the bear. Tonya collapsed again to her hands and knees, exhaustion mixing with elation and freedom of her magic, even as it still fought inside her.

*I don't know that this is better.*

Arms encircled her and pulled her into a tight hug. Tonya squeezed Diane until the princess squirmed.

"Can't breathe!" But Diane's voice teased. The sound near brought tears to Tonya's eyes.

"I'm so glad you're all right," she said.

Diane pulled away.

"Tonya!" She gave a little gasp as she tugged at the ends of Tonya's hair. White streaks coated the ends of her dark hair. A few blond strips shot through the entire length.

"You're an ice caster," a deep grumbling voice said.

Tonya slowly turned to face the bear. It lowered itself a little to look her in the eyes where she still knelt on the ground. She couldn't believe its name.

"Tonya, this is..." Diane took a deep breath as if she couldn't believe it either. "Your father. Freyr."

Deep grey eyes held her gaze. Words locked on her tongue, her heartbeat louder than each pulse of her magic.

"You grew up," the bear said.

Tonya gasped a sob.

"I'm so sorry we left you. I was supposed to come back and find both of you, and then — "

Tonya lunged to wrap her arms around his neck. Freyr sank back onto his haunches with a surprised huff. He lowered his head to rest on her shoulder. He'd wanted her. Tried to come back for her.

And he couldn't because of...

She pulled away. "Did Steinn do this to you?"

"Yes. We'd thought to use the Lights to turn me back, but I was too late."

Tonya's heart cracked. She might not truly get him back after all. "How do we undo it?"

"Thalia's touch can end it."

"She's — at the cave..."

"I know." Her father gently nudged her arm with his nose. "But there was no way for us to undo the ice."

"But now we have our own ice caster." Diane stood, brushing the snow from her knees. "She can get Thalia out, and then you can help August and Dorian."

Tonya's lungs constricted. "Are—are they…?"

Diane's features pulled down into a grimace. "August is barely hanging on."

Tonya leapt to her feet. "Let's go."

Diane ran to Arvo, tugging him back over as Freyr lumbered to his paws.

"Diane, take the caribou," Freyr said. "Tonya, with me."

Tonya hesitated, but he crouched. "Last time I carried you, you were a tiny babe. But I think I can handle it this time." A bit of humor deepened in his growl.

A smile flickered across Tonya's face and she swung a leg over his back, settling into place. A rope already wound about his shoulders and she gripped it tight as he broke into a run. Diane and Arvo kept pace alongside.

Her journey to the lights with Steinn had taken nearly an hour. It seemed to take three times that on the way back. Her magic began to settle a little, pressing out into each tiny corner to fill herself up with it. Every now and then, one would rush forward in an attempt to gain dominance. She'd double over, her nose nearly in Freyr's fur.

He stopped the first time, but her mumbled reassurance and panic to get back to Dorian and August prompted them to run on.

Each time it happened again, he chuffed a reassurance that helped her untangle another thread inside and tuck it into place. The moon crept across the sky to cast shadows across the snow by the time they arrived back at the cave.

Tonya jumped from Freyr's back, magic rushing into her fingertips at the sight of the figure waiting for them.

Steinn stood in the mouth of the cave. Dorian knelt at his feet, a knife pressed against his throat.

# Chapter 31

**B**lood dribbled down Dorian's chin from his nose and mouth. He swayed on his knees, a small cut appearing on his neck where the cold steel pressed against his skin. Fury called forth Tonya's magic, whipping around her in a miniature storm.

"Let him go!" She lunged forward a step, halted only by Steinn pressing the knife harder against Dorian's neck.

"That's what I thought," Steinn sneered. "The warding around that one is clever." He jerked his chin at Diane, who scowled back. "Surrender to me, child, or I'll let the forest faery inside die, which won't take much longer, and then kill this one."

"Why are you doing this?" Freyr padded forward, a growl reverberating in his chest as Steinn threatened Dorian again.

Steinn's lip curled further in derision. "You should know, Freyr. I told you as much before I trapped you. You can't do anything to help here and you know it. I'll deal with you after I put your daughter away."

Tonya flexed her fingers, trying to pull only the threads of ice magic. Her ocean magic leapt forward along with it, straining to be released. She looked to Dorian. A small smile crinkled around his eyes.

"You did it." She barely caught his soft words.

She managed a smile back. Her magic was free, but she had no idea how to control any of it.

"Silence." Steinn struck Dorian's injured wing. His face twisted in pain and he wavered further on his knees.

A muffled cry came from Diane. Tonya clenched her hands, sliding her foot slowly in another step. The ice trembled in response.

Dorian opened his eyes and met her gaze again. His face hardened in determination. He slowly reached his right hand toward the ground, fingers spreading wide. A thrill ran through Tonya and she opened her hands, ready to let her magic run free.

Dorian struck the knife from his throat with his left hand, bringing his right hand up in a fist at the same time. The earth rumbled under Steinn's feet, knocking him off balance with a curse. Dorian pitched himself away as Tonya flung out her hands, throwing ice shards and beads of moisture at Steinn.

He dodged, but Freyr lunged forward, knocking him to the ground. Steinn stabbed the knife at Freyr's shoulder, driving him a pace back to avoid it. He whistled and his caribou lunged forward, lowered horns driving into Freyr's side.

Tonya shouted in alarm as her father tumbled to the ground under the force of the caribou's charge. Arvo galloped forward, slamming his horns against the other caribou's and driving it back.

A quick movement snapped her attention back to Steinn and she jerked her arm up to protect against a beam of light. It burned her arm on impact, drawing a cry.

Diane helped Dorian struggle upright. Her eyes widened and she threw herself over him as Steinn shoved a wall of ice at them. Most disintegrated on impact when it hit Diane, but she and Dorian toppled back to the ground.

Tonya released another uncontrolled burst of ice at Steinn which flung him against the cave wall. He gasped a breath, but stayed on his feet.

*What do I do?* Tonya desperately let green and violet light stream from her hands. Steinn brushed it aside almost carelessly.

*Find the right words...*

Freyr lunged forward again, swiping heavy paws at Steinn. The faery dodged away as Freyr kept coming with angry snarls. Tonya looked down at her hands.

*What do I want?*

Desperate, she closed her eyes, trying to find the whispers that had called to her of magic all her life.

They rushed about her, one deeper whisper calling her toward the ice, the other lightly sighing of waves and currents. She closed her hands and whispered back to the ice.

It pressed around her heart, rushing down to her fingertips. She whispered to the ice to trap Steinn's feet. He lurched to a halt, shock creasing his features as it wrapped around his legs to his knees.

She commanded it to stay. It held under his attack.

Freyr backed away.

"What now?" Steinn sneered again. "You kill me?"

Tonya swallowed hard. Despite her anger and hate, she didn't want to kill him and plunge into the darkness beside him.

"No. I want you to answer for everything you've done to my family and friends. To me!" she shouted, then whispered another command to the ice.

It leapt from her hands and swept up from the ground to freeze his arms to his chest. Icy chains pinned him in place, locking him where he stood. He struggled against the ice, but Tonya whispered strength and binding into the ice. It held.

Fury covered Steinn's face when he could not break free. He hurled curses and imprecations at them until Diane shoved a piece of cloth into his mouth, gagging him.

"Can I hit him a few times?" Diane brandished her staff. Steinn glared.

Tonya covered her mouth with her hands, trapping a cry of relief and exhausted emotion. Her father came up beside her, letting her lean against him for a long moment.

"No," Tonya said.

"You sure?" Diane turned a disappointed frown at her.

A giggle broke from Tonya, bringing with it the sudden urge to cry.

"That's impressive binding for someone who's never been able to use her magic." Freyr's soft growl urged more tears.

"I just found the right words," Tonya said.

Dorian's smile took up half his face. He struggled to his feet. The sight of his torn wing brought back the horrible reality to Tonya.

"How's August?" she whispered.

"Not good. We need to hurry." Dorian staggered into the cave.

Diane followed after a last scowl at Steinn. Tonya took a deep breath and stepped inside.

The lantern still burned by the ice wall. Remnants of a fire scattered across the cave floor. August lay sprawled on the ground, torn out of a nest of blankets, one hand reaching toward his knife. His chest jerked in a faint gasp. Swirling patterns of frost covered his face and parts of his neck visible around his coat collar.

Dorian tried to drag him back to the blankets and Diane hurried to help him.

"Tonya." Freyr nudged her to the ice wall. "Break the ice."

She rested a hand on the wall, feeling every particle of water frozen in place along with the binding resting in between. Her mother stared back.

"How?" Her voice trembled in a whisper.

"Trace the binding back to its source. There's always a starting point left in a spell. And — and it looks like she was trying to cast back. There will be weakness there." An extra gruffness covered his voice.

Tonya broke off her stare to look down at her father. He stared longingly up at the faery trapped in the ice. Tears pressed up against her eyes. She closed her eyes against the sensation and focused on the binding.

This time she found the starting point. She moved her hand up and to the right to center over the gentle shift in the binding. Another ripple in the spell occurred around her mother's hands. Tonya pressed her other hand even with Thalia's outraised fingers.

*Break,* she whispered. *Give me back my mother, please.*

A fracture formed under her fingers.

*Wider.*

A crack echoed through the cave. She opened her eyes. The fissure ran all the way to Thalia. Her mother's chest rose and fell in a quick breath.

Tonya flexed her fingers, drawing her hands back as if opening double doors. The ice fell away. Freyr jumped forward, allowing Thalia to collapse against his broad back as the ice no longer supported her.

Tonya took her mother under the shoulders and laid her back. Another breath jolted through her, and then she breathed normally. Color rushed back to her pale face. Her arms jerked and she pushed up with a cry, hands outstretched.

"Thalia!" Freyr's voice halted her.

She lowered her hands, disbelief slackening her jaw. She leaned forward towards him.

"Freyr? What happened? It was Steinn, he—"

"I know," Freyr gently interrupted. "We're safe."

"Tonya!" Thalia's hands flew to her face. Tonya froze, heart pounding.

Freyr looked past Thalia to her. Her mother slowly turned, her green eyes widening.

"Tonya?" she asked hesitantly.

Tonya pressed her lips together to keep from crying. She managed a nod.

"You're—how long has it been?" Thalia half-turned back to Freyr.

"Seventy years," he quietly answered.

Thalia gasped, pressing a hand to her chest. "Seventy…" She reached a careful hand out to Tonya as if afraid she wasn't real.

"I wanted to be there as you grew up…" she whispered.

A tear trickled down Tonya's cheek. A tiny breath edged past her lips. Thalia grabbed her shoulders and pulled her into a ferocious hug. Tonya clung to her, burying her face against her mother's shoulder.

*My mother…*She couldn't believe it.

A nudge on her shoulder brought her head back up. Freyr leaned close.

"We need to help the others," he growled gently.

Thalia looked past Tonya and gaped at the sight of August lying terrifyingly still on the blankets, and Diane and Dorian staring back.

"Thalia," Freyr said. "Steinn made the warding on me such that only you could break it."

She pushed to her knees. "How?"

"You just have to touch me."

A smile curved her lips. "That's easy enough." She rested her hands on Freyr's face and pressed a kiss against the top of his head.

A shudder and groan ripped through his body. He collapsed to the ground, limbs spasming, then shrinking. His last growl turned more human, then a faery appeared on hands and knees, shaking and gasping.

Tattered clothes of blue and black, edged in the same red stitching as Thalia's, clung to a muscular frame. Tousled dark hair edged in white covered his head. Thalia rested her hands on his shoulders, then brought his head up.

Tonya stared at her father. His features were similar to Steinn's, but laugh lines creased around his eyes and mouth which seemed to stay quirked up at the corner. His grey eyes sparkled with laughter.

His arms buckled and he winced as he caught himself on an elbow. Thalia pulled him back up.

"What's wrong?" She gripped his tunic as he leaned against her.

He shivered, a breath blowing out in a frosty plume. Ice crackled about his fingers. He sucked in a deep breath and closed his fists. The ice vanished.

"Freyr?" Thalia whispered in alarm.

"My magic's been cut off for the last seventy years." His voice was still deep, though lacking the extra growl of the bear. "Stings a little to have it all come back at once."

"I know the feeling," Tonya said.

Her father grinned and her heart leaped at the twinkle in his eyes. She understood what had pulled her mother away from the ocean.

"Come. I might need help." He shakily made his way over to August. Tonya hurried beside him.

Diane cast wide-eyed glances between Freyr and Thalia. Tonya offered a small smile of understanding. *I think I'm still in shock myself.*

Diane had to undo August's coat and tunic, loosening the bandages underneath at Freyr's orders. Dorian propped August's head up in his lap, slumping against the wall himself. Tonya swallowed hard. She hated how grateful she was that it wasn't Dorian lying near-frozen on the ground.

Freyr pressed fingers around the biggest wound. Deep blue spread around the edges and over August's chest where it faded to the same frost as his face. Freyr closed his eyes, lips moving soundlessly for what felt like an eternity.

"Look!" Diane whispered.

The frost had begun to recede from August's skin, back towards the gashes. The frigid blue lightened, fading back into the wounds. August took a deep breath, shoulders jerking a little. Dorian pressed a hand to his shoulder and another on his forehead to keep him still as he moved again.

Freyr kept his hands in place. Threads of blue coiled about his hands. He opened his eyes and pulled his hands away. He rubbed them together and a ball of ice began to take shape. He stopped once it became as big as his fist. Then he smashed it down against the ground. It shattered, pieces skittering across the cave floor.

Another deep breath came from August and then a normal pattern resumed. Blood oozed from the open wounds, a stark contrast against his pale skin.

"Of course, they start bleeding again," Diane muttered. She reached trembling hands to try to replace the bandages. Dorian tapped her wrist.

"Let me."

"No," Thalia's firm voice interrupted. "You look drained of magic. I have a little healer training. I'll take care of him."

Dorian didn't even argue, just shifted away from August and nodding his permission. Tonya moved over to him as Thalia bent over August.

Freyr touched Tonya's shoulder. "Find the ice. The binding spell isn't as strong in him."

Tonya's cheeks warmed as she met Dorian's eyes. She gingerly reached out to touch around the cut on his cheek.

"I don't really know what I'm doing," she whispered apologetically. "My father should do this."

Dorian brushed the back of her hand with cold fingers.

"Just find the right words."

It gave her the courage to close her eyes and send a tentative tendril of magic through him. He flinched as the ice in his blood jumped in response to her call. The binding rested in a small crystal slowly making its way towards his heart.

*No, you don't,* she whispered, pulling it back toward her as gently as she would brush a hand over the waves. She opened her eyes to see a lighter blue pooling in her palm.

"Shape it like a snowball," Freyr said.

Tonya rubbed her hands together, pressing the ice together. It didn't form as big a crystal as with August, but it still gave her savage satisfaction to hurl it against the wall and watch it shatter into a hundred pieces.

She glanced back at Dorian, who still leaned against the wall.

"You all right?" She brushed her thumb against his cheek, wincing a little at the dark bruising around his mouth and nose.

"Better now." His eyes crinkled with a smile. "Not as cold anymore." He reached up and combed a bit of her hair where it still hung loose over her shoulders. "I like it."

Her cheeks heated again. The white and blonde streaks would take some getting used to.

"Thank you."

"Y-you sure he's all right, Tonya?" August's cough held amusement. "He might need some mouth-to-mouth for full recovery."

Fire engulfed Tonya's face. Dorian rolled his eyes.

Diane smacked August's shoulder. "Obviously you're feeling better."

"Ow." August stirred a little more, grabbing at the blankets. "I'm still c-cold."

"The ice had begun to freeze your heart," Freyr said. "It will take some time for you to recover fully."

"We should build this fire back up," Thalia said.

August blinked owlishly at them, bits of confusion in his face. "I missed something."

Freyr's booming chuckle brought smiles to all their faces. "Until a few minutes ago, I was a bear, so you did miss a bit."

August raised an eyebrow before turning his attention to Thalia. "You're Tonya's mother?"

She nodded, turning an almost shy smile at Tonya.

"You should be proud of her."

Tonya fought the burning in her eyes at August's words.

"I already am," Freyr said.

Then he raised a teasing eyebrow at her hand still resting on Dorian's chest. She reflexively jerked it away. But, unlike Steinn, there was no judgement or anger there.

Something like panic came over her.

"Diane, do you want to help me get more firewood?" she blurted.

Diane pushed to her feet, understanding in her eyes. She shouldered her staff and followed Tonya as she practically ran out of the cave. Tonya jolted at the sight of Steinn still standing frozen in place. She'd nearly forgotten about him in the last few minutes.

Diane scowled again and kept one eye on him until they stepped into the forest just out of earshot of the cave. The darkness settled under the trees like a gentle blanket pricked with patterns where the moon- and star-light trickled through the branches.

"You all right?" Diane rested a hand on her shoulder.

"I don't know." Tonya started pacing, flapping her hands by her sides and taking shuddery breaths. "I'm just—my parents are *alive*—my magic *works*—I don't know what's wrong with me!"

"Since that all happened in the last hour or so, I think you're entitled to panic a little. Your life just turned on its head."

Tonya pressed hands to her cheeks. "You think so?"

Diane nodded, a smile curving her lips.

Tonya shook her head, taking another shaky inhale. "Then I guess I'll panic." She huffed a bit of a laugh.

Diane chuckled and wrapped her in a hug. "I'm so happy for you."

"It wouldn't have happened without you." Tonya's heart steadied a beat. "Thank you."

Diane gathered a breath, and Tonya thought she'd shrug it off. But then she said, "You're welcome," in a shaky sort of voice.

They clung to each other for a long moment, before Tonya sniffled again and flicked her hand across her nose.

"We should probably get some firewood."

Diane squeezed her shoulders and then released, wiping at her own eyes. Tonya unfurled her wings to give some extra light as they gathered fallen branches and sticks in silence. Tonya straightened and adjusted the wood in her arms.

An unfamiliar sensation rippled across her skin as a breeze wafted by to stir the branches. Her skin prickled and she shivered.

"You all right?" Diane hurried to her side in concern.

A smile crept across Tonya's face. "I'm—cold?" She laughed. "I'm cold!"

"Usually that's not something to be excited about." Diane raised her eyebrow. "The novelty will wear off soon enough."

But she chuckled as Tonya headed back to the cave with a spring to her step.

Now that the warding was gone, she could *feel* everything more. Tonya tipped her head back to the sky. *Thank you.*

# Chapter 32

Inside the cave, Dorian lay on a pallet next to August. His chest rose and fell evenly in sleep. Thalia stood at the entrance to the passageway.

"There's another room back there with more blankets and things," she whispered. She wore a coat that was a size too big for her, and she'd tucked her hands up into the sleeves.

Tonya and Diane stacked the wood as quietly as they could. Diane gingerly gathered the half-burned logs back together and set about trying to bring the fire to life again. She met with little success until August reached out a hand and set them ablaze with a wave.

"You should be resting!" Diane scolded.

"I am," August mumbled back.

Tonya rubbed a hand over her sleeve, shyly meeting her mother's gaze. Thalia seemed just as unsure now. Her mother lifted a tentative hand and gestured to the cave wall furthest from the shattered ice.

"Could we talk for a few minutes?"

Tonya nodded, stepping her slow way over. "Where's—Father?" She stumbled a bit over the words.

"He went to go see to the animals. And make sure Steinn couldn't get away." Thalia twisted her fingers together, looking nervously at the cave mouth. "I almost didn't want him to go."

Tonya nodded, a small fear taking hold that her father might not walk back through the entrance. They sat down on the ground. Thalia pulled a blanket over her lap, offering an edge to Tonya. She scooted closer and let her mother tuck it around her legs.

"I never quite got used to how cold it can be here." Thalia offered a smile.

Tonya returned it. "How long were you here before—everything?"

"Almost two years. If we'd not been attacked, we might have stayed here."

Tonya rubbed the blanket's furred edge between her fingers, wondering what it would have been like to have been raised in the north, with her magic free.

"Kostis took you to the Reef?"

Tonya nodded. "Aunt and Uncle looked after me."

Thalia's face brightened. "I'm glad."

Tonya didn't have the heart yet to tell her that it hadn't been all that wonderful.

"They have a daughter, Sophie. I didn't know if you knew that."

Thalia gasped. "A daughter! Oh, I can't wait to meet her! Tell me everything about the ocean and the Reef. I've missed it so much. And Freyr says you have ocean magic as well. We'll have to see what you can do. And—"

She pressed a hand to her cheek. "I'm sorry, I'm going so fast. I'm just—I can't believe you're here and grown up."

"It's all right." Tonya smiled. The panic was abating, to be replaced by the urge to tell her mother everything about her life, and in turn hear everything about her mother and ocean magic.

"Where do you want me to start?"

Thalia reached for her hand, squeezing hard. Tonya kept hold of her hand when she made to release. Thalia smiled and tucked a bit of Tonya's mismatched hair behind her ear.

"From the beginning, maybe?"

*

Tonya stared at the cave ceiling and the patterns the flames cast on the craggy surface. Diane shifted beside her and nudged her side with an elbow under their blankets.

"All right?" she whispered sleepily.

Tonya slowly nodded. She and her parents hadn't talked long. Her father had walked back in, stomping snow from his boots, and come to sit beside her mother.

"Started without me?" He'd smiled.

Tonya had suddenly become tongue-tied sitting next to them, watching Freyr's arm draped around Thalia's shoulders, while her mother snuggled into his side like they hadn't been parted for the last seventy years.

She'd finally complained of fatigue—not so much a lie. More blankets had been found, the fire stoked higher, and they'd turned in to join the boys in sleep.

That had been nearly an hour ago. Her parents' soft murmurs had died down across the cave where they slept together. Despite the fatigue that weighed at her, magic still thrummed through her, keeping her awake.

"It's just—strange," she admitted softly.

"Give them some time." Diane yawned. "I'm sure they don't know what to do with the daughter who went and grew up without them."

Tonya half-turned towards Diane. "What if they don't like what they see?"

Diane rolled over to face her. She arched her eyebrows.

"I think the only thing you have to worry about is them absolutely smothering you in affection. Freyr would have spoiled you rotten." She poked Tonya's side.

A small smile curved Tonya's lips.

"Get some sleep," Diane said, and rolled back over.

Tonya stared over Diane's shoulder at the bits of sky visible through the cave opening. Freyr had warded it against the cold and any malicious magic since they'd left Steinn still bound outside. The stars winked back, cold and bright and reassuring.

She closed her eyes, letting the ebb and flow of her magic around her heart lull her into sleep.

# Chapter 33

"**W**ill you two be able to head back to Konungburg today?" Diane asked August and Dorian over breakfast.

August sat up against the wall, slowly eating some bread. He'd kept two blankets wrapped around him. Tonya didn't like the paleness that lingered in both their faces.

"I can try," August said. Dorian looked like he might argue, but he finally just shrugged his uninjured shoulder.

"As long as you ride one of the caribou," he said.

"It'd probably be easier if it still weren't so cold outside," August muttered, tugging the furs around him.

Tonya bit her lip. She had her magic, but still no idea how to break the ice.

"I think we can probably do something about that." Freyr looked to her. She rubbed her jacket sleeves, afraid to voice her complete and utter lack of ability to use her magic other than in uncontrolled bursts.

"I'll walk you through it," he said, as if sensing her fear.

She slowly nodded. Her mother sent her an encouraging smile. It bolstered a bit of confidence in Tonya.

"What about Steinn?" Diane asked.

Tonya's gut twisted at the name. *Can we just leave him?*

Freyr's features hardened. "He goes with us to answer to the king and the council."

Thalia rested a hand on his forearm. He looked down at her, a faint smile barely softening his eyes.

"So, seven of us, two caribou." Diane arched an eyebrow at August. "Plenty of blankets..." August halfheartedly glared at her from his mound of furs.

"Dorian, how are you feeling?"

Dorian opened his mouth, then sighed and slumped back against the wall. "Tired. I could probably walk for a bit."

"He gets the other caribou," Thalia interrupted. "You gave up too much of your magic." She jabbed a finger at Dorian as if lecturing a small faery. He looked slightly taken aback, and Tonya stifled a small smile.

"Freyr, you and Tonya go do something about that ice. I think Diane and I can handle the rest of this." Thalia made a shooing motion at Freyr.

Diane beamed at Thalia and scooted over to her, already rattling off a list of their current supplies.

"Come, I think we'd better leave them to it." Freyr extended a hand down to Tonya. She hesitantly took it and let him pull her to her feet.

She followed Freyr outside. He ignored Steinn where he sat against the cave wall. Tonya paused, having half-expected him to have disappeared sometime in the night. He shivered a little in the icy chains, but Tonya couldn't muster up any sympathy for him. He glared at her and she walked away.

Her father led the way from the copse of trees and back out onto the tundra. He propped hands on his hips and took a deep breath of the chill air, tilting his face up to the sun. Tonya shyly came up beside him.

"I don't really know how to control my magic," she admitted. "I don't know what to do to break the ice."

Freyr opened his eyes and looked down at her. "Half of it is knowing what you want. You seemed to do all right last night."

Tonya tucked her hair back. "I was just panicking, really."

He nudged her shoulder gently. "Some faeries take years to master what you did in a panic."

Heat tinged her cheeks before the breeze whisked it away. She took a breath and squared her shoulders.

"So what do we do?"

Freyr knelt and placed one hand in the snow. He beckoned her down beside him.

"What do you feel?"

Tonya closed her eyes, settling her fingertips against the snow. Beneath the initial chill, swirls of her magic lay with the ice. But over-lacing it all was a warding and a warning to stay away from the ice. *From me.*

"My magic and the warding you and mother placed on me." She looked to him for confirmation.

He nodded. "We thought it would just hide your magic from anyone trying to find you. We didn't know it would hide your magic from you. I'm sorry."

Tonya blinked hard. What a difference that would have made.

"It's all right."

Though her entire past screamed that it wasn't.

Freyr rested a hand on her shoulder. "No. And we shouldn't have left you like that."

"He took you away from me." Tonya forced the words in a trembling voice. That she knew for certain. "You were just trying to protect me the only way you knew."

He brushed a hand over her hair and pressed a kiss against her temple. "I'm still sorry."

She leaned into his touch. "I forgive you."

Freyr blinked a few times and smiled.

"It told me about this place," Tonya said. "The warding. I've dreamed of seeing the north for as long as I can remember. Seeing you."

"I hope the north won't disappoint you." A bit of her fear shone in his grey eyes.

She squeezed his hand. "Never."

His quick laugh sounded more like a faint sob. He kissed her forehead again before turning back to the ice. He cleared his throat once and indicated she should touch the ice again.

"Just like before, find the starting point."

"Wouldn't that be all the way back in the ocean where I was attacked?" Tonya tried to convince her ice magic to come forward and investigate the ice. Her ocean magic rushed in and out of her fingers like the tide.

She waved her hands in irritation.

"What?" Freyr asked.

"It's just—I can't figure out how to make both magics cooperate!" She frowned at her fingers as if they were responsible.

He pressed her hand. "It'll come, trust me."

Tonya raised an eyebrow. "How do you know? No one's ever been born with two different kinds of magic before."

"Maybe, maybe not." Freyr shrugged. "I sensed a few drops of ice magic in August last night."

"What?" Tonya stared at her father.

"It's probably happened before, but not for a very long time. I'll help you figure it out." His hand tightened around hers. "Try again."

Tonya shoved away memories of instructors saying the same thing to her, albeit in a more weary and frustrated tone. They hadn't been at this long enough for her father to feel the same way yet. *No.* She shook herself. *I can do this now.*

She closed her eyes again, imagining the tide withdrawing into the ocean. The whispers of waves and breezes and currents obeyed this time, making way for the ice magic in a surly rush. The magic of ice and lights and glaciers leaped eagerly from her fingers into the ice, scurrying around the warding to find the weakness she needed.

It resided in a swirl of her magic, where the ocean and the ice clashed together, repeating their fight over and over again through the spelled ice.

"You found it," Freyr said.

Tonya nodded, afraid to open her eyes and lose it.

"My warding was specifically against an attack from Steinn, so it's the strongest warding magic in the ice. I'll cast against it and you target your own magic."

Tonya nodded, hoping she understood what to do.

"When you're ready."

She felt a rush of strange, yet familiar, magic ripple into the ice, shaking off the warding and letting the swirls of her magic move more freely. She focused on the nearest weak point. *Find the right words.*

Gently nudging the fighting magics apart from one another, she whispered *break. Melt.*

A crack startled her eyes open. The ice ripped open in front of her, exposing a long swathe of green and a few purple flowers that lay flat against the ground.

"Good!" She looked up into her father's smile. "That's a start."

A surge of triumph filled her. "How far did you cast?"

"All the way to the Strait. You can work as we go."

She shook her head. This was what she'd come to do. Her magic roared in agreement. She plunged her hands back down, sending out tendrils and pushing them over the hills and tundra, as far as she could sense the ice. Then she commanded it to break.

Dizziness swept over her and she nearly smacked her nose against the ground, but her father's arm encircled her and pulled her up.

"Easy!" He half-laughed.

But Tonya smiled, watching spiderwebbing cracks spread out in every direction, widening as the ice shrunk and melted.

The air warmed noticeably. A sweet scent overtook the air and she inhaled deeply.

"What is that smell?" she asked in wonder.

"Summer on the tundra," Freyr replied.

Green spread out in every direction. Swathes of vibrant reds and purples lay across the clumped grass. The trees behind them shook free of the snow clinging to their branches.

Tonya turned further. The mountains freed themselves from the ice and snow in a rippling wave rushing up to the peaks.

She staggered to her feet. "I think I used too much magic at once."

Freyr laughed. "Aye, you did, but I wager you cleared the ice all the way to the Strait. The Lights must have given you some extra strength last night."

He let her lean on his arm as they began to walk back to the cave. Tonya barely had time to brace before Diane hurled herself forward in a hug.

"I knew you could do it!" she squealed.

Tonya laughed. "I had some help."

Diane leaned back, her hands on Tonya's shoulders. "Doesn't matter. You're amazing!"

"I didn't clear it all," Tonya said. "Everything past the Strait is still under ice."

Diane's face fell a little. "All the more reason to start heading back."

She turned back to the cave, a spring to her step that had been missing since they'd first set out from Chelm.

Under Diane's direction, Freyr and Tonya readied the caribou. Then Freyr helped August from the cave to slowly mount Steinn's caribou. Thalia followed to make sure blankets were tucked around him. Tonya watched anxiously as he sat slumped in the saddle, nothing like the confident, careless posture he'd ridden with only a few days ago.

Dorian limped outside by himself, blinking a little in the sun. Arvo cornered him until he had to mount just to settle the animal. Tonya caught a little grin from August and shook her head at the faery. August shrugged and blinked innocently back at her.

She held her breath as Freyr approached Steinn and undid the ice that held him to the ground. Steinn said nothing, just started walking when Freyr gestured. They all fell into a little procession. Diane stepping out in front, Freyr guarding Steinn several paces away from the rest of the group as they walked. Tonya shyly walked with her mother beside the caribou.

After a half hour of walking, she rolled up the sleeves of her coat. Thalia unbuttoned hers as well, letting her arms swing free by her sides.

"I barely knew that time had passed in the ice, but I feel like I still missed the sun for every minute of these years." She lifted her chin to the sky with a sigh. "I can't wait to see the ocean again."

"Father taught me some ice magic. Will you show me some of our ocean magic?"

"Of course!" Her mother waltzed forward a few steps.

"I hope I'm a little better with it now that the warding is gone. I can't even fix coral," she admitted sheepishly.

Thalia chuckled and wrapped her in a hug. "Can I tell you a secret?" She lowered her voice to a whisper. "I can't either."

Tonya drew away in shock. "What? But fixing coral is the easiest use of magic. That's what everyone told me!"

"Maybe for some. But I find it boring. I'd rather dance with the waves any day."

Tonya giggled. "That sounds wonderful." Her ocean magic surged in agreement. "I wish there were something you could teach me right now."

"Me too. But I will as soon as we get back to Konungburg and the salt water."

"Freyr?" Diane's cautious voice sounded.

They looked up to see figures approaching. They morphed into six faeries riding caribou. Tonya watched with bated breath until her father visibly relaxed. He waved them to a stop to wait for the riders.

Within minutes, the caribou slid to a halt. The foremost rider jumped to the ground, and Tonya stared at King Birgir.

"Steinn, what is—" His jaw dropped. "Freyr?"

"Birgir! Still king?" Freyr's voice came oddly light.

Birgir shook himself and hauled Freyr into a hug. "You're alive?"

"No thanks to my brother," Freyr said as they pulled apart.

Birgir cast a glance over them and half-turned to the closest rider. "It seems you were right, Lilja."

Lilja dismounted, scowling at Steinn. "I wish I wasn't." She looked past him and her expression brightened. "Thalia!"

Thalia accepted a hug from the faery before curtseying to the king.

"Tonya, it looks like you succeeded, then?" Birgir smiled at her. "Was it you who undid the ice this morning?"

Tonya nodded. "Father helped."

Birgir smiled. "I'm glad to hear it."

"What are you doing out here?" Tonya finally blurted, unable to keep the question at bay.

"Lilja has long had some suspicions concerning what really happened to your parents. She had an eagle follow you. August was supposed to send in reports with other animals, but you look a little worse for the wear, lad." Birgir nodded at August, who still sat hunched in the saddle and wrapped in the furs despite the warmth.

"Had a little run in with some ice." August mustered a smile. "It kept me busy. Sorry." He looked to Lilja. But the faery commander had turned a stormy glare on Steinn.

"You dared to attack them with ice spells you learned from us?" She lunged forward, and only Birgir and Freyr grabbing her arms halted her advance. Steinn said nothing, just turned his face away.

"When we didn't hear from you by yesterday's noon, we rode, fearing the worst. Then this morning, we caught trace of a magic we thought long vanished." Birgir looked to Freyr. "When the ice vanished beneath our feet, we didn't know what to think, except to ride faster."

"Are those extra caribou I see?" Diane pushed up on her toes to look past the other riders.

Birgir laughed. "They are indeed."

"Perfect." Diane beamed. "I was dreading walking the entire way back."

"Aye, mount up," Lilja said. "It looks like there's a long story to be told after we get back to Konungburg."

# Chapter 34

Tonya tiptoed over to Dorian and August's room. Upon arrival back at Konungburg, they'd been once again housed in the same quarters.

She knocked softly on the open door. She hadn't had a chance to see either of them since arriving back at the city two nights before as they were immediately taken to the healer. No answer greeted her, and she gingerly opened the door a little further.

August slept in the bed closest to the door, curled up under a pile of blankets. Color had finally started coming back to his cheeks, but the occasional shiver still wracked his body.

Dorian lay in the other bed, his back to the door. Blankets had been tucked up around him, not quite hiding the bandages wrapped around his muscular torso. His right wing lay folded up neatly against his back. The left draped over his side and arm, the rips skillfully repaired.

She stepped around the bed, just wanting to make sure he was all right before she left. His eyes slowly blinked open. She froze, caught between wanting to stay and wanting to run.

The last time they'd actually been face to face, she'd been pulling ice from his blood.

A faint smile creased his cheeks.

"How are you?" she whispered, scooting a stool closer to the bed to sit.

"Fine." He shifted his wing with a slight flash of discomfort and slid his hand toward her. She pressed her hand over his, and then somehow, he was holding her hand with their fingers twined together.

"How are you?"

"Fine," she teased. His smile grew a little. She sobered. "Today wasn't really though."

He tilted his head inquisitively. Tonya bit back a sigh. He wouldn't have heard.

"They held the trial for Steinn."

His grip tightened over hers for a moment. "What happened?"

"My parents told their entire story. It was awful. He turned my father into his bear form and made him forget everything, except for a tiny memory of my mother to spend the rest of his days searching for her without really knowing why."

She blinked several times. Watching her parents' faces during the trial had been one of the hardest things about the day.

"Then he caught my mother when she came looking for Father, and trapped her in the ice prison."

A sob hitched over her words and she took a breath to steady herself. "Diane and I had to tell everything that happened."

"Someone came and talked to both of us yesterday to get the full story of his ambush." Dorian shifted a little, wincing again as his wing moved.

"They read the account out loud. It was awful to hear it."

"We're fine." He brushed his thumb over the back of her hand.

"Now you are," she retorted. "You both could have died! And you, giving so much of your magic to August!"

The corners of his eyes crinkled, destroying any sort of irritation.

"What was the final decision?"

"Some other faeries admitted to helping him. Steinn didn't deny anything and didn't show any regret for what he'd done. They declared him Draugur and banished him to the crevasses in the north until he repents of what he did."

Another involuntary shudder cut through her. Steinn hadn't looked apologetic at all, and took his punishment with a strange sort of eagerness.

Sadness creased Dorian's face. "It's all right to hope that he'll turn back."

Tonya sniffed. Somehow, he'd managed to find the reason for the lingering bits of sadness again.

"My father is banished," Dorian said. "I still tell myself that I hate him for everything he did, but some part of me doesn't want him to die here."

She moved her other hand to press over his. "And that's all right, too."

He glanced away, clearing his throat.

"So now what?" His voice noticeably lightened.

She lifted her hand to push away the strands of her mismatched hair. "Father has been teaching me a little bit more about my magic. Tomorrow we're going to go to the Strait so we can clear some of the ice across the water."

Tremors shook her stomach. She'd worried incessantly that she wouldn't be able to recreate the way she'd broken the ice. But her parents' and Diane's unfailing optimism had managed to keep her anxiety slightly at bay.

She'd been told that she wasn't to clear more than a few miles so as not to drain herself of magic. They'd begin a more regimented clearing once they began the journey back south.

"I should go with you tomorrow." He shifted as if ready to sit up and ride right then.

Tonya shook her head. "No. You need to keep regaining your magic."

His mouth quirked in a displeased frown, but he didn't argue. A small miracle.

"You're coming back here right after?"

A small laugh teased her chest. "Yes. And my father and Lilja and about ten other faeries are going with us, so we'll be perfectly safe."

He settled back down with a satisfied look. She stared down at their entwined hands. The sight seemed to say the things that hadn't been said yet. That she'd wanted to wait to say until her magic was free.

But it didn't feel right to not say it.

"Dorian," she began slowly. He tilted his head against the pillow to better regard her. She swallowed, suddenly nervous.

"I—you saw me when no one else tried to." His smile started to form around his eyes. "After I break all the ice, my parents and I are going to the southern ocean. My mother wants to see home again. You—you could come with us, if you want."

Her words stumbled and tripped as if slipping across ice.

It wasn't really what she wanted to say, but she didn't quite know what those words were supposed to be yet. Or maybe just afraid that there might not be enough room in her heart for both him and her parents.

He gently squeezed her hand again.

"I'd like that," he said simply.

Tonya smiled. He wouldn't push, just wait for her to find room for everyone.

A knock announced Diane as the princess leaned into the room. She wiggled her eyebrows at the sight of Tonya sitting with Dorian. Tonya flushed but didn't jerk her hand away. Diane stepped over to August first, gently nudging his shoulder.

"Why?" August grumbled.

Another smile flickered around Dorian's eyes.

"I volunteered to come see if you two felt up to coming to dinner tonight?"

The blankets shifted and August emerged, sitting up against the carved headboard. "Food might help me forgive you for waking me up."

Diane tipped her head back with an exaggerated sigh. "How much longer are you two going to sleep?"

"Forever, if those two keep whispering to each other." August crossed his arms with a mock scowl.

Tonya wrinkled her nose back. Her flush didn't come as bright this time. Dorian rolled his eyes and released her hand to push himself up. Once upright, he let his uninjured wing stretch for a long moment. She resisted the urge to brush her hand along its soft surface.

"How's your wing?" Concern lined August's face as he looked to Dorian.

Dorian gingerly shifted his patched left wing. "They told me I'd likely have to be forever careful how I use it, but it's healing."

Tonya slid her hand to press around his where it rested on the blankets. It wouldn't have happened but for her.

"So, dinner?" Diane clasped her hands hopefully.

Dorian rolled his eyes a little. "I think so."

Diane stifled a squeal and bounced on her toes. Tonya wasn't the only one who frowned her direction.

"You seem unreasonably excited for a meal," August said suspiciously.

Diane tilted her nose in the air. "Food happens to be a passion of mine."

"Since when?" Dorian asked.

"Since now." Diane tossed her hands in exasperation. "Just get your wings down to the dining hall, will you?"

"Fine!" August made a shooing motion at her.

She beckoned to Tonya and yanked her from the room. She shut the door and hopped up and down twice more with a laugh.

"What is happening?" Tonya tugged at Diane's sleeve.

"Absolutely nothing." But Diane's grin belied her words. She pushed Tonya farther from the boys' door. "All right. It's a bit of a surprise dinner in our honor. Don't say anything!"

"I think you've already spoiled it." Tonya smirked, dancing back a few steps as Diane jabbed a finger at her with an expression of mock outrage.

"Come on, we have to go change." Diane grabbed her hand again and pulled her into their room. A new dress lay across Tonya's bed, blue bodice and full skirt trimmed in stitched polar bears.

"Your mother snuck in here with it a bit ago." Diane came to stand next to her. Tonya brushed a finger over the patterns stitched into the waistline. Her parents had stolen as much of her time as they could, and she'd been more than happy to let them. They knew most of the truth now about what her life had been, and she'd hated the anger and sorrow mixing in their eyes.

But seeing them together, the hugs and smiles bestowed on her, more than made up for it.

Her grandparents—at least her grandmother—had been happy to meet her. Another thing Steinn had lied about. He'd deliberately kept them apart in the days before they'd left for the Lights.

Tonya shuddered a sigh. She wouldn't change anything she had now, but over the past two days she'd had the urge to crawl under her blankets and just hide and wonder at it all for a few hours.

Diane nudged her shoulder, bringing her back to the dress. She was Ísbjörn. She could wear it with pride.

They washed and dressed, Diane fussing a little more with Tonya's hair than she thought was strictly necessary.

"I'm just going to leave it down." Tonya finally pushed her hands away.

"Just hold on!" Diane took a small comb and used it to tuck some of the hair away from her face. "Perfect."

Tonya didn't understand the fuss until she stepped back out and felt Dorian's eyes on her again. He seemed almost— nervous to see her.

Tonya flushed and glanced down at the ground.

"Thank you." She squeaked a whisper to Diane.

"You're welcome," Diane whispered back in a light laugh before moving past to straighten August's collar. She smoothed the fabric over Dorian's shoulders next.

"Honestly, don't you two know how to dress?" she chided.

"If we knew what we were dressing for, maybe we would." August leaned back as she reached for his collar again.

Diane just moved to the door, opening it with a flourish and ushering them into the hallway. They made their way slowly down the stairs and through the wide corridors until they reached the closed doors of the dining hall.

The two guards pushed the doors open in response to Diane's imperious wave. Crowded tables laden with platters of food came into view. Tonya immediately sought out her parents, standing at the head table along with Birgir and Lilja and her grandparents.

Cheers broke out as Diane led the way into the hall. August came up short.

"Diane…?" he gritted around a frozen smile.

"You'll be fine." Diane tugged at his arm.

Dorian stood just as still and uncomfortable as August. Tonya reached out and took his hand. He looked down at her and a smile eased its way forward.

She led him forward to the four empty chairs at the head table.

"I really didn't do anything special besides get frozen." Tonya caught August's muttered complaints to Diane.

"Just smile." Diane prodded her elbow into his side.

"I pity Ralf, I really do," he retorted.

She reached up to cuff his head, ignoring the horrified looks the younger female faeries gave her. Tonya grinned. Diane was stirring up sympathy for August, intentionally or not. He likely wouldn't lack for any admirers later.

Freyr and Thalia both reached out to August and Dorian as they arrived at the head table.

"So glad to see you both up." Thalia smiled, squeezing their hands.

They settled into seats and the feast began with the ring of the great bell.

"Tonya said you're going across the Strait tomorrow." Dorian turned to Freyr.

Tonya's father nodded. "Not far. We'll clear a little of the ice and then come back. Birgir didn't want us going too far the first time."

She smiled into her glass at the agreement that showed plain on Dorian's face. A smile tugged the corner of Freyr's mouth.

"Don't worry. I've already been assured that anything after that will include the two of you."

"You can bet your life on that, sir," August spoke up from piling food on his plate.

"Slow down," Diane chided.

"All right, Mother. You're one to talk." August looked pointedly at Diane's own overflowing plate. She pursed her lips back, and dug in.

"I like them." Thalia leaned close to whisper to Tonya. "I like them all." She glanced to Dorian.

Tonya smiled shyly back. "Me too."

Thalia squeezed her hand. "Is he coming with us?"

A flush warmed Tonya's cheeks as she nodded.

"Good," her mother said, and freed Tonya's hand to allow her to begin eating.

The feasting stretched late into the night, long enough for the Lights to dance and shine through the clear ice panes in the ceiling, bathing the hall in the brightly-colored hues of the Creator's love.

# Chapter 35

**D**iane stood a little taller in the stirrups, shielding her eyes from the bright summer sun as she searched, again, for any sign of Chelm's red shale rooftops in the distance. Disappointed, she sank back into the saddle.

"We're getting close." August trotted beside her on Niko.

"That's what you said three miles ago." Diane glared back. "I've been remarkably patient the last few days, so I think I'm allowed today."

They'd left Konungburg two days after the feast, Dorian and August declaring themselves well enough to start traveling. Birgir lent them the caribou that had found their way back home again, a guard of six soldiers captained by Lilja, and supplies, and sent them on their way.

They'd been traveling for almost a week, cutting a diagonal path across Durne this time, and striking into Calvyrn to break the ice, before turning back into Myrnius. The border had been empty, except for a lone wolf that came and stood at a distance to watch Tonya and her father break the ice.

It howled once and August lifted a hand in a wave before it ran away in a dark brown streak towards Lagarah Lake. She'd already decided to try to ask Lord Darek about it next time she saw him.

Now, three days later, Tonya had freed the last bits of Myrnius from the grip of the ice. Weeks ago, they'd set out over snow and ice-covered hills. Now they returned over lush green coated in wildflowers that seemed none the worse for the wear for having been trapped under ice.

Diane's patience vanished with the warmth of the summer breeze and she stood in the stirrups once again, drawing a huff from Raakel as she continued on in her clicking gait.

*There!* Symmetric red roofs and the bulky ruins of the castle spread over the hills.

She kicked Raakel up to a gallop, unable to wait any longer.

Bells rang out as guards noted their approach. Gathering crowds cheered and shouted welcome once she was recognized, forcing her to slow Raakel back down to a walk. Townsfolk and soldiers and even faeries parted to make way for the strange animal and the unfamiliar faeries who had finally begun to catch up with her.

But Diane didn't pay any attention. She pushed Raakel on to the manor house, searching the crowds for a face that she hoped would already be trying to meet her there.

She reined in, sliding from the saddle and starting for the door. Maybe Matilde would know where he was.

"Diane!"

She whirled to find Ralf pushing his way through the crowd. He stumbled to a halt, staring at her, checking her over in the short, quick glances that meant he was trying to make sure she was all right and not hurt in any way.

Diane lunged into a run, slamming into his arms and burying her face in his tunic. He folded his arms around her, pressing his lips against the top of her head.

"You're back," he said softly.

She pulled back a little. The words she'd rehearsed over and over for the last few days stuck in her throat. She moved her hands up to his collar and tugged him forward into her kiss. Once he got over his surprise, he did a thorough job of kissing her back.

They finally parted, a little breathless. He cupped her cheek in one hand.

"I've been wanting to do that awhile now," he admitted, a little sheepishly.

She smiled up at him. "Sorry I'm so oblivious."

"I think I'll forgive you."

"I'm a little offended that I had to wait for a hug," Edmund broke in.

Diane turned in Ralf's arms to see her brother standing with hands on hips, but a ridiculous smile stretched across his face. It made him look years younger and more carefree than she'd seen in a long time. Ralf released her, and she ran into Edmund's arms.

"Told you we'd break the ice," she murmured.

He held her tightly. "So you did." His voice tightened oddly for a moment. "I was worried about you. I'm glad you're back."

Diane stepped back. "Worried? I was only in mortal peril *most* of the time."

A sort of strangled noise came from Ralf and she smirked at him.

"I agree." Edmund nodded to Ralf. "I want to hear everything, starting with what on the Creator's good earth is *that?*" He pointed to the caribou still standing patiently on the cobblestones. "And who are they and how many places to sleep do we need to find?"

He turned next to the ice faeries who gathered around Tonya and her parents.

Diane giggled, and looped her arm in his. "Don't worry, I'll help."

But Edmund gently detached her arm. "I know you don't want to be holding my hand right now," he said and nudged her toward Ralf.

She opened her mouth to protest, but Ralf beat her to it.

"Edmund, I—" His face took on a slightly panicked look.

Edmund rolled his eyes. "Ralf, you're the only one who can keep up with her. And one of the few I'd trust to look after her." Reluctant understanding showed in the upwards pull of his mouth.

A smile spread across Diane's face and she stepped closer to Ralf.

"But…"

"Your father was a noble, Ralf. Besides, we're not exactly living the courtly life." Edmund gestured to the manor house behind him. "And I'm the king. I can make whatever rule I want."

Another step closer, and Diane took Ralf's hand. He looked down to her.

"You shouldn't argue with him. You know how stubborn he gets." She shook her head.

Ralf relented with a smile and laced his fingers through hers.

Diane turned to find her companions. The sight of August embracing his parents brought a lump resurfacing in her throat. Almost as much as seeing Dorian's family again when they'd stopped for a night back at Csorna Hold. Adela reached out to Tonya to wrap her in a hug as well.

Diane motioned Edmund forward, pulling Ralf with her, as she was not about to let go of his hand, and began introductions. August finished for her, only because she was interrupted by the sobbing whirlwind that was Matilde coming to crash into her.

Once the tears and hugs and greetings were over, and caribou stabled and accommodations found, they moved inside the manor house to tell the story again.

Chairs were pulled from the dining room, the smaller sitting room, and bedrooms to accommodate Tonya and August's parents, Lilja, Edmund, Ralf, and Diane and her companions. Diane pulled Matilde down into a chair after she helped bring out drinks and fresh-baked scones.

Diane claimed a chair next to Ralf, who sat like he'd rather be standing back in the shadows and listening. But he relaxed slightly when she took his hand again.

Tonya and Dorian sat next to each other, hands entwined. They'd been nearly inseparable during the course of the trip and August had taken it as his solemn duty, along with Diane, to tease them about it whenever they got a chance.

They paused in the telling of the story only to balance plates on their laps as dinner was brought out. Adela paled and pressed a hand to her mouth when they relayed the bit about the ambush. Damian clamped a hand on August's shoulder as he leaned a little closer to his parents.

After Tonya assured them that the ice was gone for good, Edmund sat back with relief showing plain in his features.

"You don't know how glad that makes me," he said. "Thank you for everything you did."

Tonya ducked her head, faint red spreading across her cheeks.

"Although some good came of it all." Edmund looked to Damian and Adela. "It made humans and faeries work together again towards a common goal. It's done more to foster some real peace among our people and countries than these years without war."

Diane leaned against Ralf's shoulder. Edmund's words chipped away at a weight inside her and she understood the change in her brother. There was still work to be done, but maybe they could finally start building and moving forward again.

Ralf brushed a kiss against her forehead. She tilted her head enough to smile up at him. Between him and Edmund, she'd have the courage to keep standing tall and doing her part.

# Chapter 36

Tonya wiggled her bare toes deeper into the sand. She closed her eyes, listening to the gentle hiss of the waves against the shore as they strained to reach her just beyond the tideline. With the ice gone and in the heat of the summer sun, she'd done away with shoes. Her mother had done the same with a wearily amused smile from Freyr.

Her ocean magic tingled in her fingertips, begging for release. Her ice magic settled into the background, content finally to share her with the ocean. She waded forward into the waves, the warm water sloshing around her knees, nudging her and chuckling a welcome in each swell. She spun around, flinging her arms wide to send the water dancing around her in ribbons and myriad droplets.

She turned back to face the beach. Dorian stood in the sand, watching her with his smile. The caribou nosed the salty grass higher up in the dunes. Arvo had refused to leave Dorian, and the ice faeries had laughingly parted with him and the other caribou that she and her parents had ridden.

It was just the four of them that left Chelm together to head towards the southern tip of Myrnius.

"Are you coming in?" she called.

He rolled his eyes a little, but bent to shuck his boots and roll his trousers up to his knees. He waded in, reaching out toward her. She danced away with a smirk, fluttering her hand and sending a small wave to crash over him and leave him soaked.

He wiped water from his face in a deliberate motion, the smile building around his eyes. She backed away, a laugh bubbling on her lips. He slammed his foot down in a splash of water. The sand shifted and rumbled beneath her feet in response.

A laughing scream broke from her as she lost her balance. A gust of wind from his wings knocked her the rest of the way into the water. His triumph was short-lived as she doused him again with another wave. Abandoning magic, he tackled her into the waves.

They came up breathless and laughing. He helped her to her feet and pulled her into a kiss. It was better than when he first kissed her two days ago beneath the midnight sky. She wrapped her arms around his neck and tangled a hand in his damp hair and kept kissing him.

There, knee deep in the waves, wrapped in his arms, with her magic settling around her heart, she was wild, and wonderful, and whole, and home.

# The End

# Acknowledgments

I never really know how to fill out these pages. I know I'm going to forget someone. And for being a writer, I'm very bad at putting my appreciation into words.

To my family who has unfailingly supported me over the years, and have accepted my writerly tendencies with grace. It means more to me than I can tell when you ask about my books, or want to discuss them with me. And thanks for not batting an eye when I casually mention torturing characters. Y'all are the best.

To Katie Phillips, my editor, who reassured me that this story wasn't a complete mess, and once again, helped me shape it into something more coherent.

To Deborah, who has become an amazing cheerleader over the years. Thanks for the word sprints and the fangirly comments.

To Paige, my best friend and encourager. There's a little bit of you in Diane.

To my beta readers Skye, Elisabeth, and Hazel—thanks so much for the feedback and the encouragement.

It takes so many people to get a book out, and this wouldn't be complete with several more people. Rachael for saving me from the headache of formatting. LoriAnn for stunning with me with your cover design once again.

And thanks to you, reader. Thanks for making it this far. For telling me that you've enjoyed my other books and encouraging me to get to this point of releasing another book. Couldn't have done it without you. Stay courageous, friends.

# Adela's Curse

*The Faeries of Myrnius Book 1*

**A curse. A murderous scheme. A choice.**

*"Reading this feels like coming home."* – Kendra E. Ardnek, author of *The Rizkaland Legends*.

# The Wolf Prince

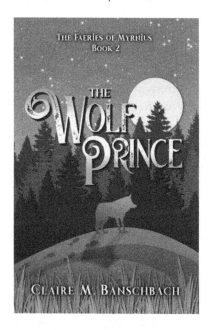

*The Faeries of Myrnius Book 2*
2019 Realm Award Finalist – YA category

**One prince. Two brothers. Three companions to prevent a sorcerer from destroying the faeries.**

*"Should be the next Disney film!"* Kyle Robert Shultz, author of the *Beaumont and Beasley* series.

# More books by Claire M. Banschbach

*The Rise of Aredor Series*

**A lost prince. A runaway chieftain's son. A sweeping war that threatens their countries' very existence.**

*"Ben Hur meets The Horse and His Boy meets Robin Hood."*
- EB Dawson, author of *The Lost Empire* series.

(The Rise of Aredor Book 1)

(The Rise of Aredor Book 2)

# New Adult/Adult Fantasy Fiction

with grit and snark from
**C.M. Banschbach and
Uncommon Universes Press.**

*Oath of the Outcast*
The Dragon Keep Chronicles
Book 1
*A lost brother. An unwilling
outlaw. A rising enemy. An
unusual alliance.*

**Y**ears ago, Rhys MacDuffy was brutally cut off from his clan, stripped of his name and inheritance, and banished to the remote Dragon Keep. Perched high above the Shang Pass in the land of Alsaya, he assumed the mantle of the Mountain Baron, serving out his sentence as the overseer of the worst outlaws and outcasts.

But one day he receives a desperate message from the clan who disowned him: MacDuffy's Seer — his beloved brother — has been taken by their enemies. With his band of Mountain Brigands and an unwelcome sidekick, Rhys leaves his mountain stronghold to find and rescue his brother.

The tide of war is rising amongst the Clans of Alsaya, fueled by the magic-wielding sect of Druids who seek to unleash a dark force the world has long forgotten.

Can the bond of blood run deeper than banishment?

# Blood of the Seer

The Dragon Keep Chronicles Book 2

**Coming Fall 2020!**

# About the Author

**Claire M. Banschbach** is a native Texan and would make an excellent hobbit if she wasn't so tall. She's an overall dork, pizza addict, and fangirl. When not writing fantasy stories packed full of adventure and snark, she works as a pediatric Physical Therapist where she happily embraces the fact that she never actually has to grow up.

She writes New Adult/Adult fantasy as C.M. Banschbach.

She loves to connect with readers on Facebook and Instagram where you can find dorky life and writing updates.

Twitter: twitter.com/cmbanschbach
Facebook: facebook.com/cmbanschbach/
Instagram: instagram.com/cmbanschbach/

Made in the USA
Monee, IL
21 August 2023